Lovely Vines

Tondria Leatrice

TONDRIA LEATRICE

Fulton Books, Inc.
Meadville, PA

Published by Fulton Books 2020

ISBN 978-1-64654-485-1 (paperback)
ISBN 978-1-64654-486-8 (digital)

Printed in the United States of America

To my lovely mother, Ada Thomas.

I love you with all my heart, and I remember you said, "And you better finish that book," and I did it for you.

May God continue to bless your family with your beautiful memories. I know you are missed by many, and this void we have can never be replaced.

We love you, Ma.

In loving memory of Vernada and Zola.

CONTENTS

ACKNOWLEDGMENTS

I acknowledge the dominant system that took a part of me in three ways, leaving my mind wandering and acknowledging I couldn't do anything at all. I learned the power of patience through this system and a mother's emptiness to the fullest, not being able to give a hug through a call. The power of lonely nights without a call can break the most influential person, not knowing what's going on behind the walls that I acknowledge took three from me.

I also acknowledge the power of love for the child can turn into prayers which led me to write this book in those long three years, with only three people telling me that I would not fall.

I acknowledge the phone calls from my mother and father telling me everything was gonna be okay and my sister Melissa Shaw for telling to my face, "I see the pain through the fake smile," and I want to acknowledge them for knowing a mother's pain.

I also acknowledge my little brothers Richard, Calvin, Dakar, and Eli and my uncles Freddy, Anthony, Raymond, and Bill for being some of the realest men I know and teaching me the value of a man. I give thanks to my best friend Theo for listening to me vent, reading my ideas, telling me I could do it, and staying true through it all.

PART 1

Who Am I

CHAPTER 1

Samaya
Saria Is My Stage Name

"Run, Samaya, run!" Queen shouted as they ducked behind the car. Samaya saw the shadows getting closer and moving past swiftly, and heard the whistle sounds go past her ears as the shadows disappeared. *Bang, bang, bang.* "Get down, Samaya!" Queen screamed again.

The shooters jumped in the car speeding off, shooting, and each time they shot, a window shattered right next to her face.

Every time the disco lights on the ceiling glared in her face, she thought about that night, seeing the flare from the gunfire.

When the money hit the stage, she knew she'd never put her life in danger over moola again, seeing how easy ass and titties made it fall, but Rocky was always into some shit.

As she slid down that pole looking into the dim room, she saw nothing but darkness, a few lights, and people cheering her on.

The colored lights glared onto her moistened body, and the money falling onto the stage made her hustle even harder. Making her ass shake and looking at her surroundings at the same time became her norm.

When she danced, all she thought about was growing up looking at her grandma pushing a cart, picking up cans off the streets.

Grandma's routine was cooking anything, cleaning, fighting, canning fruit, gardening, drinking, and not working.

She didn't grow up around her runaway dad, or his beautiful family, and Grandma tried hard to fill the empty void.

Her mom was fifteen years old when she had Samaya, so Grandma's routine is all she saw, and that lifestyle made her twerk even harder.

She didn't start figuring shit out until she turned twelve that their family was poor and accustomed to the system.

Not only that, the crack epidemic took over the whole motherfucking hood and the ones she looked up to in her family tree. That thought alone made her climb the pole again, coming down fast into the splits and barely thinking about her runaway mom.

That street shit had her mom missing, so she went looking for her daddy's missing ass. *Fuck that hungry shit*, she thought. Searching alleys where she heard he gambled, his mother's house, the clubs, and to find out he was the lead crackhead dealer. The realization alone made her count her money with pride, not caring about shit but the height of the stash.

Eventually, running the streets was all she knew, which blew by like a breeze, missing the last few years of high school to get naked for a dollar. Teaching herself how to hustle from the first period to the six-hour turning could be As into a sum of banknotes.

Never giving in to doing drugs, being she saw it take over some of the strongest in the game, which had her doing headstands to get the powerful dollar.

By sixteen, she was not giving a fuck about feelings or life, period, running away from the empty home into the streets that pretended to love her.

Shaking her ass to the latest bounce music made her forget family function and values to the point family started to shake and forget about her.

Learning the power of money was her main focus, and stacking it by any means necessary was the only goal she had. Breaking anyone that came in her path made her careless of who she was.

Being overpowered by the dollar pumped through her blood, and best believe it was all she knew and to hustle.

*****

Samaya stood on the corner, cold as hell, as the customers came and went, while she watched Queen sit in the car. Queen counted the money, listened to music, and flamed, as usual.

Samaya was more focused on being happy that the hunger pangs were gone, she forgot to eat some days. The money was coming so fast. She was blinded.

*****

When Ginnie from the block approached Samaya, she was relieved as hell knowing that all these hours standing out here was worth it. Everybody knew that Ginnie bought all your shit when she came from turning tricks.

Samaya said, "What's up, G? What you need?"

Ginnie said, "*I need all that shit! What you got left, girl?*"

Samaya said, "Quit talking so damn loud! I'll give you this for one eighty."

Ginnie said, "*Okay! You're hustling tonight? Here you go!*"

*****

All the negative things that occurred in her life made her focus while trying to keep her breath. *Is she running,* Samaya thought. *Not falling to the streets again* was all she thought about when chasing this bitch down the alley. "Queen, she took our shit!" Samaya yelled as she punched Ginnie in the back of her head. "What the fuck is wrong with you, Ginnie? Give me my money, and get yo monkey ass on somewhere, bitch!" Samaya shouted. Queen jumped out the car running behind them all out of breath and late, "Get that bitch, fam!" hitting the flame and trying to yell at the same time.

*****

Samaya rushed to the back after watching Queen get all her money off the stage. As she gathered what Queen didn't, she rushed to the dressing room and saw DJ coming from behind the booth to talk like he always does.

"Saria!" DJ shouted, but the door closed in his face just like that chapter of chasing crackheads down the streets and his simple-as-baby-mama lines.

*****

Samaya said, "Roll up, my nerves getting bad. The mouse face chasing me with his musty ass."

Queen said, "Oh, one day he's going to bite yo ass. You know Rocky doesn't allow smoking anymore."

Samaya said, "His mouse ass is going to bite the tip of my nine. Da fuck! Well, Rocky knows I don't follow the rules. Fuck him!"

Queen said, "You dropped out of school and started shaking that ass at fifteen for this club. He knows damn well, you could have been shut down this club a long time ago."

Samaya said, "Stop it! I'm going to finish school eventually, and shaking my ass fed us, deary."

Queen said, "You're always saying that shit!"

Samaya said, "Me doing the splits got you through high school and out of the car."

Queen said, "I'm just saying, damn! Thank you, Ms. Bouncy."

Samaya said, "Bouncing, and twerking in the air getting on my nerves."

Queen said, "Girl, you been needing a man to bounce on for a while now!"

Samaya said, "I wouldn't know the first thing about how to treat a man, let alone myself."

Queen said, "It's easy. All that shit you're doing on the pole, you do on his dick, then follow his lead with your eyes open."

Samaya said, "Bitch! You sound dumb as fuck. Hit this shit so that you can come back to earth."

Queen said, "You don't have no filter. At least give it a try or something."

Samaya said, "With no direction, or structure, I'm a hot mess for anybody. Sliding down this pole to get this paper is all I know, and a man will slow that down. Have you ever thought about what our life would be like if our parents raised us, or Granny?"

Queen said, "I don't think about them. We came from nothing, but look at us now, bitch!"

Samaya said, "I've never seen our family work a nine-to-five, attend college, or have rules."

Queen said, "We ran away from home into the streets to get away from Granny's army rules, or we'd probably be college graduates by now."

Samaya said, "Girl, please! We didn't give a fuck about anything just loose. Chasing people in that old blue Chevy."

Queen said, "My dumb ass was right there with your hungry ass stealing and shit. Girl, remember Granny tried hard to get us out of that damn car, but we kept dodging her. I didn't want to move across the country and shit."

Samaya said, "She had the police looking for us, and we hid in the car for hours. We'd probably be running like my mom did, if we went. Poor Kacee and Kasie, they're trying to leave now."

*****

Samaya looked at Queen sideways when Sunshine came into their changing room. "Thanks for knocking first," Samaya said. Queen knew Samaya wasn't fucking with any of the females or men that stepped a foot in that club.

Sunshine said, "Let me hit the flame, Queen."

Queen said, "Huh? What you need?"

Samaya said, "You got money, right? We don't know where your mouth been. Da fuck!"

Sunshine said, "I do…I wasn't talking to you to begin with."

Queen said, "Slow your roll, Sunny. What do you need?"

Samaya said, "This bitch said, 'Sunny.' You funny as fuck, girl."

Sunshine said, "It's Sunshine. I'll see you later before you leave, Queen."

17

Queen said, "Here, girl! Let me get that hundred first. Did Rocky raise your premium?"

Sunshine said, "What the fuck is a premium?"

Samaya said, "Hell naw! This shit funny, G! It's your rent!"

Sunshine said, "Y'all using all these sadity-ass words. And no! He didn't raise shit! I'm gone, Queen."

Samaya said, "I can't stand her jiggly ass. Anyways, we went from pushing pushcarts down the street to rolling on rims in this bitch."

Queen said, "Girl…every time you get high, yo ass go down memory lane. Come back, bitch! Come back! Look at the situation now, we're good. But jiggly?"

Samaya said, "Whatever! I can't wait to count all this money my beauties, techniques, and Saria made tonight."

Queen said, "We did bank tonight! I'll call you tomorrow. I'm out."

Samaya said, "Hold up! Did you hear our premiums went up in this bitch?"

Queen said, "Yes. I was serious when I just asked her that. He so money hungry, I can't stand him."

*****

The smell of smoke, stale alcohol lingered in her hair and clothes, but counting all that money made her forget about that shit.

She danced four nights out of the week and shopped the other three. In her mindset, she didn't have time to fuck with a nine-to-five, that school bullshit, or these simple-ass men. Money turned her on, and people that made it, period.

Samaya hustled hard to get her apartment on the top floor of the Canyon Club Condo, never wanting to be hungry again. Taking everything off as she walked through looking at her all-white fur-nished Grayson Luxury collections, she was reminiscing about living out of her car with her sister and Queen.

The warm water hit her body, relaxing her mind as she massaged herself with Eau Du Soir in the all-white marble shower, moisturizing her caramel skin, perky 38D pierced breasts, thirty-four-inch waist, and apple booty. She loves her moneymaker, thinking about how they used to take baby baths in restaurants, to the movie theaters.

She lay across the top of her white Batiste European goose down comforter, with her white laced bodysuit on, in her oversize king bed by herself again, which was solely hers.

She loved the softness of her skin, feeling the silk sheets ravel as the tightness came then relaxation. *Beep. Beep. Beep.* She did not pay the notification no mind, because only a few people had her number, so if it rang, she answered. *Beep. Beep. Beep.*

She ignored the sound and continued to slowly rub her nipples in a circular motion to intensify the effect of the tightness, never letting a release to the fullest, relaxing the clitoris just enough for a daily wall exercise. She finished and checked her notifications, knowing damn well it wasn't Prince Charming with the glass slipper.

*****

Queen's text to Samaya: "Love you girl...Wyd?"

She noticed that Chad finally got out his feelings, texting the same thing over and over again; a few notifications on Lovely Vines; and her manager fat ass from the club.

When she responded to Chad, she instantly got mad at herself giving in to her past.

Samaya's text to Chad: "What's popping?"

The last time she had drinks with Chad, they became partners in crime. He tried to wife her because he liked how she got down with him, but they went their separate ways when he couldn't fuck.

Chad's text to Samaya: "When can I see you?"

She ignored Chad's text, wishing she hadn't said anything to him. She continued to check her notifications until she saw one that stood out from the rest. She decided to text Queen because she knew she had something to do with it.

Samaya's text: "What's up, Queen?"

Queen's text: "What are you doing?"

Samaya's text: "Looking at this site 'Lovely Vines' you know, the one I joined. Are you coming over?"

Queen's text: "Got some new flame! This shit fire! The twins called earlier wanting to come live with me, but granny not going."

Samaya's text: "Girl please, you see Tara left when she turned sixteen."

Queen's text: "You are always trying new shit! I'm bringing fast food. Why would you try a site that cost money and all these free fine men out here."

Samaya's text: "It's a VIP page for ballers only."

Queen's text: "YEAH! IT DOESN'T COST TO MEET MEN."

Samaya's text: "A one-time registration fee and they make sure funds are legit. And, I can look all I want to without them all in my face…"

Queen's text:: "That's too much! You can pay a fee to get in a nightclub and see men in the flesh. Lol."

Samaya's text: "If someone comments or likes your pictures only you can see it. My inbox, always full of nude photos, and long-ass paragraphs of horny fuckers."

Queen's text: "I hope you don't respond to that horny bullshit! It seems like the more money a person has, the freakier."

Samaya's text: "Well my Sketch only has a little information."

Queen's text: "Then they know all your business, NOPE!"

Samaya's text: "I have one face picture, one full body in that long white dress Jai designed. My hair straight as usual, and you know my body moistened down, French tips, and my lip gloss shining."

Queen's text: "You're always extra."

Samaya's text: "Want me to set you one up?"

Queen's text: "HELL NO! I'm good. Omw!"

*****

They sat around the fireplace sipping on wine, flaming, looking over her Lovely Vines page, and laughing at all the alerts she was getting.

Queen said, *"Look, girl! Look!"*

When they saw the new alert coming from him, they both smiled hard. Samaya was waiting for Queen to snitch on herself because she tried setting her up with him before.

Samaya never paid attention to how fine he was, but she knew the name well.

Samaya said, "I should give his fine chocolate ass some time. He liked a few of my pictures to get my attention, I see."

Queen said, "Look at the other fellas compared to him."

Samaya said, "They're all saying the same lame-ass shit. He looks familiar."

Queen said, "Let's check out his sketch. Let's be a little nosy!"

Samaya said, "Check him out. He's a business owner, with almond brown skin, brown eyes, six foot four, an elegant taper with a full beard, mustache, solidly built body, and single."

Queen said, "*Go to the other pictures.* I think you should breathe, bitch! Quit drooling and shit."

They started checking pictures for females and kids.

Samaya said, "Should I hit the 'like' button to this one?"

Queen said, "*Yes, bitch! Get his attention!*"

Samaya said, "Anyways! Have you been to the storage?"

Queen said, "I went last week! It's your turn! Yes, I know! We're going to move it soon."

Samaya said, "No! Let's repackage it, so it doesn't mildew."

Queen said, "Or, we could just put it in the car and move it. Problem solved!"

*****

That morning, Samaya went for her morning run around the lake and saw Chad doing pull-ups on the bars. The sun shined on the lake and glared onto his body, making his monkey ass look good.

She kept jogging past him all cool, not noticing that Chad was right behind her, picking her up off her feet from behind. She screamed until she saw Chad's face as if she didn't notice him.

Samaya said, "*What the fuck, dude!*"

Chad said, "Calm your pretty ass down."

She yelled while hitting him in his chest in a playful way, noticing his fake empty smile. *This bitch fine as fuck*, Chad thought. Chad laughed, knowing he's never had a chance with her anyway, so he enjoyed the hitting while it lasted.

Chad said, "Bet your ass don't run past me no more, acting like you didn't see me. What you've been up to, Samaya?"

Samaya said, "*Shit, Chad!* You scared the fuck out of me."

Chad politely grabbed Samaya's hand and began running with her to complete the run around the lake, trying to convince her to hit another lick with him.

When he walked her over to her car, he opened the door for her. He placed his business card in her sports bra, seeing that she was rolling better than him, and that made him want her more.

Chad said, "This time, use it! Hopefully, I get a yes for an answer."

Samaya said, "I get busy."

Chad said, "Why are you scared? It's quick money."

Samaya said, "I'm not the same young thirsty-ass girl anymore. I make real money now!"

Chad said, "It can be between us, Samaya."

Samaya said, "I'll think about it."

*****

Queen went out that morning and picked up some groceries while Samaya was out running. When she returned, Queen had breakfast and coffee ready for them.

Queen said, "Bitch! How you got money and no food? I don't get it! How are you thick in the ass like that, seriously?"

Samaya said, "I buy when I'm hungry, okay! Let's go before the gym gets crowded."

Queen said, "Yo ass want to see that sexy trainer. Horny ass!"

Samaya said, "He is fine! I know he's probably fucked half his clients already. I saw Chad irritating ass."

Queen said, "Please don't deal with him. He's bad news. Had us running for our life type shit."

Samaya said, "I'm not thinking about hitting any licks. I'm past all that dumb shit."

Queen said, "I've seen that look before, Samaya. You have a lot of money, so there's no need for that thirsty shit."

Samaya said, "We were hungry and desperate back then. The fuck! I'm not stupid for no nigga."

Queen said, "Bringing him up done spoiled my appetite. The twins called again today. They're ready to come up here with us."

Samaya said, "We need to go find your mom and daddy's ass."

Queen said, "Your mom said she'll be out of treatment in three months."

Samaya said, "Well, hopefully, Pops get out of jail and stay out of the streets this time."

Queen said, "He ain't my pops. He left us for the streets and turned my mom out."

Samaya said, "We have to learn forgiveness, baby girl."

Queen said, "Fuck that! Forgive your daddy then."

Samaya said, "My daddy on the street, still chasing false dreams. Yours is locked up for trying to put money into the house. It's a big difference, cousin!"

Queen said, "If he's that perfect, Granny shouldn't be raising his children. Oh, I forgot! Who do they want to come live with?"

Samaya said, "I love you! You're still my baby, but they're running from discipline, probably. Tara forgave our parents for sending her with Granny."

Queen said, "*You like my mama, girl!* Tara ran away at sixteen too."

Samaya said, "Well, you don't like them! I don't either!"

As soon as Samaya smashed off, Queen leaned over, hugged her, and kissed her face, leaving lip gloss all over her cheeks, knowing Samaya hated shit on her face.

Samaya said, "Stop it! Before you make me crash this bitch."

Queen said, "Ugh! There that bitch go. She never speaks when I come to the shop. I can't stand that bitch!"

Samaya said, "What bitch?"

Queen said, "She just pulled out the garage in that raggedy-ass car."

Samaya said, "Girl, we weren't always rolling and eating. Stop that!"

Queen said, "One day I came looking for you at that store, and it took forever for the bitch to tell me you left. Then the bitch rolled her eyes, and sipped her coffee."

Samaya said, "She told me about that. She said, 'Some girl came looking for you, Ms. Samaya,' plus, she always speaks to me."

Queen said, "Little turtle-head-ass bitch. Eyeful-watching ass!"

Samaya said, "Girl, yo ass funny! Leave that girl alone."

Queen said, "Her sister needs to make her some damn clothes. How the hell you fly, and your twin look like a rag doll."

Samaya said, "Jai is outgoing and classy, and her twin is laid-back into her books. Just because she wears oversize flannels doesn't mean she's a rag doll."

Queen said, "So what! If she's into her books, she missed the part of good customer service."

*****

Man 2 said, "Told you, my nigga!"

Samaya put in the code and waited for the gate to open. She discussed with staff already about it opening and closing too slow, so she was pissed to see they hadn't fixed it.

She hated going by herself which Queen complained about, but they both went by themselves most of the time.

Man 2 said, "She's not giving up any play, so you might as well get the bitch."

Chad said, "I told you to give me more time. I'll convince her to be mine, and we can get the shit easily."

Man 2 said, "Look! She has a briefcase, and Queen has the duffel bag. It never changes! Then, you think she's gonna fall in love with you and give you her password and hand you the money."

Chad said, "If I can get in her crib, then I can look for it. You look! Ain't no way we're getting in this storage unit without a unit."

Man 2 said, "That's the smartest shit you've said. Let's call and get one!"

Chad said, "We're going to need a few more people."

Jai
Doing Me

Jai was one of the coldest designers on the rise in California. This bitch kept her shit tight with her skin always glistening. She stood at five foot seven with long-ass legs, had a nice bump in the back to complement her figure and boobs sitting high at a 36D after her surgery. Her stomach was flat, and her makeup was always on point.

The bitch's hair was shiny and jet-black, hanging to her ass, which made her stand out. She had clothes to die for, and her outfits showed off her buttered-down skin, with no scars or tattoos anywhere.

Only a selected few exotic dancers knew about Jai, and the rest were some funny Wall Street bitches with big-ass noses.

Her identical twin sister Jez worked as the cashier and her assistant part-time. Jez always smiled and greeted the people she liked, but Jai couldn't let her go, knowing she was rude at times.

*****

Jez said, "Hello, Samaya. How are you doing?"

Samaya said, "I'm okay, twin. How are you doing?"

Jez said, "I'm good, girl. Thanks for asking."

Samaya said, "Likewise. Where twin at?"

Jai noticed Samaya immediately walking into the shop. *I see money today. And prices don't matter*, Jai thought. She would have sit-downs with Samaya and sketch designs to her liking.

Jai said, "Come to me, beautiful! I have so much to show you."

Before she could say hi, Jai pulled some new designs from behind the white curtain, and the twin was pouring her a glass of champagne. After trying them all on, Samaya bought them all and chatted with Jai.

Samaya said, "You know my style, girl?"

Jai said, "Very simple, and elegant. How are you doing with the man search?"

Samaya said, "You never ask questions to why I want my outfits to come off so easy. And, this man situation needs to find a way into my universe. I'm not looking or chasing shit."

Jai said, "Are you still down with the business proposition?"

Samaya said, "Yes! I brought the down payment, and we can meet at the bank on Thursday when everything goes through. Right?"

Jai said, "Correct! Here are the business agreement and insurance papers. Sign these, and we're in business, girl."

Samaya said, "I need a few minutes to read it over."

Jai said, "I'll be right back! Take your time!"

Jai and Samaya attended fashion shows; went to brunch, wine tasting, body painting events, movies; gone fabric shopping, spa treatments; and shared the latest gossip.

Samaya considered Jai a friend, so she decided to open up more and handed Jai a business card.

Samaya said, "Meet me tonight around nine thirty, so we can celebrate. I'm in business now! I'm proud of myself."

Jai smiled as she read the card, knowing damn well she'd never been to a strip club before. *I never have known for a stripper to have a business card, but I like her hustle,* Jai thought.

Jai said, "I got an invite? I feel special as fuck. See you tonight, Saria."

Samaya said, "Bring your A game, girl. I see your friend still sending flowers."

Jai said, "Yes, girl! These are the old ones. Since I let him smell this muthafucka, he's been sending flowers on a weekly."

When Jai went to hug Samaya, she saw the delivery man approaching with a big bouquet of fresh white tulips, knowing who sent them already. "Look at this shit!" Jai whispered to Samaya as she let her go. "You got that soup cooler," Samaya said as she walked off, and Jai giggled so hard, she teared up.

Jez said, "Bye, Samaya. Seriously, how many dates have you been on with him?"

Jai said, "We went on a few dates. He's sending flowers before the other ones go bad. Thirsty ass!"

Jez said, "Did you have sex with him? What does thirsty mean?"

Jai said, "I cannot deal with you. Sis, you need to get out more."

Jez said, "If your ass doesn't speak proper English. Don't go around the question."

Jai said, "We've had some good conversations. He's been to the shop a few times. He's watched me model my designs, a few movies, and some lunch dates. I already know he wants sex, but who doesn't?"

Jez said, "Well, he must like something about you. Always sending flowers and candy. Do you think he's relationship material?"

Jai said, "You already know sex comes easy with male, or female with me. Oh, I let him eat my pussy a few times."

Jez said, "*Oh my gosh, sis! TMI…Next, he's going to be here cutting fabric.*"

Jai said, "Sis, you're crazy. Let's step out tonight?"

Jez said, "For something to eat, I hope?"

Jai said, "No! A strip club."

Jez said, "Hell no! Not my cup of tea."

Jai said, "Loosen up a li'l bit."

Jez said, "I'm not that loose. I don't want to see loose asses shaking all in my face."

As Jai read the card attached to the flower stick, she smiled. "It must be nice, the way you're cheesing," Jez said.

> To Jai
> I hope these flowers brighten up your day beautiful.
> Meet me for lunch at our spot around the corner.
>
> From Chuck

Jez made sure Jai arranged all the orders for pickup with the receipts for each client that were picking up their orders before heading to lunch with Chuck.

*****

Chuck said, "Hey, baby girl! Looking beautiful as always. Come here!"

Jai loved hugging Chuck and smelling his cologne, and the strength of his hug made her pussy wet every time. Chuck picked her up a little bit off her feet, pulling her into him, loving the softness and smell of her skin. Chuck finally got that wet kiss he's been wanting. He wanted to start fucking in the restaurant but had to snap back into reality.

Man 2 said, "His ass happy as fuck to see her. I think we might need one of my brothers."

Chad said, "I'll talk with him! He doesn't know about the storage unit. He thinks we're following the girls for a friend over some money she owes."

*****

Chuck said, "Get up and follow me!"

Jai said, "Oh my gosh! You're crazy! They're going to see us!"

Chuck locked the door to the bathroom, picked Jai up like she was a feather, and sat her on the sink. He lifted her skirt and opened her legs as she pretended to be nervous. She was watching his head go in between her legs, and that turned her on every time. His head was moving up, down, side to side, like he didn't have a bone in his fucking neck. As soon as she squirted, they went and had a beautiful lunch like the lovely flowers he sent to the magnificent tongue he used.

*****

Chad said, "Bro, I hope you don't fall in love! We're strictly after the money."

Man 2 said, "We need a way to distract the other girl! If her sister went that easy, we need to find somebody to holla at her."

Chuck said, "Y'all didn't tell me what the stipulations were to this shit! She too fine not to fuck! Fuck that! How many more friends does she have?"

Man 2 said, "Queen is not going! She fucking with that one nigga that be at the club, and I know that for a fact he has money."

*****

Jai took the papers to the bank and her lawyer, so they could see the business arrangement through.

She was so excited to have a partner now, knowing the money would help her find a factory to make her designs. She could buy more fabric, make more designs, get better materials, and models for fashion week.

She knew some of the top designers' assistants from France would be there, so she worked hard on these designs.

Jai walked back into the shop, smiling from cheek to cheek, thinking about what she was going to wear tonight to see Samaya. She grabbed a few designs off the rack in the back of the shop that she hadn't put out yet, and headed for her office. She picked out her outfit for the night, went to the liquor store, then headed home.

She got her workout clothes then headed straight to the treadmill, showered afterward, took a few shots, and got dressed.

*****

She couldn't find a parking spot anywhere close, so she parked a block down the street, passing a couple on her way toward the club. Trying not to let them notice her looking at them argue, she tried walking faster. When the man pulled the lady's hair shoving her into the car, she turned around and glanced at his ass. She wanted to keep it moving, but to see that the lady didn't yell for help irritated her.

Jai said, "*Stop hitting women, pussy!*"

Woman's voice said, "*Mind your business, bitch!*"

Jai said, "*Dizzy ass!*"

The man said, "*Go on, bitch! Before you get popped!*"

Jai stuck her middle finger up. "Fuck you!" she shouted. She wanted to turn around and leave, but she wanted to see Samaya do her thang.

She was so pissed that the lady defended him. All she thought about was her mother getting her ass beat, yelling for help. Their mother's eyes were bruised up one day; then the next day she be hugging and kissing all on their father.

When she approached the door, the attendant looked her up and down as if she was lost. Pretty as Samaya was, she thought she was lost and looked at the business card again in disbelief.

The door attendant said, "Hello. How may I help you, miss?"

Jai said, "Hello, sir! How much?"

The door attendant said, "Fine as you are, it's free."

Jai said, "Thank you!"

The door attendant said, "Damn! Can I get your number?"

Jai said, "I have a man!"

The door attendant said, "He doesn't have to know! Why is he letting you come here?"

Jai said, "First of all, I'm grown. Boy, bye!"

The door attendant said, "He still shouldn't let you come to places like this."

Jai said, "Just how, you don't know me! He doesn't let or tell me shit."

The door attendant said, "Damn, ma! It's like that? What's your name, beautiful?"

Jai tried being polite, but he kept coming at her until the door slammed behind her. Before the door closed all the way, he got his last say in trying to whisper.

The door attendant said, "Have a good night, bitch!"

She couldn't let that shit go because that was one of her most disliked words coming from a man. She turned around so fast to open the door it almost went off the hinges.

The door attendant said, "Coming back for more?"

When she chuckled, he knew she was about to say something from how her face looked. "Let me tell you something. You short, stocky, 'coming to my chest, closer to the ground than me' fucker. Maybe you should get on all four since you're the closest to the fucking ground, doorkeeper. *Now, bitch that!* Now have a nice night, pup," Jai said in one breath.

The door attendant said, "Go on, before I bite your sexy ass. Woof, woof!"

She rolled her eyes and pushed by the door again. As soon as the door closed, her phone was beeping like a muthafucka. When she saw it was Chuck, she ignored his hootchy-kootchy-eating ass and went straight to her contacts and blocked his number for the night.

A dancer said, "Would you like a dance?"

Jai said, "Maybe later, thank you!"

The bartender said, "What can I get for you?"

Jai said, "Double shot of top-shelf tequila. Thank you!"

CHAPTER 2

Queen
Queen Is My Street and Stage Name

Queen's mom died in the streets as soon as she had the twins at seventeen. Queen was only two, and her brother Kendrick was one.

Queen was too young to remember her daddy or what his face looked like due to his magical disappearing act.

She heard he turned her mama out and had some bullshit traveling sales job selling whatever was popular on the streets. *I'm turned out easily by the pole like my mama, and showing off my goods is making me popular like whatever Daddy doing*, she thought, walking onto the stage.

*****

Trying to flame the thought away on how this man's street role could be more important than to raise his own got damn children pushed her further away.

It blew her like the flame she blew in the air, thinking of different dance moves, hustling options, and the role she played, helping Granny in any way.

When their grandmother Liz moved to North Carolina, she took Tara, Kendrick, and the twins, Kacee and Kasie, with her.

Queen sent her granny money every month for them since their parents were still lost, which made shaking her ass simple.

She also understood why her mother ran away from her grandma Liz's strict house rules, but to abandon your children, she never understood.

Watching the streets take hold of her parents instead of them taking hold of responsibilities made Queen hate both her parents.

Hearing the horror stories from her aunts made the shots go down smoother, but running from your children, she could never understand, and that alone made her not want any or anything to do with her birth givers.

Their grandma Liz didn't play when it came to rules under her roof. She locked the doors at seven thirty, homework completed by eight, and no boys were calling her house phone. That alone pushed Queen to run behind Samaya.

Running the streets with her cousin Samaya was all she knew, and being hungry made the hustle come easy until the easy hustle took her brother Kendrick. That meant no more homeless, hungry-ass nights and chasing bums down alleyways, and she still got money as it came by, making the hustle more straightforward as she crawled on all fours.

The phones she sent the twins to keep in contact with her they used every day to call her for Kendrick. The twins reminded her of their eighteenth birthday approaching, so approaching the edge of the stage came with ease.

Hearing their voices made her hustle even harder, going onto the stage with all smiles, doing the splits to get a quick dollar, knowing her siblings wouldn't suffer as she did. She did what needed to be done by any means necessary, wishing their parents would participate and make necessary moves.

Whenever Queen heard the operator end the call with Kendrick, that made her end the night with putting money on his books, and she didn't care if it came from Merch, VIP, or the pole.

Queen always wanted her own money, crib, and clothes because she got tired of stealing shit.

After sleeping in cars on long cold and hot nights, twerking on that stage half naked with pride to get a quick dollar meant no more running the streets broke. *But, I do be cold as hell on this stage in the winter months*, Queen thought.

She never had options to ask her parents for shit or help from family, so that alone made her grind even harder and not deal with that friend shit. Therefore, going to work became her bestie with unwanted developed friendships with peekaboo, "let me see the dollar" boo-boos.

Asking clients if they wanted a private dance was more accessible than writing down what she wanted to be accomplished in the next five years because the money came that easy.

Queen went to live with their aunt Teresa for a few months until her Section 8 came through and did inspections, and she got tired of that hiding shit too.

That shit never lasted long, so they had to move around without Teresa just how they moved their money around, not to be found.

Teresa had caught her boyfriend looking at them one time, and that shit got him cut up and put the fuck out sooner than he could unpack his weekly backpack. With that violation, Teresa started hustling right along with them.

Auntie Teresa didn't give a fuck about what they did as long as she got her monthly payments and flame when they rented their first house together.

Gathering her money up off that floor made her feel good that she didn't have to ask anybody for shit or sleep in nasty-ass motels again or her aunt's floor.

Flaming and taking a few shots before work every night made the performance and tolerance for some bullshit with the game go easy, so not giving a fuck about feelings came easy.

When it came to the pole, stage, or what people thought about her, she could care less. *Long as I see green and they don't get in the way of it, I'm good*, Queen thought as the sounds continued. *Poop. Bang. Poop. Bang, bang, bang, poop.* Queen screamed so loud, you'd thought they'd shot her. "*Get the fuck down, Samaya*," Queen shouted. *Bang, poop. Bang. Poop. Bang, bang.* "Queen...*stay the fuck down,*" Samaya replied. *Bang, bang, poop, poop, bang.*

When the cars started peeling off, they stood up, slowly looking around to see Rocky standing in the alley, letting his shit ring. *Bang, bang. Bang. Bang. Poop. Poop. Bang.*

Queen said, "*Stay the fuck down, Samaya!*"

Rocky said, "*Motherfucker! Don't ever come back here.*"

Samaya said, "That's Rocky shit-starting ass."

They waited for a few minutes before standing up, but Queen was mad as hell that the only club that allowed them to start dancing so young was owned by Mr. Rocky himself. "*Stupid motherfuckers,*" Rocky shouted like he had done something striking.

Samaya had her pistol in her hand, but she wasn't about to get shot or shoot for Rocky's nasty ass. As long as Queen was okay, she was staying put.

Samaya said, "You okay, baby? Make sure you're not hit anywhere."

Queen said, "I'm okay! Are you okay?"

Samaya said, "Yes. Follow me to my house. Always starting shit with his crazy ass."

*****

When they arrived at Samaya's place, they flamed and took shots all night, thinking up a plan to get more money.

Samaya said, "I told your ass to start carrying that thang with you at all times. Quit leaving it in the car and house. What good is it if you don't carry it? Damn!"

Queen said, "They just let loose on his ass. He probably on some fluky shit again."

Samaya said, "They let that shit ring on each other. I don't give a fuck. Think it's time we move around and do some new shit!"

Queen said, "Look at how I'm shaking and shit!"

Samaya said, "That man bought you the gun for safety. I bet he thinks you know how to use it, huh?"

Queen said, "I do. I always forget it in the car. What the fuck is so funny?"

Samaya said, "Your ass lying. Tell me about the frog again."

Queen said, "Fuck you, Samaya! He did jump across the lake and turn into Merch. That's how I met Merch. Bitch, I'm not lying. Quit laughing at me!"

Samaya said, "Bitch, a lake though? Every time you flame, yo ass make up shit."

Queen said, "I should have recorded the shit! You said you seen TT knife turn into a gun, da fuck."

Samaya said, "I can't deal with you. Give me the flame, bitch! Seriously, I know you didn't hear the story I told yo ass. Give it to me!"

*****

That morning, Samaya was taking Queen on a mission to get her right. They flamed, ate breakfast, and flamed again, then headed out flaming.

Queen said, "A gun range, cousin?"

Samaya said, "This will get us right. All that nervous shit gots to go."

Queen said, "Hit this shit! Let's go, baby!"

*****

Samaya just stood there laughing at Queen fumbling because she was nervous, but all that shit was about to stop.

Samaya said, "*Don't be scared! Shoot dat bitch then!*"

Poop, poop, poop, poop, poop!

Queen said, "Oh my gosh! Bitch, I'm shooting this bitch! You get over here, Trigger Finger Betsy. Let's see what you do!"

Samaya said, "*Girl, please! I was shook last night too! I would have shot back if need to. I knew what the fuck I was doing. Why are we yelling in this bitch?*"

Queen said, "That shit was right next to us. Let me shake this shit off. Watch this!"

*****

Queen kept a bag fuckin' with her friend Merch, and she loved this side hustle that came easier than taking clothes off.

He stayed 100 with her, and she stayed 100 with him, so their sideline business was business only. Being loyal to keep the bag and flame coming in was her main focus and him being happy.

Merch never wanted to get caught slipping by another motha-fucker trying to come up, so he made sure they were strapped picking up and dropping off packages to the bank and clientele.

After handling the business, they drove around the lake flaming and listening to music while she slowly massaged his dick with her tongue. Queen made sure her daddy was pleased because he gave her whatever she desired and more from a man.

Merch never tripped about her side hustle being a stripper or asked questions about her family, which turned her on even more. The fewer issues, the better was her way of thinking because that way she didn't have to think about them.

All she ever wanted was to meet someone as real as him with a lot of money, handsome, and simple with leadership skills. That made her mindset go from caring too much for him and not giving a fuck about bullshit she saw that she neglected herself.

Going from rags to riches within six months; finishing high school; owning a crib, two cars, a storage room with plenty of money; and most of all, being his lady friend.

*****

She chopped it up with her auntie for a minute, deciding on what she should do with her siblings and their living situation.

Teresa said, "The twins can stay with me until you get a bigger house. They're letting your mom out early because she's doing well.

Hopefully, she doesn't come with that bullshit 'I want my kids back' shit."

Queen said, "Auntie. Were all grown now, fuck that! I thought you knew where my dad was?"

Teresa said, "He was at the strip club the other night."

Queen said, *"Oh my gosh, Auntie! Why didn't you tell me?"*

Teresa said, "You were twerking all that ass on him."

Queen said, "Ick, TT. I'm talking about my father, not Merch. *Ick!"*

Teresa said, "Oh, okay. Could have sworn I heard you calling him Daddy. I know where your father is. Are you ready?"

Queen said, "Yes! Let me roll this flame real quick."

Teresa said, "I see you're getting nervous. Just say what's on your heart."

Queen said, "What the fuck does my heart has to do with anything?"

Teresa said, "Damn! You're really messed up, baby."

They drove around for hours looking for him, flaming back-to-back. They checked alleys, corner stores, where the dopeheads are, parks where the homeless hang out, under the bridges, and, last but not least, his mama's house.

Queen said, "We should've come here first."

Teresa said, "I don't fuck with these people like that."

Queen said, "He ain't nothing but a crackhead anyway."

Teresa said, "Excuse me! I don't know who the fuck told you that. Just because he hangs out around these places doesn't make him a crackhead. He blended in to make his money, baby."

Queen said, "Can you take me home?"

Teresa said, "Fuck it! I'll get his number. Stay here!"

When Teresa came back to the car, her eyes were all teary. She started flaming real quick, and Queen could tell she was pissed because she saw that look before and it wasn't right.

Queen said, "What's the matter, Auntie?"

Teresa said, "A bug just flew in my eye. Let me take you home."

Queen said, "Auntie! You can't lie for shit! What happened?"

Teresa said, "His sister opened the door, saw my face, and shut the fucking door in my face. Bitch, just pissed me off! Man…I wish I weren't on paper. Let me drop you off. I'll go to the barbershop and get his number from his fine-ass brother. Fuck her!"

Queen said, "Why she do that?"

Teresa said, "Your mama, Tamyra, and I jumped her brother punk ass for putting his hands on your mama."

Queen said, "So, y'all was gangbanging and whooped on my father?"

Teresa said, "I didn't say we won. His big muscular ass was slinging the fuck out of our small, frail asses. After that fight, I went and bought my first knife. Never again!"

Queen said, "Don't forget to leave the car parked, TT. I'm on my way to my baby."

*****

Queen walked into the room butt naked with her hair down just as he liked. She knew to whisper in his ear because it turned him on, and she loved doing it. *He's gonna give me more flame and money*, Queen thought.

She slowly turned around, handing him the flame as she twerked in front of him, making her ass clap and bounce. Every time he smacked her ass, she twerked harder.

Queen said, "Make sure you handle all this ass before you bounce, Daddy."

Merch said, "Bring that ass over here!"

She loved talking shit to his sexy ass for some reason that made him throw the dick faster and go deeper just like he went deeper into his bank account.

Merch said, "I'm about to put a baby in yo ass."

Her pussy creamed from the way he grabbed her ass and pulled her hair. She knew he was about to bust when he slapped her ass as usual, and she always slapped the money from the flame into her stash.

Merch said, "Damn, Q! You are throwing that ass. Get this dick!"

My baby dick stays hard, Queen thought as she jumped on top of his dark, muscular, sweaty body, six foot four, juicy pussy lips, round nose, beautiful teeth, and no ash on his body, smelling good.

She sat down and rode his dick like she was dancing to become his first-prize lady-to-be. He cuffed her ass and pulled up as she went down, hoping that a baby had made a way to blossom.

Beep.

Not now, Queen thought.

Buzz.

Not now, Merch thought.

Merch picked her ass up and carried her to the shower where they continued to grind and suck. The steamy water was glistening off their beautiful skin, and that made her indulge in him even more, forgetting about the sideline.

Merch watched her rub her body down with moisturizer, looking at every inch of her, five foot four, bright skin, perky 36D, twenty-eight-inch waist, ass big enough to sit his drink on, hazel eyes, workable lips, long dark brown hair, and Brazilian-waxed tight pussy.

He tapped her ass gently as always, playing with a stack of money, and she took it every time with no hesitation. Queen knew when he was talking shit in a jokingly way and when to stay out of his way.

Merch said, "Go get that money, Q. Can't be ashy."

He handed her the pink 9-millimeter he bought her for Valentine's Day as he watched her swish her juicy ass out the door.

Merch said, "Make sure the safety off. Don't be scared to use it."

Queen said, "I'm never scared! I've learned from the best, baby."

*****

She pulled off as if she was leaving but parked down the street next to her auntie's beat-up car that he didn't know about and switched cars. She waited for him to pass, so she could follow his ass before she headed to work.

Toonie said, "Drop me off, Queen. I don't have time for this shit. I'm not about to chase behind a man. Then to think my dumb ass waited for you."

Queen said, "You're always disappearing on us. Why don't you fuck with us?"

Toonie said, "Queen! My mama doesn't fuck with me. She's done more for you and Samaya, and I'm her only child. Just take me home before this man sees us."

Queen said, "You're special! Well, take my car, and I'll call you later."

Toonie said, "Don't call me from jail behind him. Seriously, your brother about to get out. I'm calling Samaya on yo ass."

*****

Queen pulled up to her aunt's house to handle some business. When she saw loose lips, Len, she tried to hurry and leave because she was on a mission.

Len said, "Hey…Queen!"

Teresa said, "You can leave it over there. When I get done with her hair, I'll get the money from her."

Queen said, "Thanks, TT. I'm gone."

Len said, "These kids nowadays are rude."

Teresa said, "Don't do that! My niece doesn't know you like that for all that hey shit."

Len said, "I was gonna tell her some school chick is running around calling dude her fiancé."

Teresa said, "My niece doesn't give a fuck about that. What's her name though?"

Merch
The Streets Don't Owe Me Shit

It didn't matter to Merch how much money he had as a unit with his family; he kept hustling and stayed loyal with his homeys from the beginning.

He learned a lot from their father on how to treat women with respect. He always kept their mothers in a decent home with money, best clothes, and cars.

Even though they had different mothers, he made sure his sons went to the same schools and stayed in the same house, never showing favoritism.

*****

Merch went to meet up with the club's owner to go over some paperwork and some numbers before showing them to their lawyers. He brought trigger-finger Tee and observant joking-ass Ax with him because he didn't know the scenery like that unless he was dealing with Queen.

Merch said, "This the new spot I was telling you about."

Tee said, "It's a few minutes from downtown. Then it's on the strip where a lot of walkers and travelers come. This a good find, fam."

Merch said, "It's ten minutes from the airport, hotels, and the highway. A lot of money is going to come through with the right advertisement, new management, and staff."

Ax said, "First, we need to get the construction crew to tear down the old letter and put up a whole new front. Then they got this fake security at the front with a dirty T-shirt on."

Merch and Tee were laughing at Ax's crazy ass when a skinny stripper approached them smiling, showing all her yellow teeth. They both looked at Ax because they knew he was about to say something about her.

Ax said, "Look at this shit! The front door has been kicked down a few times. Was that a bullet hole?"

Merch said, "Cuz, chill out! Aww, shit!"

Skinny Stripper said, "Hello, fellas. How can I assist you?"

"You can get your skinny ass out our face and go brush yo teeth," Ax whispered to the guys. The guys started laughing hard as hell, hoping she didn't hear him.

Merch said, "Can you please go get Rocky?"

Skinny Stripper said, "Right this way, gentlemen."

Merch placed a twenty in her G-string, and she swished away.

Ax said, "I hope she gets a steak and comes back for auditions."

Merch said, "Fuck that! We're getting all new staff."

Tee said, "Ax, man, your ass be going in. All this shit about to change real soon."

Ax said, "Man, these drugs got these bitches looking sick as fuck."

Merch said, "Right! Look at her, fam. Skinny ass popping pills and hitting the pipe in the dressing room. I've been here during the nights, and all the chicks thick as fuck."

Tee said, "They're doing it because the owner is allowing this sick shit."

Ax said, "Look at this fat fucker! He stretched the horse out on the shirt."

Merch said, "That's dude fat ass. Looking like he ate all the dough."

Rocky approached the guys with a big fake smile showing all his gold teeth. His fat-ass stomach was hanging over his belt with a sandwich in one hand, and he trying to shake their hands with the other. "I take it that you're Rocky? Nice to meet you," Merch said. "Yes, I am. What's funny? I want to laugh too," Rocky replied.

"Nothing. You got something white on your mouth," Ax said. Merch and the guys shook hands with Rocky then went straight to the business. "He just used his shirt," Tee mumbled.

"Okay! Now, I see a few ladies we should keep," Tee said in a jokingly way to Rocky. "Follow me to my office in the back, and, Jill, go get us some drinks please," Rocky demanded.

Merch saw her at his brother's spot last week but didn't real-ize she worked here because he was picky as hell. "Rocky? Does she come with the club," Merch asked.

All the guys chuckled because she was fine as hell. Merch was trying to figure out how long she'd been working there because his brother Ishmael didn't deal with strippers at all.

Rocky said, "Yes, she does. She's new here. So, back to business. Here's the number I came up with."

Merch said, "I see, you went up, like, forty thousand. What's that all about?"

Rocky said, "A new appraiser stopped from the city, said I own the empty building space on the other side. I'll show you after we finish here."

Merch said, "Well, my construction men Tee and Ax here can do the walkthrough with us. They'll see how much value the extra space adds."

Ax said, "Let's do this! Let's start with the empty side first. Then upstairs, so I can check for water damage before we go downstairs."

After the walkthrough, Ax gave Merch an estimate on how much everything would cost for renovations and getting everything up to codes. Merch, Tee, and Rocky went over numbers, had a few shots, and flamed until they came up with an agreement.

Merch said, "I'll have my lawyers look over the agreement when they get here. Then we'll meet later tonight to finish signing everything."

Rocky said, "All right, my man. Enjoy the VIP on me tonight."

Ax said, "Merch…is he serious, fam? Hopefully, they bleach it first."

Merch said, "Let us get the bottle. Thanks. We're good on the VIP though."

Rocky said, "I insist. Let my girls show you a good time."

*****

Merch called his homey to meet him at the club to handle some business. When he arrived, they met in the VIP room.

Merch said, "What's up, Swen?"

Swen said, "What's up, nephew? Baby, go get us some drinks."

"Okay, Daddy," the baby said. Swen always had a female with him to make shit look good and not draw attention to himself.

Merch said, "Same ol' shit! Learning from the best."

Swen said, "Heard Pops is coming home soon? Are you keeping your hands clean?"

Merch said, "Yeah. You can't hold a real nigga down for too long. Sorry about your little brother, Unc."

Swen said, "Thanks! That shit fucked my mom and dad up. He was on some hero-type shit."

Merch said, "I can't blame him. I'd do the same shit if someone fucks with mines."

They flamed a few before Merch made his mind up if he wanted the shit, like always. His baby came back in looking and shit. "Go find some friends," Swen told her ass. Merch chuckled as he counted out the money for Swen.

Swen knew his best friends' sons wouldn't try anything funny because they grew up thinking that he was their uncle.

They were so into their conversation that they didn't even notice that Rocky peeked in the room and turned around before they could see him. Rocky saw the pistols sitting on the table, a lot of money, and flame. His fat ass got spooked, hoping they didn't see him because a mission just went through his mind that quick.

When Swen left with his baby, Merch went on about his business with Ax and Tee, talking about a layout plan.

Ax followed Merch out the club to his car, making sure no bullshit happened. Then Tee always walked a distance from them, so it wouldn't look like he was with them. He would be the element of surprise just in case some shit popped off.

When Merch went to get in his car, he saw Samaya strutting through the back door with her nose turned all up.

Merch said, "What's up, Samaya?"

Samaya said, "Nothing, nigga! Where Queen at? Ask her what's up."

Merch said, "That's your fam. You should know, smart-ass!"

Samaya said, "Call her! Don't be questioning me, Merch."

Merch said, "Bitch! Quit playing with me before I smack the shit out of you!"

Samaya said, "Go on, Merch! Quit playing with me! Go find Queen."

Merch said, "You got a man yet?"

Samaya said, "'Do you have a man yet?' The fuck!"

Merch followed Samaya to the back and smacked the back of her head. He made her lipstick smear onto her slushy cup.

Samaya said, *"What the fuck, dude? You play too damn much."*

Merch said, "Bitch! Don't play with me. Ask your cousin with your stuck-up ass."

Samaya said, "Exactly! She's your bitch! Not me…"

Merch said, "Shut the fuck up! Give these packages to Queen and Teresa for me."

Samaya said, "This what the fuck you followed me for? I'm not a delivery service, nigga."

Merch said, "Do as you're told, smart-ass! You smoke the shit? Miss delivery."

*****

Merch's text to Queen: "When you come to work tonight I'll be here."

Queen's text to Merch: "okay! bring some money."

*****

Merch went to his mom's crib to change and talk numbers with his accountant. Then he met up with Ax and Tee to make packages. He had plans to deliver a few before heading back to the club.

Ax said, "Let me take it up? I want to see her fine ass."

Merch said, "Yeah, if I go. I'm staying there for a few minutes."

Tee said, "We're not waiting on fam tonight unless she got some friends in that bitch."

Merch said, "Run that shit, fam! We have a few more drops, and I have places to be."

When they finished making runs, they headed for the club, but they stopped for some Swishers and Backwoods first.

Merch said, "Look at the ass on her. Got damn!"

Tee said, "What her face look like, though?"

Ax said, "Turn around, turn around. *Ohhh, noooo! Fam...*"

Merch said, "Nope! Couldn't do it. Her face is all wrong."

Tee said, "You don't have to look at her face though, fam."

Ax said, "Well, she looks like a skipper. Skip my big-ass nose, skip my droopy bottom lip, skip my dark-ass eyes, and skip on to this ass. Fam! Start looking at the face too. Shit! I forgot. Look at your baby moms."

Tee said, "I told y'all! That bitch took the dick when I was drunk."

Merch said, "My dick not working if I'm not awake. He got a sensor with eyes. Pretty face, pretty pussy alert. He's not going!"

Ax said, "I don't give a fuck if the bitch ass fat. If she's ugly and we fuck, it's a possibility we can get pregnant. Nope! Hit this shit, fam. Get out the trance of her ass."

Merch said, "This the last drop. I'll be right back."

Ax said, "Fam! You know she is about to be on your ass."

Tee said, "Let me go, fam? Just wave to her from the car. I'll tell her your stomach hurt."

They laughed so hard to the point Ax started choking off the smoke. Merch was holding his stomach but went to drop it off anyway.

*****

When they pulled up to the club, they saw Teresa bending over in the trunk getting some bags out then heading into the back door.

Ax said, "If all them strippers are going through the back door, we need to hire some dancers quickly."

Merch said, "My girl, and her family, the finest ones in this piece that I've seen. It's a few that I think we should keep, but we should wait until after tonight to make our decision. The night chicks look better than the daytime dancers anyway."

Tee said, "Morning dancers get high all night, then drag dance all day. The night dancers get their beauty sleep all day, shop, and dream of hustling."

Ax said, "I'm so high that shit made sense, fam."

Merch said, "Beauty sleep? I guess we were the beast then."

Tee said, "Ask a night dancer what she does all day?"

Merch said, "Queen sleeps and shops."

Ax said, "Fam, stop it! He got you believing that shit!"

They sat out in the truck flaming until everybody else arrived. The guys went in the club like a mob, and Merch saw Queen standing at the bar talking to one of her regulars. He didn't bother her until she walked over to him on her way to the dressing room.

Merch said, "Why do you still have street clothes on?"

Following yo monkey ass, and getting addresses, Queen thought. She held that shit in because she knew he'd carry her ass to the back. She didn't want to fuck up all the money she was about to make off him and the club.

Queen said, "Just walked in, and he waved for me to come over."

Merch said, "I don't see a tip. Time is money, right?"

Queen said, "Where's my package? Follow me, so I can show you where the tip at."

Merch said, "In the back with your fam. Not right now, Q."

Queen said, "When have you ever turned down my juices?"

Merch said, "Not right now Q. Later…Quit playing with me."

Queen said, "Okay, playa!"

Merch said, "Don't say that shit to me! When have you ever saw me playing? I'll see you later."

CHAPTER 3

The Club
The Spot Where It Goes Down

Samaya had a routine when she got to the club, and it works every time. It consists of scoping out the money in the room first before she hit the stage and what clients were there, so she'd know what music she had to pick.

Queen always came late since she started fucking with Merch, but Samaya didn't complain since he was the streets and kept them with that good flame.

"*We don't clock in until we hit the stage, bitch*," Queen yelled as she entered the dressing room. Samaya already knew Queen was high off dick, and flame, when she was this happy, and happy meant they're making extra money that night.

Samaya and Queen always shared the same dressing room unless Samaya's younger sister Tara came in to make a quick dollar, which was rare. Skunk snatched her ass out the club scene, and put her on the right path. Tara received her high school diploma and graduated cosmetology school at nineteen.

"Thank you, Merch," Samaya mumbled as she hit the flame. "Girl, hush! I haven't seen him since this morning," Queen replied.

Samaya said, "Long as you're happy, we're paid."

Before doing their rounds, they took a couple of shots and flamed with their aunt, Teresa. Teresa made sure they had her best wigs on before hitting the stage so that she could advertise.

Samaya went out to greet clientele, noticing a few new faces, hoping they came to spend that bread for the main event.

When she made them wait for lap dances, it always worked for the newbies because all the other females were thirsty as fuck. Samaya would stand up and dance slowly and let them fantasize while the other females go straight to their laps bouncing, giving no tease.

Samaya said, "It's some new money out there. I need to shine when I hit the stage."

Queen said, "Yeah! I saw Merch and his friends here talking to Rocky fat monkey ass."

Samaya said, "Merch came back here looking for you with his irritating ass."

Queen said, "He told me! He said, 'She still needs a man to tame that smart-ass mouth.' I ignored his ass."

Samaya said, "He can't even tame you? The fuck he worried about me for?"

Teresa said, "I know, right! He got some fine-ass brothers. What the daddy look like? Shit!"

Queen said, "Auntie, you are so crazy."

Teresa said, "I'm serious, though. How long are you gonna make your clients wait this time, Samaya?"

Queen said, "That shit be working for her. I tried that shit, and all my clients went to somebody else."

Samaya said, "I already told yo ass you talk too much and to get butt naked on the stage."

Teresa said, "*Well, damn!* That's my cue to leave."

Samaya saw this pretty woman walking up like a model with a white short silk dress, hair pulled up in a cute bun, and body looking like a gold glimmer.

Samaya said, "Jai? Okay! I see you."

Jai said, "Yes, Saria. You look good, girl."

Jai winked her eye at Samaya like they had a secret, but she knew Samaya wasn't with that licking shit.

Samaya said, "You're working that outfit, Ms. Jai."

Jai placed a hundred-dollar bill in Samaya's G-string. "Get yo money, girl."

Samaya said, "Thank you, sweetie. I have a VIP table reserved for you by the stage with the bottle of your choice."

Jai said, "I like your outfit also. Let me see how you work, girl."

Samaya said, "Bitch finally listened to me. *Take everything off! More money!*"

Jai said, "What?"

Samaya said, "I'm thinking out loud. Come with me, girl."

Samaya was picking up Queen's money, noticing that Jai was mesmerized in deep thought watching her ass.

Queen backed up in front of Jai twerking to the beat, and Jai made it rain rain. When Merch walked up, he dropped so much money on his Queen to get Jai's attention then walked off.

Teresa said, "Damn, Queen! *Get that money.*"

Samaya said, "*Yassss, bitch!*"

Jai said, "*Okay! Work that shit!*"

Samaya said, "I'll be back, Jai!"

Samaya rushed to the back, passing Queen as she exited the stage with all smiles, and paid well. She stood behind the curtain until she heard the DJ announce her name.

She was still nervous as day one, so she would peek out to see if her regulars were at the stage.

DJ said, "Time for the main event…*Sexy-ass Saria to the stage!*"

DJ always added extra if you threw him a few extra dollars, making the ladies feel extra special. Especially if you're pretty, and he wanted to fuck. He'd say your name like you're a Hollywood actor coming out to get a goddamn Grammy.

Merch said, "Look, bro! There she is!"

DJ said, "*Ms. Saria…*"

Samaya was strolling down the stage, noticing that Merch was trying to grab Queen before she could get to the stage.

DJ said, "Fellas and beautiful women. Help me welcome Saria to the got damn stage."

She swung her head down and got on all fours, started crawling, and slowly twerking her ass to the beat. The more people that came to the stage, the faster she approached the edge, stopping and bouncing her ass for each tipper.

When Jai approached the stage, she stood next to Teresa, Queen, and a group of guys. Samaya looked at Jai like, *My bitch!*

Jai said, "*Aye, girl!*"

Teresa said, "*Get it, girl!*"

Samaya climbed the pole and came down in the splits, bouncing her ass like she was making a baby, watching Jai and Queen make it rain, but not like the man wearing all white.

DJ said, "Saria...doing her thang, fellas."

To see him better, Samaya showed out doing a headstand with her face facing his, and the pole between her cheeks giving her balance. When she saw who it was, her stomach tightened up, and her body started doing shit on its own.

Jai said, "*Aye! Get it, girl.*"

Isaiah from around the hood, Lovely Vines, done came to see her at the come-up spot. She saw him push politely past Jai and place a stack of cash on the stage, and her ass must have seen it, too, the way it started twerking.

That shit turned her on, and she gave him eye contact the whole time, not knowing if she should be mad or happy at the same time he came to the job.

Queen knew the drill, and she started picking Samaya's money up for safekeeping from the thirsty when she couldn't see it.

Seeing all that money this customer was throwing made Samaya's ass have its own goddamn brain. Her ass cheeks were talking in sign language to his brain and pockets.

She stood up, slowly massaging her body, giving his fine ass all the attention, noticing he had a few guys standing with him as if they were watching his back.

Queen said, "*Damn bitch! Twerk...twerk that ass?*"

Teresa said, "*She's snapping! Don't break your back!*"

Samaya made her way off the stage, nervous for no reason, and her family was right behind her.

Samaya said, "I'm nervous, Queen! I liked all his shit on Lovely Vines."

Queen said, "All you need is a few shots, hit this flame, and go get him."

Teresa said, "I was hoping that wig didn't fall off."

Samaya said, "*Auntie…oh my gosh!* Let me freshen up!"

Teresa said, "*What's funny? I'm so serious. You were shaking, twerking, and some mo shit!*"

Queen said, "Spray on some perfume, and brush your teeth, because your ass looked like you saw a ghost. Scary ass!"

Samaya said, "Let me lock my money up until Toonie gets here. I need to step back out to greet, and show love to the ones who tipped well."

Teresa said, "He's the only one that tipped well. He made everybody move to the side."

Queen said, "This is my first time seeing him up close. Girl, he fine just like his brothers."

Samaya said, "Who's his brothers? Don't tell me, let me guess. Lovely Vines, huh?"

Queen said, "Remember, I told you. Merch wanted to hook you up with his brother."

Samaya said, "Well, he looks like a chocolate bar with muscles. Did you see Jai?"

Queen said, "We talked for a hot minute."

Teresa said, "Well…I want to meet the chocolate bar who created their ass!"

Queen said, "Auntie, I don't know his father. He got some fine-ass cousins though."

Teresa said, "Damn! I need an uncle. Fuck these little boys."

Samaya said, "Let's go chop it up with Jai, before her fine ass leave."

Queen said, "You need to go chop it up with the dude before his fine ass leave. All that money he just placed on the stage, girl."

Samaya said, "I'm not about to look all thirsty."

Teresa said, "Y'all young girls kill me with that thirsty shit."

Queen said, "Auntie, we the same age damn near."

Teresa said, "My mama wasn't no joke. I still like them older."

Samaya and Queen went back to the front to finish up the night with private dances, and the VIP.

Teresa stayed in the back, selling wigs, making appointments, and giving out her number to the girls.

Jai said, "OMG! Girl, that man threw all that money on you. You made that shit look simple."

Samaya said, "That comes with the territory. You look, you pay! Let's go get a shot, girl."

Jai said, "Well, I'm going to mingle a little bit before I leave. It's some nice-looking men in here."

Samaya said, "You're right about that, girl! Go on and get you one."

Samaya didn't see him anywhere in the club. She wanted to thank him, but she couldn't find him, so she went about business as usual.

She made a few thousand giving lap dances, and a few VIP requests from her regulars, and that made her night a good profit.

When she made her way to the dressing room to change, she was surprised when she opened the door. Isaiah was sitting in her chair, looking at his phone as if he didn't see her walk in. "What the fuck," Samaya shouted.

Samaya said, "Are you lost? Do you want a lap dance? VIP is in the front, sir."

Isaiah said, "I know where I'm at, and when I want a lap dance, you'll give it to me. Have a seat, please."

Samaya said, "Really? How'd you get in here, sir?"

Isaiah said, "The same way you did! Have a seat!"

Samaya said, "What do you want?"

Isaiah said, "*You!* I'll call you, so be ready, Ms. Saria."

Samaya said, "How did you get my number?"

Isaiah said, "Never mind all that. I'll call you, or you can call me. Take my business card, lovely."

Samaya said, "Oh my gosh! All these monosyllabic responses."

When Isaiah went to leave out the door, Queen, Sunshine, and Teresa came in giggling as he brushed past them, and that made them laugh even harder.

Sunshine said, "*Hey, Saria!* Damn, he smelled good."

Teresa said, "Change clothes, Queen, so your slow ass can take me home."

Queen said, "Let me see what Merch talking about. I might need you to take my car."

Samaya said, "Queen, did you let that man in here?"

Sunshine said, "He was fine as hell. Is that your man?"

Queen said, "What man? Sunny, mind ya own—"

Samaya said, "You know damn well who I'm talking about."

Teresa said, "I don't know who let his ass back here. Did you get the number?"

Sunshine said, "If she didn't, I'll go get his shit. Now ignore that!"

Teresa said, "Queen, if you don't handle this scorned kneecap broad, I will."

Samaya said, "Thirsty-ass broad! Don't know who they're dealing with."

Samaya sighed loud to piss Sunshine off, so Queen ignored her only because Samaya did. Queen handled her business with Sunshine and left with Teresa.

Queen saw him all in Jai's ear, but Teresa grabbed her arm and pulled her outside. "Don't worry about that," Teresa whispered.

When Samaya was leaving, she saw Isaiah and his friends standing by the main entrance with Merch, and Rocky off to the side. When she saw Sunshine approaching the crowd of men, they all shook their heads no, so she laughed to herself, watching Sunshine turn and walk away fast with a frown.

Samaya always waited for DJ to walk with her to the car so that he could get his tip, and a little conversation that she knew wasn't going anywhere.

DJ said, "You did your thang tonight!"

Samaya said, "My thang? Thanks. What they want with Rocky, DJ?"

She always kept her pistol on her side until she got in the car. Then she put it on her lap in case someone tried robbing her for their money back, or the other strippers' stickup friends.

DJ waited for her to get in the car, as usual, so he could shut her door, and try to get some pussy.

DJ said, "I don't know, baby girl. You know all the shit he is into. He probably owes them money. Rocky in debt with everybody. I see you're going to get home safe."

Samaya said, "Always! Here's your tip. Thank you."

DJ said, "Thanks, baby. What's up with you? When can I take you out? Let me get your number? You got a man, huh?"

Samaya said, "Damn, DJ! Stop with all the questions. I'm going home. I don't go out with coworkers, and I most definitely don't give out my number. We talked about this before, DJ."

DJ said, "It's Donald, Saria. You're too smart and pretty to be in here dancing. When are you gonna stop doing this?"

Samaya said, "How do you know I'm smart? My dancing is just a hustle. I'm gone! Thanks again, Donald."

The building Samaya lived in had an underground parking lot and cameras everywhere. She felt safe once the gate closed because she knew Donald wasn't the only man that wanted her.

*****

Queen let her auntie take her car, but they waited for Merch to finish chopping it up with Rocky before Teresa left.

Queen said, "Look, TT! There his cousins Tee and Ax."

Teresa said, "I'm not getting introduced in a damn parking lot to some young thugs."

Queen said, "What does that mean? You and Samaya something else."

Teresa said, "Presentation, baby! Where you meet them matters how they treat you. Here your man come. Love you. Call me tomorrow."

Queen said, "Why didn't Toonie show up tonight?"

Teresa said, "I don't know! Samaya will find out. Bye!"

*****

Queen didn't even let him shut the car door before she started drilling him with questions.

Queen said, "What did you do today? Where did you go? Thought you were linking with me before I came to work?"

Merch said, "Hello, Queen! How are you doing?"

Queen said, "Hello, Merch! What did you do today?"

Merch said, "I handled my business. What did you do today?"

Queen said, "Fucked you, then came to work."

Merch said, "Funny you weren't here when I first came. I left and came back."

Queen said, "I know, my cousin told me. And I got that. Thank you."

Merch said, "Oh! Now you don't know what to say? Don't get quiet!"

Queen said, "I ran to the store to get some Backwoods and gum. What about—"

Before Queen could finish asking another question, Merch cut that shit short real quick.

Merch said, "Don't start asking me all these damn questions. You ready to do this or what?"

Queen said, "I guess! This what you want, right? That's what you were in her ear about?"

Merch said, "Look! We don't have to do this shit!"

Queen said, "Why her, though?"

Merch said, "You're the one that told me to pick or find somebody. Got damn!"

Queen said, "Whatever! I've been ready!"

Merch said, "Well, stop all that pouting shit, G!"

Queen said, "Not pouting! Just asking questions and making conversation."

Merch said, "At least say hi or how are you doing before questioning me, Detective."

Queen hit his arm then went back to game mode. When she leaned over and pulled his dick out, Merch already knew she was ready. No questions asked and sucked it all the way there without hesitation.

Queen said, "He's ready now. Come on!"

*****

After everybody left, Rocky locked up and called a few people to meet him at the club. They all sat there listening to him, but needed more information before going through with it because Rocky's MO was getting over on people.

Rocky said, "I know what I saw. If y'all do what I say, everything will go as planned. Now, if y'all want to be some pussies, and let this opportunity pass gone head."

Man 1 said, "*Hold the fuck up! I'm not a pussy!*"

Man 2 said, "*I'm not a pussy either. What the fuck!*"

Rocky said, "*Either! Either! Either!* Well, let's not let this pass. I'm selling the place to them first."

Man 3 said, "If everything split evenly, I'm game."

Rocky said, "Don't do shit until I say. Let me find out where the briefcase is."

Man 2 said, "What's in the briefcase?"

Rocky said, "Money and flame!"

*****

Lia wasn't about to tell everything she knew about Mr. Simms. She knew they weren't telling her everything about the case with him, so she played their game with them.

She saw Mr. Simms go in, and leave with a group of people after the club closed, but Thomas wasn't about to get promoted off her hard work.

Lia said, "I didn't see him come or go. You think he knows we're on to him?"

Detective Thomas said, "I know he's not that hard to spot. We should get a search warrant for his house also."

Lia said, "Let me figure out a way to get more concrete evidence first. I'm not letting his nasty ass get off from us fucking up as Afonso did."

Jez
Mixed Up

Jez had a schedule for every day and hated if she was thrown off because that would throw her whole day off. This morning was the gym at 5:00 a.m. sharp, so she rushed past her mother and her overly strong cheap coffee.

Jennifer said, "Good morning. Would you like some coffee?"

Jez said, "I'll pick some up on the way. Thanks."

Jennifer said, "See you tonight for supper?"

Jez said, "I don't know. See you later, Mother."

*****

Jez was leaving the gym and noticed a few men walking into the parking garage laughing, but she paid it no mind. She stopped to buy water out of the vending machine as she watched them get in a silver car with tinted windows.

As she approached her car, she noticed another note from the mystery man that kept putting love notes under her windshield wipers. She grabbed it and started crying, immediately opening her car door and watching her back. "*What the fuck,*" Jez cried out.

> I've been watching you!
> You are so beautiful
> One day you'll be mine!
> I will love you forever!

After reading it, she threw it in her console with the rest of them. She started thinking hard about who it could be, wondering what was so funny with the men that just passed her in the gym to the few guys that spoke to her in the gym, and a lot that just looked.

It couldn't be the guy at the coffee shop because she's never seen him at the gym, and the only men in her cosmetology class were into men.

Back to the coffee shop by 7:00 a.m., finished with her class at ten thirty, coffee again at ten forty-five, and off to help her sister at her shop by 11:00 a.m.

When the shop closed, she went home to her parents' house by six thirty every night faithfully.

Whoever was leaving the notes either knew her schedule or worked out at the gym, and she hoped they didn't know where she lived.

*****

Jez didn't have to worry about money, so she saved all her money from working at the shop and the clients she had at school.

Right before graduating from cosmetology school, she signed up for business management, and her parents paid for school and transportation.

*****

When Jez entered the class, a few girls were looking at her, smiling all hard, so she turned her back to them and set her station up. She wasn't about to fake it with their whispering ass, knowing they didn't like her, and she didn't care for them either.

The teacher said, "Hello, everyone. Let's get ready to open the doors. We're past all the color testing, so relax. *You can test on clients or friends with the cut and style. Did everyone hear me?*"

"*Yes,*" all the students said simultaneously.

Student 1 said, "Jez, do you have a client or friend coming today?"

Jez said, "Why? Client and friend are the same shit!"

Tara said, "Jez, my sister coming."

Student 1 said, "Just asking. Tara. How'd you do on the coloring?"

Tara said, "I took that before you started. I'm done with everything. I'm here getting clients and money."

Jez said, "That's a good idea."

61

Student 1 said, "I asked my baby daddy's sister to come, but they act funny when he does."

Jez said, "Act funny? The teacher said we could use clients. Didn't you hear her?"

Student 2 said, "Here she goes. Girl, quit talking to her."

Jez said, "I would act funny if she wanted to do my hair. If she stops talking and listens to the damn teacher, she'd have clients."

Student 1 said, "Hold on, bitch! I do listen!"

Student 2 said, "You're a mean bitch, Jez!"

Tara said, "Your lips are loose with that bitch word. Act pretty and professional, so you can pass this time."

Student 1 said, "Fuck you, Tara!"

Tara said, "You need to fuck this test."

Jez said, "You're talking, but you're the one that told us she failed every test and had to repay for a retake. Not to mention, they're getting rich off her dumb, not coloring, no cutting, or styling, ass."

Student 2 said, "I didn't say all that. You're adding extra, just like your extra ass."

Student 1 said, "*All y'all ass fake!*"

Tara said, "Watch that y'all shit."

The teacher said, "*Excuse me, ladies! I'm opening the doors. Smile.*"

Jez said, "Now we're fake, because y'all talk about each other. Get the fuck out of here."

Teacher said, "Jez, you did a nice job on that color yesterday. I'll be making an appointment with you soon. Keep up the good work."

Jez said, "Thank you, I really appreciate that."

Tara said, "Hey, girl. I'm proud of you."

Jez said, "Thanks, Tara."

Student 1 said, "Teacher always amping."

Student 2 said, "You know she has to amp her pets."

Jez said, "You need to amp your girl, so she can get some pet clientele and graduate."

Tara said, "*Not* 'graduate,' Jez, stop!"

Jez and Tara laughed, clinking their combs together.

Teacher said, "Now. Now. Ladies, let's keep it cute."

*****

Jez headed to the coffee shop before going to work with her sister.

Jai said, "Hey, twin, how's it going this morning?"

Jez said, "Here's your coffee! Surprisingly you're here early."

Jai said, "What's with you, *no hello*?"

Jez said, "Sorry, sis! It's just, this is like the fourth note left under my windshield, and I don't know what to do."

Jai said, "You reported it to the security office already. You should call Daddy's crazy brother, or get a gun."

Jez said, "Uncle not crazy, he's defensive."

Jai said, "Go to the police, as I told you before."

Jez said, "*Okay*. The manager said they would keep an eye open because the security cameras been down for a month now. I just looked at their ass, like, okay."

Jai said, "If a muthafucka were stalking their daughter, they'd fix the cameras."

Jez said, "It has to be somebody that works there, or following me. What the hell?"

Jai said, "OMG! They got you cursing all out of your element. Quit going to that location, period. That's some fluky-ass shit."

Jez said, "I'm quiet, but I don't want a man that can't approach me."

*****

Jez picked up her clothes from the dry cleaners every Tuesday before going to the shop.

The cashier said, "Hello. How can I assist you today, beautiful?"

Jez said, "Hi. Here's my ticket."

The cashier said, "You don't talk much, huh?"

Jez said, "I'm fine. Thank you!"

The cashier said, "My name is David."

Jez said, "Well, you know my name. Nice meeting you."

David said, "Lift your head up, beautiful, it's okay."

Jez said, "How much?"

David said, "You have five items. It's on the house today, miss."

Jez said, "That's nice, but I insist on paying. Thought appreciated!"

David said, "See you again. Have a nice day."

Jez said, "Yeah! Yeah!"

It couldn't have been David leaving a note because the gym is across town, and I barely speak to him. He can't get my information or my whereabouts just from my credit card, Jez thought.

*****

When she approached the house, she saw the lights still on, so she knew her mother was still awake and full of questions.

It used to piss her off when her sister said, "You are acting like our mom," but she saw it herself and didn't like it.

John said, "Hello, daughter. How was your day?"

Jennifer said, "She's coming in later and later each night."

John said, "Honey…leave her alone."

Jez said, "Hello, Father. Hello, Mother. How was your day?"

Jennifer said, "He asked you first. You didn't say much this morning. What's going on?"

Jez said, "My day was productive. I passed my styling and coloring so far. Mother…come in and get a style from your daughter tomorrow."

John said, "That's a good idea! I'll bring her."

Jez said, "Dad…Mom knows how to drive, right? See you in the morning, Mother."

Jennifer said, "Hmm. Yes, daughter."

CHAPTER 4

Tara
Finding My Own Way

Tara never had to worry about money since Skunk scooped her from the club.

Skunk said, "Baby? Come help me count this money before I leave."

Tara said, "You know…I need my allowance."

Skunk said, "Ass, always begging! I see you're showing that fresh wax off. You can have all this shit! Spread that butterfly open."

Her job was to keep her hair done, body waxed, hands and feet manicured; finish school; and keep him happy.

Skunk made all the money for the foundation, so she kept it maintained and hired all the help to keep everything lavish.

She made sure everyone left by 5:00 p.m. so she could have some private time. "I love your silky cocoa skin tone," Skunk said.

Tara always giggled when Skunk kissed her stomach, slowly making his tongue go in a heart motion. She loved watching this tough man on top of her, blowing, licking, and sucking her clitoris like there's no tomorrow. His head moved up, and down, slowly indulging into her heart, making her fall for him even more.

Tara said, "Skunk…OMG!"

As soon as her legs began to shake, Skunk put his arms around her thighs in a locking position, so she couldn't run as she climaxed.

Beep. They both ignored the sound of the phone.

Skunk said, "T-turn over."

Tara said, "Okay, Daddy!"

Tara loved that demanding shit, especially with the nickname calling; she turned over fast as hell.

Tara's phone started ringing, and they both ignored it, knowing damn well it was her mom anyway.

Skunk loved hitting it from the back, watching her ass he paid for jiggle.

"Damn, T," Skunk said as he flipped her over onto her back, pushing her legs open. The head of his dick went in, out, in, out, and he knew her pussy would grip his throbbing dick, like always.

He pushed her lower back down with his hand to form her arch better, then he went in stroking, holding Tara's hand so she couldn't push his thigh.

He loved watching her boobs he paid for jiggling up and down fast as hell smashed on the bed. "Hold on! Baby, you are clowning me," Tara said. "Quit begging then," Skunk replied.

She turned around and pulled him closer, "I'm taking all that," Tara whispered. They French-kissed while rubbing each other softly, grinding hard, about to start a fire, breathing heavy, and moaning. When Skunk began sucking her nipples, they both climaxed at the same *damn* time.

Buzz. Skunk ignored the sound. "Fuck that phone," he whispered.

"Come here, Daddy," Tara said. "*Damn, baby!* Daaaaamn," Skunk mumbled. "Shh, relax! Let me clown you for a minute," Tara said, getting on her knees, making smacking sounds while kissing the tip of his dick. *Who taught her this shit*, Skunk thought. When she started licking, spitting, and making smacking sounds, his body went numb just like she wanted.

Skunk said, "When you learn this shit? Got damn!"

Tara said, "Practice makes perfect! Right?"

They finished with "I love you," exiting the shower, but Skunk was still thinking who in the hell she's been practicing on.

Tara replied to Samaya's text, "I'll be there in a hot minute."

Skunk replied to Isaiah, "Yup bro, at the spot."

Skunk said, "Don't be scared to use it."

Skunk hit Tara's ass when she passed, handing her the pistol he bought her for her birthday. "Never scared! I'll see you later, babe," Tara said.

Tara giggled, getting into her cotton candy Maserati Quattroporte S Q4 that Skunk scooped her for Valentine's Day. *She just sucked the skin off my shit*, Skunk thought as he watched her pull off waving and shit like she just did something.

*****

It was Tara's turn to drop the package off to her parents' house, and she hated going alone because they pushed for information about Samaya and Queen.

It got so bad to the point where she'd put the package in the mailbox to avoid one-way conversations and questions.

She wasn't worried about it getting stolen because the envelope went straight into the house on the porch so she could dip off quickly.

*****

Tara's text to Samaya: "I shouldn't have to call three times for you to answer. I'm on my way to see you."

Samaya's text to Tara: "I'm at Queen's house. Wait, wait! Get some Backwoods…"

Tara picked up some pizza and drinks because she knew her sister barely went shopping for food.

The ladies sat in the kitchen flaming, taking shots, talking shit to each other, and playing spades.

Queen said, "You have a lot of clientele already, so you're going to make money."

Tara said, "I was thinking, maybe Auntie and I could open a shop."

Samaya said, "I don't know about all that."

Toonie said, "You're talking about my mama? Girl, please!"

Queen said, "Don't do my aunt, Toonie!"

Tara said, "My aunt got skills! Now, her tolerance for BS is on another level."

Toonie said, "Skills to find, fuck up, and destroy."

Samaya said, "Damn! I'm not knocking her skills, but Auntie?"

Tara said, "Okay! She'd have to put up the knife, gun, ax, hammer, and Mace."

They laughed so hard, but Toonie was serious as hell, but Toonie really didn't like her mom's fucked-up ways and how she put everybody before her.

She always felt her mom played a role in favoritism and always said, "It was Toonie's mouth she didn't like," so Toonie gave the same energy.

Queen said, "You didn't speak to Sunshine the other night at the club, so she was talking mad crazy about you."

Samaya said, "I don't like that thirsty bitch. Period!"

Queen said, "Auntie crazy ass tried to grab my thang out the box in the parking lot. Luckily Tee and Ax weren't out there yet to see all the commotion going on, because she knew they'd tell Merch."

Tara said, "I don't like that bony bitch! Always bouncing when she walk and talk."

Samaya said, "I heard her speak to me, but I don't like the sneaky-looking bitch. Should have let Auntie pistol-whop that ass."

Toonie said, "Listen to this nonsense? That's why I stay to myself. I'm going home."

Tara said, "Well, Skunk and I supposed to be moving together soon."

Samaya said, "Thought y'all already lived together?"

Queen said, "Right! I thought the same thing."

Tara said, "Nope! I haven't met his parents yet."

Samaya said, "What's the wait? He met ours. Hell, he's paying most of their bills."

Tara said, "It's his mean mama. When I went to the hotel to grab some papers with him, she rolled her eyes at me. I smiled and waved at her."

Samaya said, "Ugh! I would have rolled my eyes back. Da fuck!"

Tara said, "When he got in the car, I asked him, 'Who was that?' When he said, 'My mother,' I was shocked. She's short and pretty as fuck."

Queen said, "I would have asked, 'Why you didn't introduce us?' The fuck wrong with him?"

Tara said, "He said, 'It wasn't the right time,' so I just left it be. Toonie really left? Hell naw!"

Queen said, "When does she ever stay around? His mom must be evil, or he's a mama's boy?"

Samaya said, "I can't say shit! I've never met a man's mother either."

Tara said, "*You've never had a man. Let alone some dick!*"

Queen said, "I know where they live."

Tara said, "*Seriously, bitch! Not the mama house?* Where they live, though?"

Samaya said, "Stop it, Tara! Queen, you followed the dude there?"

Tara said, "He didn't take her."

Queen said, "Bitch, you thirsty! Talking about where? What yo scary ass gonna do?"

They chuckled, knowing damn well Tara was sneaky, crazy, and dick whipped.

Queen said, "I know all his spots...He's a very busy man."

Tara said, "Well, if you go looking, you might see something you don't like."

Queen said, "If I see something, it just means I'm informed."

Samaya said, "I'm staying out of this. I'm not following no man."

Tara said, "Get one, then talk. Your mean, horny ass need something besides your hand and toys."

Queen said, "I'm staying out of this one. But, *true...lonely ass!*"

Tara said, "*True indeed!* Eventually, you'll have to follow somebody or *rules.*"

Samaya said, "Since you're taking it there. First of all, I make and follow my own rules. Second, the following is intended for bitches that want to be pimped. I'm more of a side-by-side, or back-to-back type, bitch."

Tara sighed loud as hell, and they both looked at her in disbelief because she does whatever Skunk says to do.

Tara said, "First of all, Ms. Saria. I meant following each other's hearts. Always jumping to conclusions. I see why Toonie doesn't fuck with y'all."

Queen said, "She used Toonie as an example as she stands for something. Hell naw!"

Samaya said, "Make that shit clear. I'm not about to be reading between the lines, putting shit together. My bad, follower of Toonie special ass."

Queen tried not to laugh, spitting her drink out across the table.

Tara said, "How about you two laughing bitches quit following each other, and do your own shit. I'm gone!"

Queen said, "*Hold the fuck up, cousin!*"

Samaya said, "Bye...And, we follow each other to the money."

Tara walked off, heading to the door. Before the door shut, Queen had her last say-so because she hated when people said, "She followed up behind Samaya."

Queen said, "*You used to follow the money with us, Tara. Come back to the light.*"

Tara said, "*Whatever! Whatever! I'm getting mines, best believe that! Don't you got some investigating to do?*"

Samaya said, "Let's leave my sister alone. You know she loves hard."

Skunk
Making Moves for the Family

Skunk said, "May I see that one, please?"

Clerk 1 said, "This is a nice one. She's a lucky lady."

Skunk said, "She's special to me. Let me see it with the other two I picked out, please?"

Clerk 1 said, "Here you go, sir. I had him bring out the new arrivals."

Skunk said, "Thank you, miss."

Clerk 2 said, "Here's the new arrivals."

Skunk said, "I'll take that one."

Clerk 1 said, "That one stood out? Lucky woman!"

*****

Skunk went to meet his realtor friend at this property he wanted to buy at the busy end of the strip that he's been watching for a while. He already ran it across the table at the meeting with his brothers before making any moves on buying it.

He met up with her for lunch to talk about numbers while they waited on his cousin Tee before heading over to the property.

Tee said, "Everything looks good. I got to go, Skunk. Nice seeing you again, Ms. Adana."

Adana said, "It's just Adana. Nice seeing you as well."

Tee said, "Well, Adana, take my card if you have other clients that need my services. Thanks."

Adana said, "Sure will. Here are the papers."

Skunk said, "I'll take the papers to my lawyer, and we'll send you over the check if everything looks good."

Adana said, "So, What's up with you? You look tense as always."

Skunk said, "I need some sleep…I've been running around all morning."

Adana said, "Okay, Skunk. Here are the keys. I trust that everything is as said. How's Tara doing?"

He didn't do too many questions, but he's been knowing Adana and her little sister Anema since second grade. Their mother moved next door to his mother's when they were kids, and they've been friends ever since.

Anema dated Merch in middle school and high school then moved to Minnesota where she attended college.

Skunk said, "She's around. How's your family? I mean, your fiancé."

Adana said, "You're still the same, barely talking. You know my mother stays at your mom's house, gossiping. They want us together so bad."

Skunk said, "I know they talk about everybody. I'll talk to you later about all that being together. I have a meeting in a few hours, so I'll call you later."

Adana said, "Skunk always running."

Skunk said, "Running from what, Adana? Acting like I don't hear questions when being asked."

Adana said, "Shits, embarrassing! I just moved my business back home to start all over."

Skunk said, "You just smoothly went around that question, again. Huh?"

Adana said, "We've divorced already, split up, or whatever you call it. He had a baby with someone else and got married, I heard."

Skunk said, "Damn! He cheated and married on your ass. He's a beast."

Adana said, "He can beast and leave me alone. I left him with his happy little family. How's Tara doing, besides being around?"

Skunk said, "You can ask her! I'm not her personal therapist. Ask her assistant."

Skunk knew she knew what she was doing, licking her lips all slow, asking about another chick trying to throw him off. Her juicy ass lips were tempting, but that made him look over the papers to see if she was trying to sneak something different on a line or two.

Then she wore the blouse with her boobs all out with the blazer all tight, pushing them up. She saw Skunk glancing at her boobs that her ex-husband purchased, but it wasn't enough to keep him.

"Let me show you who's the beast," Adana said as she squatted down in front of Skunk. She unzipped his pants while giving him eye contact while pulling his dick out. When she sucked the tip, he jumped back really quick, amazed at her wet grip.

Her face was down in the back seat of her truck with her ass up, and he was banging the shit out of her in the doggy style. She was moaning so loud that he thought he was hurting her. "*Skunk? Skunk? Skunk?*" Adana shouted. She grabbed his shirt to get his attention, but he wasn't budging.

Adana said, "Skunk, you are always getting quiet when we talk. If you don't want to talk to me, fine. *Skunk.*

Skunk said, "Shit! My mind was somewhere else for a minute. My bad, Adana. Get your fine ass out of here. I'll call you later."

Adana said, "Are you okay? It looks like you were in a trance again. You're always drifting off when we're together."

Skunk said, "I'm good. Just thinking about this meeting."

Adana said, "You should see a doctor. You might be experiencing blackouts."

Skunk said, "Adana, I see the doctor on a regular. It's no blackouts. I'm good!"

She hugged him and kissed his cheek and left. Adana knew damn well she made him feel some way, and she loved it. He watched her until she pulled off, then went on about his business.

He walked around the building looking around until he found some file cabinets, and that took his mind off Adana's fat ass.

He waited for Tee and his crew to come back and help clear out all the rubbish. They took so long, he started opening the files and reading them. Before they arrived, he found the key taped to the top of the cabinet in the inside, so he locked them up.

*****

Tee said, "This a nice find, fam. What do you want me to do with all these file cabinets and furniture?"

Skunk said, "Take it to your warehouse. This building has been empty for a while. The previous owner passed away and didn't have any family."

Tee said, "That's fucked up, fam. Some of these items are antiques. Look at this!"

Skunk said, "I'll pay an antique expert to see what we found. I don't know what the fuck I'm looking at, fam."

Tee said, "When do you want me to start knocking walls down?"

Skunk said, "Hold on, fam, let me see first. We can go through the cabinets at your warehouse first. Look at these files, fam. This man had money everywhere. I need my lawyer to look at all the files in these cabinets."

*****

When he finished, he went over to his mother's house to eat and meet up with his brothers, and they gathered around the big table talking, and no phones or electronics were allowed.

Marsha said, "I'm pleased with the business profit. I know your father is going to be pleased."

Jean said, "Pass me the wine, please. Where are your brothers'?"

Merch said, "On the porch using their phone before coming in."

Marsha said, "Well, let's eat. When am I going to be a grandmother?"

Jean said, "Long as...it's not by none of them stripper girls."

Marsha said, "Amen to that."

Skunk said, "I'm not having kids until I'm married."

Jean said, "Hey, son!"

Marsha said, "Hello, son!"

Ishmael said, "Hi, Mothers. Isaiah had to go meet up with his coach. He'll be right back."

Skunk said, "Mom want grandkids."

Ishmael said, "I'm not ready for all that."

Merch said, "I'll give you some when I find some wives. I meant wife."

Skunk said, "Look at this."

Marsha said, "Who is that for?"

Jean said, "Seriously. Who? That ex-stripper girl?"

Ishmael said, "He about to get beat by both moms."

Marsha said, "I didn't hear or see anything funny."

Jean said, "No! Merch about to get beat. He keeps trying to sneak diss."

Merch said, "What I do? Mama Jean, I wouldn't dare sneak diss."

Merch chuckled because he knew his brother loved Tara. She was one of the good girls just trying to fit in and make a quick dollar. He also knew his mothers weren't going for no ex-stripper.

Merch saw the look in Jean's eyes when he said "wives," so he knew to shut the fuck up.

Skunk said, "Never mind."

When everyone finished supper, they went about their way in the house, packing for their mother's move.

Skunk saw Lois in the kitchen drinking with his mom, and he just knew Adana wasn't far behind.

He made his way out the door because every time he saw her, it made Skunk want to fuck her more. He didn't want to start day-dreaming and get his dick hard in front of his mom or hers, so he went to the car to blaze.

Skunk's text to Tara: "I was having supper with my family, sorry I missed your call. What's up?"

Tara's text to Skunk: "Nothing…just checking on my baby :)"

Skunk's text to Tara: "I'll see you tomorrow, GN."

Tara's text to Skunk: "So, you're not coming over? :("

Skunk's text to Tara: "I'm tired, and I don't feel like driving that way baby."

Tara's text to Skunk: "YEAH, WHATEVER! I'LL JUST STAY AT QUEEN'S TONIGHT…"

Skunk's text to Tara: "Take your ass home."

Skunk's text to Tara: "I'm not playing."

Skunk's text to Tara: "Tara? You see me texting you."

Skunk's text to Tara: "I'm on my way to Queen's think I'm playing."

*****

Skunk said, "*What the fuck!*"

"Open the door," Adana said, as she banged on the window. "Stop banging on my window," Skunk shouted.

Adana said, "I saw you come out. Put that thing down before it goes off."

Skunk said, "Woman....don't be walking up on me like that."

Adana said, "What are you smoking? May I get in?"

Skunk said, "Get in! When you start smoking?"

Adana said, "When we were in the eighth grade. What do you have that thing for?"

Skunk said, "For protection. Niggas won't catch me slipping anymore. Then muthafuckas are walking up knocking on windows."

Adana said, "What's your problem? I'm not a muthafucka, Sem."

She punched him in his arm. Little did she know that shit turned him on.

Skunk said, "Baby-ass punches. When you get tough? Here's a flame for you, and I'll finish mines."

Adana said, "Oh. You can't smoke with me?"

Skunk said, "Your DNA, fiancé DNA, and his new bitch DNA. Here's your flame."

She went to punch him in his arm again, and he grabbed her hand, placing it on his dick so she could see how hard it was.

Adana said, "You play too much."

Skunk said, "I'm not playing. This what your hands are for, Adana, not hitting."

Adana said, "I see you act shy around me, but you're nasty."

Skunk said, "I'm not shy shit! Showing you what your hands for is not nasty, baby girl."

She finished her flame and pulled his dick out, and kissed it slowly, letting the tip go halfway into her mouth; then she pulled back doing it again, going faster each time. He watched her head go up and down as the light on his phone kept flashing. He put the phone on the dashboard then put his hands over her backside so that he could finger her pussy.

Adana said, "You like this DNA, Sem?"

Skunk said, "Shh, keep doing that. Damn you swallowing this muthafucka!"

Adana said, "Let me go in the house. The check went into my account today. Let me know when you're ready for another property."

Skunk said, "Adana, get yo ass over here and ride this muthafucka."

Adana said, "Whatever! Are you ready for all my DNA?"

She already knew what she was doing, trying to give him a little tease to see what his response was going to be.

She jumped right over onto his lap, bouncing and kissing his neck and ears. He started sucking her nipples and gripping her ass, not paying the phone notifications no mind. He started helping her go up and down, and the way he gripped her cheeks made her think he wasn't going to let go.

Adana said, "Don't nut in me, Sem."

Skunk said, "Shut the fuck up!"

Adana said, "Oh, Sem… Oooh, Sem…Sem!"

He lifted his head, and she placed her lips on his as the flash from the phone gave them enough light to see into the eyes of each other. They began French-kissing until they both climaxed, not caring or thinking about the missed calls of disappointment from the other end.

Skunk said, "You want another flame to relax that fat ass?"

Adana said, "Yes! If I can hit yours?"

They sat in the car, flaming, talking, and listening to music until she started going to sleep.

Skunk said, "Go in the house, you're falling asleep."

After she fixed her clothes, she leaned over and kissed him on the neck. As soon as she opened the car door, his brothers were walking up to their rides, laughing.

Ishmael said, "What's up, y'all?"

Merch said, "Look at all that smoke. Do you need help, Adana? Don't fall, goofy!"

Adana said, "What's funny? I'm good, monkey ass! Don't tell my momma, though. Bighead!"

Merch said, "Scary ass. Aw, shit! She fell!"

*****

That morning Skunk walked past the kitchen and saw his mother talking to Marsha, Lois, and Adana sipping coffee. Skunk rushed to the bathroom, and before he could shut the bathroom door all the way, Adana pushed it open.

Adana said, "Thought you went home, Sem? Why are you looking like that? They didn't see you pass."

Skunk said, "Whoa…What the fuck! They right in the kitchen."

Adana said, "They're not worried about us! They're talking about politics. Shhh! Let me do this so you can have a good day!"

Adana washed her face and went back into the kitchen as if nothing happened. She eyeballed Skunk as he walked in the kitchen, trying not to look at her. Adana jumped right up and poured him a cup of coffee.

Skunk said, "Thanks! Hello, ladies…"

Marsha said, "Hello, son! Thanks, Adana!"

Adana said, "Welcome, Ms. Marsha! Anything for Sem…"

Lois said, "Your mother told me everything. Congratulations, Sem!"

Skunk said, "Thanks! Well, I'm going to take this coffee to go, Mother, and I'll see you, beautiful ladies, later."

*****

Skunk just sat there looking over the papers ignoring his phone and on his second flame. When he went to flip the paper over, he noticed Ax all in his face.

Ax said, "Are you that disgusted, fam? You looked over the papers three times already. You don't even smoke like that, fam. Some women are bold like that and need a man to keep up."

Skunk said, "She just grabbed him! I couldn't even enjoy it knowing our moms were right there in the kitchen. Then she was pouring coffee and shit."

Ax said, "Shit! She's a freak! She's turning my fam out. Because y'all have maids, don't knock a female that will serve yo ass. Has Tara ever poured yo ass anything?"

Skunk said, "No. We have maids for all that, or I got her a maid."

CHAPTER 5

Isaiah
Making It Harder Than It Is

All he wanted was to see baby girl in the flesh to see if she was as beautiful as her Lovely Vines photo. This woman was pure fucking beauty with a hustle, just like he wanted. He planned to get her out of that club scene and make this bad bitch his wife. Plus, he wanted to see if she could bounce that ass on his dick like she was dancing.

*****

Isaiah arrived at the Manhattan spot off the water where they met weekly to handle the family business and speak the shits. From day one, the table seated Isaiah, Ishmael, Merch, and Skunk only.

Isaiah and Ishmael's mother is Jean. Merch and Skunk's mother is Marsha, and all the children have the same father, who is Isaiah Sr. Their father made sure they all grew up together in the same household and wasn't any half this, half that shit in his house. Their pops taught them all how to hustle books and the value of family first, no matter what.

Merch said, "Isaiah always late! No pussy-getting ass!"

They all laughed as Isaiah walked up smirking, and he knew they were talking shit like always.

Isaiah said, "What's up? What's up? I see y'all started before me...What's so funny?"

Skunk said, "You threw all that money on shorty. Hope you got the pussy?"

Merch said, "Bro, about to marry her smart-mouth ass first."

Ishmael said, "It's about time bro gets some play. I don't see how you go so long without some pussy."

Skunk said, "We told you! She is fine as hell, with a smart-ass mouth."

Isaiah said, "Yeah, she bad! Soon as we get that paperwork back, I'm snatching her out of the club. I'm about to tame all that smart shit. Can't take a stripper to meet Mom Dukes though."

Merch said, "Told you! Bro about to marry her mean ass. She is fine as hell, though."

Skunk said, "The paperwork right here, once we sign it, she's yours. Oops! I meant it's ours!"

Ishmael said, "I don't like the idea unless we're flipping it?"

Merch said, "You don't like strippers. That's why you don't like the idea."

Isaiah said, "All that mean shit about to stop! Let's get back to business. The club is ours already. We're just signing the agreement with the zoning shit. Right?"

After handling all the business ideas on how to bring in more revenue, they looked over numbers. They all listened to Isaiah when he talked about investments and stocks because he studied hard on it. When signing the employee's paychecks, all their names had to be on the bank receipts before taking them in. Ishmael hated bringing up the street money because it made Merch upset, but it all had to be cleaned up before moving forward.

Ishmael said, "When moms find out we bought a damn strip club, they're gonna trip big time."

Skunk said, "It's our money, and we are adults. We have other things to take care of, right, Isaiah?"

Isaiah said, "No more street shit, right? Everything is running legit from now on."

They agreed that everything would be legit but the flame they got to blaze. "What the fuck y'all looking at?" Merch mumbled. "You," Skunk uttered in disappointment.

Merch said, "I'm not going for all this daddy-role shit! So, let's slow this shit down. Back to business, as usual."

Ishmael said, "This ain't no daddy-role shit. These your big brothers speaking facts to you that could jeopardize the family."

Merch said, "I wouldn't put the family in danger. We all flame! Right?"

All the waitresses loved when they came in for meetings because they left generous tips. Some days Isaiah would stop by on a Thursday evening for a few drinks or get wet.

Isaiah said, "Hold this shit down! I'll be right back to finish signing my portion."

Waitress 2 said, "Hello, would you like a refill?"

Merch said, "Yes. For everybody, and thank you!"

*****

Rachel would bring Isaiah his drink, fold the napkin down, then walk off smiling. That was her way of letting him know that the office was okay for him to come back.

Isaiah didn't play any games. He pulled his dick out immediately and palmed Rachel's head, not having no emotional attachment. When she got on her knees, she opened her mouth, trying to get all his dick in her mouth. She was going back and forth fast as hell, holding the other portion with her hand.

Isaiah said, "Slow down, Rachel!"

Buzz. Buzz. When Isaiah glanced at his phone and saw the text, "Aww, Samaya," he whispered.

Samaya's text to Isaiah: "Hey Sai, this Samaya."

Isaiah said, "*Stop*, Rachel, stop."

Rachel said, "Why?"

Rachel was never told to stop, hoping that she performed well enough to get a business card this time. She slowly released his dick out of her mouth and was upset to even go along with someone she barely knew. Rachel stood looking at him, not getting any eye contact, and feeling pissed off that the plan was to find and fool, but not suck. When she went to grab at his pants, he pushed her hands away politely, not thinking of her feelings, period.

Isaiah said, "Clean yourself up."

Rachel said, "What's wrong? What did I do? Why you stop me?"

He placed some money in her bra before Rachel could get another question out. He put his two fingers over her lips and looked her straight in the eyes.

Isaiah said, "No questions beginning with W, remember?"

Isaiah walked back to the table with a big smile on his face.

Ishmael said, "What's taking bro so long?"

Skunk said, "Here he comes cheesing and shit!"

Merch said, "Let bro cheese all he wants. He makes them numbers multiply easily."

Isaiah was the last to sign the papers for their new club, thinking of ways he was going to win Samaya over. He texted her back, liking that she called him Sai. He's still undecided because he never thought about dating a stripper, knowing his parents would disapprove, but he followed his first mind.

*****

Isaiah's text to Samaya: "Meet me tonight at the beachfront, Samaya."

Samaya's text to Isaiah: "What time Sai? I work tonight at eight pm."

Isaiah's text to Samaya: "Seven!"

Samaya's text to Isaiah: "I'll get back to you. No promises."

Isaiah's text to Samaya: "text me when you ready."

Samaya's text to Isaiah: "okay!"

*****

Isaiah said, "Good news! Skunk bought a building that was sitting for a while. The findings in the building tripled what he paid for it."

Merch said, "I still can't believe the bank or realtors didn't go clean it out."

Ishmael said, "All they saw was trash and spiderwebs."

Skunk said, "I'm glad Tee was with me. I was about to have all that shit put in the garbage."

Isaiah said, "That find added a nice decimal in the bank. We need you to go find more."

Merch said, "What's up with Adana, bro?"

Isaiah said, "Who's the ring for?"

Skunk said, "Bro...the ring for Tara!"

Merch said, "Tara was pulling off last night when I pulled up to Queen's."

Skunk said, "I told her to take her ass home. Trying to do grown-up slumber parties."

Ishmael said, "Bro was doing slumber parties in the car."

Skunk said, "We just talked, bro. Adana is not like that. How're the numbers looking, Isaiah?"

Isaiah said, "If we keep flipping these properties, we'll be needing more staff. Bro tried to go around his slumber party in the car."

Skunk said, "Adana's a sweetie! What's so funny?"

Merch said, "When Pops get home, he can finish where he left off."

Isaiah said, "He can't be on that street shit with Uncle Swen anymore."

Merch said, "You think Pops just gonna stop his business with Unc like that? Basketball fame or not."

Isaiah said, "Pops don't have to lift another finger anymore."

Skunk said, "You know Pops always took to the streets. He always took care of the home, and never played about his paper."

Ishmael said, "He always told us. Never trust another man to your finances or your home."

Isaiah said, "Damn right! Bitches too! His words, not mine."

Skunk said, "We know you love women enough not to disrespect them."

Ishmael said, "It's to each's own on that bitch shit! What's up with our father?"

Merch said, "Pops's friendship with Swen is way stronger than the streets. He's not going for this property shit."

Isaiah said, "Well. That hustle helped us out with all these families we're taking care of, and not to mention the females. Let's put them to work."

Skunk said, "Have y'all ladies ever poured you a drink?"

Isaiah said, "Where did that come from? Mines gonna do all that, and more."

Merch said, "Bro, we need to hurry up! I need to run. All mines do except for Queen."

Ishmael said, "When we got signed, Dad left the streets alone. The side hustles are good for our family. Let's see if Swen will get into business to persuade Pops."

Merch said, "Swen is a hustler for life."

Isaiah said, "Well, my brothers, I have to run."

Skunk said, "Hold on! You're always the last one here. Now you're leaving before us?"

Ishmael said, "Hurry up and go if it concerns some pussy."

Isaiah said, "I don't see anything funny. I'm out! Love y'all. Oh, Skunk? You should talk to Ishmael about women and pouring drinks."

Ishmael said, "Come on, bro! You know that's a must, dealing with me. There's nothing wrong with an obedient woman. Plus, they're hard to find these days."

*****

Isaiah arrived at the beachfront early so he could have everything arranged to his liking. He waited for her at the bar and had a few drinks until she came.

He had the waitress walk her to their table to be seated as he watched one of the most beautiful woman he ever saw approach gracefully.

Isaiah didn't ask any questions at first. He just sat there staring into her face as she looked at her phone giggling and answering text. He didn't want to come across rude, so he just sipped his drink and waited to see if she had any questions for him.

After ten minutes had passed, the waitress came with their appetizers, and she still had nothing to say.

He wanted to hear this jazzy mouth everyone talked of and, most importantly, her speech skills. He decided to break the ice and say something because she didn't thank the waitress, and it made him mad.

Isaiah said, "Put your phone down, Samaya!"

Samaya said, "Excuse me? You're not saying shit!"

Isaiah said, "You heard me! While you're with me, we talk, communicate, and find things out about each other. Put your phone down! Thanks."

Samaya said, "What do you want to know? You know, I shake my ass already."

Isaiah said, "Lift your head, beautiful! Look at me when you talk to me. Just how you looked at the picture, you liked on Lovely Vines."

Samaya said, "Look. Look. Look. You liked mines also, then showed up at my job."

Isaiah said, "There we go! We're communicating now. Feels good, doesn't it?"

Samaya said, "You're funny, huh? What do you want from me, Sai?"

Isaiah said, "Now we're getting somewhere. I want you, Samaya. To know everything about you."

Samaya said, "Just like all the other men wanting to get in my panties? I don't have time for that right now. My money comes first."

Isaiah chuckled, knowing damn well she needed some dick the way she was twerking in his face at the club.

Isaiah said, "Samaya? We were created to want each other. What man wouldn't want a beautiful woman like you? Explain to me. Where's the hostility towards men coming from?"

Samaya said, "I'm not giving my virginity away until I'm ready. I run into rude men all the time. Nothing personal. Why are you acting all proper and shit?"

Isaiah said, "I'm not acting shit! I was raised to respect women and people until my boundaries are overstepped. You're uptight, I see, for?"

Samaya said, "Almost time for me to go to work. Can't miss my money."

Isaiah said, "Look at me, Samaya, and breathe. Relax your mind for a moment, then realize everybody is not out to harm you or prevent you from getting money, baby girl. How much money would you make tonight that has you this uptight? Besides, money shouldn't ever take over your feelings. That shit come and go."

Samaya said, "Oh, wow! On a slow night, I've made over five stacks. On a good night, you should know, since you're one of my first-time good tippers."

Isaiah stood up and walked over to her holding his hand out. "Come on," he said. When she placed her hand in his, for some reason, he knew she was obedient and he liked it.

"Jump on my back! Here, wrap your legs around me," Isaiah said. He gripped her legs then ran off through the sand and water up and down the shore.

He heard her giggling, and he knew to keep it up and let her see that he was serious about her.

She wasn't thinking about money or work at the time. She was enjoying his smell, and how this giant man just swept her up off the earth, making her feel secure.

Samaya said, "Oh my gosh! My clothes and hair are all wet."

Isaiah said, "Let me wrap this blanket around you. Would you like another drink?"

Samaya said, "Something to keep me warm, please. I'm late for work, Sai."

Isaiah said, "You're not dancing anymore. Thought I told you that? Follow me to the car for a moment."

Samaya said, "Really, Sai? What's up with you? Who are you? What do you want from me?"

What the fuck? Samaya mumbled with her hands on her hips, trying not to notice her pussy was wet as fuck from playing like a big kid.

She knew if she'd taken the money, he'd have his way, and deep down, her uterus screamed at her to take it. She thought about walking away, but she'd be a dummy to walk away from a stack of hundreds, knowing there was more to come.

Isaiah said, "Time will tell. Just take the damn money, and quit asking questions."

Samaya said, "Thank you. Do you want a lap dance? Where you get money to give away?"

Isaiah said, "Welcome. No lap dance needed right now. My money and finances are my business, and I think your time is money, as mine is."

Samaya said, "You told me to ask questions, Sai."

Isaiah said, "Let me put it this way. My businesses make money, and my finances make up a system acquiring money."

Samaya said, "Well said! With this stack of money, I can set up a financial system."

Isaiah said, "Good comeback! Each one teaches one!"

They lay on the beach looking up into the sky, talking, and laughing all night.

Ishmael
Only the Real Can Survive

Ishmael got robbed once, and after that, he only dealt with his brothers, cousins, and a few females.

His female friends cooked, cleaned, picked up clothes from the cleaners, shopped, and drove him around. All his lady friends knew from the beginning that no feelings were allowed, no pictures, no fighting, follow the house rules, everybody gets paid for their services, and threesomes are a must.

He's bought hair, boobs, asses, cars, clothes, and paid for a few tummy tucks to keep his lady friends happy.

When he bought his first house, he had the downstairs refurbished into a man cave with crisp light gray walls, a few paintings, full-service bar, three hundred-inch flat TVs, soft dark gray leather furniture on every wall, and with matching lounge chairs.

He had two separate walk-in showers, three bathrooms, Jacuzzi inside and out, two pool tables, three stripper poles, and a stage with mirrors.

When you step down a few stairs to the lower level, it leads to the patio doors and the outdoor pool and Jacuzzi. The guys played basketball on his court a few times a week.

They reminisced about the come up, laughing and flaming.

Tee said, "Skunk crazy ass punching on everybody that looked at the family wrong. Glad my uncle got you into the books."

Mac said, "Ishmael always was a smart-ass thug. Merch was quick to pull the trigger for no damn reason."

Merch said, "After that shit happened to bro, I didn't trust nobody, fam. I'm not getting caught up for nobody."

Ishmael said, "I know Mac ain't talking. You act like all of us, put in one."

Mac said, "You don't even like strippers, but you have a pole?"

Ishmael said, "For my family! It's funny watching my females play on it, knowing damn well they can't dance."

"That shit ain't funny! Why is y'all laughing? Y'all pops raised me too," Mac said in a soft manner of respect.

Tee said, "Isaiah has always been the quiet, observant one."

Isaiah said, "Observing is the key to everything."

Ishmael said, "Did you count it? Here's your check from that find."

Tee said, "It's all here. I'm going straight to the bank. That find makes me want to start buying properties."

Mac said, "Smart-ass. I'd probably have thrown that shit out."

Ishmael said, "We need to have a family meeting about that. We were thinking about letting the family run the business when we start playing."

Mac said, "My family about to be mad...rich. Damn!"

Isaiah said, "I need my family to be on some positive movement now. All that running the street shit dead. You hear me, Mac?"

Mac said, "What should I do with what I have? I'm not trying to lose money."

Isaiah said, "I'll holla at you when these females leave."

Ishmael, Merch, Skunk, Isaiah, Tee, and Mac were flaming back-to-back when they noticed the females taking pictures of each other. They all looked at Ishmael because they already knew the drill, and he took shit way too serious.

Ishmael said, "Slow up with that! Erase the pictures."

One of the ladies said, "You're not in the photos. Here, take a look!"

Ishmael erased all the pictures she took in his house. He let her grab her items then escorted her to the door. They went on talking as if nothing happened because she wasn't the first to be put out.

Mac said, "It was some dimes in the club the other night."

Skunk said, "When I came to the spot, they were pulling all on my clothes doing any and everything for attention."

Mac said, "Cousin, hit this shit! This flame is the new shit I was telling you about."

Merch said, "This shit fire, I see. Got you coughing!"

Mac said, "When I saw Queen's crazy-ass friend trying to pull that thang out, I wanted to give that bitch my number."

Skunk said, "Yeah, we need to get them out of the club before our value goes down."

Merch said, "Fam, that's her aunt. Remember that beautician tried to cut her client when she didn't want to pay? That's her!"

Tee said, "That shit was on the hood news. You know he likes older women."

Ishmael said, "Fam…what the fuck is the hood news?"

Merch said, "He making up shit again."

Mac said, "Auntie got a fat ass, trigger finger, and a pretty face."

Tee said, "Come on, bro. I'm not about to go to jail over this woman, trying my little brother."

Mac said, "Man! She pulled that thang faster than some of my boys."

Merch said, "She retired the knife! Be careful with that one."

Mac said, "She told my ass my pockets have to be deep, the tongue has to be strong, and feelings in check. Then walked off on my ass."

Isaiah said, "Don't hand that shit to Skunk. He's flamed enough, talking about they're gonna make our property value go down."

Skunk said, "I'm good! But they are…"

They all laughed so hard, they started choking off the flame. "I like women bold, but not crazy," Isaiah said.

"You're messing with the wrong family, bro. You know that's Samaya's aunt also?" Merch said, laughing.

Tee said, "I'm scared of bitches like that. I'd be in jail for body-slamming a bitch. Fuck some property value."

Ishmael said, "Damn! She's beyond feisty. 'She is digging in your pocket while you fuck' type shit. Gangsta shit!"

Mac said, "I'd have to choke the bitch den! Fuck that!"

Tee said, "Ole girl that had that yellow bodysuit on was fine as hell. I got a few lap dances in VIP."

Ishmael said, "I saw her too! Looking like a ripe banana. Hell, I got a few lap dances too."

Merch said, "How much she bank from you, fam? I spent a few hundred."

Skunk said, "I paid her too! Anyways, let my auntie know we're walking across that stage next week. Moms should have sent an invitation."

Mac said, "Skunk, you drunk as fuck! Take that cup from him."

Skunk said, "I'm good! I'm...good! I called Tara to pick me up."

Tee said, "We already got the invitation. Congratulations, too, two of my favorite cousins."

Ishmael said, "Thanks, fam! I need a break from all that studying. Now, I can focus on my game."

Mac said, "What about the bitches?"

Merch said, "Whoa...They're not bitches...They're women, son! What's so funny?"

Mac said, "My fault, Isaiah! When you start dunking, they're going to come from everywhere. Watch!"

Isaiah said, "I can't wait to dunk on their ass! I'm ready to kick it!"

Everybody just looked at Isaiah. "He must have got some pussy," Skunk said. Isaiah has never been the going-out type just book smart, so when he stood up, they sat there.

Isaiah said, "Y'all tripping! I'm just trying to step out and see the scenery."

Mac said, "I've never seen you do anything but study, fam. I always looked up to you."

Skunk said, "What's your plan for your graduation party, bro? You know our moms doing the formal shit for us on the beachfront."

Ishmael said, "Haven't thought about it. We should do something in the new spot. Bro, take this shit! I'm high as hell."

Merch said, "I saw your girl Jill at the club the other day."

Ishmael said, "She said she started working more, but not at a damn strip club. Good looking, bro. Acting like she too good for that life. Always putting the other females down."

Merch said, "Well, her ass and boobs were all out just like the other chicks."

Ishmael said, "You don't have to lie to kick it."

Merch said, "These females lie and be sneakier than us."

Ishmael said, "I guess she thought I'd look at her differently if she danced. Being sneaky doesn't get any respect from me."

Tee said, "Watch who you give respect. Everybody doesn't deserve it, or your time."

Merch said, "You sound like my pops. He always told me, 'Listening and observing can tell you a lot about people. Most of all, keep eye contact,' so, moving around comes easy for me."

Ishmael said, "Pops said, 'If you have to second-guess, you don't need them around you.' That's why I don't bend my rules."

Tee said, "My uncle, the truth! Don't stress the brain. Use it for productivity."

Isaiah said, "Productivity has been good to our family."

Ishmael said, "All my friends get treated the same. Regardless if you're going to school, working a nine-to-five, or a stripper. A liar, I can't do."

Merch said, "Bitch doesn't have to front to be treated."

Tee said, "Face value ass!"

Mac said, "All that laughing shit got y'all wasting the flame. Fam...do you miss playing ball?"

Ishmael said, "Hell yeah! Six weeks left of physical therapy, then I can practice again."

Skunk said, "His ass was trying to dunk, for them face value—ass cheerleaders, and broke his damn ankle at practice."

Ishmael said, "My shit was sprung, bro. Quit adding shit! Bro ass, a comedian."

Skunk said, "The way you fell on the floor and rolled around, I thought the whole leg was gone."

Ishmael said, "I'll get up with y'all tomorrow. Jill is coming through!"

Isaiah said, "Be careful with her lying ass."

Merch said, "Well, I'm trying to go be productive in some guts...Call y'all tomorrow!"

*****

"See, I told you, bitch," Queen whispered as she ducked down in the back seat. "Why are you ducking? They can't see you," Toonie yelled. "Follow him," Queen shouted.

Samaya said, "They can't see or hear us, silly. How do you know where they live?"

Queen said, "Long nights and days. With plenty of flame, snacks, and tissue."

Toonie said, "Didn't know I was coming out to play hide-and-seek without getting tagged. Quit calling me for this shit, Queen!"

Queen said, "You need to get out of the house and live a little bit. I was going to introduce you to Tee, but Merch didn't hit me back."

Samaya said, "You play all day, Queen. Why Tee?"

Queen said, "She likes chubby boys! Plus, he's making money."

Toonie said, "*I don't like fat boys! Drop me off, Samaya!*"

Queen said, "He ain't fat, fat! His stomach healthy, though."

Samaya said, "Aw, hell naw! Bitch, you're silly…Toonie, he is okay looking."

Toonie said, "*Girl! I don't give a fuck, fuck! I don't want a man…* Besides, I met someone anyway."

*****

After everybody left, Ishmael called for Jill to come over so she could play on the pole for him.

They sat around, watching videos and looking over some of the papers found in the file cabinet.

Jill said, "Where did you get this from, Zaddy?"

Ishmael said, "In the building we purchased. I kept this one to look over, the rest are—"

Before he could finish his sentence and tell her the bank bought most of them, she cut him off too quick.

Jill said, "There's more of these? Wow! How many?"

Ishmael said, "Yeah. Someone is looking them over for me. What's up with all the more and many questions?"

Jill said, "Just curious! This file alone is worth two hundred thousand. If the person is alive and wants to repurchase it, that's good, Zaddy. One question. Did all the files look like this?"

Ishmael said, "No. I see you know your shit. Bring your smart ass over here, Professor Jill."

*****

That morning Ishmael went to the club to meet up with Rocky before handing him the signed papers.

He wanted to see if Merch was right about the profit it'll bring, and from what he saw the property value was already down.

He sat in the parking lot, waiting for Rocky taking notes on what he thought would be excellent for renovating.

After waiting fifteen minutes, he got out and walked around the outside of the building, looking for cracks in the foundation.

He noticed there were a few other bars on the block that weren't as big, but they were updated.

As he walked by the side entrance, he noticed that the building was attached to an empty, abandoned building in the back.

When he turned around to go back to his truck, he noticed a woman coming out of the side door.

Ishmael said, "Hello. Is Rocky in there?"

Woman 1 said, "Hi. No, he's not. He should have been here ten minutes ago."

*****

Rocky said, "I thought he was going to bring his other brothers. They'll be here tomorrow."

Man 1 said, "I saw a few of them the other night spending that bread. How many is it of these pretty modeling-looking muthafuckas?"

Rocky said, "Stay put! I'll be right back."

Rocky walked over fast, so Ishmael couldn't see which car he came.

Rocky said, "*What's up, Ishmael?* Sorry about that. I was running late."

95

Ishmael said, "What's up? I was just about to call you. Time is money, man. Maybe you need an assistant."

Rocky said, "I do! She's busy this morning gathering information for me. Let's go through the front so you can see the entrance. Then we can come out the side."

Ishmael said, "The purpose for you selling? If you don't mind me asking. Let me see the other building."

Rocky said, "At my age, I'm ready to retire and travel, young man. I didn't know that the back was my property."

Ishmael said, "That's real! Did you owe money on the place?"

Rocky said, "No. All it needs is some minor remodeling, but I don't have the time or patience right now. I mentioned to Merch that I had to sell quickly."

Ishmael said, "Just checking on what we bought and the location. Do you have all the keys with you?"

Rocky said, "Yes! Do you own other properties? Is this your first time buying? Are you going to keep it as a gentlemen's club?"

Ishmael looked at his ass sideways, like, *Pause, bitch*.

Ishmael said, "What's with all the 'you' questions?"

Rocky said, "Awh, man! Just wondering, because you look so young. Last potential buyer was a young man playing games."

Ishmael said, "We're keeping it as a club, just changing the name. Buying and selling are in my blood. Anyways, this is a nice place. We'll meet you later on."

Rocky said, "How'd you hear about this place? I hadn't even put it on the market yet."

Ishmael said, "My friend Jill!"

Rocky said, "I don't know of her. She must have heard about it from the last guy."

Ishmael said, "Word of mouth travels fast. I'll call you later."

Rocky said, "That's real spit. I'll keep you posted, and nice meeting you."

Ishmael said, "You as well."

*****

Mac said, "Hi, beautiful. What's your name?"

The lady said, "Hi. Do I know you? You look so familiar."

Mac said, "No. I'm not from around here. What's your name?"

The lady said, "My name is Jillian! Is this your first time coming here?"

Mac said, "Second time. Have lunch with me, Jillian?"

Jill said, "Sure will! You can pay as well! What brings you to this lovely city?"

Mac said, "I'm a businessman trying to get around the block without being seen."

Jill said, "What's your name, businessman?"

Mac said, "Lil Cam! Nice meeting you, and thanks for having lunch with me. What do you do for a living, beautiful?"

Jill said, "I'm self-employed. I try to bend my body around this pole, trying to be saw…What's so funny, Cam?"

Mac said, "I like that! Real creative comeback. Do you like your job?"

Jill said, "Not really! Honestly, I don't know what I want to do. Do you like going around blocks?"

Mac said, "Nope! I'm starting a realtor company soon, so I can relax and be on my time. Would you like another drink?"

Jill said, "Let's take a shot to our 'Not really' and 'Nope.' We both look like we need a pep in our step this late morning."

Mac said, "What time do you need to meet up with the pole?"

Jill said, "You're funny! I like that…I'm off today. What about you being seen today?"

Mac said, "You got some nice comebacks! Do you flame?"

Jill said, "Hell yeah!"

The flame was in the air, and they decided to hit up the mall and finish talking, which she thought came easy with him.

Mac said, "Go try it on?"

Jill came from behind the curtain, dancing and laughing, "What do you think?" Jill said. "You are going to make somebody a happy man," Mac mumbled, trying not to forget why he was here.

Jill said, "Why are you looking like that? I'll try the other one on, then we can leave."

PART 2

What Made You

CHAPTER 6

Samaya
Letting It Go

She didn't deal with banks, nor liked the fact that other people knew your business with some shit called routing, and account numbers. Besides, she loved counting her shit, knowing she'd never finish. The thought of looking at it when she wanted to made her feel secure that she wasn't going to be homeless and hungry again.

*****

Early mornings on the balcony watching the sunrise over his muscular body made her happy. *I should go sit on his face,* Samaya thought.

All the breakfast dates, lunch dates on the beach, and late suppers had her nose wide open.

They went shopping, to the movies, walks around the lake, amusement parks, on boat rides, and more.

These were the dates she always wanted from someone and more, yet missing her money coming in every day was on her mind. *He's paying me, but I'm missing the pole,* Samaya thought as he massaged her booty cheeks.

When they spent time together, Isaiah made her laugh, tried to make her forget about the pole, and having feelings without having sex was beautiful, but she was starting to develop a fondness. She didn't want to stop spending time with him, but the impression he gave her is something she's never felt before from any man.

She decided to get all the ladies together, so she sent a group text, hoping Queen would come out, knowing she didn't fuck with too many females.

Samaya's text to the ladies: "Let's meet at Moque's Place around two pm :)"

All the ladies had their hair wrapped in a towel getting massages from head to toe, laughing about the men at the club going from tippers to wanting them to be their wives.

Jai said, "I like the smile and glow, girl! I haven't seen you in the shop lately?"

Samaya said, "Getting some alone time. Thinking about my future."

Jai said, "Hey now, that's what's up."

Tara said, "Why be alone and you could have a man or friend. You should have met a man in that club or somewhere."

Queen said, "Our motto! In one ear, out the other, when it comes to the men in that club."

Samaya said, "Our motto was not to give out each other's number either, but in this case, I don't mind anymore."

Queen said, "You do like him because I haven't heard from you in a few days."

Tara said, "Let her bond with the man. Is it a man?"

Samaya said, "Don't play with me, sis! I like him, okay…"

Jai said, "Who? What's his name?"

Toonie said, "Can she speak? Damn!"

They finished their massages, then went to get a pedicure and manicures as Moque poured them some champagne. When she went to pour some for Queen, she said, "No thanks."

Jai said, "I hope he's a good guy because I see you're falling for him."

Tara said, "Sometimes you might need to listen and follow your heart. Not all men are bad or cheaters. If they see you half naked, of course, they want to fuck."

Toonie said, "Say it again, so they can hear you. She said, 'Falling for him.' Girl, please."

Queen said, "Who are they? Toonie, don't start that shit!"

Samaya said, "Anyways, do you remember the guy that threw all that money on me?"

Queen said, "Yes, bitch! What? Hope you got the digits."

Samaya said, "Queen, you gave him my number, quit playing."

Jai said, "He placed the stack of money down all politely while everyone else threw theirs."

Queen said, "No, I didn't, cousin! I stayed in the VIP with Merch all night after you danced. Seriously."

Jai said, "I saw him talking to some big dude with a beard after you left the stage. What's his name?"

Toonie said, "Here we go with this telling shit! I hope you're happy, Samaya."

Queen looked at Samaya, like, *Rocky fat ass gave it to him*, thinking he probably got a tip with his thirsty ass always begging.

Tara rolled her eyes because she wasn't there, and deep down, she didn't care because Skunk made sure she was happy, plus secure.

Samaya said, "He was waiting in the dressing room for me."

Tara said, "Quit playing, sis! He bold as hell for that."

Queen said, "*Bitch, I saw him leaving.* What he say?"

Samaya said, "That shit scared the shit out of me thinking the dressing room was empty."

Jai said, "Did you fuck him? What's his name?"

Toonie said, "Really?"

Samaya said, "No, bitch, but I will, with his fine chocolate ass, smelling good, and he dresses nice."

Queen said, "You're the oldest virgin, I know."

Jai said, "Damn! You're a virgin still?"

Toonie said, "Nosy ass! Samaya? How do you deal with this shit?"

Samaya said, "I'm not a fucking virgin. Quit saying that shit!"

Tara was all on her phone smiling, but still had something to say. "Who you fuck, Samaya?" Then she finished up with her text, as if she didn't say anything.

Queen said, "*Tara?* Put your phone down!"

Tara said, "I need to check in with mines. That's why y'all bitches lonely. *Hello!*"

The manicurist said, "What color, miss?"

Tara said, "Cotton candy, please! Because my *man likes it*!"

Queen said, "Whatever, Tara! Finish the story, Samaya."

Samaya said, "He said, 'I'm going to call you,' but I didn't give him my number."

Jai said, "Oh, shit! Did he call?"

Toonie said, "Duh! Samaya, seriously? What's her name again?"

Samaya said, "Yes! We've been hanging out a lot lately."

Queen said, "Funny, because I don't like her sister, and she's irritating you."

Jai said, "Excuse me? My friend invited me along. Therefore, I could care less who likes me."

Queen sat there sipping her juice like that damn frog on the memes, knowing damn well Rocky didn't give him the number. She also knew Samaya wasn't about to tell Jai his name and Toonie was the wrong tree for Jai to be barking up.

Tara said, "It's about time she gets some real dick."

All the ladies laughed because they knew how uptight Samaya was about her feelings and personal business.

Samaya was the only one that wanted to wait until she found a husband, but the men that approached her lately had been dicks.

Her mother even tried introducing her to men at the church, grocery store, motel attendants, and the men at her dad's job.

Samaya said, "Dick can't make me money or happy."

They all turned and looked at Samaya then laughed again when her purse fell on the floor, and her book fell out.

Tara said, "A book on how to love? Wow!"

Toonie said, "Let her be! We need to learn from somewhere. I hope you leave and live happily ever after."

Queen said, "She's not going nowhere. Stuck-up-ass bitch."

Samaya said, "Why are you so harsh, Queen? We've been on a lot of dates, bitch."

Tara said, "My sister is not stuck up! Maybe a bitch! But stuck up, never!"

Jai said, "Why do you ladies call each other bitches?"

Toonie said, "I'll see y'all later, fam! I can't do dumb!"

Queen said, "You're worse than me! Yeah, you should leave…"

They all looked at Jai and started laughing because she was serious and decided not to say anything else until she had Samaya by herself. "Excuse her," Samaya whispered as Toonie walked off.

Jai said, "So…where have you've been with him?"

Tara said, "Do you like him?"

Queen said, "Have y'all kissed? I need details!"

Samaya said, "For the record, I'm just picky. He wants to see me again tonight, ladies, for all the questions. We've been everywhere. Yes, I like him. He smells good, and our kisses are short but passionate."

Jai said, "Damn! It sounds like a love story."

Queen said, "Well, have you seen him naked? Does he have any bullet wounds or tattoos?"

Samaya said, "I've seen him in his swimming trunks. His body is perfect, with no tattoos or scars. I like how he picks me up, carries me on his back, and runs through the water when we're on the beach."

Jai said, "Okay! Are you going out? If so, have fun tonight, sweetie."

Queen said, "You're falling in love. Damn! Merch never ran on a beach with me on his back."

Tara said, "Y'all dating? Sounds good."

Samaya said, "I consider us dating, Tara. Yes, I'm going, Jai! I like how forward he is, and he knows what he wants in a relationship, Queen. Love though, Queen?"

Tara said, "Being forward is called pimping, sis…What's funny?"

Jai said, "I've been taken to bathrooms, my office, and hotels. Never on the beach. Damn!"

Tara said, "Shit! Skunk hasn't taken me to the beach either."

Queen said, "Go out, so I can make all the money tonight. Thank you!"

Samaya said, "Tara can cover for me tonight. *Right?*"

Tara said, "Quit playing! Skunk is not letting me dance."

Samaya said, "*Not letting! Sounds like pimping, sis.*"

"What's funny? Y'all spitting drinks everywhere, damn!" Tara said.

Queen said, "*Get that dick, girl.* It'll be money when you return."

Samaya said, "Queen? Take Jai and break her in."

Jai said, "*Dancing?* I'm clueless! Been done bust, my ass."

Queen said, "I'll teach you, baby! After a few flames to loosen you up, and some shots. You'll be all right."

Jai said, "*No!* I'm scared, bitch!"

Samaya said, "See how you just used 'bitch'? There's nothing to it."

Queen said, "Form of expression. Call Toonie back. She gets it now."

Samaya said, "Yo ass funny! Let Toonie be!"

Jai said, "Sitting around y'all for too long got me saying that shit. My bad!"

Tara said, "Scared of what? Dance like you riding a dick!"

Jai said, "Seriously, Tara?"

Tara said, "Seriously, Jai! It got me some money, and I don't know shit about dancing."

Samaya said, "Fake it until you make it."

Queen said, "I need to call Toonie and tell her to come tonight?"

Samaya said, "I told her to come the other night, but she's still tripping over the other night."

Queen said, "Shhh…We got to many ears. I don't know Jai like that."

Jai said, "What you say, Queen?"

Queen said, "I said, 'I need Jai to design some clothes for me.' I might make more money."

Jai said, "Oh…Thanks! Come through. I got you."

The ladies kept laughing at one another, throwing shots at one another until they left and went shopping at the mall. Jai stopped and grabbed Jez on her way there, so she could help her pick up some fabrics.

Jez said, "Why are you grabbing all of the panties?"

Samaya said, "You can never have too many panties, Jez."

Queen said, "You should grab some and quit watching, folks."

Jai said, "Please stop, Queen!"

Jez said, "Do you feel pressed or something, huh?"

Queen said, "Press your goofy ass over there. Better yet, quit asking little-girl-ass questions."

Tara said, "Can you both behave and shop. Damn! Grab some panties, Jez."

Jez said, "Queen, you don't want none!"

Samaya said, "I'll buy them all in my size if I like them."

Before anybody could speak another word, Queen grabbed a handful of panties and threw them at Jez, making sure they hit her in the face.

Jez said, "Told you! You are pressed, for what?"

Queen said, "I'll press my fist through your face, skinny bitch!"

Samaya said, "Okay...Time to go. I'll see you ladies another day."

Jai said, "Yeah! All this trying behavior is unnecessary."

Queen said, "Whatever! I'm about to bounce, ladies. My Merch calls for me."

Tara said, "She said 'trying behavior.' I see you're slick with your words, Jai?"

Samaya said, "Flying helicopter thongs? We're acting a fool in lingerie. They're about to put us out this bitch in handcuffs. Go to Merch, Queen!"

Tara said, "I'll talk to you ladies tomorrow before my behavior becomes unnecessary with the slick talk."

Jai said, "Nice hanging out, ladies, and I'll call you tomorrow, Samaya. Come on, Jez!"

Jez said, "I'm not a damn pet or your kid. I'll meet you at the shop later."

*****

Samaya couldn't wait to wear her new one-piece for Sai. When she got home, her concierge Coral greeted her every time, which was her best friend.

Samaya said, "Hi, Sai!"

Isaiah said, "Hello, beautiful. It's this charming hotel on the other side of the beach. I'll text you the direction and time."

*****

Coral said, "Hey, girl! Who was that? You hung up all quick!"

Samaya said, "Hey, boo! What time you get off tonight?"

Coral said, "Same time, girl. What's up with you missing in action? I miss my friend."

Samaya said, "Come up after you clock out. I'll tell you all about it."

She told Coral everything from when she first met Isaiah, running into Chad, the drama between Queen and Jez. When she mentioned how Jai irritated Toonie, she noticed Coral got pissed at her from saying Toonie.

Coral said, "Baby...Mr. Isaiah is a keeper. I'd wish a man would pay my salary for me to kick it with him."

Samaya said, "And, he knows how to kiss, bitch."

Coral said, "*Oh, Lort! You know what that means?*"

Samaya said, "You're nasty!"

Coral said, "Anywho! Have you ever asked Queen why she doesn't like Jez? You know, Queen is my baby."

Samaya said, "No. You know Queen doesn't like nobody, and it took her a minute to fuck with Jai."

Coral said, "I need to know before I investigate this broad. Are you sure she's not the people? What? Quit looking at me like that!"

Samaya said, "All this time, I thought Jez was quiet and shy. She snap back with the shits! Make you want to choke her ass."

Coral said, "She's one of them, huh? Well, she's met her match with Queen, baby. What's up with Toonie since you mentioned her?"

Samaya said, "Toonie is not fucking with us like that. Jai is the cool one, and Jez is one of them. The thing about it, I don't invite Jez. Her sister brings her along."

Coral said, "'Them quiet, pretty girls are evil, and always thinking up a plot."

Samaya said, "That's a lie! We're all cute, and I'm not evil."

Coral said, "See, baby, you're brown! There's a difference between evil and crazy. You know I love you, but we've done some crazy shit."

Samaya said, "Yeah…Bitch, you right. You should go to the shop and see her."

Coral said, "I'd beat that bitch ass she try me, baby. I got you!"

Samaya said, "I don't need you getting a domestic. Never mind, crazy."

Coral said, "What's up with Chad? You know he's bad news, so don't even think about it because I'll get your ass straight real quick."

Samaya said, "I told him I'm not stressed anymore, and he still wants to pressure me."

Coral said, "See, if I beat his ass, I can't get a domestic charge. I bet' not find out you're plotting with this mothafucka either."

Samaya said, "I'm not! Let me show you my outfit for tonight."

Coral said, "Where's the rest of it? Oh, you're trying to get some dick, dick? Finally!"

Samaya said, "Oh my gosh! All of you irritating as hell. I'm not a virgin. You like it?"

Coral said, "*Who you fuck? No…Seriously, don't be stomping off!*"

Samaya said, "Whatever! I'm about to get dressed. Call you later."

*****

Man 2 said, "Told you she's fucking him now. You don't have shit coming."

Chad said, "I see! Fuck, her…"

Man 2 said, "You thought she was about to fuck yo broke ass?"

Jai
Always Down

After Jai stopped in on Samaya's performance the other night at the club, she made sure to pass out her business cards. She even acquired some men that came in shopping for their women and more dancing clients that night.

She started making drop-off visits if the money was right for the travel and taking orders in one run.

Clientele started expanding, so she had Jez ordering more fabric, supplies and assisting with the drawings. She hired Kimberly and Daisy part-time to give Jez a break.

Jai said, "I thought about dancing, sis. Seeing all that easy money fall for shaking ass, but you know my scary ass."

Jez said, "Fuck that! Dad would kill you, then wake you up, and Mom would kill you again!"

Jai noticed that Queen beeped her line, and thought about calling her back, which she barely did after seeing people on certain levels. "You're going to ignore me just like that?" Jez muttered.

Jai said, "Hey, Q! What's up, girlie?"

Queen said, "Come to the club around eight PM!"

Jai said, "See you later."

"What are you rolling your eyes for?" Jai laughed. "What's going on with you?" Jez said in a concerned voice.

Jai said, "Sis? Why don't you like Queen?"

Jez said, "Ugh! That's who you were talking to? Ask her! Bitch always observing me and what I say."

Jai said, "I will ask her! She's cool people, just give her a chance. That's just her demeanor. You see her family laughs at her."

Jez said, "Her demeanor needs to be checked, and I'm not that bitch's family."

*****

Jai threw back a few tequila shots then started closing the shop up. She sent Daisy an e-mail to meet with her, knowing her sister and Kimberly weren't going for more help.

Kimberly said, "*I'm finished! See you ladies tomorrow.*"

Jez said, "*Bye!* What's the rush for, Jai? Who's texting you?"

Jai said, "*Good night!* Thought I'd get a few lap dances in VIP from Queen. She knows how to kiss, and she could teach me how to dance."

Jez said, "*Quit playing!* Now you like girls? And, I bet' not ever hear about your dancing, period."

Jai said, "You sounding just like Mom. Break loose, sis!"

Jez said, "When you get to your destination, text me."

Jai said, "Okay, Dad! Break loose! I'm heading home first. You are coming with me?"

Jez said, "When I'm ready to break loose, I will. Thank you! Let me call Mommy dearest and tell her, so she doesn't worry."

Jai said, "*Break loose!*"

*****

Jez watched Jai get all cute wishing she dared to live like a rock star, knowing damn well she couldn't hang. The more Jez watched her twin dance in front of the mirror, she started believing her sister wanted to dance. The thought made her not like Queen even more, and one thing she knew for sure was Jai couldn't get turned out more than she already was.

Jez said, "When did you make that outfit? That's revealing."

Jai said, "I have a lot of them on the rack in my room. I haven't brought them to the shop yet, Mom."

Jez said, "Stop it! I'll look at them later. We're some pretty twins!"

Jai said, "You need to stop smoking that shit! What is that?"

Jez said, "Flame! Don't knock it until you try it, sis."

Jai said, "Let me take another shot because that shit stank and I need to smell my perfume."

Jai said, "Anyways, I have a young lady named Daisy coming for her second interview tomorrow. I need you and Kimberly to be nice."

Jez said, "Oh, really? Sounds good, I guess."

Jai said, "I need more help with these new orders, especially when you are with Tara."

Jez said, "Don't do that. You knew I was finishing school and Tara is cool."

Jai said, "I'm not jealous. I'm planning on opening a new shop across town, so I need to train someone soon."

The other night Queen introduced Jai to Merch's fine ass at the club, but she saw them talking beforehand and played it off like she didn't see shit and just asked for more flame.

Jai had followed them to the hotel that night, and she wasn't expecting Jai to go, but she did, and that's all she wrote. Jai became her bitch, Merch's side piece just like the rest of them, and they didn't even know it and Merch didn't either.

*****

Merch was fucking the shit out of Queen doing doggy style as Jai lay on the bed with Queen's face in between her thighs. He backed off and walked over to the extra big lounge chair, motioning his hand for them to play with each other as he watched them through the smoke.

He told Queen to suck her nipples then he walked back over and started fingering her. Queen got up and pushed him over and sat down slowly onto his tongue. She motioned for Jai to sit down on his dick.

Jai was riding his dick like it was hers until Queen switched positions with her. Jai went to sit on his face, and he pushed her politely to the side, and he knew if he had let Jai sit on his face, they'd both be dead. Queen and Merch climaxed at the same time, then headed for the shower, and Jai followed.

*****

Jai's text to Queen: "On my way!"

Queen's text to Jai: "I reserved you a table, so when you get to the door tell them you have a table then they won't charge you."

Jai's text to Queen: "Thx sweetie…"

When Jai walked up to the entryway, everyone noticed the lady in all red. "What's your name, ma?" Man 1 shouted. "I'm good," Jai shouted as the door closed behind her.

Jai approached the stage slowly when Queen came off the pole into the splits. When Queen saw her approaching, she crawled slowly toward her. Jai placed a stack of money on the stage as instructed, and a few men came to the stage as they had planned. *That shit worked just like Merch said it would,* Jai thought, so she proceeded to make it rain on Queen as she tapped each ass cheek with cash.

Queen made her ass move to the music then the men started cheering her on, and Merch stood at the bar watching his girls show out as he flamed.

Jai was surprised that Queen could move like that with such ease because she wasn't very flexible in bed.

She saw Queen coming from the back toward her, but Merch cut her off, whispering something in her ear, then she walked over.

Queen said, "Hey, girl! Thanks for the tips."

Jai said, "No problem! Both of y'all can dance."

Queen said, "We've been doing this for a while. Practice makes perfect."

Jai said, "I'm about to get out of here. I have a long day tomorrow at the shop."

Queen said, "You should meet me at the hotel from the other night in an hour?"

Jai said, "Okay, girl, I'll be there!"

*****

Queen was greeted with a smile from ear to ear, knowing this bitch thought Merch was here also. When Jai noticed it was just them two there alone, she didn't care because she wanted to talk to her alone.

Queen said, "Merch had some business to attend, so it's just you and me."

Jai said, "That's fine with me, sweetie. You can teach me how to dance."

After a few shots and a hot shower, Queen, didn't waste any time flaming and taking shots.

Queen said, "What's up with you and my cousin? I see she's been inviting you to a lot of functions lately."

Jai said, "Nothing, really…We've been associates for a while, we hung out before she introduced us, and she's a loyal customer that spends good money."

She started massaging Jai's thighs, kissing her neck and ears, wanting to choke her, but whatever Merch wanted, she did. Jai couldn't take any more, so she started sucking Queen's nipples, politely pushing her onto the bed. As she spread Queen's legs open, she tapped her pussy. "I need my man here for this," Queen said.

When she pushed her fingers inside Queen, she moaned out loud. Jai saw that she liked it, so she kept moving her fingers in a circular motion.

Queen said, "Stop! Turn around, Jai."

Jai lifted her ass in the air then turned her head, so she could look at Queen. She wanted her to lick her pussy from the back so bad, but Queen stood there staring.

Queen grabbed her nipples hard as hell, watching her moan out loud, then backed off and picked up her flame.

Jai noticed that Queen wasn't into all this threesome shit from the way her face looked, but Merch had a hold on her. She knew Queen was only doing this to please Merch, and he was very fruitful for her to be around.

Jai said, "It's your turn to teach me some moves."

Queen showed her some dance moves in front of the mirror like she was onstage. "It's okay to touch yourself," Queen whispered dancing to the music.

Queen said, "Hit this flame. It'll loosen you up."

Jai said, "I've never flamed, sweetie."

Queen said, "It's a first time for everything. Quit calling me that, like I'm an old bitch."

Jai said, "Give it to me, because this looks different from what my sister was flaming."

She inhaled the flame so hard, she started choking and coughing. Queen handed her the bottle, then she took some more shots. "This is called Backwoods," Queen said as she exhaled, blowing the smoke in her face.

Queen said, "See...Now, arch your back a little, and toot your ass up."

Jai said, "Girl, my ass moving now. Aeeeee..."

Queen said, "Your twerking good enough for amateur night."

Jai said, "Hey, my shit moving. *Hey...*"

Jai was high as hell laughing at Queen, cheering her on, until Merch walked in the room. He eyed both the ladies naked on top of the furry rug twerking on all four.

Merch said, "Don't stop because I walked in. Continue!"

Queen said, "Come here, Daddy?"

Merch said, "Hold on! Let me flame real quick. What is y'all drinking?"

Merch went to shower, and the ladies followed him. Queen made her way back to the room and went through his pockets and tried to unlock Jai's phone. She heard them coming, so she quickly put his things back in his pants.

Merch said, "Lay down, Jai! Go on and get that, Q. That's what I'm talking about. Lift that ass more, Q."

Jai rubbed her nipples while Queen licked and fingered her at the same time. Merch was banging the fuck out of Queen to the point she kept coming up moaning until Jai held her head down.

Jai said, "Keep going, Queen, don't stop!"

Merch said, "Come this way, Jai!"

Queen said, "Daddy not playing tonight."

Merch said, "Go on and get that, Jai."

Queen lay down and let Jai indulge into her juices, while Merch looked her straight in the eyes.

Queen said, "Hold on! Hold on! Move, please..."

Jai said, "What's the matter, Queen? She must be feeling sick again."

Merch said, "She's a big a girl. Come here until she comes back."

When Merch finished, he went straight to the shower and saw Queen going through her phone.

He came out, and they both were sleeping on the lounge chair, so he flamed one and went right to sleep with them.

*****

That morning Merch pulled Jai's hair soft enough to wake her up. He sat on the edge of the lounge couch flaming, as he watched Jai's head go up and down. He liked that she didn't choke like a pro. She was enjoying the pulling of her hair, but she wanted more. Jai stood up and turned around. When she bent over, Merch slid his manhood in, and Queen woke up from the moans of Jai.

Queen said, "I see you're enjoying yourself without me. Weird shit!"

Merch said, "Come here, Queen! Quit playing with me."

She began massaging Jai's nipples, as Jai fingered her slowly. Merch loved how Queen was down for anything when it comes to pleasing him. After they finished, they sent Jai on her way and jumped in the shower.

Merch said, "You outdid yourself last night. Do you hear me, Q? I heard you've been sick lately. Q? Queen?"

Queen said, "Oh, yeah! Something I ate made me sick."

*****

Jai left her sister a voice mail that night to open the shop because she already knew she was going to be late. When she got home that morning, she fell right back to sleep.

She woke up in the late afternoon, rushing to the shower. While brushing her teeth, she noticed her sister left a note.

She put on the silk jumpsuit with matching pumps her twin left out for her and headed for the shop, hoping she didn't miss any customers needing sizing.

Jai said, "Seeing the open sign light on made me happy that I have a twin sister."

Jez said, "Of course, twin. Looking nice."

Jai said, "Thank you, sis. I'm so grateful for you."

Jez said, "Good morning, Jai. Your coffee is in the microwave."

Kimberly said, "Hi, Jai…"

Jai said, "Sorry, so late. Good afternoon, ladies."

Jez said, "All your orders were picked up, your materials came this morning, and Chuck sent more flowers. Hopefully, Queen doesn't get mad."

Jai said, "Your ass silly, sis. Here are your checks with a bonus. This coffee tastes different."

Jez said, "It's your usual, Thanks."

Jai said, "I know, you know!"

Kimberly said, "Thanks, Jai. Your mother called earlier."

Jez said, "Queen dropped your wallet off right before you got here. She was with some fine-ass dude."

Jai said, "Oh, shit! I didn't even realize I left it."

Jez said, "The guy stayed in the car with his fine ass. She has good taste in men."

Jai said, "Your ass crazy, but he is fine."

Kimberly said, "Yes, he is!"

Jez said, "Samaya called. Here's a list of people that called the shop."

Jai said, "I didn't hear my phone ringing. I was knocked out."

Jez said, "Why are you trying to go around that bighead girl then she brought your wallet here."

Jai said, "I'm not. I left it at the club last night."

Jez said, "Are you sleeping with her or her man?"

Jai said, "Stop it, twin. You don't like her. Do you really want the truth?"

Jez said, "No! I want you to be safe. I put your mail in your office."

Jai said, "I'm okay! I made us hair appointments today for one PM."

Kimberly said, "Can I go?"

Jai said, "Of course…I'll be ready in a minute."

*****

Jez walked to the back and peeked into Jai's office, noticing her head was bent over onto her arms. She was knocked out, so Jez closed the door.

DJ said, "*Welcome Ms. Jai to the stage.*"

She crawled slowly down to the front of the stage with her back arched, twerking her cheeks to the music one at a time like Queen showed her.

When she made it to the pole, she flipped over into a headstand, bouncing her ass in midair, copying Samaya's move. She flipped over into the splits and noticed Merch and Chuck sitting at the same table, laughing.

Jez said, "*Jai? Wake up! Jai? Jai? Wake up, twin!*"

She was tapping and shaking Jai until she woke up.

Jai said, "Stop! What time is it, sis?"

Jez said, "Seven PM. I let you sleep. You need to stop smoking that shit. You can't even handle it."

Jai said, "Why didn't you wake me up?"

Jez said, "I checked on you a few times, you were snoring, so I let you sleep. I smoked the rest of your flame. What you know about Backwoods? I'm telling Mommy!"

Jai said, "Tell her, and I'll tell her you gave it to me. Sorry, I left all the work for you. I'm so sorry, sis. Let me take you out to eat."

Jez said, "Good, because I have the munchies. And, who in the hell gave you flame? Matter of fact! When did you start smoking?"

Jai said, "Why? And last night. Kimberly left already? Damn!"

Jez said, "I already know Queen turning your ass out. Let me find out you're auditioning for the amateur night. I'm going to fuck you up."

Jai said, "First of all, I'm grown. Can't nobody make me do shit that I don't want to? Secondly, If I decide to dance, make sure you make it rain."

CHAPTER 7

Queen
Damn! Not Again

Her face had been hanging over the toilet all morning, throwing up everything she drank or ate.

She pissed on three pregnancy tests, and each one was positive. The tears just ran down her face like a faucet. *"I can't...I can't...I can't...,"* Queen cried out.

Merch always said he wanted Queen to have his daughter because she had cat eyes, and she let that shit go in one ear, and out the other, never taking him seriously, plus, she didn't have an education or career, and she took that seriously.

Queen wanted a future with him, but the money came regularly, and that's all she wanted right now.

He's the only man that she's been with since they started messing around, and he rides without a rubber since day one.

Queen sneaked out and had two abortions behind Merch's back and pretended to be sick when he touched her. When she had the miscarriage, he was right there through everything, consoling her.

She started feeling bad about killing these babies, but now she's not homeless, she has more money, and she knows he would help.

Queen said, *"Who the fuck knocking this early?"*

She grabbed a rag and washed her face, trying to throw everything away at the same time panicking. She looked through the peephole again, trying to hold her tears back, hoping Merch walked off.

Queen said, "Aww, shit! Merch! *Where the fuck is his key?*"

Merch said, "What the fuck! Open the door."

Queen ran back to the bathroom, trying to hide the test strips and the empty boxes in the garbage. Knowing she wouldn't have a choice in the matter if he knew. He started banging on the door again, hard as hell.

Merch said, "*I hear your ass running the fuck around. Open the door now!*"

Queen said, "*Quit banging. I'm coming. I was using the bathroom, damn!*"

Merch said, "*Open the mooootherfucc—*"

Before he could finish his sentence, the door swung open, and he pushed past her, walking in all fast, looking around as if somebody was there.

Merch said, "Who are you yelling at, Q?"

Queen said, "I was using the bathroom. Where's your key?"

Merch said, "What's up, Q? I heard your ass running around and shit."

Queen said, "Nothing. What the fuck are you waving your pistol around for? Damn! Ain't nobody in here. You're spazzing."

Merch said, "Don't be speaking on what I'm doing like you're warning some goddamn body. What the fuck!"

Queen said, "*Oh my gosh!* I'm not crazy enough to have another man in my house, knowing damn well you have a key."

Merch said, "Don't get fucked up, punk!"

He sat in the lounge chair they fuck in all the time, breaking his blunt down, noticing Queen's eyes were watery as soon as he walked in, so he tried handing the flame to Queen, and she waved him off. "No, Merch," Queen mumbled.

Merch said, "When did you start refusing the flame?"

Queen said, "Just flamed before you came."

Merch said, "I don't smell shit. Lying ass!"

Queen said, "We're going to sit here as if you don't have your key. Where's your key?"

Merch said, "Queen, start cooking, I'm hungry."

Queen said, "Where is your key, Merch?"

Merch said, "I don't know! Probably lost it playing basketball."

Queen said, "I don't know how to cook either."

Merch said, "Go cook some chicken."

Queen said, "Yeah…Let me go fry up some keys."

Merch said, "Funny ass. Damn! Them panties are looking right."

Queen said, "My funny ass got my keys, though."

She switched off hard, knowing that the boy shorts were rising in her ass cheeks. She wasn't trying to hear shit he said, but her ass went to the kitchen to prepare some fried chicken, baked macaroni, lemon asparagus, and a lemon cake.

Merch flamed like two blunts and went to shower as usual. While brushing his teeth, he noticed a pink box on the floor behind the toilet, and he picked it up.

He just stood there looking at the lines comparing them to the instructions, and his body went numb. Once he figured it out, *This is why she was crying*, he thought. He wanted to storm out of the bathroom, but he held his composure. He started going through the garbage can rumbling for more tests. After he read the results for the other tests, he was happy as hell that they all read positive.

Merch said, "*Positive. Positive. Positive. What the fuck!*"

His phone started ringing, and Nyala's name popped up. He sent it straight to voice mail, thinking he's finally getting his baby girl and wife. "Fuck these other females," he whispered to himself.

He wanted to see if she'd tell him, so he put all the boxes back the way he found it. Now he knew why she was running around crying and hiding shit.

Merch said, "That chicken smells good, bae."

Queen said, "I tried a new seasoning called 'keyless,' it's okay."

She looked at him walking out of the bathroom with his white wifebeater, white basketball shorts on, looking fine as hell and loving how his manly power showed through the shorts, and his big-ass muscles glistening from the water, looking like a piece of melting chocolate with juicy lips.

He walked up behind Queen kissing her neck, pressing his manhood into her juicy ass, rubbing her nipple with his fingertips, and as soon as his other hand ran into her wetness, Queen closed her eyes.

Queen said, "Boy, stop! Before this food gets ignored!"

Merch said, "Turn around, Queen, and look at me."

He slowly gripped Queen's face with his big hands, pulling her face to his lips, kissing her slowly and passionately with his tongue all down her throat. Backing off slowly, they pecked each other's lips, then she grabbed his dick.

Queen said, "Hold that thought, baby, until after you eat."

Merch walked off like he's the man, thinking to himself, *I have a daughter*, then he turned around and faced Queen.

Merch said, "Queen? Do you have something to tell me?"

Queen's mind was somewhere else from all the grabbing her nipples and kissing her neck. In deep thought about the kiss, she didn't hear him say anything.

Merch said, "*Queen? Queen?* Do you hear me?"

Queen said, "What? What did you say? You are throwing me off."

Merch said, "Do you have something to tell me?"

Queen said, "No…Where's your key?"

Merch said, "Quit asking me the same shit. I told you. I left them at my mom's."

After they ate, Merch flamed with his hands wrapped in Queen's hair. He watched her head go up and down to the rhythm of the music.

He loved the smacking noise, the wetness, and how she made her lips tightly grip his tip.

When she climbed on top of his muscular thighs, she slid down, trying to go down on all ten inches of dick moaning, but she only mastered her rhythm on four.

Merch grabbed Queen's cheeks, moving her up and down, trying to make her take a little more, but he started thinking about the test.

Merch said, "You good?"

Queen said, "Shut up, missing keys!"

"Yo ass funny," Merch said. He was amazed at the wetness and creaminess but mad she didn't mention the test results. Then he lifted Queen up and softly sucked her clitoris until she screamed out. "Why are you crying?" Merch asked. She motioned her head in a no motion and rolled to the side.

She heard him snoring and went to the bathroom, hoping he stayed asleep while she took the garbage out.

*****

That morning she woke up with Merch sucking her boobs like he was scuba diving and running out of air. She just looked at his ass like, *First, you lost your keys playing ball, then you left them at your mama's house, and you lie on somebody that I haven't met.*

Merch said, "You woke now?"

Queen said, "Yes."

Beep, beep.

Merch said, "Let me answer that. Hold on, Q."

Queen said, "Who is it? You've never told me to hold on. Why are you covering up the phone?"

Merch said, "What's up? I was busy last night. I'll be over later...I need to run somewhere. I'll be back, Q."

Queen said, "Before you go, can you leave some money to go shopping? And thank you."

Merch said, "Take it out my safe. I don't feel like running back in here."

Queen said, "Aight! Don't forget your keys. I might not be here."

Merch said, "Quit playing with me. Make me another set, punk...Ouch! I'll give you something to pinch."

*****

As soon as he left, she showered and put on her clothes, took some money, and went to her aunt Teresa's house.

Queen said, "I didn't look at his phone. When I said something, he shh my ass."

Teresa said, "What are you gonna do? Fuck up all the bitches he fucks? If you can't handle it, move around. I see that you put some more money in that safe."

Queen said, "Master gave me some more shopping money. Do we need some more packages?"

Teresa said, "Always. Now, let's count this *money*…so I can put some money in my account too, shiiid. What about the baby?"

Queen said, "How do you know, Auntie? I haven't said anything."

Teresa said, "Girl, please. Are you keeping this *one*?"

Queen said, "*Samaya telling ass.* Why did you emphasize one?"

Teresa said, "No. Your attitude changes, you start showing feelings, and you stop smoking. When your sisters come, they need to know that dancing is out of the picture for them."

Queen said, "Where'd that come from? I don't want them dancing either. The fuck!"

Teresa said, "If you're gonna keep having abortions, you need to start using condoms or birth control. Poor babies! If he's allowing this shit, he's wrong as well."

Queen said, "No, he doesn't know. He only knew about the miscarriage because he was there."

Teresa said, "All I can say is don't tell him. Seems like the type that'll snap."

Queen said, "Why are you coming at me?"

Teresa said, "First of all, if my sister were here, she'd tell you the same thing. Secondly, I don't want my niece chasing behind somebody that doesn't want a relationship, or knows when his chick is pregnant. And thirdly, I do care. Besides, this hustling shit doesn't last forever. Get what you need, and move around. If you love him, suck that shit up, and claim yours. Let his ass know, *we not no bitches.*"

Queen said, "Anyways, have you talked to your daughter?"

Teresa said, "This is gonna wallop you keep playing with his babies. Now, anyways that!"

Queen said, "And if it does? You'll be right here like always."

Merch
Floating

Ax walked through the building, letting the renovators know what walls to knock down and the look they wanted to achieve. Tee showed the movers the things he wanted refurbishing and the things they were throwing away.

Ax said, "We're getting rid of everything here, so take everything to the warehouse."

Tee said, "When we pulled the old lockers out the dressing room, look at what we found, fam."

Ax hired Teisha as his assistant, so she had interviews in the back for new staff, commercials on the radio, advertisements in the paper, and new business cards and flyers handed out for the grand opening.

Merch said, "What's up, Ax and Tee? I see your girl handling business."

Ax said, "Once you point her in a direction, her mind's set. Rocky came by looking for you, and he pulled one of the strippers out the back door by her hair."

Tee said, "He's about to be exposed, and he's pissed."

Ax said, "Short arm, nasty ass!"

Merch said, "*Damn!* He doesn't come across as the violent type. I'll call his crazy ass later. Which female?"

Ax said, "He snatched her ass so quick, I didn't see her face. Come back here and look at this shit."

Tee said, "Damn! He had cameras behind the mirrors."

Ax said, "He got pictures and videos of everybody. Nasty bitch!"

Merch said, "Where did you get this shit? Like what areas specifically?"

Tee said, "Found it in the locker room when we pulled the old lockers out. That's not it. See this shit! It was more in the VIP."

Merch said, "What the hell? Secret closet mothafucker."

Ax said, "All this shit! Then he watched them change and shower. Nasty fat fucker."

Merch said, "I'll have my boy look over these documents. Now these pictures and tapes, I need to make sure my girl and her family not in this shit before I give it to him."

Ax said, "Hope I'm not in them motherfuckers, while I'm laughing."

Tee said, "Shit! I was in the VIP the other night getting good head. Erase me, too, fam."

Merch said, "Fam, that's why I'm taking this shit. We won't be on this shit or the breaking porn news. I was back here, clowning on several occasions."

Tee said, "What about all these guns?"

Merch said, "Don't touch that shit without gloves, fam. Put it all in a bag. What's on them DVDs?"

Ax said, "I'm not trying to get you sick right now."

Tee said, "That's why he snapped on ole girl. She was supposed to get this shit before he signed them ownership papers."

Ax said, "Well, I do have good news!"

Tee said, "It's more space now the walls are coming down upstairs. The lady's dressing room and the customers' bathroom is bigger without all the peepholes. We took out the benches on the wall, and that made the dance floor bigger around the stage."

Ax said, "I need them two offices in the back knocked out, that'll add space for the bar and VIP area. We can keep that front office by the entryway for the managers and staff."

Tee said, "I'll get the guys on it."

Merch said, "Well, here's the credit card for the business use."

Ax said, "Let me show you this wall they knocked down upstairs and the new security system."

Teisha said, "Hello, fellas…How are you doing, Merch? Ax, I handled everything. Can I get the dollars?"

Merch said, "Hello, Ms. Feisty. I'm good. How about you?"

Teisha said, "I'm not feisty, Merch. Just defensive. I'm good."

Ax said, "Here's two hundred, I'll get you the rest tomorrow."

Teisha said, "I have things to do, and this is not enough."

Merch said, "Hold on, Teisha!"

Teisha said, "I'll be back tomorrow to finish the interviews."

Merch said, "Let me know if you need anything else, Feisty?"

Teisha said, "Oh, it was a fat man back there searching the ladies' locker room earlier. When I walked by, he left in a hurry."

Merch went in his pocket and pulled out so much money that Teisha couldn't stop looking. "That shit made my pussy wet, boy," Teisha whispered. He counted out two thousand and handed it to her and shook his head at her mindless boldness.

Ax said, "I had Teisha fill out an application for herself as well, so if we need anything else, we'll call you."

Teisha said, "Okay, Mr. Ax. Bye, Merch…"

Merch said, "See you later…What the fuck he all up in here for? The business is ours now."

Ax said, "Damn! Fam, look! That new bartender fine as hell!"

Merch said, "Yes, she is! What make dude think he can keep coming in here unannounced? We found your collection and stash tapes. Now ask for it, nasty ass."

Ax said, "When Teisha told me, I had already seen him leave. I went to check his ass, and he had pulled off too fast."

Merch said, "This nigga came outside his body coming here without calling first. *Fat ass!*"

Ax said, "Trying to get his shit out the locker room, and he didn't find it. He's taking it out on a female. Pussy shit!"

Merch said, "It's too late now! Do you need anything else before I bounce, fam?"

Ax said, "I'm good! My moms said thanks for the package. I'll call you later."

Merch said, "Family first."

*****

Merch made a call to meet up with one of his friends that lived on campus. He needed a break from all the renovations and peeping toms shit. Then his family coming at him about his side business was pissing him off, knowing damn well they flamed right along with him.

Nyala said, "Come in, Daddy. *I miss you, sexy.*"

Merch walked in and immediately hugged her, grabbing her ass tight while pushing her into his hard manhood. She jumped up, wrapping her arms and legs around him.

Merch said, "Hey, baby girl. Kiss me!"

They kissed for like two minutes straight before he carried her into the living room.

*****

Samaya said, "*Look, bitch! He moving around.*"

Queen said, "I told you...I wasn't lying about all these females."

Tara said, "Cousin, I thought you were lying...Seriously!"

Samaya said, "You saw how she jumped into his arms?"

Queen said, "She does it every time. I got something for his ass, though."

Tara said, "Have you gotten tested? Don't be looking at me like that. When your ass gonna be in a secluded camp somewhere, and don't call me."

Samaya said, "I wouldn't be able to hold my composure. Fuck this!"

Queen said, "Honestly, I don't see how he has the energy to fuck all of us."

Tara said, "Have you thought about who's paying her tuition and rent."

Queen said, "Right. I stormed up to the door one night. Thought about my sisters and turned my ass around."

Toonie said, "Is he your man? Like, did he ask you to be his woman? You can't trip over something that is not yours."

Queen said, "Hold the fuck up! You sat back there this whole time with yo quiet moo—"

Samaya said, "*Queen...stop! Toonie...shut up! Damn!*"

Queen said, "Since you're talking now. Did you tell her you went to some club the other night for an audition?"

Toonie said, "Whatever, private eye! Drop me off! Get out the car and peek through the window. Scary ass!"

Queen said, "Yo ass gonna have a black eye you keep talking, li'l girl."

Tara said, "I think we need on all-black to do that."

Toonie said, "Little enough to have since not to be following a man..."

Samaya said, "Y'all tripping! We're going to all have on orange we get caught. The way she jumped in his arms is proof they're fucking."

*****

They flamed back-to-back while he counted his money, and she did her homework for law school.

Merch waited patiently, as he rubbed his fingers through her hair and poked her in the ears, trying hard to distract her. She wasn't going because the last time she let him have his way, she almost failed her test.

As soon as the glasses came off, he knew what time it was, and he always followed her to the shower.

When she tried to put her hair up, Merch gently grabbed her hair in his palm, turned her head around, and pushed her head down. She kissed his tip, slowly massaging it with her tongue, opening her mouth, and letting it all go in like a pro.

She stood up to face him, and she watched his tongue swirl around her nipples. Not being able to take it anymore, she turned around, arched her back, raised her ass, and poked it out.

The water hit her body as he stroked passionately back and forth with pleasure, watching her moan as she tried to take the dick, and pushing him back with her hand.

He let her get away with pushing him, just as he got away with taking her time from finding someone that would love her the right way.

Nyala's personality made her a different type of pretty from his other friends. She was book smart and pretended to be tough, which turned him on.

She stood at 5 foot 5; weighed 125 pounds; and had a 34D bra size, a nice round ass that sat up high, pale light skin, pretty feathered brown highlighted hair, good manners, and manicured hands and feet.

Most of all, she never judged him, and Nyala took him for the man he was. She brought out a patient side to Merch that no other female has never seen or done.

Nyala said, "It'll be nice to spend more time together."

She made him laugh, talk about his future, family, other chicks, and his current accomplishments, giving him ideas to help his business grow, and that's what made her unique in his eyes.

All his other chicks had their hands out for money, mouths open, and she had a full scholarship off her brains alone.

He didn't mind taking her to movies, out to eat, and shopping when he had time for her, so he made sure she kept money and flame in her bag for extra cash and to keep her around.

The flame sold so quick on campus that she was his number one hustler. He paid some of her tuition with her profits and made sure she put the other money in the bank with her allowance from her parents.

Nyala said, "I'm going to need an extra package. Everyone's partying since finals are over."

Merch said, "I'll make it happen."

Nyala said, "My parents want to meet you. Don't look at me that way, Merch."

Merch said, "Really? You speak on me like that?"

Nyala said, "Yes! They ask questions about the money and my future. They saw my car and wanted to know how I afford these things without asking them."

Merch said, "I'll see what my schedule looks like, because I'm not ready for all this, Nyala."

Nyala said, "Excuse me...I thought we were past all this? Every time I mention my future, you leave."

*****

Queen said, "Look how long he's been in there. I've sat out here before, watched him take this bitch to a five-star restaurant, movies, and shopping sprees. Auntie stopped me from shooting at their ass."

Tara said, "Auntie stopped you? I'm surprised she didn't shoot. *I have to fuck him up.*"

Toonie said, "*Oh, no! Now, we're talking about life sentences… Samaya drop me off!*"

Samaya said, "Chill, ain't nobody shooting shit. Toonie, stop!"

Tara said, "I couldn't fuck him freely and raw knowing he's dicking down everybody. That's too many juices."

Queen said, "Anyways, she told me to get as much money from him as possible and stack that shit. I've been on my fake shopping sprees and movies by myself on his expense. Getting my hair done by Auntie, while I put that shit in my safe."

Samaya said, "Text his ass to see if he responds."

Queen said, "Tried that with Auntie in the car, and he doesn't respond until he gets in his car. Auntie was so mad. She told my ass to double the amount of flame I get from him and give it to her. She went and bought me a strongbox to keep at her house."

Toonie said, "Sounds like my mom. Thirsty!"

Samaya said, "She's right, Toonie. Use this shit to your advantage, Q."

Tara said, "Get tested!"

Queen said, "I am! He goes in empty-handed and comes out with a nice size bag. I'm getting mines with my thirsty ass."

Toonie said, "She can say get tested, but I can't?"

Samaya said, "Toonie…stop it! *Damn!*"

Tara said, "We should jump this nigga?"

Queen said, "Bitch, please! He has a gun, and will use it."

Samaya said, "I'm not about to get shot over some pussy."

Toonie said, "Me either! But, he's leaving…Look!"

Queen said, "Good looking! He always stays with her longer than the other females."

Toonie said, "*Others? Wow!*"

Merch pulled off, and they all ducked down, forgetting that the rental had some tint. Before they could say anything, Samaya jumped out of the car and walked up to the door. She had her hat pulled down with her tinted sunglasses on.

*****

Nyala said, "*Hold on! Did you forget something?*"

Samaya said, "Hey, girlie. Can you tell me where the rental office is located? I start next year, and my parents sent me down here to do their work."

Nyala said, "Um. Sorry...I thought you were my man coming back. I believe they closed two hours ago."

Samaya said, "Darn it! I thought the brochure had eight PM on it. Do you know any nice hotels around?"

Nyala said, "My fiancé owns a hotel. Let me write it down for you."

Samaya watched her walk over to the table. *Damn, this bitch fine and thick*, Samaya thought. When Nyala walked back over, she smiled so hard, showing all her pearly whites.

Samaya said, "Thank you, girl. We need more nice people out here because a few people flicked me off."

Nyala said, "No problem, see you around. And never mind these pricks. They did that to me my first year."

Samaya said, "Oh! I'm sorry. My name is Nancy."

Nyala said, "I'm Nyala. See you around."

*****

Samaya ran and jumped back in the car. She stared at Queen for a minute before saying anything, then started the car, and pulled off.

Samaya said, "Let's go, before you jump out this motherfucker and beat her ass."

Queen said, "*Say something.* Don't leave anything out either."

Samaya told Queen everything but left out the fiancé shit. Tara started crying with her emotional ass.

Toonie said, "It's not the girl's fault. Why are you crying, Tara?"

Queen said, "I got this. I'm fucking him up. *Oh my gosh! I hate him! Go back. I want to ask her something.*"

Samaya said, "The last time you said that we were shooting at people."

Queen said, "Tara, stop crying. Acting like you just saw Skunk. Da fuck! Besides, Merch ain't the only real man out here."

Samaya said, "Seriously! Don't fight him. Fuck up his pockets."

Toonie said, "*Yup! Yup! You have to get like us li'l girls! We don't get mad! We chase the bag!*"

Queen said, "Yeah! Drop Toonie off first, Samaya. Suck that shit up, Tara!"

Tara said, "I'm crying because I'm mad. I would have knocked and went in to see some shit. Da fuck!"

Samaya said, "I'm confused. Why these fuckers got y'all yapping at each other? Da fuck! Treat they ass how they treat you."

Toonie said, "Exactly! Simple shit!"

CHAPTER 8

The Club
Business as Usual

Samaya and Queen walked up to the club noticing significant changes that they didn't see coming.

Samaya said, "Did Rocky hit the lottery in this bitch? He's doing good."

Queen said, "Girl, please, I know for a fact he didn't do this."

They had valet, switched the name to Cupid, which was plastered on the top of the building with working light bulbs. The entryway had red velvet ropes to form lines for entrance, and four big bouncers were holding the front door down.

As soon as you walked in, it was all white everything, with a complement of gold. New white leather furniture wrapped along all the walls that were bare before, lovely crystal vases were complementing the modern end tables, then white sheer curtains separated the seating areas for lap dances. They even had some clear stool chairs surrounding the bar.

Queen said, "When they get guards at the VIP section?"

Samaya said, "Now they want to make sure we're safe. Where Rocky at?"

Queen said, "I don't know! But, they got new paint, glasses, waitresses, and bartenders."

Samaya said, "Rocky should have been done this. I see a lot of new faces tonight."

Queen said, "They put extra poles on the stage. Look!"

Samaya said, "We got competition now."

Queen said, "All I see is fake boobs and butts."

Samaya said, "That's trending now. They look good though. I'm going to get some boobs and ass."

Queen said, "You always say that. Well, when you go, I'm going."

All the chicks had beautiful manicures, pedicures, nice hair, colorful wigs, smiles, and outfits.

Queen said, "You think your friend is here?"

Samaya said, "I hope not! We've been seeing each other since that night, and I'm starting to like him."

Queen said, "He's got your nose wide open. Hope he's not like his brother."

Samaya said, "Ugh...No, he doesn't! Who the fuck is this?"

Teisha said, "Excuse me! I don't remember you from the interviews?"

Queen said, "Just like we don't remember you from no damn interview, bitch."

Samaya said, "Our dressing room supposed to be right here!"

Teisha said, "I'm not your bitch for one, and you don't have a dressing room or job here."

Queen said, "Where all my shit go that was in here?"

Teisha said, "*Chick!* The manager is upstairs, but y'all need to wait at the front while I finish with my business."

Queen said, "*Bitch! What the fuck you mean y'all? You ugly bitch!*"

Samaya said, "Like I said!"

Teisha said, "Get your dusty asssss ooouut!"

Bop. Bop. Bop. All you could hear was "Bitch, bitch, bitch," Queen yelled, as she threw fist after fist. Teisha tried to say something, but she couldn't get all the words out her mouth before Queen punched Teisha in the nose. Teisha tried swinging back, but Queen was punching to fast. Queen knocked her down, then she went to stomp her, but Merch picked her up.

Teisha said, "*Bitch! I got something for your ass, period.*"

Merch said, "*Hold on! Hold on!* Queen…get the fuck off this girl. I had my people put you a room in the back. Damn!"

Ax grabbed Samaya and held her until Merch got Queen off Teisha.

Samaya said, "*Bitch, better watch her mouth. Where is Rocky?*"

Teisha got up, ran at Samaya, and Ax moved out of the way. Samaya stood to the side, and let Teisha run straight into her fist, swinging hard. She knocked her ass down to the floor again. Samaya let her get up, so they could square up. Even though Teisha was taller, Samaya was drilling her face until Teisha fell back.

Queen said, "*Get that bitch, cuz! Let me go, Merch!*"

Merch said, "Calm the fuck down, Q!"

Merch laughed because he knew his fam didn't give a fuck about these females fighting. Merch waved for security to come. "Grab Teisha, man, they got her ass leaking," Ax said to the guard.

Security grabbed Teisha off the floor and kept the ladies separated. Teisha tried pushing past the security guard.

Security said, "You need to stop, ma!"

Teisha said, "*Fuck you!*"

Security said, "They fucked you up."

Samaya said, "Where's Rocky?"

Ax said, "He's not here no more."

Samaya said, "What's going on, Merch?"

Security said, "You good, sir?"

Queen said, "Who is this oversized-hulk-looking motherfucker? Yes, he's good!"

Merch said, "I'm good! Quit insulting staff, and calm your ass down."

Samaya said, "The professional staff insulted us first. Merchie…"

Merch said, "*Shut the fuck up, Saria!*"

Merch finally got Queen settled down then escorted them to the back. Ax stayed in the front to calm down Teisha, so she wouldn't call her sisters and cousins because they didn't need drama at opening night.

Merch said, "Rocky doesn't own this building anymore. Y'all fighting on people?"

Queen said, "Y'all need to check these new bitches. She was out of line."

Merch said, "You know better than to tell me what to do. Slow your mouth down."

Samaya said, "She ran at us, talking loud. Giraffe ass."

Merch said, "Bring y'all ass in here! Y'all too pretty to be fighting and acting a fool."

Samaya said, "Whatever, nigga! Control y'all horses from galloping in people faces."

Queen said, "This is nice and clean. This for us?"

Merch said, "Yes! Before you change, someone is requesting for you in the VIP, Samaya."

As soon as she opened the door and saw his face, she was all smiling. Samaya was happy to see him sitting in the private VIP room, waiting for her.

Samaya said, "So, what do I owe the pleasure of your company, Isaiah? Females were running up on me, and my family yapping at the mouth. Then I come in here. You don't want me working. I'm not falling for this 'sweep me off my feet' shit."

Isaiah said, "I don't want you working in a strip club, I made that clear? All that shaking-ass shit about to stop."

Samaya said, "What am I supposed to do for money? Answer that! I don't know where you are from, but hustling is in my blood."

Isaiah said, "We'll start from where you left off, putting your future first. School, college, setting goals."

Samaya said, "Money brings income, and bills need to get paid is all I know. School and college didn't put me in a condo, new car, or clothes."

Isaiah stood up and looked down at her. When he picked her up, she wrapped her arms around his neck, and she thought about that lady jumping in Merch's arms the other night.

Isaiah said, "Shut the fuck up! Listen for once. It's called structure and guidance."

When he put her down, she put her hands on her hips, smiling, knowing that shit made her heart melt, because no one ever really cared enough about her future, just her money.

Samaya said, "Damn! Shut the fuck up though? Sounded so harsh!"

Isaiah said, "*No!* You keep rambling on because you're scared. I got you, baby girl. It's okay."

Samaya said, "If I don't like something about you, will you make a drastic change?"

Isaiah said, "If it's for the better, Samaya, I'm not scared of change or failure because we can always get back up. Allow me to show you a different life for the better. I don't want anybody seeing mines. I'm not sharing you with the world. Get your things together so that we can leave."

Samaya said, "What does 'mines' mean? How many mines do you have?"

Isaiah said, "We're going to talk about that when we leave."

When Samaya was walking down the hall, she saw Teisha crying to Ax, smacking her hands together.

Queen said, "You're leaving me?"

Samaya said, "I don't know what's going on with this new club Cupid or whatever. Isaiah is trying to love me or something."

Queen said, "Follow your heart, girl. Remember, we still need money to survive."

Samaya said, "He's giving me the money I miss here, believe that. Mama didn't raise me, but I'm not a fool."

Queen said, "Go on, before I follow yo ass out of here. Call you later."

Samaya packed up her things and waited for Isaiah upstairs in the newly renovated office. While waiting, she checked her Lovely Vines page and went straight to Isaiah's page. *He removed his account, slick ass,* Samaya thought.

Merch said, "What's up, Rocky? Thanks for coming on short notice. My lawyer said you forgot to sign this last paper."

Rocky said, "What's up, man? I like what you've done with the place. What's your plan for the additional building?"

Isaiah said, "We haven't thought about it yet."

Merch said, "I heard you stopped by the other day. Did you find what you were looking for?"

Rocky said, "Aww, I was looking for my briefcase and a box I left here. Did you find it?"

Isaiah said, "No. For future reference, call before you come. We can't have the previous owner just popping up like this establishment is still his."

Rocky said, "My bad, brother! Did you find anything?"

Merch said, "We threw everything away when we gutted the place out."

Merch was surprised that Isaiah spoke up and checked Rocky's ass real smooth. Rocky didn't look at the paper; he just signed it, not knowing he just signed over permission for the videos and pictures to be released. They could do whatever they wanted with them now.

Merch said, "I'll return the paper to my lawyer since you went up on the price. Isaiah…"

Isaiah said, "We can meet at the bank tomorrow around ten AM. If that's okay with you?"

Rocky said, "That's fine with me."

Samaya got tired of waiting, so she went to look for Queen. When she passed the other office, she noticed Isaiah, Merch, and Rocky talking. Rocky was handing Merch a piece of paper, and her mind started wandering. *What the fuck is going on here*, she thought, trying to listen, and didn't notice Ax walking up.

*****

Merch said, "Nice doing business with you."

Rocky said, "Likewise. It was some important papers in that box."

Isaiah said, "Do you know where you left it exactly? What color is briefcase?"

Rocky said, "Brown box, and the briefcase is all silver. I'll see you tomorrow."

Isaiah said, "Just letting you know again. For future references, when we bought the club, you should have taken all your belongings, no more stop-ins without calling first. Thank you!"

*****

Ax said, "What's up, Saria?"

Samaya said, "Nothing! I was about to go look for Queen and changed my mind."

Ax said, "I guess. Let me get my fam for you…seeing you can't sit still."

Samaya said, "Fuck you, dude!"

Ax said, "Watch ya mouth! You're not in the family yet. Rabbit-face ass!"

Samaya said, "That's what you think. Fetch master! Thank you."

So it wouldn't look obvious that she was busted, she turned around and went back into the office and waited for Isaiah. Ax just walked off, because he knew his fam liked her.

Merch said, "What's up, Ax?"

Ax said, "What's up! Your girl was getting antsy over there."

Isaiah said, "Can you escort Rocky to the front, please. Thanks!"

Merch said, "Can you have Teisha come upstairs for a moment."

Ax said, "Yeah, let me escort him, so he doesn't snatch any more ladies by their hair out the back door."

Rocky looked surprised as hell, Merch chuckled, and Isaiah just nodded in agreement.

Rocky said, "Man, it wasn't like that at all. You know these women get out of hand."

Ax said, "Yeah! Come on, peeps."

Merch and Isaiah couldn't stop laughing, hoping Ax didn't slip up and say too much. "Let me walk you out," Ax said.

Merch said, "Fam funny! I told y'all he needs to be a comedian. Let me get downstairs before they start fighting again."

Isaiah said, "Hold on, bro! This man said papers, lying right in our face. Like we're just going to hand him over a briefcase full of nasty pictures and tapes of these women."

Merch said, "I'd be embarrassed thinking y'all saw the shit. Why didn't he mention the guns?"

Isaiah said, "The first thing he should have done was take that fucked-up camera system down, then take all the evidence. This thirsty, nasty fuck left all the shit like he tried to set us up."

Merch said, "See, I didn't look at it like that. We didn't touch none of that shit."

Isaiah said, "He's in a rush, leaving shit like that. The people don't know we found the shit, but Terrence knows what to say. I'll see you later, bro."

Isaiah walked in the office and sat in the chair behind the desk. Samaya walked over, leaned in, placing her hands on his thighs. When she put her lips on his, she slowly began pecking until both their mouths joined into French-kissing. He gripped both her ass cheeks pulling her to sit down on his lap. She started moving her ass in a circle then backed up slowly.

Isaiah said, "Sorry, it took so long."

Samaya said, "That's okay! I'm hungry, though."

Isaiah said, "Hold that thought! Let's get out of here. When I pull to the front, follow me."

Samaya said, "I came with Queen, so I'm riding with you."

Isaiah said, "That's even better. Do you have a car?"

Samaya said, "Yes. We were out rolling around. I don't like driving anyway."

Isaiah said, "Damn! Thought I found a driver!"

Samaya said, "Boy, please! We can get a driver."

*****

Rocky went straight to the truck mad as hell, thinking they found his shit, but he was willing to do any and everything to get it back. When he jumped in the truck, everybody was waiting for their descriptions before they went in.

Rocky said, "Make sure you get a lap dance and throw money. They might have it sitting around or something."

Man 1 said, "They don't come across as stupid. And, why would they have a briefcase full of money just sitting around?"

Rocky said, "Go in there and try to get a bitch to give you some head or pussy in the back. *Find my shit!*"

Man 2 said, "Look at Saria stuck-up ass."

Rocky said, "That's one of them with her. I didn't know she fucked with that man."

*****

Isaiah took her to the movies, out to eat, then to the beach house he rented for the week.

Isaiah said, "Get comfortable, baby girl."

Samaya said, "Whose house is this?"

Isaiah said, "I rent it out when I want to look at the ocean."

Samaya said, "Makes sense. Why don't you buy it?"

When she walked out of the bathroom all wet, with a towel wrapped around her, he was hoping that the cloth fell so that he could massage her fat ass. He knew she was still a virgin, but he took a chance and walked over. He started massaging her feet with lotion, and he watched her fall asleep.

*****

That morning Isaiah ordered breakfast and had flowers delivered. He even had some clothes delivered for her to wear from his little cousin's boutique.

When Samaya woke up with everything sitting at the side table, she saw him sitting at the desk, looking over the newspaper, and drinking tea. She walked over to him, then took the paper out his hands and dropped her towel.

Isaiah said, "Baby girl, we don't have to do this right now."

Samaya said, "I'm ready. I want you to be my first."

She grabbed his dick, squeezed it a little bit, leaned over, and kissed him.

Isaiah said, "Shit! I want to be your first, but this is not the time. Go home, get dressed, and meet me later."

Samaya said, "You know you want this pussy, Sai. Quit playing!"

Isaiah said, "You're a bold virgin."

Samaya said, "Being a virgin doesn't mean I'm scared."

*****

"What the fuck is she banging on the door like that for?" Ax whispered to himself as he watched the woman on the screen.

He was the only management there, so he didn't have any meetings set up, and wasn't about to be set up. When he zoomed the camera in, he got up and went to the door. He talked through the intercom to see who it was at first.

Ax said, "How can I help you?"

Toonie said, "Management didn't call me after my auditions."

Ax said, "Hold on!"

He opened the door, and she was standing there with her hands on her hips, looking dull and straightforward. "What do you need that for?" Toonie laughed.

Ax said, "Better safe than sorry! Come in, beautiful."

Toonie said, "I gave her my information already. She was supposed to call me yesterday."

Ax said, "Do you have time to come in now?"

Toonie said, "I'm here! Right?"

Ax said, "Would you like a drink? You can come in. I'm the only one here."

Toonie said, "Sure. I don't drink like that."

Ax went and grabbed the applications then came back and sat down with her as he went through his pile.

Toonie said, "This is a good drink. Are you a bartender?"

Ax said, "No. I've watched and learned. Once the hat and glasses go, you'll be ready. Would you like another drink?"

*****

Teresa said, "I said to put two drops...He's hanging out the chair drooling and shit."

Toonie said, "He came back too fast, so I just poured the shit. Get what we need so that we can go."

Teresa said, "Let me check to see if he's breathing. Where did he get the applications from?"

Toonie said, "In there...I hope you didn't tell my cousins about this?"

Teresa said, "I hope you didn't take that hat and glasses off? Okay. Okay. Let's go...Make sure you switch glasses and take yours."

Toonie said, "Mom? You said we came for some papers. I should have known."

Teresa said, "Let's go. This is the best kind of paper."

Jez
Mistaken Simplicity

Jez went to work out at the gym on campus, which opened at 7:00 a.m., so that gave her a few hours to work out before class and flame.

She was hitting the punching bag when a gentleman walked up and held the bag for her. "Excuse me?" Jez mumbled. She was about to walk off until she saw his name tag showing that he worked for the school.

Jez said, "Thanks, Coral. I don't need a personal trainer."

Coral said, "I'm here to assist and give advice on what machines or exercises you should use. No harm intended."

Jez said, "What should I use for my legs and burn calories?"

Coral said, "Follow me, sweetie!"

Coral started walking toward the treadmill, and Jez followed, knowing she didn't need assistance. She just felt bad for being rude, but after he opened his mouth, she knew he wasn't into females anyway.

Coral said, "I'll set you up. Let me know if you need any more help, miss."

Jez said, "My name is Jez. Nice to meet you! And thanks."

Coral said, "Likewise. I'm Coral...Damn, you are a beautiful girl!"

Jez sat thinking about it. She had switched gyms because the school gym opened too late for her schedule, and Coral didn't know anything about her switching gyms. It couldn't have been him leaving the notes unless the sick fucker followed her.

She was thinking about all the men she gave her name to was becoming frustrating. She didn't have any friends, no social media accounts, no club-hopping, just work and school.

The only female she talked to besides her sister was Tara. She's been knowing Tara since they attended cosmetology class. Tara was Samaya's sister, but she never hung out with them, so whoever was leaving the note wasn't anybody they knew.

Jez was looking through books in the school store for her new class in accounting. She went to put the book back on the shelf. A gentleman grabbed the same book out of her hand before it touched the shelf.

Jez said, "What are you doing?"

"Ahem. Ahem." The man was trying hard to get her attention. "Ahem."

Jez said, "I'm adding up the cost for my classes, plus supplies, then here you go interrupting me with this stupid shit."

"Hi, my name is Bill! Who may I have the pleasure of meeting this beautiful morning?"

Jez said, "Excuse me, sir. I'm trying to put the book back. Then you can grab it. If you want it, it's plenty more copies, instead of grabbing this one out my hand. Why are you licking your lips like that, dude?"

Bill said, "What's your name, beautiful? You're too pretty to be all mean. I'll see you around on campus another beautiful day."

Jez said, "Bill. You will see Jez around campus. Have a nice day."

Bill said, "Nice meeting you, Jez."

Jez's mind was racing like a mothafucka. *It could be Bill leaving the notes, but he already approached her. Why would he do some pussy shit like this?* Jez thought.

*****

Tara said, "What does your schedule look like?"

Jez said, "I don't know! What are your plans for graduation?"

Tara said, "Let's throw a party for ourselves? It's a nice lounge downtown."

Jez said, "My parents have a family function. You're welcome to come. I don't have too many friends to invite."

Tara said, "We could get a booth and invite a few people, but you and my cousin can't be arguing."

Jez said, "I'm good, long as she doesn't come at me. Every time I make conversation, she says something."

Tara said, "Girl, please, I've been tried by some of the best, and I'm not going."

Jez said, "I know! I know! You can say what you want, but you're not going to move me until you keep trying me. I try to ignore her, but she keeps coming. Well, I'm gone! See you later. Love."

Jez tried to find something at the shop, but Samaya always bought all the cute outfits, so she went to her sister's house to get one of the new dresses.

After she picked out the dress, she went straight to the mall to grab some shoes and accessories. As she was looking through the glass, she saw his ass approaching all fast, hoping he'd pass, and go about his business. *Fuck, he saw me*, Jez thought.

Coral said, "*Hey, Ms. Jez. How are you doing, beautiful?*"

Jez said, "Hello! I forgot your name. You're the trainer, right?"

Coral said, "It's Coral, sweetie, and I'm not a trainer. I was offering assistance that day. I go there in the mornings before work to relieve some of this stress, girl."

Jez said, "Nice seeing you again, Coral. I'm in a rush, so I'll see you again."

Coral said, "Well, that bracelet you're holding is not what's up, so, if you're buying this for your granny, girl, go on 'head. Does it even match the shoes in your bag? Let me see what you have."

Jez said, "No. For your information, I'm wearing it tonight to Skyline. Funny, because I didn't ask for your opinion?"

He wanted to punch this bitch in the mouth, but Samaya asked him for this favor, so he sucked it up. He pointed to the other tennis bracelet and matching diamond earrings.

Coral said, "Let me help you be the baddest bitch in Skyline tonight. Free of charge."

Jez said, "I didn't ask you for nothing, so why would I pay?"

When she opened the bag and showed him the shoes, he immediately swooped his arm through hers and started walking off. *Choke the bitch*, Coral thought.

Jez said, "Whoa! Let me go, please!"

Coral said, "Let me help you, baby. Do you have time?"

Jez said, "Help me with what?"

Coral said, "What color is the dress? I like the shoes if you're going to prom. Let's go back to the store. Hold on! I know you got money, right?"

Jez said, "Damn! Hold on. The dress is white. I'm not going to prom, crazy. Yes, I have money."

Coral said, "Watch the language. I'm just offering assistance."

Coral helped her pick out some shoes, and he made sure she bought the jewelry he picked out.

They finally made it to the makeup counter to buy some lipstick, and she was mad as hell for following him.

Coral said, "Baby, the nails and feet need some attention. Follow me on the first floor. Do you have time? The club doesn't get lit until after eleven PM anyway."

Jez said, "You sure do know a lot about fashion, Coral. Thanks for your help. I feel like Jez'erella."

Coral said, "She wants French tips on both, and I'll take my usual. The works with no color. Thank you, Sue."

Jez said, "If you're not a trainer, what made you talk to me that day?"

Coral said, "You looked like you had a lot on your mind. Plus, you were walking around looking at all the machines like you didn't know where to start, honey. Girl, besides, the men in that gym looks good. Gets me through my day all the time."

Jez said, "It's a few nice-looking ones, but I don't be hearing nothing they say to me. I keep it moving."

Coral said, "Why are you so mean? You've probably passed up on some good men and friends."

Jez said, "I'm not mean. I recognize bullshit. Most of these females expect shit, instead of getting their own. In class, all I heard was females talking, 'If he has this or that.' That shit gets on my nerves."

Coral said, "So, would you just fuck a nigga for nothing?"

Jez said, "Why must men be niggas? When I choose to have sex, it's going to be special and because I want to. Not because of some fucking money."

Coral said, "I think you took it the wrong way. Sometimes you have to join the conversation, baby, to understand where people are coming from."

Jez said, "Anyways! What are you doing tonight? If you don't mind me asking."

Coral said, "I'm going downtown to hang out with a few friends."

Jez said, "Where are you from?"

Coral said, "I'm from Minnesota, born and raised. I moved to California four years ago. Why do you ask?"

Jez said, "Just making conversation. My family is from Portland, born and raised. We moved here because my dad's job relocated him."

Coral said, "Do you like it here? I have three older brothers and one sister. They disowned me when I came out about my preference, so I left and never looked back."

Jez said, "Wow…It's a little too fast for me, but I'm learning to keep up. I have one sister, and she's accepting of me, and I let her be."

Coral said, "My family is so judgmental that they run you away. I wish they'd accept me for me, and let me be. Enough of that! Do you flame or drink?"

Jez said, "Hell yeah! My family is the same way…"

*****

Coral picked out some red lipstick, red peep-toe heels with diamonds over the front strap, with the matching clutch. She pulled her hair back in a slick ponytail, put on the jewelry he picked out, and headed out the door.

*****

Jez walked up to the booth that seated Jai, Tara, Samaya, Queen, Toonie, and a few people from their cosmetology class.

"I'm glad you came. Congratulations, beautiful," Jai whispered in her ear as she hugged her. Jez took in all the love her sister was pouring out because she saw how Queen was mean mugging her for no damn reason.

They danced, took shots, and bounced around to music, having a good time until Jez noticed Coral walking around the club with a man. She waved for him to come over, but he was already approaching them. He gave her a big hug, noticing she took his advice on everything, but she lied about the dress being white.

Coral said, "Hey, beautiful ladies...Nice seeing you, Jez. Looking good, girl. My friend, Bobby."

Jez said, "Hello, Bob! You look good too."

Bobby said, "It's Bobby! Not Bob, dear."

Jez said, "Excuse me! No harm intended."

Bobby said, "You're excused this time."

Samaya walked over and gave Coral and Bobby a hug, and Jez was shocked at their greeting. "Come here, Queen," Coral screamed.

Jez said, "I didn't know you guys knew each other. What a surprise."

Samaya said, "Yes. We go way back."

Queen said, "*Hey, Coral.*"

Jez said, "Small world, I see."

Coral said, "Told you, I was meeting my girls."

Tara said, "Hey, Daddy."

Coral said, "Skunk let you out? *Wow!*"

Tara said, "I can still have fun. Damn!"

Coral hugged Toonie, and Bobby instantly got mad. He knew Coral and Toonie tried the dating thing until he told her about his true feelings for men. "Hey, C," Toonie whispered in his ear.

Bobby said, "Hi, Toonie."

Toonie said, "Hello!"

Samaya said, "I had to drag her out. Toonie, this is Jez. I forgot to introduce. Jez, this is my li'l cousin Toonie."

They both dragged out the hellos. "Well, damn!" Coral muttered.

Jez said, "*Okay! Let's get some drinks.*"

Toonie said, "Why didn't you tell me it was two of them?"

*****

Jez left early and went home, not knowing that her parents were still up. She tried to open the door slowly without it squeaking.

Jennifer said, "Hi, Jez. Looks like you're going to be needing your own home soon."

Jez said, "Hello, Mother…I had fun celebrating my graduation with my sister."

John said, "Dear, leave her alone. Hi, Jez."

As soon as Jez went into her room, she pushed the door behind her. Before it could close, it swung open fast, hitting her arm.

Before she could turn around, her mom slapped the shit out of her. "Who do you think you are? Don't come to my house, all times of the night, like some whore. What's your problem?" Jennifer yelled out in one breath. "I'm sorry, Mom," Jez said softly as the tears ran down her face. She wanted to push her to the ground, but she knew her father would shoot her.

John said, "What did I tell you? Leave my girls alone…"

*****

Jez arrived at the gym early, trying to get some running in and wanting to run away from all the unwanted abuse from the abused victim.

*****

Man 2 said, "You're gonna pass out you keep overdoing it. Here."

Jez said, "Thanks…I'm used to it. Had to get my frustration off. Thanks again for the water. See you around."

Man 2 said, "You're welcome."

*****

"Damn! Here he comes," Jez muttered. She wasn't dealing with anybody that dealt with that family.

Coral said, "Hello, beautiful! Did you get his number? He was handsome."

Jez said, "Not my type, and he only gave me some water. I'm about to run. I have class in a bit. Nice seeing you."

CHAPTER 9

Tara
Coming Out

As soon as Tara graduated high school, she tried stripping with her family, but that shit didn't last long. She got her beautician license one year after. Everything was going as planned, but trying to find a place to work without haters was hard.

*****

Tara and Skunk pulled up to this abandoned brick building that used to be a family store with cardboard on the windows, and it had a parking lot with no other businesses attached.

"Several for-sale signs, I see. Let me inform my realtor," Skunk said. *Buying everything*, Tara thought.

Tara said, "What's this place, bae?"

Skunk said, "Wait, baby! I'll show you because I need your ideas."

Skunk noticed Tara looking all crazy, so he smacked her ass as he opened the front door. Tara held Skunk's hand tight as they walked through the building.

Skunk said, "I could do a lot with this space. What do you think about a clothing store? Should I fix it up and flip it for sales. Yeah, day care or something."

Tara said, "I don't know, bae! A corner store, but what about all the empty rooms upstairs?"

Skunk said, "Well, Tara. It's your new beauty shop. Congratulations on graduating."

Tara started crying in disbelief because no one has ever done nothing big for her except for him.

Tara said, "This is all I ever wanted, Skunk."

"Quit crying, boo, and you deserve the world," Skunk said. Tara jumped in his arms, hugging, kissing his face and neck with excitement. Decorating was all she thought about with every kiss of amazement and glad she left the pole alone.

Skunk whispered in her ear, "What's next, Ms. Beautician," with his hands under her skirt, massaging her ass.

Tara said, "Let me start with the designs and color schemes, bae. The name can come during the decorating process."

*****

The next day Skunk and Tara walked through the shop with a contractor and designer giving her everything she wanted without hesitation and no questions asked. Tara was on point with everything she planned the night before because she was so excited and geeked that she couldn't go to sleep.

Skunk said, "Whatever you want, baby."

Tara said, "I'm so happy, I can't believe this."

Tara started crying like a baby from feeling overjoyed. "Oh my gosh," Tara cried out.

Skunk said, "Quit crying, baby. I need you to be happy and busy."

Skunk had already told the contractors and designers that Tara could get whatever she wanted from the roof to the basement, no questions asked.

She had the outside wood trim painted white, the brick cleaned on the outside, and a new roof, and the parking lot was paved and painted. The four apartments upstairs were gutted and finished into some beautiful office and storage rooms. The chairs, blow-dryers, the combs, and the most significant office which was Tara's office was cotton candy.

*****

Tara said, "*OMG, everyone…It's so beautiful!*"

Skunk said, "You outdid yourself with the decorations."

Samaya said, "Come here, sis? Don't cry, you deserve it."

Queen said, "Hit the flame, you'll be all right."

Merch said, "Bro, you snapped. Tara, can I make an appointment before I leave?"

Queen said, "She's booked up until next year. I wish somebody would snap for me."

Tara said, "This is not the right time or place for that. Please, stop!"

"I see they're not broke if they're buying buildings back-to-back," Toonie whispered to her mom. "I told you they're not gonna miss anything," Teresa whispered back. "Besides, I heard some girl out here saying that Merch is her fiancé and shit," Teresa muttered in an angry voice. Toonie looked in disbelief, and glad Queen was getting hers from his monkey ass. "We should go down there," Toonie said.

Skunk thanked everybody for a job well done as they left because Tara was too emotional to talk. Skunk tried to lock the door to Tara's place as they pushed Samaya, Queen, Jai, and Jez out the door.

Queen said, "I need a man like that! Shidddd!"

Jai said, "Don't we all!"

Samaya said, "That's real love, y'all."

Jez said, "What her pussy look like to get all this?"

Queen said, "Must be glitter, with a sprinkle of gold, with diamonds on top. You should ask her to see it."

Samaya said, "Stop it, Queen! Y'all funny as hell."

*****

Skunk poured them another drink as they sat at the receptionist desk, talking for hours and looking over her goals.

Skunk said, "Baby, I see that your plans for the next five years are gonna keep me busy."

Tara said, "Making sure were happy."

Tara couldn't stop staring into this man's eyes, for he was doing everything in his power to treat and make her feel loved.

Tara said, "I want a baby, and, and, sorry."

As she wiped her tears away, she noticed Skunk getting on one knee, and that shit almost made her throw up.

Skunk said, "Will you marry me, Tara?"

Tara said, "Yes. Skunk! Oh my gosh. I love you so much."

Skunk said, "I love you too. I will always make sure your heart desires are secured."

As Skunk took a piece of her clothing off, he kissed each part of her slowly. When he pulled her bra down, he kissed each nipple slowly, picking her up. He carried her to a beautician chair, placing her down softly, giving her comfort as her heart melted in his hands. When he put her legs up over his shoulders, her eyes opened wide. He ate the shit out of her pussy like he was in the Olympic tongue movement contest.

Skunk said, "Tara? This my pussy?"

"Yes, Daddy. Yes, Daddy," she moaned, slowly trying to answer. Skunk heard her response and tried to put a baby in her at that moment.

They cleaned up, locked the shop, and finished their night at the uptown bar, taking shots all night.

*****

That morning Tara had a surprise for Skunk. "You know, I don't like surprises," Skunk said.

Tara said, "Come on, bae, we're going to be late."

Skunk said, "Hmm, you smell good. Let's go back to bed."

They drove up the dirt road, and Skunk couldn't believe this girl just went way out in nowhere land. He was nervous as hell but couldn't tell her, he was afraid of heights once they passed the flying signs. She noticed he was hitting his flame fast the closer they got.

Tara said, "Are you okay, bae?"

Skunk said, "You know, I don't like shit like this. What the fuck."

The pilot said, "Hello, you're my eleven o'clock. Ms. Tara?"

Tara said, "Yes. I'm excited."

The pilot said, "I'm your pilot. Have either of you ever flew in a hot air balloon?"

Skunk said, "Never thought about it. Tara, what made you think of this?"

Tara said, "You asked me what I wanted in the next five years. I'm about to show you."

Skunk said, "A simple sketch and sketch would have been nice."

The pilot said, "You're in good hands, sir. Let's get started here."

Tara hugged Skunk so that he could get comfortable, but she felt him shaking.

Skunk said, "What the fuck is that?"

The pilot said, "This keeps us up."

Tara said, "Bae, look. I want the world with you. Look, so you can get over your fear of heights."

Skunk said, "We over water. Hell naw! Pilot, turn around, please."

The pilot said, "As requested."

Tara said, "Look, bae, it's beautiful."

Skunk said, "Yup. We can also have the world together on the ground."

*****

That evening Tara met up with Queen and her mom. She tried calling Jez, but she went straight to voice mail.

Queen said, "What made you take that man up in the air?"

Tara said, "Well, if he can propose to me and think he's ever to cross me, I'll remind his ass of the balloon ride."

Tamyra said, "Why think negative? Has he ever shown any interest in someone else or cheated?"

Queen said, "She's only saying that because we saw Merch cheating."

Tamyra said, "Just because you lay with a man and run his flame doesn't make you his woman. Have you ever talked to him about this?"

Queen said, "No, Auntie. Flame, though, Auntie?"

Tamyra said, "I'm not stupid, baby. I hate that y'all dance, but I know dancing alone is not bringing in that much money. Please be careful and not a fool."

Tara said, "Mom, please, no lectures. The girl already feels betrayed by this man, and don't nobody know what they talk about or do."

Tamyra said, "That's my niece. You or nobody else can tell me what to say to her. I've seen your father with different women, but I upped my game. The fuck you mean lectures? Hopefully, my sisters would give you advice. Queen, doesn't anybody know how you feel until they've been through it, baby. Pick your battles, baby."

Tara said, "Sorry, Mom. I didn't mean it like that. I don't know what I would do if someone did it to me."

Tamyra said, "If you're in a relationship, you shouldn't have to question your love or feel betrayed. And, if that someone is Skunk? Baby, that's a good young man."

Tara said, "Mom, no disrespect. How do you know what Skunk is?"

Tamyra said, "Are you happy, daughter? Don't answer that, because I know my child."

Queen said, "Let's go get in the hot tub, TT."

Tara said, "Queen! What made you follow him?"

Queen said, "When he started turning down sex. Sorry, Auntie."

Tamyra said, "Baby, I done heard it all. Ask yourself do you love him, then you decide."

Tara said, "Okay. Enough about these men. Let's go get in the hot tub."

Queen noticed that Tara was thinking about what her mom said, and it touched a nerve. Tara's face turned purple, and then she pretended to brush it off.

Tara's text to Skunk: "Hey bae, miss you :)"

The waitress brought over drinks for the ladies as they sat in the hot tub. When her mom went to reach for her glass, she noticed that Tara kept picking up and putting down her phone.

Tara's text to Skunk: "I'm out with mom still. What's for supper tonight?"

Queen said, "Tara? Have you thought about where the wedding will be?"

Tamyra said, "Tara? *Tara?* Girl, put the phone down and let's enjoy the day."

Tara said, "I'm sorry. What did you ask again?"

Queen said, "Have you guys decided on where the wedding will be?"

Tara said, "No. I want it in a church, and he wants it on the beach."

Tara's text to Skunk: "What are you doing?"

Tara went shopping and picked a cute purple lingerie body-suit then headed to the beachfront to grab some fresh seafood. She stopped at the Low-End Store and bought some candles.

When she got home, she cooked, had a few shots of tequila, had the music on blast, lit all the candles, and danced around the house.

Tara's text to Skunk: "Where you at bae?"

She showered, rubbed her skin down with gold glimmer oil, put her hair up in a bun, put on a little makeup, slipped on her black heels, threw a silk wrap around her body, and sat down waiting. She kept opening the box, looking at the watch, noticing that Skunk hadn't texted her back all day.

When he walked in, all the candles were burned out. He stood looking over Tara asleep on the lounge chair. He pulled the silk wrap up and saw the purple lace and got hard immediately.

He gently opened her legs and unsnapped the bodysuit. He started kissing her vigorously until she woke up moaning. Noticing she didn't jump up real quick, he knew she had too many drinks.

She grabbed his head, and he knew she wasn't going to say shit about the time. She pushed him up, unbuckled his pants, and he helped her pull them down. When she went to sit on him, he palmed her ass cheeks, lifting her; she rode the fuck out of his face until she climaxed.

Her body went limp as soon as her back hit the chair. Skunk lifted her legs and began stroking until she opened her eyes again. "Daddy. Aww. Aw," Tara moaned loudly.

*****

The house was clean when she woke up in the same purple lingerie outfit half off. All the candles and food were put up, and somebody put her up as well because she didn't remember going to bed.

The maid handed her a cup of coffee as soon as she walked in the kitchen, looking lost and feeling hungover.

Marjorie said, "Hi, Ms. Tara. Come, let's eat."

Tara said, "Hi, Marjorie. Where's Skunk?"

Marjorie said, "I don't know! He left. He left this for you."

*****

Tara's text to Queen: "Where you at Q?"

Queen's text to Tara: "What's up?"

Tara's text to Queen: "Come over…"

She threw on some jeans and a tank top. She grabbed her bag, filled it with what she needed, and ran out to the car when Queen pulled up.

Queen said, "Damn! What's up, fam? I haven't seen you in tennis shoes in a minute, hair all up, and ya nude lipstick popping. What's up?"

Tara said, "Waiting for his response."

Queen said, "Do I need to pick up your sister?"

Tara said, "We can grab her on the way."

Skunk
Moving Around

Skunk went to pick up his hat, gown, and tickets for admission from the school. He ran into this cheerleader named Chaste he had a thang for before he met Tara. They had a few classes together, studied, and went to a few movies but nothing serious to him.

Chaste said, "Hey, Sem. How's it going?"

Skunk said, "What's up, Chaste? I'm good. How are you?"

Chaste said, "Fine...Picking up my things for graduation. Congratulations."

Skunk said, "Congratulations to you as well. So now we've finished, what's your plans?"

Chaste said, "I'm still looking to start a firm, but I need at least one other person with money because Shelly changed her mind. Do you want to go have lunch to catch up?"

Skunk said, "I have a few hours to pass. Where to?"

They went to the pier to have a seafood lunch. Chaste and Skunk talked and laughed at the times they cheated on their test.

Chaste said, "Sem?"

Skunk said, "Yes, Chaste?"

Chaste said, "Why didn't we ever get serious?"

Skunk said, "You know I don't do questions beginning with W. Remember, I asked you where do you see yourself in five years your answer was?"

Chaste said, "I said I don't know. I didn't know you were talking about us."

Skunk said, "So, why ask me that? Well, I have to run. I'll see you again."

Chaste said, "Can I go with you?"

Skunk said, "What's your purpose?"

Chaste said, "See what I mean, you always seem reserved. I want to have a purpose, but I keep getting shut down."

*****

Samaya said, "*Bitch, what the fuck is all that?*"

Queen said, "*Grab her ass, Samaya. Tara, wait!*"

Tara said, "This muthafucka proposed, ignored my text, ate my pussy, then left me in bed half naked. He said, 'I'm going to my school for a minute,' not to have some bitch follow him to this nice-ass restaurant he never brought me to. *Who is this bitch?*"

Samaya said, "Maybe she's a client. We don't know yet."

Tara was sobbing hard as hell, and Queen looked at Samaya like, *What to do?*

Queen said, "You can't walk up there with a pistol in your hand, knife in your bra, and Mace in your back pocket. Hide the shit!"

Samaya said, "Queen, stop. Don't do it, Tara."

Tara said, "*He left me hanging a few times. Mom said, 'You shouldn't feel like this.' I can shoot from right here. Roll the window, Queen.*"

Samaya said, "*No. No.* Let me think for a second."

Tara said, "*All I need is a second. Roll the window down.*"

*****

Chaste said, "What's your plans. I could use you to open the firm."

Skunk said, "Use me? That's cute. We can use each other, depending on the numbers. Have you put anything together yet?"

Chaste said, "Oh my gosh. These lobster cakes are so good. Taste it?"

*****

Tara said, "Is he eating off this *bitch* fork."

Queen said, "*Oh no. She feeding his ass.*"

Samaya said, "Queen, please don't amp her. *Did she wipe his mouth?*"

*****

Skunk said, "It's good. Nice choice. How many lawyers have you asked? And, have they backed out?"

Chaste said, "What's that? Let me taste."

*****

Queen said, "*Grab her. Let me pull off before we all go to jail.*"

Tara said, "*She's eating off his plate. Let me go, Samaya. I'll stab the bitch and walk off.*"

Samaya said, "Text him."

Tara's text to Skunk: "Just woke up. wya now?"

Queen said, "Call his phone."

Samaya said, "He looked at it, and put it back in his pocket. *Okay.*"

Samaya jumped out of the car and rushed over to where they were sitting. She made sure she walked past him so that he could see her face, fake smiling and all.

Tara said, "What the fuck is she doing?"

Queen said, "Keeping yo ass out of prison."

*****

Samaya said, "*Hey, Skunk. How are you doing?*"

Skunk said, "What's up, sis? Where's Tara? Oh, my bad. Chaste, meet my fiancée's sister, Samaya. Samaya, meet Chaste. We went to college together."

Chaste said, "Nice meeting you. Sama, right?"

Samaya said, "It's Samaya, Chase. To you as well. I'll let her know I saw you."

When Skunk chuckled, Chaste rolled her eyes at him.

Samaya said, "I just stopped to get some lobster cakes. Bye, Skunk!"

Skunk said, "Bye, sis! Well, I'm about to bounce as well. Chaste, call me when you're ready to open the law firm."

Chaste said, "I'll give you the file to look over. It's in my truck."

Skunk and Chaste went the opposite way of Samaya. When she jumped in the car, all she heard was sobbing.

Samaya said, "Pull up over there."

Queen said, "That bitch got a nice-ass truck."

Tara said, "Shut up, Queen. She's pretty and well put together. *What happened?*"

Samaya said, "That bitch a lawyer, or they got their lying down to pack. *Stop right here!* He asked about you in front of her and introduced me as his fiancée's sister."

Queen said, "We're too close. If he acknowledged you, that's good."

Tara said, "She's handing him something. Acknowledgment *brought him home at three in the morning.*"

Samaya said, "I heard him say something about a law firm when I walked off."

Tara said, "*What? He wants a prenup? He got me fucked up!*"

Queen said, "If he were getting a prenup, he would have discussed that with you."

*****

Chaste was mad as hell that he said "fiancée," and she was ready to say fuck everything, but she knew he had money and the degree she needed to get things started.

Skunk said, "Aight. I'll look over it and get back to you."

Chaste said, "Congratulations. When's the big day?"

Skunk said, "Haven't got that far. Hug me, sexy, so I can handle my business."

Tara, Queen, and Samaya all spoke at once, "*What the fuck.*"

Queen said, "*This bitch just hit his chest. They fucking, Tara.*"

Samaya said, "Yeah! That hug alone didn't have anything to do with a prenup. They held long enough to smell each other and shit."

Tara said, "Hope y'all don't have plans. We following his ass. I want to see if she follows him."

Queen said, "Okay, bitch! That's what I'm talking about."

Samaya said, "Chaste went the other way...Don't get so close, Queen."

Tara said, "Chaste, huh? I'll put her name on the list. Fuck it! Follow that bitch...He's going to make his way home eventually."

*****

Skunk was meeting up with Isaiah to see what the crew did with Cupid, making sure that the money they spent was worth it.

When he arrived, he checked the outside of the building to make sure they fixed everything stated on the bill. He was pleased with the work when he made his way upstairs to the office. He finally sat down, and read over the file Chaste had given him.

Skunk's text to Isaiah: "Bro meet me in two hours my schedule changed."

Isaiah's text to Skunk: "I'll be there around two."

*****

Skunk's text to Tara: "What's up, baby?"

Tara's text to Skunk: "Woke up and you were gone. I miss you."

Skunk's text to Tara: "I'll be home later!"

*****

Skunk's text to Adana: "When you pull up, text me."

Adana's text to Skunk: "Two minutes away."

He opened the door for her, then locked it after she entered.

Skunk's said, "Get up there, so I can see what you can do."

Adana's said, "What's so funny? Let me roll up this flame first."

*****

"*Hold on*," Queen shouted. As soon as they found out where Chaste lived, they went straight to the club.

Samaya said, "*Sis...don't do it! Stay in the car!*"

Tara said, "I can't do this! *I told y'all! He was coming here.*"

Queen said, "Quit crying! Think about the money. 'Up your game,' like your mama said."

Tara said, "I know she's not a lawyer. His days consist of pretty bitches with fat asses, I see."

Samaya said, "Queen…take that gun from her, before we go to jail."

Queen said, "Fuck jail! We're going to prison, prison. Give me the gun. I have shit to do later."

Tara said, "Y'all fake as fuck! Queen, you shoot at everybody… Sis you be right there with her. I see why Toonie said, 'Y'all one-sided.' I'm about to shoot the fucking door open and kill them."

Samaya said, "*Hold her ass! Tara…I'm calling Dad.*"

Queen said, "*Pull off! I didn't know you were crazy, bitch!*"

Tara said, "Okay! I'm good. I'm good. *Let me go, Queen! Damn!*"

*****

When Adana got on the stage and bent over, she was trying to make her ass cheeks move one at a time. Skunk went and stood over her, patting her ass while he flamed to her non-dancing ass. When he went to hand it to her, she turned around, sat down on the edge of the stage. He pulled up a chair so that he could sit in between her legs.

*****

Tara said, "*Guess he in here feeding this bitch vodka cakes.*"

Samaya and Queen tried to hold their chuckles back, but this was the first time Tara ever went off.

Tara's text to Skunk: "let's meet up."

Queen said, "Skunk doesn't come across as the cheating type."

Samaya said, "Queen, can you go get us something to eat from across the street."

*****

Adana laid-back on the stage and pulled her sundress up. He started fingering her slowly until he felt her walls tightening up. He nudged her knee for her to get up, and she followed his lead. His long, strong arms lifted her off the stage right on top of his dick, and she fell in love at that moment.

Adana said, "*Oh my gosh, Sem. Hmmm.*"

Skunk said, "This pussy creamy. *Damn!*"

Beep. Beep. Beep. Beep. He was so into her riding and bouncing on his dick that he didn't see her grab his phone.

Adana said, "Look! Your wife is calling."

He grabbed the phone from her and put it on the table. "Fuck that! Get this dick. I haven't said 'I do' yet," Skunk said.

He went right back into fuck mode, pulling her boobs out. She leaned her head back, put her hands on his knees and arched her back a little, and bounced while he sucked her boobs and kissed her neck.

Skunk said, "Stand up, baby?"

Adana said, "My legs are numb."

Skunk said, "I gotcha. Turn around."

When she bent over her ass, spread apart, he went ham. He was stroking the fuck out of her, and she was throwing that ass back like a pro.

*****

Tara said, "Sis, I can't take this anymore. I don't like this feeling."

Samaya said, "Baby, I know. Let's go!"

Tara said, "I need to see her leave, so I can have all my facts before I front his ass."

Queen said, "We've been out here for almost two hours. Here's your food."

Samaya said, "*What the fuck!* I'm getting sleepy. I'm not doing this shit anymore…This shit for the birds."

Tara said, "What the fuck is he doing in there?"

Queen said, "Don't look at me like I know. The fuck."

Samaya sat right up when she saw Isaiah walk into the club. "I see you're not sleepy anymore," Tara whispered.

*****

Skunk said, "Let me handle my business, baby girl. I'll call you later, Adana."

She looked up and watched as this handsome, strong man bent over and kissed her forehead with his juicy lips, longing for the next time. *I just swallowed his shit, and all I get is a forehead kiss,* Adana thought, maybe because his brother was here.

Isaiah said, "Hi, Adana. How are you? What's up, bro?"

Adana said, "Hey, Isaiah! I'm good. Thanks for asking. How are you doing?"

Isaiah said, "I'm well. Bro, I'll be upstairs."

Skunk said, "Aight, bro."

After Adana left, Skunk locked the door and went upstairs to talk numbers with Isaiah.

*****

Queen said, "Y'all calling me detective. You are taking more pictures than you have of yourself."

Tara said, "I need evidence. I should whoop her ass. *Why this bitch hair down? Her shit was up in a bun before she went in there.*"

Queen said, "They fucked. *And he pulled the bitch hair!*"

Queen handed the flame to Samaya, then jumped out the car. She ran across the street, screaming and waving the woman down.

Samaya said, "*Aw, shit! Make sure she left the gun?*"

Tara said, "It's sticking from under her shirt on her back. Bitch! We're going to jail."

Samaya said, "Well, weren't you about to do the same thing. It's prison, sis, not jail."

As Queen ran up to her, she said the first thing that came to mind. "*Hey, girl. Excuse me, miss? Excuse me, miss? Are they having auditions right now?*" Queen said, panting.

Adana said, "Oh, no, miss. I was visiting a friend."

"Damn," Queen mumbled as she pulled the locked door.

Queen said, "It's locked, girl! Thought you were visiting a friend? Do you dance or something?"

Adana said, "Sorry. I should have explained myself. It's closed. I was visiting my close friend that owns the club."

Queen said, "Ain't you special, get it, girl. Do you think they would hire me?"

Adana said, "Without the hat, yes. You're pretty and nicely shaped."

Queen said, "Thank you, uh?"

Adana said, "It's Adana."

Queen said, "I'm Keisha. I'll just come back when they open. Thanks, Adana."

Adana said, "You're welcome, Keisha."

Queen just sat there hitting the flame, not saying shit.

Tara said, "Say something! Why the fuck you just sitting there? Should I marry his devious ass?"

Queen said, "Bitch said, 'I'm visiting a close friend,' smiling cheek to cheek. When I went to open the door, it was locked."

Samaya said, "She could have auditioned for a job."

Tara said, "Please, sis. All their ass some whores. Why did he propose? Buy me a whole fucking building, car, pay my mama's rent, and still cheat. I, the fuck, don't get it."

Samaya said, "Don't speak for my Sai. She left when he came. Besides, Skunk loves you."

Tara said, "Ugh…You sound like Mom. *Take me home please?*"

Queen said, "I think you should keep following him until he goes home. Oh, put Adana on your list."

Tara said, "I can't be any more hurt. I've done seen too much."

Samaya said, "Well, we didn't see him do anything, but give a hug and grip her ass. Then this jolly bitch went in, and got a new hairdo."

Tara said, "Fuck it. Let's wait?"

They each took turns running to the bathroom down the street. They flamed back-to-back, trying to make conversation so that Tara wouldn't cry, but that shit made her cry even more. They all must have saw him coming out at the same time because they jumped up in attention mode.

Tara said, "Start the engine up, now!"

Queen said, "They're both leaving. Who should we follow? Your man, Samaya?"

Samaya said, "No. He texts me. He's trying to see me soon. Follow Skunk, please!"

Queen said, "She said 'engine,' hell naw."

They followed him to a condo building with security, looking like a gated community, knowing they couldn't get in, so they just sat there for a few minutes, texting his phone to see if he would text Tara back. When he texted and told her he was at home, she was mad that he never told her about this place.

Tara said, "He's never brought me here."

Queen said, "I've never been to Merch's house either. The fuck!"

Samaya said, "All this time, and you mean to tell me, that y'all never went to their houses? They just got keys to your shit? Can pull up whenever they want? Get the fuck out of here!"

Queen said, "When you say it like that, it sounds like we're some dumb bitches. I never asked to meet up at his shit, but I am now."

Tara said, "Let me text him right now and see what he says."

Samaya said, "Don't listen to me and get your feelings hurt. He spent a lot of money on you."

Queen said, "I'm not about to get shit hurt. I'm not following for no reason, and you know that."

Samaya said, "But you're acting like your feelings are getting involved. I still can't bring myself to follow a nigga if it ain't concerning money."

Queen said, "They might be! I'm more mad that I've been raw fucking his ass."

Tara said, "I'm not on the same page as y'all. Y'all need to stop doing dumb shit and find love."

Queen said, "Dumb shit been keeping money in my pocket, and don't act like you didn't roll with us before. Ms. Goody Two-shoes... ass."

Tara said, "I stopped following a long time ago. It's time for a new hustle, don't you think?"

Samaya said, "*Tara? Why must you always be combatively right? Darn!*"

*****

Tara's text to Skunk: "Are you coming over tonight?"

Skunk's text to Tara: "I don't know yet."

Tara's text to Skunk: "I'm coming to see you if you're not too tired from running around."

Skunk's text to Tara: "I'm going to bed. I'll come to see you tomorrow. Love you, baby."

*****

Adana's text to Skunk: "Where should I park?"

Skunk's text to Adana: "Park in the visiting area, then come to the main entrance, and the concierge will bring you up."

*****

Queen said, "I know I'm not that high, but that's the same bitch from the club."

Tara said, "*Lying fucker!*"

Samaya said, "When did you start talking like this, Tara? I'm appalled!"

*****

Tara's text to Skunk: "Where are you? Coming over to see you?"

*****

Samaya said, "Sis, look! This man done switched cars, and they are riding off."

Queen said, "Want me to shoot the tires out? This gun not traceable back to us. Fam, run they ass off the road."

Tara said, "He's not responding. Hit they ass, Samaya."

Samaya said, "Y'all crazy! I'm not doing that shit. Roll that god-damn window up...Put the gun away, Queen. What the fuck!"

Queen said, "I don't see the bitch no more. Did she jump out the fucking car?"

Tara said, "*Oh my gosh! This bitch giving him head.*"

Samaya said, "*Give me the gun!*"

Queen said, "Oh, now you want to shoot, shoot? Nope! Keep driving."

Samaya said, "Aww, he taking this bitch to a five-star restaurant. He likes this bitch."

Tara said, "Follow valet to see where they park his car."

Queen said, "Shid! You want to hit the flame, fam?"

Samaya said, "*Oh my gosh! Hurry up, Tara!*"

Queen said, "She jumped out of a moving car. Hell naw!"

Tara said, "Let them walk home. Fuck! I cut my hand. Take these bags with y'all."

Samaya said, "She took the girl stuff he bought. You are a smart, crazy..."

Queen said, "I would have taken it also. The fuck!"

Tara said, "Have you seen Merch take a bitch shopping and out to eat?"

Queen said, "I plead the Fifth right now. I'm taking this shit to TT. She'll get some money for it."

Tara said, "Yes. Yes. Correct. I left. I kept them with me. I didn't know. Thanks."

Samaya said, "Know you didn't just have his shit towed? He's gonna know it's you."

Queen said, "Damn! Why didn't I think to have Merch shit towed."

Tara said, "I blocked my number, and I told them I took my keys and to call me when they get to the shop, and I gave them the club number."

Once Tara saw that he was kicking it with her, she had enough and went straight home. She sat crying and weighing out her options on what to do first because she wasn't about to let these bitches stop her from getting money. Trying not to fuck him up was going to be a challenge, so she came up with a plan.

*****

Skunk said, "What made you come back here, Adana?"

Adana said, "I told you already. Heard you were in a serious relationship with someone, so I wanted to see how serious."

Skunk said, "You wanted to see if you still had feelings for your childhood crush? You know, I love her, right?"

Adana said, "Childhood, huh? If you love her, then why are you here with me?"

Skunk said, "I love you too. You got some fire-ass pussy."

Adana said, "Oh. Are you trying to be like your father?"

Skunk said, "Don't mention him in this type of discussion. You love me too."

Adana said, "My bad. I've always loved you, Sem."

After they ate, they went straight to the movies, and then the family hotel.

Skunk said, "Get naked, Adana, and go to the shower."

He just flamed, watching the water flow off her skin as she washed up. "Do you need some help?" he said as he looked at Tara's text and turned his phone off.

Adana said, "Are you getting in with me?"

Skunk said, "I'm fine with watching how you wash that fat pussy."

Adana said, "You can learn how. Come here, Sem?"

*****

Detective Phillips said, "What they lie for? I've been watching Rocky ass too."

Lia said, "They don't want us working together. They know we'll solve this case. I lost him in the warehouse district. The only way I'm calling Thomas is if his ass on the way to the airport."

Detective Phillips said, "They want us working separately, so we can gather all the information for them. You need to be careful when you see him, Lia. Don't let him know who you are."

Lia sighed and looked at him sideways.

Lia said, "You sound like Afonso punk ass. I'm not that stupid."

Detective Phillips said, "What about Jill?"

Lia said, "Since I've been following her, I know who bought the club from Rocky. They don't know anything about him. They're some property buyers and college graduates."

Detective Phillips said, "Keep me posted on that. Are you sure Jill doesn't know?"

Lia said, "No. This girl and I are like besties. Afonso is who we need to watch."

Detective Phillips said, "You looked right in that bodysuit though."

Lia said, "Fuck you, Phillips! And for the record. I'm keeping all the money I make from this case. Luckily, Ishmael didn't see me."

Detective Phillips said, "Shit! I would keep it also. They don't pay us enough for this shit."

When they finished their conversation outside the club, they went their separate ways. Lia knew something was up with Afonso because she saw him watching Rocky the other night at the club after he told Phillips he was gone.

*****

The valet rushed to Skunk in a panic not knowing what to say or do. "I'm so sorry, sir, but did you switch tickets with someone? I can't find your car," the valet said.

Skunk said, "Why would I switch tickets? I kept the ticket with me the whole time."

175

The valet said, "Your car is gone! You had a white charger? Let me get my manager."

Adana said, "Yes, he did! Let's call a cab."

Skunk said, "I'll call for us a ride. This shit crazy! The whole car just disappeared? Is it parked in the wrong spot?"

The valet said, "I checked the whole parking lot, sir. My manager will be out in a minute."

CHAPTER 10

Isaiah
Allowing Direction

Man 1 said, "Rocky said wait for him, so, what the fuck are we doing here?"

Man 2 said, "I'm not getting into this shit not knowing what the fuck is in this briefcase or box he's looking to find. Then he got the other set shooting at him. I need to know what the fuck we're getting into."

Man 1 said, "What's the plan? Why didn't we follow the other dude when he left?"

Man 2 said, "Fuck him. The other dude is the one. If they just bought this fucking club without hesitation, nigga they paid."

Man 1 said, "That's not the dude that met up with Rocky."

Man 2 said, "I know, muthafucka! They're all paid, and he's the easiest to follow. He's in love with Saria fine ass."

Man 1 said, "I know you loved some Saria. She got a lot of your money, right?"

Man 2 said, "Fuck you! I still think we should get all their asses."

Man 1 said, "He's leaving! How do you know what they got?"

Man 2 said, "I've been following him and his stripper bitch."

Man 1 said, "If they can buy a club, they got money as you say, nigga. What the fuck is really in the box and briefcase? Rocky not telling us something because these fuckers don't need no petty cash."

*****

She was shocked at how big this house was, and the decorator did a fantastic job. Expensive furniture in each room, swimming pool with an attached Jacuzzi, pretty cream walls with gold trimmings, and outside, the bar.

Isaiah said, "Come on in, Samaya, and make yourself at home."

Samaya said, "Is this a rental property?"

Isaiah said, "No. It's mine."

Samaya said, "I get to see where you live? I like this. Is there a reason why you go through the back?"

Isaiah said, "If you're mines, you're supposed to know where I live. Right?"

Samaya said, "Do you live here alone? Can I see the front entrance?"

Isaiah said, "Yes. I like peace. Plus, I like to walk around as I please. Follow me!"

Samaya said, "What made you get a big house like this? Who decorated?"

Isaiah said, "No more questions beginning with Ws, okay. I like space, and I picked out everything."

Samaya said, "Smart-ass! It's nice, though. Do you know how to cook?"

Isaiah said, "I can boil water. I'm glad you received your GED."

Samaya said, "Thanks, Sai! I signed up for business management. Seriously, Isaiah, how I'm supposed to make money?"

He had everything planned from when he first saw Samaya on Lovely Vines. He remembered her from staying at their hotel under a fake name. He tried talking to her back then, but she kept walking and talking on her phone.

Samaya said, "I was thinking about going for cosmetology like my sister, but I don't like females like that."

Isaiah said, "Explain that to me, Samaya?"

Samaya said, "We talk too much, complain about everything, and I couldn't deal. My sister has patience, and I don't."

Isaiah said, "Once we figure out what you like to do, we'll make something happen. While you attend school, we can make something happen. What did you do before you started dancing?"

Samaya said, "The streets raised me...I was a hustler."

Isaiah said, "Your pretty self stood on corners?"

Samaya said, "I had to. I wasn't a prostitute! Ugh..."

Isaiah said, "I know what you meant. I can't see it, and I'm not knocking anybody's hustle. You could prostitute, strip, or be a street pharmacist. Who am I to judge?"

Samaya got up and started dancing in front of him, playing around.

Isaiah said, "So, you like dancing, I see? Come do that on the dick."

Samaya said, "Like this? Come show me the rest of the house, Sai."

Isaiah always had his way with everything, from the business they bought to women. He never mixed business with pleasure, and Samaya was the only female that he brought to his home that he was about to incorporate both. Something about her glow, personality, and the want for love in her eyes made him want her more.

After showing her the house, he carried her into the dim-lit room where he had edible rose petals all over the lounge chair, candles lit, a bottle of champagne on ice, and body oils warming.

When he placed her on the lounge chair, he took off her clothes and placed a gold two-piece bathing suit next to her. "Put this on, and join me in the Jacuzzi," Isaiah said softly.

They sat in the Jacuzzi kissing, laughing, talking, sipping until their skin wrinkled, and the want for each other intensified with each look into each other's eyes.

Samaya said, "Do you have any kids?"

Isaiah said, "No. I want two of each by the same woman. Can you handle that?"

Samaya said, "Too soon to know. Do I have to worry about anybody coming to me about you?"

Isaiah said, "I wouldn't put myself in a predicament like that, let alone someone I want."

Samaya said, "I'm not sharing you with nobody. I will cut a bitch..."

Isaiah said, "Fuck cutting, I'll shoot a bitch. Let me quit playing. You're mines from this day on."

Samaya said, "I'm not playing, Sai. I have a list of dos and don'ts."

Isaiah said, "Hold up! All that list shit applies to kids. I know how to treat a woman, and I'll show you how to treat me since you've never had a man."

Samaya said, "Excuse me! I know love doesn't come with rules."

Isaiah said, "Let's make this clear! I don't have to ask to do shit. Being with someone means you make each other happy. That's it!"

They showered for like thirty minutes as he watched her wash her body with the satisfaction of her beautiful skin and chunky ass.

Everything moved in slow motion as he helped her rinse off. He took his time kissing her nipples, then her neck, and caressing his hand through her hair. As the warm water ran over their bodies, he rubbed her ass in a massaging motion while she indulged into his chest.

They lay across the lounge chair, and he rubbed the oils over her entire body, squeezing her nipples every chance he got. She turned around and watched him put the edible rose petals on her nipples, as he gently sucked them off.

Samaya said, "Oh my gosh! I can't take this anymore."

She gently pushed him over and took a piece of ice out the bucket. He watched as this virgin put the ice in her mouth, and placed it on his chest. She went down slowly to his navel until the ice melted, and his body showed pleasure in wanting more.

As soon as she came up, he turned over to the side and blew the candle out. He played with her hair until the wax cooled down. He poured the warm wax on her stomach, watching her body squirm with excitement. When she put her hand around the back of his head, he leaned in and sucked her nipples, and played with her clit at the same time until she couldn't take it anymore.

She climbed on top wanting more, so she grabbed his hard dick and put it in her mouth, salivating with a rhythm.

Isaiah said, "You a virgin? Right?"

Samaya said, "I was. I've watched some movies. Don't look hard at all. How am I doing so far?"

Isaiah said, "You're good! I'm sorry, keep going, bae!"

*****

Man 1 said, "Rocky lying about a damn box with money in that club. Look how big this house is?"

Man 2 said, "I told you, my nigga. We need one more person to handle this shit with us. Then this bitch Saria always with him. We can kill two birds with one stone."

Man 1 said, "We could get Man 3, but he might tell Rocky."

Man 2 said, "Let's bounce. If Rocky saw all this shit…he'd be game for whatever."

Man 1 said, "I don't know. When he mentions the box, his eyes get all bucked and shit."

*****

Isaiah's dick was all in her throat. He started looking all crazy thinking, *This girl ain't no damn virgin,* when she grabbed his shit with her hands, and he pulled her hair a little bit. She kept licking and kissing his dick with her juicy lips.

He pulled her up and thought, *This little bitch a professional,* and he wanted to see what her walls were like now.

Isaiah said, "Hold on! Turn over, Samaya."

Samaya said, "Did I do something wrong?"

Isaiah said, "Shut up!"

He opened her legs slowly with eye contact, then grabbed a piece of ice out the bucket, and put it in his mouth.

When he placed the ice on her clit, she moaned loud as hell. He pushed the ice inside her, making her body jump with excitement.

Samaya said, "*Oh my gosh, Sai. More!*"

He was licking and sucking her pussy like a strawberry swirl pop.

Isaiah said, "You okay, virgin?"

Samaya said, "You're irra! I've never felt that before."

Isaiah said, "Want me to stop?"

Samaya said, "*Hell no!*"

Before she could squirt, he got on top of her and slid his man's inside her slowly as he watched her eyes roll. He started stroking faster until they heard something pop, and she screamed out, "*Oww*," loud as fuck.

Isaiah said, "Damn! Let me stop."

They paused a moment then she jumped on top, and rode the fuck out his dick like she was dancing for a semifinals competition.

Samaya said, "Don't start something then stop. Lay down, Sai."

Isaiah said, "Don't hurt yourself now."

Samaya said, "I can't go all the way down. It hurts."

Isaiah said, "It's okay, save some for later. You're drunk, baby girl. Chill for a minute before you rupture some shit."

"You play too much," she said as she fell to the side, and hit his chest going straight to sleep. He couldn't help but think, *Is she a virgin*. The way she just deep throated was not like a first timer, but her riding skills could do some video watching as well.

*****

He rolled over to turn the alarm off, and Samaya woke up smiling. He moved his body over, cuffing her from behind, and she moved up enough so his dick could slide in.

Isaiah said, "Such a good morning."

Samaya went outside to shower in the sun, and he watched her for a few minutes, loving that his plan was coming to real life.

He stepped behind her as the water ran down their bodies while the thoughts of intimacy took over. He saw some blood as she was rinsing and the concerned look on her face.

Isaiah said, "You on your period?"

Samaya said, "*No.* It's just a little blood. I feel sore and crampy."

Isaiah said, "Your cherry got popped, baby girl. You'll walk it off."

Samaya said, "Oh, thanks for telling me…Mr. Popper…"

When he picked her up, she wrapped her legs around his waist, and he hugged hers. The water ran down their faces as they kissed passionately and slowly.

*****

They finished cleaning, having a long breakfast of laughs, him chasing her through the pool and the house.

They went to the bank to open a checking, savings, and a business account in her name.

The banker asked her what she did for a living; she didn't have shame in the world telling them she was an ex-stripper. Isaiah sat there proud of his baby girl and her confidence.

*****

Rocky said, "That was not my briefcase they carried there. Mines is black!"

Man 1 said, "How do you know they didn't switch it? When I walked past, she was doing all the signing."

Rocky said, "What made you follow him? I told you we need my briefcase and box."

Man 2 said, "I need to find it, right? I'm doing what I need to do so I don't look stupid when I run in somewhere looking for it."

Man 1 said, "If you knew who had the shit, we wouldn't be sitting the *fuck* here. We've been following all of them to get this damn box."

Man 2 said, "If they both going into the bank, they both got money."

Rocky said, "Once we get what we're looking for, I don't give a fuck what happens."

Man 2 said, "I need to know if that case went in with money, or came out with money in it."

Man 1 said, "I thought we were all looking for money? What's going on?"

Rocky said, "Motherfucka, you're going to get paid. Just find my shit! I'm out."

Man 1 said, "I'm not your motherfucka either, nigga."

Man 2 said, "Come on now, y'all, I'm going to find the shit and more. Here's your ride. I'll keep you posted."

Man 1 said, "I don't believe it's money, bro. Did you hear him? 'What are we looking for.' He's lying."

Rocky jumped out of the truck and slammed the door not before getting his last word, *"Find my shit!"* and stormed off to his car.

Man 2 said, "I'm not looking for his shit anymore. He can get his shit. I need what's in their briefcase though."

Man 1 said, "You are right! He's lying his ass off. He's sweating and shit."

Man 2 said, "I told you I've been following Saria and Queen for a minute, my nigga. They go to a storage unit across town making drops. They got security like a motherfucker at that bitch."

Man 1 said, "Did you mention this to Rocky?"

Man 2 said, "Hell naw! I'm telling you I've been watching them come up for years now. They paid, nigga, and you know it."

*****

The invites to dinner were to celebrate Samaya's graduation. The table seated her parents, Tara, Queen, Merch, Skunk, Jai, Samaya, and Isaiah, as planned.

Tamyra said, "This is a nice restaurant. My baby is doing thangs now!"

Samaya said, "Thangs, Mom?"

Tamyra said, "What's funny? Well, Dad and I thought you'd never find a man. You finished school, and I'm proud of you."

Isaiah said, "She's getting high scores on these tests, Pops."

Sammie said, "She's always been a smart girl. Just a few bumps in the road."

Samaya said, "Daddy, stop."

Queen said, "I'm so proud of you."

Tara said, "Cheers to a wonderful evening with the people I love the most."

Merch said, "Smart as her mouth is, she should be a lawyer."

Skunk said, "Congratulations, Samaya."

Tara glanced at Queen and Samaya, trying to hold her composure. When they saw her look, they took a quick sip of their drinks, hoping she didn't have that damn pistol and the rest of that shit with her.

Jai said, "Congratulations, girl. Here's your gift."

Samaya said, "Thanks, everyone. Whatever, Merch!"

Isaiah said, "Sorry, my other brothers couldn't be here. They're busy. You'll all meet them soon."

Tamyra said, "Have you decided on your major?"

Samaya said, "I was thinking about taking my generals until I figured something out or accounting, Mom."

Skunk said, "Accounting is good. You'll always find a job with that under your belt."

Tara giggled because she wanted to jump across the table and stab his ass with her butter knife, but jail was not in her plans. "Account for is a big factor," Tara whispered.

Queen said, "May I have a bottle of your best wine, please?"

Sammie said, "Take your time, baby girl. Don't rush into something then regret it. Maybe you should be a lawyer. Merch does have a point."

Queen chuckled, sipped her wine, and watched them all laugh in enjoyment. She was moving her legs under the table tapping Tara and Samaya, so they could follow her to the bathroom to talk for a moment.

Queen said, "I followed Merch and one of his bitches to this restaurant, and this is fucked up!"

Samaya said, "What the hell! We should start playing Duck, Duck, Who's a Cheater? Raise your got damn hand."

Tara said, "This is not funny, sis."

Queen said, "Then his brother invited me out to eat before he does for my family. I'm so pissed right now."

185

Samaya said, "We can leave this bitch. Give me a hug, baby."

Tara said, "Shit! He invited me too. I didn't tell Skunk anything about this. Matter of fact, I haven't seen or talked to him since the other night."

Queen said, "I'm not going to make a scene. It's about Samaya tonight. Hell, I didn't know Merch was coming until we both said our goodbyes this morning."

Tara said, "This man is introducing my sister to his family, having dinners, and shit. I can't even get my fiancé to introduce me to his mama, let alone all his brothers."

Samaya said, "We need to talk about this, but not here. And I haven't met his mama yet. Let me check y'all purses and pat y'all down."

Tara said, "You play too much!"

Queen said, "I'm getting mines! Fuck them females. Who's paying for this shit, so I can go order up some shit?"

Tara said, "I'm good! You are not checking me though, sis."

When they came back to the table, everyone was laughing.

Isaiah said, "I have something to say. In the little time that I've known Samaya, I know she's a great person with a big heart. I can't wait until all her goals are accomplished and I'm going to be right by her side."

Sammie said, "My man..."

Out of nowhere, Tara started crying, and when she saw that everyone was looking at her, she sucked that shit up real quick.

Tara said, "I'm sorry. I'm just happy for you."

Samaya said, "Thanks, sis...I love you."

"Hmm, hmm. Love you, too, sis," Tara said as she opened her purse. Queen's and Samaya's heart almost stopped.

Skunk said, "You okay, baby?"

Tara snickered as she held the trigger, but she couldn't pull it out the purse in front of her family. Then she'd have to shoot all the witnesses, and she knew his family stayed strapped.

Tara said, "He said 'baby.' Hell naw!"

Queen said, "*Tara? You* okay?"

Tara pulled out some Kleenex and blew her nose. Samaya looked straight at Queen and grabbed her heart in relief.

Tara said, "Yes…I'm fine, Queen. How about you?"

Queen said, "I'm fine! Miss, can I order something to go? Thanks."

Isaiah said, "Let's finish eating. We're planning a trip to Cancun if y'all are interested."

Samaya said, "Thank you, Isaiah. Come sit by me, Tara."

Tara said, "I don't feel well. I'll call everyone tomorrow. I need to leave. Congratulations again, sis. Love you."

Tamyra said, "Tara, come to the bathroom with me?"

Skunk said, "Let me take you home."

Queen said, "Aw, shit! Unc…"

Sammie said, "What's the matter, baby girl?"

Tara said, "What? Home…" Tara sighed softly. "I can't do this. I'm gone."

Tamyra said, "What's the matter, baby?"

Sammie said, "Let me walk you to your car, baby girl."

Skunk went to get up, and Merch shook his head no, but Skunk still didn't catch on to what Merch meant until he hit the table. Then he sat his ass back down and let her dad walk her out quietly.

They were all leaving, and Queen jumped in her ride. Jai knocked on her window, hoping she'd talk to her in front of everyone because she's been ignoring her text. When they started talking, Tamyra and Samaya walked up, so they switched up their whole conversation.

Merch pulled off with Skunk because he got the call to where his car was. "Who the fuck did this shit," Merch asked. "I don't know, bro. They're calling me with an estimate. I didn't even call their ass to set up anything," Skunk said. "Maybe, valet was joyriding in your shit and fucked it up." Merch coughed out as the flame clouded the car. "Well, they need to pay for this shit," Skunk demanded.

Sammie and Tamyra stood to the side, talking to Isaiah until the valet pulled up with their car.

Sammie said, "We appreciate everything you are doing for my baby. With a little guidance and love, she'll stop hanging out at that club."

Isaiah said, "She's not there anymore. Thanks for coming out, Sammie."

*****

Isaiah said, "Is there anything you'd like to do before we go home?"

Samaya said, "Go to this address, please? I saw my dad talking to you. He asked something?"

Isaiah said, "Yes, you did! He's a good man. He didn't say much."

Samaya said, "Well, my mom likes you."

Isaiah said, "Good...I don't see any parking spots over here."

Samaya said, "Pull around to that gate. The parking spot number will show after you enter the code, then the gate will open."

As soon as Coral saw Samaya walk past with Isaiah, he winked his eye for approval.

Coral said, "Good evening, Ms. Samaya. Hello, sir!"

Samaya said, "Good evening, Coral."

Isaiah said, "Hello, sir!"

Coral said, "Ms. Samaya, you have a message."

Samaya said, "Thanks!"

When they got on the elevator, she could tell that Isaiah was sizing up his surroundings because he always pushed his jacket back for a quicker way to pull his thang.

She always kept her pistol on her side or in her purse, so she was never worried, and that made her like him more.

She wanted to ask him why he carried it everywhere because she had a reason to, but *What was his*, she thought.

Samaya said, "Come on in, Sai. Make yourself at home."

Isaiah said, "Okay. Nice place. How long have you lived here?"

Samaya said, "Almost three years. I bounced around for a while until I got tired of moving from place to place."

Isaiah said, "Why would a young lady be bouncing around?"

Samaya said, "That's the life of Saria and Samaya. Okay, come into my place."

Isaiah said, "Damn! I like this layout. All white everything, huh? Samaya, come here?"

Samaya said, "Oh my gosh, your hugs are firm and comforting. Makes me feel secure."

Isaiah said, "You got me, I got you. Start the fireplace, so we can sit down and talk."

Samaya said, "What is there to talk about. We have plenty of time."

Isaiah said, "When's your birthday? What's your favorite color, besides white? Do you have any fears? Tell me, what do you want from me?"

Samaya said, "Okay. Okay. I get it."

Isaiah said, "There's more to a relationship than fucking and sucking."

Samaya said, "Were in a relationship now? Oh, I forgot."

Isaiah said, "You already knew that. When I first told you, you weren't dancing anymore and you listened, you became mine."

Samaya said, "Makes it seem like I'm following directions or orders."

Isaiah said, "No. That means you're a woman. Don't get me wrong. Men listen to their women also, but man is the head, period."

Samaya said, "Women, huh?"

*****

Jill, Chad, and Man 2 sat outside, watching and waiting.

Chad said, "Look, bro starting to like that broad. I'm not feeling this shit anymore."

Man 2 said, "This don't have shit to do with Rocky anymore. Have you told him, Jill?"

Jill said, "I didn't say shit. Fuck him! If he knew I was following them, he'd trip."

Man 2 said, "This building too secure to be running up in. How many is it of these fuckers?"

Chad said, "I told you Rocky on some BS since you've met him, sis. I don't like him, Man 2."

Man 2 said, "Fuck him! How many, Jill?"

Jill said, "You asked me to follow them from the bank. That's my first time seeing him. I only dealt with Ishmael, and he never introduced me to anyone. Why am I following them? You sure Rocky don't know you text me?"

Man 2 said, "Why the fuck would I tell his fat ass anything we do? You sound nervous!"

Chad said, "Chill, dude, with all the disrespect. I'm going to look at the storage unit."

Man 2 said, "That's what I'm talking about, making moves."

Jill said, "You could have told me he was in the car with you before I pulled up to the bank. Got me ducking and shit."

Man 2 said, "I had to drop him off, and I saw you hit the corner, so I pulled off. He was too busy arguing with Man 1 anyway."

Jill knew she had to lie to see what Man 2 was on because she didn't want to get involved, knowing this family didn't play games, and now Chad was involved.

Jill said, "What does he want with this family? Because they're not into any mess."

Man 2 said, "I was following them for Rocky at first. He's looking for a briefcase and box with money in it. Who the fuck is Ishmael? And why the fuck would I tell him about our arrangement?"

Chad said, "I'm gone! I'll holla at y'all later."

Jill chuckled in disbelief because she knew what Rocky was looking for and he had them fooled just like everyone else.

Jill said, "That's what he told you? I'm not about to get involved in all this. This too much."

Man 2 said, "Bitch, you're already involved, stupid. When they left the bank, I need to know everywhere they went?"

Jill said, "Some big-ass house where the rich people live. Then they both went to this restaurant, and this place we're watching. They were together all evening. Take me back to my car, and I need my money."

Man 2 said, "Take this! I'll get the rest to you later after you finish helping me."

Jill said, "What the fuck! This not enough. *Just drop me off.*"

Man 2 said, "Shut the fuck up before I put you out."

Jill said, "Ain't no point in sitting out here all night. They're making love. Let's go."

Man 2 said, "What the fuck you know about love?"

Jill said, "The way he chased her through the grass playing, picking her up, and the way he held her hand all day. She smiles of happiness when she looks at him like nobody's watching them, or a care in the world but him."

Man 2 said, "Aw, yeah, let me drop your cupid-wannabe ass off."

*****

Samaya lay across his chest, watching the fire crackle as he played with her hair.

Isaiah said, "Where's the food? How the fuck you get all that ass with no food in the fridge or cabinets?"

Samaya said, "I buy food sometimes. Queen buys the food and cook for me."

Isaiah said, "Damn! You don't know how to cook? We'll fix that."

Samaya said, "That's funny! My birthday is May 12th, my favorite color is orange, and I fear deep water. What do I want from you? Treat me as you want to be treated. When's your birthday, and the rest of all that good stuff?"

Samaya said, "*Ouch! You pinched me?*"

Isaiah said, "Stuff? September 19th, gray or green, and I fear God only. What do I want from you? I want you to be happy. That means you'll make me happy."

Samaya said, "That's simple. Thanks for the outing tonight. I appreciate that."

Samaya started sobbing softly, and he kissed her forehead.

191

Isaiah said, "What's the matter? It's okay. Don't answer that. Let that shit out."

Samaya said, "You play too much."

*****

That morning when Samaya came back from her morning run, she saw her door propped open with a grocery bag.

Coral said, "*Thank you, sir!*"

Isaiah said, "Welcome. Hello, baby girl!"

Samaya said, "Really, Sai? Thanks. I'm not going to ask."

Isaiah said, "Good, because I wasn't going to tell you. See you later."

Samaya went straight downstairs to talk with Coral, as soon as Isaiah left.

Ishmael
Family First

He lay there watching the silk sheets go up and down while they played under the covers with each other, giggling. He waved for Jill to come over, but she was hesitant and stubborn. When she jumped on the bed and started playing along, he was surprised.

When his phone rang, he pushed the girls away. "Chill out for a bit," Ishmael whispered.

Ishmael said, "What's up, bro?"

Isaiah said, "When are you getting out?"

Ishmael said, "All that construction, remodeling, and my finals got me tired. Cupid looks good, bro."

The ladies were wrestling around with each other, giggling like little girls."

Isaiah said, "Yeah. I was there the other day grabbing that paperwork and chopping it up with Skunk. Are you coming to Mom's house tonight for supper?"

Ishmael covered up his phone. "I said chill for a minute. Hold on," Ishmael demanded in a low tone.

Ishmael said, "Stop, Jill! Claudia, start the shower and let me finish this call. Lia, baby, bring me something to drink."

Isaiah said, "Well, Mom rented out the beach resort for you and Skunk's graduation party, pimp. It's an all-white event."

Ishmael said, "These women are my friends, bro. No pimping involved. Merch wants to meet up after at Cupid."

They both laughed at the fact Ishmael always kept several females, and they never complained. His brothers swore he made them sign a contract."

Isaiah said, "My girl birthday next week, so I'm going to throw her a party at the hotel ballroom."

Ishmael said, "She fine, bro. You should keep that one. I think you should do it in something we don't own."

Isaiah said, "I might do that, playa."

Ishmael said, "I don't make these females do anything they don't want to. It's that simple, bro."

Isaiah said, "I can't believe you just said that with all the women friends you have. They are in the crib all at the same time, having a grown-ass slumber party."

Ishmael said, "It's all an understanding. They know the deal. No feelings involved. Don't knock it until you try it."

Isaiah said, "Father like sons."

Ishmael said, "Bro, you know damn well, you are not like him."

They laughed because the whole family knew that Isaiah was the only one that was uncomfortable with their father's arrangement.

Isaiah said, "Anyways, we need to figure out what we're doing with the empty building."

Ishmael said, "Tear it down, and make it the super strip club."

They both laughed so hard, Ishmael choked off his flame. "Not super." Isaiah laughed.

Isaiah said, "I was thinking we should keep the upstairs offices, make the other building a club, or tear the wall down and expand the VIP. Let me know what you think when we all meet, and what the numbers are. Congratulations again, bro."

Ishmael said, "Thanks, bro. Learned from the best."

Ishmael walked straight to the shower where both his lady friends were. One started washing him down, Lia began to wash her up, and the favor returned.

Ishmael sat on his patio while two of the girls swam topless in his pool, and Jill prepared lunch. The ladies knew not to bother him while he was on his computer, on the phone, while he did his paper-work, or when company came.

Ishmael said, "Lia…come here?"

Lia said, "Yes, Ishmael…What's up?"

Ishmael said, "I need your management skills at this strip club I just bought. Let's go over your pay."

Lia said, "I'd have to think about it. I've never worked in a strip club before."

Ishmael said, "It's a first time for everything."

Lia said, "Does this require me to get naked? My family wouldn't approve of me working in that kind of environment."

194

Ishmael said, "You don't have to get naked unless you want to. As the manager, you'd make sure everything is coming and going. I do expect you to dress nice, though."

Lia said, "Where is it located at?"

Ishmael said, "Downtown off Highway 85."

Lia said, "I thought the fat creepy dude owned that? I'll still have to talk to my family first."

Ishmael said, "That's cool? I'm not creepy nor fat."

Lia said, "Well, can I get a bonus to go shopping?"

Ishmael said, "Your family approved quickly."

When his phone started ringing, he shushed her. "Give me a minute, Lia," Ishmael said. He already knew she had money because he paid all his friends for their services whenever they come over or did him favors. He just looked at her sideways, because he hated "can I get"-type females, knowing damn well time is not free.

Ishmael said, "What's up, bro? I was letting Lia know that we need her at the club to work with Teisha crazy ass."

Merch said, "I'll let feisty and Ax know she's coming. Teisha's mouth is jazzy, but Queen beat that ass in the club, bro."

Ishmael said, "Queen got them hands, bro. Told you she was whopping on some nigga at the corner store from grabbing her ass. That nigga lucky I put her ass in the car because she was about to use that thang."

Merch said, "Queen knows not to try me. When are you stepping out, bro?"

Ishmael said, "I'm about to go pick my suit up, and have a cab drop these females off."

*****

At the station house, Detective Thomas said, "*What? So, he sold the club. He must know where on to him?*"

Lia said, "I'll see because they offered me a job. Maybe they bought into the club with him. Rocky can't know anything, and Jill most definitely doesn't know anything. The last few times I was with Ishmael, she wasn't there as usual."

Detective Afonso said, "You were supposed to be following Rocky. How the fuck you end up following Jill? Now, he's on the run."

Lia said, "*He don't know shit! I thought this was a meeting? Where the fuck is Phillips?*"

Detective Afonso said, "He's not here to fix your fuckups anymore."

Lia said, "Fuck you, Afonso! I'm gone."

Detective Thomas said, "I need Rocky off the streets. I'm not about to be chasing his nasty ass."

Lia said, "*Stop it, boss!* We'll get him if the other side doesn't get him first."

Detective Afonso said, "Please don't go falling in love blowing my got damn case."

Lia said, "*This is not just your case. I need to go shopping for my interview.*"

Detective Thomas said, "Now. Now, folks. Let's try to keep our bubbles from popping. We're all in this together, and be careful, Lia. Soon as you lay eyes on him, contact us immediately."

*****

Jill said, "What should I do? All I want is for Rocky to go down."

Chad said, "I'm not feeling this. Robbing these people and taking from a storage unit is two different things."

Jill said, "I'm starting to care for this man, and they're not some random as people you fuck over. They will kill if they have to, Chad."

Chad said, "We need to tell Charles to stop before he gets too involved. Why did you involve Rachel?"

Jill said, "She needed extra money. How you sound questioning me, and you told Charles to fuck that twin?"

Chad said, "Do her family know? These some creepy mothafuckers, Jill. Leave Rocky alone."

Jill said, "What about Man 1 and Man 2? They're planning on something, but they won't tell me who they're going after first."

196

PART 3

When It Started

CHAPTER 11

Samaya
The Life

Samaya had been staying at Isaiah's house lately, so she invited the girls over to hang out at her condo.

She put on her all-white cotton dress, with no panties so she could air out, and put her hair in a bun. She pranced around, listening to music and flaming until they arrived.

Samaya said, "He's streetwise, book smart, knows how to cook, dress, smells good, and he knows how to fuck."

Jez said, "You found a good man. I'm happy for you."

Queen said, "I wish they were all good men."

Jez said, "They're probably good men needing real women in their lives, or to be treated right."

Queen chuckled because she knew she was sneak dissing. "Rhinoceros-nose ass," Queen said softly.

Tara said, "Whoa, ladies…I love a man that smells good."

Queen said, "See…this bitch doesn't even know me?"

Jai said, "Okay! I like a well-groomed man as well, that knows how to throw the pipe."

Tara said, "Don't we all…With a li'l head game. Wallah."

Samaya said, "Isaiah told me to count my money and to take my ass to college. He's teaching me about having good credit, stocks, bonds, buying property, and investing."

Jez said, "That's what's up, girl. Jai needs to find a man like that."

Queen said, "I need a few shots."

Jai said, "Quit coming at me. You sound like Mommy dearest. You need a man."

Jez said, "I'm not your mommy, but I do not sound horny, either."

Tara said, "Wow! I need a shot, too, cousin."

Samaya said, "I put a lot of bubbles and oils in the tub, so I could soak my sore body. I need a shot also."

Jez said, "Why are you so sore? Exercising will do that."

Samaya said, "Ask a question, then answer the question. Where they do that at?"

They all laughed, but Queen did some extra shit, trying to piss Jez off.

Queen said, "*Damn, bitch! Do you like hearing yourself? You talk too much!*"

Jai said, "Chill out! That name-calling is not cool."

Jez said, "That's called conversation, but you do that with your ass, right?"

Tara said, "Whoa, Jez. Let's be respectful now."

Jai said, "Stop being so judgmental, and live a little, sis. Damn, this shit is irritating!"

Queen said, "Don't warn her. I have exactly what she needs right here. Keep it up!"

Jez said, "Tara? See what I mean."

Samaya said, "So…I picked up some groceries, Swishers, and some board games on my way home. I know everyone likes shrimp, right?"

Queen said, "I thought your man bought groceries? Did you call Toonie?"

Samaya said, "She missed the outing the other night. She left a letter saying she went to see Granny."

Queen said, "I know what that means. She's going to give her the 411 on our ass."

Samaya said, "Hopefully she'll be back before we leave for Cancun."

Tara said, "I don't know if I'm gonna make it. Have fun, though."

They started in the kitchen then ended in the living room, sitting around the fire on the white furry rug, laughing, taking shots, flaming, and talking for hours.

Jez said, "It's frustrating not knowing who's putting these notes on my *damn* car. Then the police can't do shit without evidence."

Jai said, "I'm terrified, sis."

Samaya said, "If it were their family, they'd find his ass."

Queen said, "I would know if someone was following me."

Jai said, "Baby, stop it."

Tara said, "Can you both stop the bickering and take a shot."

Jez said, "*How the fuck would you know? If I knew, I would handle it. Shit sound dumb.*"

Queen said, "Dumb, huh?"

Samaya and Tara looked at each other, knowing their cousin didn't do that smart-mouth shit. Everything is one way with Queen, and she started more fights than a boxing ring announcer.

Tara burst out, "I'm not getting married anymore," taking off her big ring, trying to distract Queen from fighting Jez.

Tara said, "Sis...I hope you didn't spend too much money on my gift."

"I haven't bought anything yet," Samaya chuckled as she tried passing the flame to Queen.

Samaya said, "Nope. You play all day!"

Tara said, "Queen...did you get me anything?"

Queen said, "Yes. I returned it after we found out everything, but I like how you think I'm going to let this frail bitch raise her voice at me."

Tara sighed hard as hell, covering her face. "See, this the shit I'm talking about." Tara muffled her voice out in her hands.

Jez said, "*I'm not your bitch, Queen! Quit coming at me.*"

Samaya said, "Okay, we're not doing this here. Jez? Queen? Let's keep our voices at a normal level, and no more name-calling, please."

Tara said, "What's wrong with y'all?"

Queen said, "Girl, please. You better ask your twin who I am."

Jez said, "Exactly. You picked the right one, my twin."

Queen said, "I'm going to smack this Z-shaped head ass."

Jai said, "*Stop it! Stop it!* Queen, stop. Jez, hush! Damn! Can you sit back down, Queen?"

Queen said, "I got you, Jai!"

Samaya said, "Well, I quit stripping, got my GED last week, and signed up for business management. Can we focus on that than all this bickering."

Queen said, "He must gonna pay you then?"

Samaya said, "We're past all that. Best believe I'm getting mine."

Samaya noticed Queen was flaming a lot and kept looking at her phone.

Jez said, "I don't understand, as people, why can't we get our own money?"

Jai said, "Stop it, *twin*! *Got damn!* Come on, so I can walk you out."

Queen jumped over Tara's legs, rushing Jez, swinging. Before Jez could do anything, Queen had hit her in the face several times. When Jez realized what was going on, Queen was choking her. Jai and Tara were grabbing Queen, then Samaya tried to grab Jez loose from Queen's grip. Samaya let Queen get a few more hits before pulling her off.

Jai said, "*Baby, no! No, Queen!*"

Everybody started looking all crazy like, *Did she just call her 'baby' again*, because she kept saying it. After they separated them, Jai escorted Jez out immediately.

Jai made plans that night to meet up with Queen earlier that evening. She wanted to talk to her about the drama without losing her friendship. She knew her sister's mouth was terrible because they fought all the time growing up.

Samaya said, "I'm glad she left, but she knows how to pick a fight. I'll see you tomorrow, Jai."

After everyone left, Tara stayed and helped Samaya straighten up.

Tara said, "So, he's buying groceries? You got a storage room of money and don't buy food."

Samaya said, "Shut up! He doesn't need to know everything about me yet. Besides, when have I ever bought food?"

Tara said, "Do you think this ring is worth a lot of money? I'm selling it tomorrow."

"You're not gonna marry him? Give me a hug, sis. Hit this," Samaya said as she choked off the flame.

"I'm not staying home while he runs the street grabbing asses, fucking, and sucking on everybody," Tara said. "Take this shit before I go find his ass again," Tara cried out. "Quit looking for shit. What made you follow him anyway," Samaya said.

Tara said, "Ignoring my text and phone calls. You saw the shit. Take this shit, and it's too strong."

Samaya said, "Before you started jumping in the car with me and Queen, everything was fine. Quit doing what you see others doing. He can't marry all of y'all, da fuck."

Tara said, "You're high! Can I stay here tonight? I need some time to think. I'm hitting the flame again, drinking like there's no tomorrow."

Samaya said, "You're more than welcome, but my baby is coming over tonight."

Tara said, "You won't even know I'm here. Besides, I need to give Skunk some of his own medicine."

Samaya said, "If you think he's playing games, then you start playing mind games, the shit's gonna clash. Tara, your relationship is different from Queen's. Don't go doing shit. You can hurt him to the point he won't fuck with you, period. Ask his ass why he asked to marry you. If you saw him fucking and sucking, that's different."

Tara said, "Bitch! You don't sound black or hoodish as you act."

Samaya said, "I know who I am. You're allowing his actions to dictate your feelings."

Tara said, "What would you do? He's hurting me, shit."

Samaya said, "Quit following his ass, and let that shit come to light on its own. You were the happiest bitch I knew a few weeks ago.

Following and doing the shit you're not cut out for. Got you acting like a bottom feeder."

Tara laughed so hard, she almost pissed on herself.

Tara said, "So...now my cousin a fish?"

Samaya said, "No. When you're on the top, you get the fresh shit that hasn't been picked over. You don't have to look for scraps and settle for anything that drops to the bottom. Best believe, Queen is getting hers, and more. She can feed the bottom feeders, but she chose to get out there, and that's something you're not cut out for."

Tara said, "I didn't understand shit you just said. You don't give me any credit. Look at this shit."

Samaya said, "Whose account is this? Tara? Tara? How'd you get all this money?"

Tara said, "Yup. That's my name on this account, this one, and I have cash put up. I understand everything you just said, but I had to see some shit. I'm not about to catch shit from him or them. I'll sleep upstairs in your guest room."

Samaya said, "And, I thought you were stupid. For the record, them some smart-ass fuckers. I'd put it in somebody's else's name."

Tara said, "Hold on! Let's backtrack! Did you call my cousin a pimp or fish?"

Samaya said, "She's getting hers any means necessary doing all that following up behind him. Best believe that!"

Tara said, "I get it! I get it! She's a bottom feeder swimming around trying to come to the top."

Samaya said, "I can't stand you...I believe we've achieved that. Daddy called asking about you. Call him!"

Samaya texted Isaiah so he could come over after the ladies left, which was a done deal. She decided to go pick the rest of her things up from Cupid before he came over.

She threw on a white cami, some tight-ass jeans, and some slip-on heels. She grabbed her handbag and made sure her pipe was in there, her truck keys, and the flame for the road.

Tara said, "I see why he's all in your ass. *Sexy bitch!*"

"Sis...you're crazy," Samaya said with laughter. Samaya said, "Sis. You are silly, but thanks."

Tara said, "Leave me some flame. *Thanks!*"

Samaya said, "Go your high ass to sleep. I've never seen you this drunk or high."

Tara said, "*Whatever, sis!* I see them nipple rings poking and a fat-ass camel toe and your lips shining. Matter fact, I'm going to get me some tomorrow."

*****

"Who is it? Samaya is not here," Tara shouted. "Come in. She's coming back later. What are you doing here?" Tara slurred out.

Toonie said, "Coral, let me in! I changed my mind about going to see Granny. Give me the address to where Samaya's at?"

Tara said, "Girl, please! She'll be back. Here, hit this shit!"

Toonie said, "Give me the address or take me there."

Tara said, "Here, take my keys. Oh, have fun, but you should let me fix you up. Let's go raid her closet."

Toonie said, "Tara, please...I have my own shit!"

Jai
Sneaky

Jai thought she was reading the test wrong, so she tried again and again, thinking she needed to try a different brand. She ran to the kitchen, drinking a whole bottle of water. *One more, one more,* Jai thought.

Jai said, "Fuck this! No. No. No. Not now! This shit can't be happening to me right now. I don't need any extra bills, and I haven't met my own goals. *Oh my gosh!*"

Jez said, "What's your plan? You know Mommy dearest was expecting for us to be married first."

Jai said, "When are you going to learn that Mommy doesn't run me. I'll accept all the love she has, but trying to dictate my life is a no-no."

Jez said, "She was mad at me for missing supper with them. I just backed off from arguing with her and left."

Jai said, "You know Daddy will back her up or slam our ass for his wife. Don't play."

Jez said, "Yeah, you're right. Not trying to fight his muscle-face ass. Whose baby is it?"

Jai said, "I've only had threesomes with them, and I'm not trying to have him or her in my life, or come in between what they have going on. I can't do this threesome or fuck with him anymore. What the fuck was I thinking, not using a condom?"

Jez said, "It only takes one time. What about Chucky?"

Jai said, "Yo ass silly! I told you he only eats."

Jez said, "Okay...Scared to ask you if it's anybody else you might say, 'All he does is fingers me.' Let me know if you need me."

Jai said, "See, you are trying to make me laugh! I fucked up! Damn!"

Jez said, "I see some bags in the back. Where'd you go? And a baby is not a mistake."

Jai said, "I met Tara at the mall. We went through fabrics and got her opinions on my sketches for the wedding dresses. I have six months to finish."

Jez said, "Sis! Please don't stress yourself out. She just said, 'I'm not getting married,' right?"

Jai said, "Skunk told me his fiancée didn't have a budget, which made shopping easier. Now she's not marrying him. I don't get it! I'll call her later."

Jez said, "He must love her? Was he there?"

Jai said, "No, he wasn't. I think they were going through something because she was rude at dinner. Girl…she started crying, got up, and left."

Jez said, "She seems happy when we're at school or work. She loves talking about him and showing off all the things he buys for her."

Jai said, "The money he gave me alone for doing the job didn't have anything to do with the purchase of the fabric. I saw him give Tara a black card, then she turned and walked away. After we finished shopping, Tara and I had lunch."

Jez said, "I think you should get your money and leave that family alone. They all seem like users."

Jai said, "Hold on! But you deal with Tara? That's not fair, because you don't like Queen. What the hell is a user?"

Jez said, "I scheduled all the appointments for their fittings except for Queen. She might change her mind."

Jai said, "I know, with your mean ass. She's coming by the shop to get fitted shortly. Answer my question, Jez."

Jez said, "Someone that uses people for material things or money. Self-gain. Then their feelings get hurt after they find out that person getting used is doing them all along. Now the users, feelings are hurt because they find out the side chick is prego. Hmmm."

Jai said, "Stop it! You can ask her since she's your friend's cousin. Thanks!"

Jez said, "When did you start using that word, let alone calling me out by name."

When Jez saw Queen coming in, she started getting her bags together because they did not get along. Jez helped the last client check out before she left.

Jez said, "I'll see you later, sis. I'm going to help Tara at the shop."

Queen said, "*Bye, twin!*"

Jez said, "Get your friend, sis. You don't have any cheerleaders with you today, so bye my ass!"

Queen said, "Bitch…I will slap the fuck out of you."

Jez chuckled with a black eye and all from the other night.

Jez said, "I'm not either one of y'all, bitch! Have fun."

Jai said, "Come on, girl! I need to get you fitted. Damn!"

Queen said, "Let me go, Jai. She's fucking irritating!"

Jai said, "I'm not about to let you fight my sister. She's leaving. Come on, girl."

Jez said, "Whatever, threebie. Bye!"

Jai said, "*Seriously?*"

*****

Queen headed for the sizing area in the back, and Jai followed. Queen slipped into the sheer slip and came out walking like she was on a runway.

Queen said, "What's funny? You know, I look good. You wanted me over here because you know my cousin is not getting married."

Jai said, "Until they tell me differently, I was paid to do a job. You and my sister need to stop it with all this nonsense."

When she went to measure Queen's bust area, her hand brushed over her nipple ring, causing it to get hard. Her crazy ass touched it again with her fingertip, making Queen smile. Queen went to kiss Jai, but she backed off.

Jai said, "Hold that thought. Let me go lock up."

Jai rushed to turn the open sign lights off. She saw Merch's ass approaching all fast, so she opened the door sporadically. When he walked past her, he smacked her ass, and she grabbed his hand.

Jai said, "Hello, Merch. What's up?"

Merch said, "Where is Queen?"

Jai said, "She's in the back getting measurements for her dress. No hi? Damn!"

Merch said, "My bad. What's up with you, sexy?"

Beep. Beep. Queen looked at her phone, noticing that Rocky kept blowing her up, asking for some flame. She ignored his ass, knowing damn well he never asked for so much.

Rocky's text to Queen: "What's up, Queen? I need something."

Queen's text to Rocky: "I'll bring it tonight, Damn!"

Rocky started calling her phone, and Merch heard her phone ringing, but Queen sent his ass straight to voice mail.

Man 2 said, "If the bitch comes, don't freeze up."

Rocky said, "When she gets out the car and start walking up to me, just grab the bitch."

Man 1 said, "I know what the fuck to do. You get the bitch here."

Rocky said, "Make sure you grab me from behind, so she thinks we're both being set up."

Jill said, "All they ass stay strapped so that y'all know."

Man 2 said, "Make sure you grab that muthafucka before she grabs it. I'm not trying to get shot over some flame."

Man 1 said, "We're just grabbing bitches now? This shit crazy!"

Rocky said, "If we get the shit, it's a profit any way we go about it. I know that nigga will give it to her. Let me call her again."

*****

Jai said, "What's up, Merch?"

Merch looked at Jai's boobs then headed toward the back. She knew damn well what the business was, and he wasn't about to say more with Queen in the other room.

Jai noticed Merch's face in disbelief that she asked that behind Queen's back, but she didn't give a fuck. She went to grab his hand before he got too far away, and he snatched back.

Jai said, "Merch, I'm pregnant."

Merch said, "Pregnant by who?"

Jai said, "Why would I tell you if it's not yours."

Merch said, "Do Queen know?"

Jai said, "*No.* What the fuck would I tell her for."

Merch said, "Don't let her find out, Jai."

Queen walked out to the front to find Merch standing there with Jai whispering. They both had a look like she interrupted something they shouldn't have been doing. She turned around and walked back into the dressing area.

They both followed behind her with her mind wandering. "What are you doing? Put that back in your purse," Merch said. "Seriously, quit playing with me," Queen replied.

Jai said, "Merch came in when I was about to lock up looking for you."

Queen said, "What's up, Merch? Haven't seen you in a few days."

Merch said, "I've been busy. I called and texted you, though. We'll talk when we leave here."

Jai said, "I'm sorry. I didn't know!"

Queen said, "Sorry? And what should you know? You know something I don't?"

Merch said, "Chill, Q! Finish what y'all was doing."

How the fuck does he know where I'm at, Queen thought. Queen looked shook. Did this bitch Jai tell him behind my back? The way he was looking, she was scared to ask him because he looked like something was bothering him.

Jai said, "Once I get your length, I'll be done, Queen. Turn this way."

Merch said, "Make sure you measure around all that ass."

Queen said, "My ass doesn't seem like it's enough nowadays."

Merch was so into Jai bending over measuring the length of the dress he didn't hear shit Queen said. Jai noticed Merch walk up and sit on the lounge chair next to them flaming, all comfortable, and she instantly got excited. When Queen turned around, Jai saw that she wasn't feeling this shit from the look on her face.

Queen said, "You're moving around all comfortable."

Merch said, "What's up, Queen?"

Queen said, "I'm in a rush right now. Can this wait, Jai? Merch and I need to drop something off."

Merch said, "Come here! I'm not trying to hear that shit. You, too, Jai."

Beep, beep, beep. "Is that notification the rush?" Merch asked.

Beep. Beep. Bringg. Bringg. "Quit looking at the phone! We'll get it later," Merch said.

Queen said, "It might be important!"

He put his hand up Queen's slip, fingering her while she stood there. He motioned for Jai to come down on her knees. She unzipped his pants, grabbed his dick out, and began sucking his dick like a pro. When she stood up and sat on his dick, she rode it like it was hers.

Queen thought about punching her in the back of her head, but she just pretended to enjoy the shit while it lasted.

Queen said, "Get the fuck up! I need to go."

Jai said, "What's the problem, girl?"

Bringg, bringg. "Silence that shit!" Merch demanded. *Bringg. Bringg.* "You mean how y'all two were talking in silence?" Queen hissed out.

Jai got up and moved to the side because she thought while Merch and Queen watched her bounce up and down, it was for their pleasure.

"Queen? Get dressed! You can finish this fitting another day. Who the fuck keeps texting and calling you like that?" Merch shouted. "Business as usual," Queen responded with irritation.

*****

Jai pulled out the yellow pages as soon as they left and turned off everything like that chapter in her life of threebies with them. Jai didn't want anything to do with Queen, or anybody knowing what she was about to do.

She fell asleep on the couch looking through her old designs until she heard her phone beeping, which woke her up.

When the man arrived, she opened the door for him to come in, and he followed her to the back. The man took off all her clothes, and let her take off all his.

The man said, "Let me see what that mouth do."

Jai said, "Tell me what you want, Daddy? I got you."

The man said, "Hmmm. Suck this dick then. Yup, get it wet. Hmmm, shit. Don't stop. Get it all. Yeah, like that. Whooo, shit."

The man sat in the chair, watching as she got on top. She rode his dick while he sucked and bit her nipples. When he pulled her hair, she moaned so loud that the whole block could hear her. "*Yes…yes…yes, Daddy*," Jai moaned in satisfaction.

*****

Man 2 said, "How the fuck did you know he was coming here?"

Jill said, "I need my money now! I started following each of them as they left that punk-ass club."

Man 2 said, "Queen didn't show up. Now, Rocky is getting pissed."

Jill said, "What the fuck is wrong with him?"

Man 2 said, "It's all there. I'm seeing all types of shit that I could blackmail a nigga on."

Jill said, "Here you go sounding just like him."

*****

Coral said, "Hi, how can I assist you today?"

Jai said, "Can you check to see if Samaya's here? Please…"

Coral said, "Aw, she doesn't do pop-ups. I'm sorry, let me ring her."

Jai said, "Thanks."

Coral said, "She's not picking up. Can I leave a message for her? Are you okay? Have a seat. Let me get you some water. You look dizzy."

*****

Coral said, "Oh my gosh! You never pick up on the first ring since you've been with him. Some girl in the front lobby is looking for you. I gave her thirsty ass some water."

Samaya said, "Can I please speak? Coral, you know I'm not home. Don't be saying all this extra stuff to me with yo jealous ass."

Coral said, "You're talking in codes because you are with him. I get it! It's the twin, and I'll get rid of her for you. She's beautiful enough to bring me back to my manly days."

Samaya said, "You are silly…He's in the bank, and I didn't tell her to come over. She's getting a little too comfortable. And, I said she looks different from her twin. Besides, she's fucking Merch and Queen. Hello. Hello. *Hello…*"

*****

Coral said, "Here, drink this. She's not here, so maybe you should go get some rest."

Jai said, "You don't remember me from hanging out with Tara and my sister downtown?"

CHAPTER 12

Queen
Quit Trying Me

The doctor said, "You're pregnant. I'll write you a prescription for vitamins, and I'd like to see you back next month."

Queen said, "Wow! Thank you."

The doctor said, "Are you okay? We have counselors at this clinic if you need someone to speak with."

Queen said, "I don't need a counselor, therapist, shrink, or head doctor listening to me."

The doctor said, "That's fine. We're always here to assist you when you're ready. Is this your first? Ms....Ms. Kya, don't leave. I have a few more questions."

*****

Queen's text to Jai: "Let's meet up so we can get our nails and feet did."

Jai's text to Queen: "okay baby, I'll be free in an hour."

Queen's text to Jai: "okay, same spot."

Queen watched as Jai walked into the shop looking like a perfect woman and someone she'd fuck up over her family and Merch if it came to it.

Jai said, "This orange will be pretty on your skin tone, baby."

Queen said, "That is pretty. Let's go shopping so I can pick up Samaya a gift for graduating?"

Jai said, "That's fine. I need to call and let Kimberly know I'll be a little late. What did you have in mind for her?"

Queen said, "Who's Kimberly?"

Jai said, "My new assistant is replacing my sister. Baby? Why don't you like my twin?"

Queen said, "What's up with this baby shit? She's just too quiet for my taste, and she seems sneaky."

Jai said, "You don't like me calling you that? I'm sorry. My sister can come off as if she's an ass, but she's cool. Have you met her before?"

Queen said, "I don't like the baby shit! No, we haven't met. She only asks questions and doesn't make conversation. Have your customers ever complained?"

Jai said, "I don't know what that means. Asking questions is how you get to know someone. When she first started working for me, yes, they complained."

Queen said, "So…it's not just me. Instead of her saying, 'How are you?' She asks, 'How do you know that's how you feel?' type shit."

Jai said, "No. They said she wouldn't smile, never spoke, turned her nose up, and threw their change to them," so, I checked that shit early. Maybe she doesn't know how to make conversation, so she asks questions to learn people. I need the arguing to stop on the strength of us."

Queen laughed at her, with no feelings whatsoever. "Strength, huh," Queen replied softly.

Queen said, "She tries too hard to fit in. I like people that go with the flow. Always asking questions, and observing like she's somebody mama."

Jai said, "That's understandable, but everybody is not the same. She's pushy at times, but attacking her for it is not cool."

Queen said, "Right. Do customers ever get tired of seeing the Doublemint twins?"

Jai said, "You are so funny. I see you like chewing on Doublemint though."

This bitch just turned my stomach, Queen thought as she rushed off to the bathroom, not noticing Jai was right behind her.

Jai said, "I saw that you looked dizzy, so I came to help you. You okay?"

Queen said, "I haven't been feeling well lately."

Jai said, "Go to the doctor!"

Queen said, "I did this morning. They gave me some medicine, but everything is okay. Don't look at me like that. I'm just pregnant, bitch, and you don't got nothing to worry about."

Jai said, "*Wow*...You're pregnant? Congratulations."

Queen said, "Bitch! You thought I had something. Your face turned red as fuck."

Jai said, "Well, you said medicine, shit. We have been fucking like rabbits, and you're laughing."

Queen said, "Okay, bitch! They gave me vitamins for the baby. Now you're acting like your sister with that corrective shit."

Jai said, "I don't act shit like my sister at all. I do have a reason to be concerned, damn."

Queen said, "Stop acting extra, girl. You're not tough!"

Jai rubbed her back to comfort her as she kept throwing up.

Jai said, "It's okay, girl, I got your tough ass. Can you make it home? If not, I can take you."

Queen said, "I feel dizzy and light-headed. I'll make it, but you can follow me. Thanks."

Jai said, "Drink this water. I'm taking you home. We can shop and come get your car later."

Queen said, "Why are you so nice to me?"

Jai said, "You're a human. Besides, you are my pretty baby."

Queen said, "Yeah right, bitch, you too. There you go with that baby shit!"

Jai said, "Oops! Do you mind me asking if it's Merch's baby?"

Queen said, "Yes, it's his! I don't fuck other men. I deal with you! Oops. Can it be yours, bitch?"

Jai said, "See, you're rude, Queen. I'm your bitch now?"

Queen said, "Thought you knew it was his? Y'all females come and go when it comes to me and Merch."

216

Jai said, "So...y'all do this all the time?"

Queen said, "Why? For the record, I didn't say shit funny. You're the first threesome. I'm talking about females in general. When I find out about them, he leaves them alone point-blank."

Jai said, "Pattern, I see! How do you know he leaves them alone? I'm not laughing at you. These men have a lot of control when they think they're running you."

Queen said, "Bitch, I don't know. His word is good enough for me. Don't make me whoop yo ass, Jai. What's the giggling for?"

Jai said, "Queen, please! I'm not worried about an ass whooping. You're making threats over a feeling somebody is probably giving to plenty of women, which is sad."

Queen said, "And, you are still chuckling...I don't see shit funny."

Jai said, "No harm intended. I saw my mom going through this as a child, and she still does to this day. I hate going around seeing her eyes healing from being blackened. I'm so tired of crying that I laugh to hide the frustration and pain I see women objecting themselves to..."

Queen said, "Damn! It's a story behind everyone's eyes. I wouldn't have thought you saw such a thing how you carry yourself. My parents ran away, but to see physical abuse to your mom is some mental shit. Sorry to hear that..."

Jai said, "I don't see how my sister stays there knowing that shit. Anyways, let's go."

*****

Jai sat and watched Queen wash up in the tub from head to toe. Jai rubbed her down with lotion and made some chicken noodle soup.

Queen tried to eat, but she was overwhelmed with all the decisions she's going to make knowing Merch would love to help. She felt awkward because she never had a woman pamper her like this, and Jai watched as she cried.

Jai said, "What's the matter, baby?"

Queen said, "Quit calling me that shit! You're not my mama."

Jai said, "Why keep everything to yourself? Let that shit go, Queen. For real."

Queen said, "Makes me feel good that people don't know my business."

Jai said, "Holding everything in makes you sick. It's okay to have friends to talk too. Do you trust anybody?"

Queen said, "*Yeah. I trust my got damn self.*"

Jai said, "Girl, you are something else. I see why you and my sister clash. Y'all both hold everything in and take it out on others."

Queen said, "That's funny! I'm nothing like her. Who do you trust?"

"Nobody," Jai replied as she laid her head next to Queen's boobs. She started caressing them with her tongue ring. When she clicked her nipple ring harder, it made a vibrating sensation, then Queen grabbed her long pretty hair and pushed her head between her legs.

When Merch walked in, he sat on the couch, and Queen didn't see him until she opened her eyes, jumping hard as hell, scaring Jai. "Somebody found their key," Queen whispered.

Jai said, "What's the matter?"

Merch said, "Did I miss anything? Come here, Queen?"

Jai said, "No. Just in time."

Queen said, "You can leave, Jai. Thank you for the soup."

Merch said, "She's not going anywhere."

Jai said, "No problem, Queen."

Merch said, "Hold on, Jai."

Queen said, "What I say? If you want her to stay, y'all both can leave. *Right now!*"

Queen walked over to Merch and stood in front of him and motioned for Jai to come over also. Both the ladies stood there naked. "You're saying this bitch name all comfortable in front of me. Now take her and get the fuck out," Queen shouted.

Queen went to grab at Merch, and he grabbed her hands before she could land a hit. He couldn't believe that she just tried him in front of Jai.

Jai said, "Let her go, Merch! Please."

Merch said, "Calm the fuck down, Q! It's not like that, baby girl."

Jai said, "She said leave and I'm leaving. Bye."

Queen said, "Hold on, Jai. I've been thinking about this situation we enjoy, and it's going to stop. You're enjoying this more than expected, so don't ever think you can get the dick while my eyes closed. Merch is mine. From now on, you only do what and when I say. If I find out you have his number, I will fuck you up. Do you hear me, bitch?"

Jai said, "I forgot, I'm your bitch, huh? I was having fun. Call me later, Q."

Queen said, "Merch? Do you want her or me?"

Merch said, "Jai…leave as she told you."

Jai said, "Don't you see me getting my shit? I'm gone."

Queen said, "Watch your tone, baby…"

As soon as she left, Queen rolled the flame up for her baby and made him a stiff drink. She sucked the tip of his thick dick while he blew his smoke and moaned.

Queen said, "Merch…do you have her number in your phone?"

Merch said, "No, Q. No, Q. Damn, Q. Don't start this shit with me."

Queen said, "I bet' not find out you fucking that bitch behind my back, period."

Merch said, "Why you keep stopping? She left. I'm done with that bitch, as you said."

Queen said, "I'm so serious, Merch! We're so done with that?"

Merch was moaning so loud, the whole neighborhood could hear him.

Merch said, "Fuck her! Where is this shit coming from, Q? Finish! Damn!"

Queen said, "I'm done sharing you with everybody. I'm not doing no more threesomes."

Merch said, "All this questioning shit needs to stop. Get on the bed, so I can fuck the shit out of you."

*****

Man 2 said, "I've been following these females for a while now. They're leading us to some big cash."

Man 1 said, "I thought we were getting his stuff back? If your ass wasn't so in love with her, we could have been got her stuck-up ass."

Rocky said, "It's not my fault the bitch didn't come. I told y'all to leave them alone. Long as they worked for me, they were my girls."

Man 1 said, "They became potentials when you sold the club."

Man 2 said, "I know they got cheese because I've followed them to their big safe."

Man 1 said, "Who is this bitch coming out?"

Man 2 said, "I saw her at the club the other night talking to Saria sexy ass."

Jill said, "That's the other girl they hook up with, and I followed her to a store.

Man 2 said, "We can take her and him. I've followed her all day. Ain't nobody else in there."

Rocky said, "This nigga just walked in the crib with his pistol on his side. He's going to bust soon as a motherfucker kick the door. We need to catch these motherfuckers alone."

Man 1 said, "Be stupid and get shot, the fuck if you want to. We should stay following Saria and dude punk ass."

Jill said, "They all got money. Take a pick."

Rocky said, "Bitch! Shut the fuck up! Speak when I ask you something."

Man 1 said, "Let's go! I'm not about to sit outside this bitch house the whole night while they're laid up."

Man 2 said, "I'm telling you. Hitting the houses is a mistake. That storage unit is where the big money is. They go twice a month. Queen goes in with a duffel bag and Saria with a silver briefcase. Sometimes they come out empty-handed like they made a drop."

Man 2 said, "I'm getting tired of talking about it. We know what we discussed, and that's it."

Rocky said, "Y'all fucking with the wrong ones. I could have been robbed they ass on a good night, but they were my girls."

Man 1 said, "Your girl's nigga's got yo shit? Right?"

*****

Queen went to the clinic that next morning and sat in the parking lot, deciding on what she should do. All she kept hearing over was Merch saying, "Fuck her," and she didn't believe none of that shit.

Coral said, "Baby! You can cry all you want, but you go in that building, he's gonna kill yo ass."

Queen said, "Who says I told him."

Coral said, "*You done lost yo got damn mind! Pull off, Queen! Now!*"

Queen said, "No! You're sounding disturbed? I'll be back."

Coral said, "If I had known you needed a ride from here, I wouldn't have come."

Queen said, "Quit yelling! You love me? Don't tell anybody, not even your bestie. I'll be right back!"

*****

Man 2 said, "We could write a book on this bitch."

Jill said, "If I'd known she was coming here, I wouldn't have called you. Damn!"

Man 2 said, "Why the fuck are you crying? It's not yours."

Jill said, "You heartless…Let's leave, please?"

Merch
Doing Me

Merch went to check on the hotel twice a week to see if the employees were keeping the company up to codes.

He made the reservation under a fake name, checking the room for cleanliness, called down with complaints to see how they handled them, and room service.

India loved meeting Merch at the hotel every chance she got. Free stays at a presidential suite, money, and a shopping spree made her answer every time he called.

Loving how he pleased her and his pay for complaining to the staff was more than she made modeling part-time and at the bank in a month where she met him a year ago.

Merch made sure India checked in under the fake name he reserved, with a checklist of things she needed to do, check-in and change her mind after the paperwork printed.

She'd ask about extending the stay to see if the staff was courteous after she changed her mind again. Call for more towels and clean sheets to see how long it takes for the team to arrive. Complain about the bathroom and hot tub being dirty.

India made sure she ordered a lot of food and champagne right before Merch came so that he could eat with her.

Merch sat in the Jacuzzi sipping champagne, flaming, and listening to music.

Merch said, "India? Come in here."

India said, "I'm coming, Merch."

India came in with a silver one-piece thong swimsuit on with a rose in her mouth, and her body was all glittery and shiny.

Her body was slim, with a little butt and small boobs to complement her frail body. She was five foot nine, which was taller than what he usually liked, and her face was so pretty, she didn't need any makeup. Her hair was long and curly, with highlights to match her skin color.

Merch said, "Hit the flame with your sexy ass."

India said, "Quit playing! You know I don't need any mind stimulators. Happy birthday, Merch."

Merch said, "Damn! You remembered?"

India handed him a box before jumping in the Jacuzzi with him, knowing damn well that wasn't going to make him stay with her the way she wanted.

She studied everything about him, too, his favorite color, cologne he wore, the food he ate, but he was just a business partner with a big dick that paid very well.

India said, "This is for you. I hope you like it."

Merch said, "I told you not to buy me anything, sweetie."

India said, "Much as you do for me, I don't mind."

Merch said, "You're the only female friend that's ever bought me anything. Everyone else always has their hands out."

India said, "Don't get me all mushy. You do a lot for me."

Merch opened the box, amazed that this young woman managed to buy him a Rolex on her budget. Queen never bought him shit or said, 'Happy birthday,' and he knew she could afford it.

Merch got out the Jacuzzi, picked her up, and carried her slim body over to the oversize king bed. Gently massaging her clitoris with his finger, sucking her nipples slowly at the same time, and watching her body squirm made him want her even more.

She looked at his chocolate body like it was a piece of candy before indulging his manhood into her mouth. She jumped on top of his body and rode his dick like she was competing for a first-place prize in the rodeo bull contest.

They lay on the bed finishing up their champagne, tasting foods, and discussing her experience with staff and her pay.

She always tried to keep the conversation long, because she hated seeing Merch get dressed, making his exit.

India said, "When will I see you again, Merch?"

Merch said, "You can always call me, India. Don't start feeling all rueful."

India said, "I need a huge favor?"

Merch said, "All depends on the favor. Get dressed, India, then meet me downstairs. I'm meeting someone."

India said, "I have an audition coming up next week. Hoping you can pull some strings to get me in this show. It's going to be one of the biggest shows of the year where all the upcoming designers and top modeling agencies come out."

She loved hearing him say her name, but Merch wasn't into her like that.

Merch said, "Give me the information, and I'll make sure everything goes through for my friend."

*****

Merch sat in the hotel lobby talking to Tee about security for an event he was having while waiting for India to come down, and his phone kept going off.

Tee said, "How many people does Cupid hold?"

Merch said, "With the new renovations the capacity changed, so you have to ask Ax."

Tee said, "I'll send you the information on the dates."

Merch said, "Hey, beautiful. Let me introduce you to my fam, Tee."

Tee said, "Hello, beautiful. How are you doing?"

India said, "Hello. I'm fine. And thank you. It's India."

Samaya, Teresa, Toonie, and Queen were hiding across the lobby where Merch couldn't see them standing behind the beam.

Teresa said, "This a whole new bitch. Did he kiss this bitch?"

Samaya said, "Auntie. Shhh."

Teresa said, "Shhh, my ass. We're getting more now. Fuck this!"

Queen said, "Fuck this shit! I'm done fucking his strong move-around dick."

Samaya said, "Grab her, Auntie!"

Toonie said, "I think y'all should grab her fanny pack."

Queen said, "He just lied to me that easy."

Teresa grabbed Queen, covering her mouth. Queen was sobbing at the point. This was a whole new bitch walking up to her man, hugging him.

Teresa said, "I'm going to let your mouth go. You bet' not say shit! Turn these got damn tears into dollars, got dammit. You hear me?"

Samaya said, "Do you want me to follow them?"

Toonie said, "Mom, let her mouth go so she can speak!"

Queen said, "Yes! I'm good."

Toonie said, "We're not going to be shooting at people, right?"

Teresa was pressing the gas trying to keep up with them, ignoring Toonie and watching Queen clean her face up. "Ain't this some shit! This nigga got you stressed," Teresa mumbled.

Samaya said, "Don't get so close."

Teresa said, "You scared? Go yo ass home for real, for real. He all up in this bitch ass. He's not paying us no mind."

Queen said, "*Ooooh*...He taking bitches to malls, out to eat, and shit. Okay! When they get out, pull up on his ass."

Samaya said, "Auntie G thang said *no*."

Teresa said, "I gotcha, I gotcha on this one. You can put that pipe up. I'm not going down over a bitch shaped like a lollipop."

Queen said, "Samaya, you said, 'I need to know what they look like.' This shit about to turn into a drive-by."

*****

After he finished up with India, he dropped her off at the hotel. Teresa waited for him to pull off before jumping out of the car. She ran through the lobby with a baseball cap pulled down.

Teresa said, "*Excuse me, miss. Excuse me.* Hey, girl. How are you doing? Is this a good hotel to stay? I'm here for a few weeks, and the ones I've looked at been messy."

India said, "Oh. Yes, it is. Very respectful staff, and clean."

Teresa said, "I'm sorry, girl. My name is Becky. I'm up here for a family reunion, so I barely know anything about here. You are cute."

Teresa was talking so damn fast, India didn't have time to say shit.

India said, "Thank you, I'm India. Nice meeting you, Becky. Have fun at your reunion."

When Teresa jumped back in the car, she told Queen her name, and they left.

Teresa said, "He spent a good thousand on Ms. India's new bag. Cheap bitch!"

Queen said, "This shit making my heart hurt."

Toonie said, "Make his pockets hurt."

Samaya said, "That's the smartest shit you've said tonight. Let's do this."

*****

Merch finally called Nyala back to see why she kept calling. He didn't call Queen back, because he was going to her when he finished with his running around.

Merch said, "What's up?"

Nyala said, "I got robbed. All my money, jewelry, and flame are gone. I didn't think to check my safe when I returned home the other night. The whole safe is gone. I don't know what to do, Merch."

Merch said, "This isn't Merch. You got the wrong number." *Click.*

Merch didn't play that shit. He wasn't about to incriminate himself, crying or not for nobody. He hung up the phone, went straight to her apartment, sat outside for a minute, and watched.

He didn't see himself anyone watching, no unfamiliar cars, so he finally got out of the car and went to her door.

Nyala said, "*Merch*...they took all my money, purses you bought me, my jewelry, and the flame. Why did you hang up on me?"

Merch said, "Stop it! Who the fuck are they? Quit crying! I'm here now."

Nyala said, "My roommate said the exterminators were here and some people handing out flyers earlier. Besides, we were both gone all evening, so I don't know when it happened."

Merch said, "I'm not about to go into who did what. Did you tell anyone you had it here?"

Nyala said, "No! I'm not stupid! My roommate doesn't even know."

Merch said, "Your lease ends at the end of the month, right? Pack a bag, go to my hotel until someone can come to help you move your things. I'll call the hotel and set everything up and I'll wait for you to pull off before I bounce."

Nyala said, "Thank you. If I tell my parents what happened, they'll make me transfer schools."

Merch said, "You are grown, right?"

As soon as Nyala pulled off, he went straight home to Queen, hoping she was okay.

*****

Merch walked into the room with candles lit, slow music playing loud, and the smell of food lingering in the air.

Queen had on some booty shorts that hid in her ass with a sports bra, knowing that was one of his favorite looks. He rolled his flame and went straight to the shower, not saying shit.

He sat at the table, and Queen brought him a plate then joined him. He was looking at her skin glow, trying to finish up his food before he handled her.

Queen said, "Is it good? You haven't said much since you've been here."

Merch said, "Sorry. I am just thinking about something. It's good. Not as good as your aunt's though."

Queen laughed because she knew her aunt Tamyra could throw down.

Queen said, "I like that watch. Here, I got this for you."

Merch said, "Thank you, Queen. This a nice bracelet. Damn!"

Queen said, "Happy birthday! I love you. Come see your other present."

Merch said, "Why are we going out here? Nooooo. Queen. You bought me a motorcycle?"

Queen said, "Yes. I never buy you anything. For this birthday, I wanted to go all out for my baby. One more surprise."

He just knew she was about to say "I'm pregnant," but she grabbed the bag off the shelf, and he had to make himself look surprised.

Merch said, "You got the leather jacket and gloves? You're trying to turn me into a rough rider now?"

Queen said, "My ruff rider, only…I've been selfish lately, thinking of myself. I want to thank you for everything you've done for my family and me."

Merch said, "Come here, bae! I'm all yours, but I'm about to rough you up with them little shorts on looking all plumptious and shit. Tell your crazy ass family to stay out of my business."

Queen said, "You must be talking about my TT? Her clients are running their mouth, so you know she's gonna come to you."

Merch said, "Really? I was talking about Samaya. She's running her mouth to my brother."

*****

That morning he noticed a lot of missed calls and texts from India. His phone kept ringing, so he silenced it until he got in the car. When he answered, all he heard was sobbing.

Merch said, "Slow down."

India said, "Merch…I got attacked last night. They took my purse, my bags, and made me strip down right in front of my house."

Merch said, "Quit crying. Did you see anybody?"

India said, "*No.* They rushed me from behind. The police said they couldn't do anything without a description, and they took everything."

Merch said, "Glad you're okay. Let me call you back."

*****

He rushed back in the house to see Queen before she left because he'd snap if someone tried her.

Merch said, "Queen? Queen? Make sure you take your pistol today and don't be scared to use it."

Queen chuckled because she's never been scared of shit, but he came back so fast that shit scared the shit out of her. She jumped so hard, she threw her phone down because she was about to tell Samaya he's on to them.

Queen said, "I will. You came back to tell me that? Good looking, baby. See you later. Love."

Merch said, "What the fuck is good looking? Don't say that shit to me anymore."

He watched her bend over, rubbing the lotion up and down her legs all slow, and that shit made him change his mind real quick.

Queen said, "See you later! Right?"

Merch said, "Where you going all buttered down wearing a sundress? You got panties on?"

Queen said, "Yes, I have panties on, silly. I'm meeting up with Tara, so I can get my hair done. Then we're going to the mall. Want to contribute?"

Merch said, "Come to the car. I left my money in there rushing last night."

Queen said, "I'm going to need some more flame too."

Merch went to the car and came back in real quick.

Merch said, "Buy something sexy! I hope you're saving all this money."

Queen said, "What made you say that? I am...See you later!"

*****

Rocky said, "*That's the one I saw with the flame and money. I can't stand that smart-mouth nigga!*"

Man 2 said, "We can hear you. No point in yelling. Damn!"

Man 1 said, "Was it his? I thought we were looking for your stuff?"

CHAPTER 13

The Club
Smoothly

Merch made sure Cupid had all his brothers, cousins, frat homeys, and uncles there for the graduation party. They had the whole club to themselves for the night with no outside distractions.

Didn't none of the guys invite their main chicks, because it was a family event? They all were flaming and drinking, waiting for Ishmael to arrive with his slow ass.

*****

Queen said, "*He just walked this unknown bitch into the club where I work.*"

Teresa said, "*I know it's hard, baby, but turn your feelings off right now. Let's go!*"

Queen said, "Hold on, TT. Now this bitch dropping clothes off. No wonder why he told me I'm not working tonight. Thought I was just gon' sit home."

Teresa said, "Fuck her! Let's make these drops and get paid. We're not fucking with Master Merch tonight. Besides, that's her twin…ain't it?"

Samaya said, "That is her. I'm trying to see which one it is. Jai didn't mention she was selling clothes here to me."

Teresa said, "Damn! You taxing hos, niece?"

Queen laughed, trying to hold her tears back, knowing her auntie would talk plenty of shit. Samaya knew her cousin's feelings for him was strong, and she needed answers for her on the strength of their bond.

Samaya said, "Hold on! I got this shit tonight. I'll be right back!"

Teresa said, "*Oh my gosh!* She's about to take too much time chasing up behind someone that is putting money in all our pockets saying the wrong shit. If you love him, you need to tell him before this shit gets too deep."

Queen said, "I didn't tell her to jump out of the car. I'm already deep in his pockets. How deeper can it be?"

*****

Ishmael walked in Cupid thinking he was dropping off some paperwork to Ax and saw a lot of his family. After the greetings and hugging most of the family, he went straight to the stage to see some ass.

Ishmael's eyes weren't caught by many, but this beauty had his attention as she walked to the back with some clothes in her arm, rushing by as if she was shy.

He followed her to the back, spilling his drink and handing his blunt to his cousin Tee. *She looks familiar,* Ishmael thought as he chased the woman with the oversize flannel and saggy jean shorts.

He waited patiently for her, but it took too long, so he walked in the dressing room, watching and waiting for her to collect the money from the dancers.

She noticed him walk in, but pretended as if she didn't see him standing in the doorway, waiting patiently.

The lady said, "Excuse me, sir. I'm trying to leave."

Ishmael said, "I take it you're not a dancer here? *Damn,* you're beautiful."

The lady said, "No. Sir, I'm just dropping clothes off. Thank you for the compliment. I need to get home. It's too late."

Ishmael said, "Don't run off! What's your name, beautiful?"

Lady said, "I don't want to give out my name with stalkers putting notes on my car. I...I...don't have time for this right now."

Ishmael said, "Whoa. Slow down, baby girl. I'm no damn stalker with notes."

The lady said, "Look at the time? I have to rush home now."

Ishmael said, "Time is cherished, not rushed. Wasting your time is not intended. Don't make up time issues when someone is trying to introduce themselves. Don't allow numbers to dictate your every move...Have a good night."

A dancer said, "Excuse me, handsome..."

The lady rolled her eyes at how the dancer brushed on him, so the lady started walking off. He handed her a business card before she could get away. She smiled kindly, not knowing what the hell he meant about numbers, but she took it anyway.

*****

Man 1 said, "She just went in with all the clothes and probably sold them."

Man 2 said, "I'm not robbing a bitch for petty change."

Man 1 said, "All money adds up."

*****

Queen took Samaya home and went her way. She let Samaya deal with the situation as she said.

Samaya rolled up some flame, grabbed her big bag out the back seat, then headed toward the big muscular bouncers.

They let her in with no problem thinking she still danced there, plus, she was fine as hell. She walked toward the back, and before she could get to the hallway by the dressing room, someone snatched her up from behind by her neck softly.

Isaiah said, "What are you doing here?"

She screamed loud until she saw Isaiah's face, slowly letting her grip off her pipe. When she stuck the pistol on her waist, she went to hit him in his chest. Before she could hit him again, he grabbed her by the face, and they began kissing passionately for at least three minutes, not caring who's seeing them.

He picked her up, and then she wrapped her legs around his waist. He pushed her back against the wall, and they stood there for a few more minutes. He whispered in her ear.

Isaiah said, "What I tell you?"

Samaya said, "I'm here to pick up Queen. What are you doing here, Sai?"

Isaiah said, "My brothers are having a private party tonight."

Samaya said, "Well, have fun. I'll see you later."

Isaiah couldn't stop looking at her pussy print in them tight jeans and her nipple print through her T-shirt.

When he put her down, he grabbed her hand and led her to the upstairs office. "You can release your pipe now, and Queen is not here," Isaiah said.

Samaya said, "Where are you taking me? We can't be up here, Sai. They're going to see us."

Isaiah said, "Hush, woman! We got the whole building to ourselves."

Samaya said, "Oh! You are trying to get it on up in here? Okay. Okay."

Isaiah said, "Whatever you want, Maya. Come here!"

He bit her nipples through the shirt while patting her pussy through the jeans, and she loved his shy boldness. They both got naked caressing each other's spot until they couldn't take it anymore.

Isaiah said, "Who's pussy is this?"

Samaya said, "Yours, Sai."

Isaiah said, "Don't let me see you in this building or area without me anymore unless I tell you to come. Do you hear me?"

Samaya said, "Okay, Sai. Okay. Okay."

Isaiah started rubbing her back from the bottom, making his way up to her neck. He kept stroking as he pulled her hip with his other hand and guided her to throw her ass back to his rhythm.

The more he squeezed her neck, she moaned in excitement, forgetting to text Queen on the scenery.

*****

Ishmael was thinking about that beautiful lady he just saw, trying to pay attention to this fat ass in his face twerking, while the family threw money.

*****

Man 2 said, "How the fuck did you know they were gon' be here?"

Jill said, "I just know, damn!"

Man 1 said, "Only person we haven't seen go in was Queen."

Jill said, "How long have y'all been following these girls? When it's obvious that the men have the money."

Man 1 said, "Quit asking shit! It's none of yo damn business."

Jill said, "Clearly, the men are the ones tipping. Meaning, they have the funds. Look at him!"

Man 2 said, "Shit! You saw that nigga go in with another bitch. How many he got?"

Jill said, "I don't know! But don't tell Rocky. I'm with y'all asses."

Man 2 said, "Bitch! Fuck him! Clearly, yo ass scary. Scary ass. Look, there they go!"

Jill said, "Whatever! I'm not scared, nigga. What nigga you know rob females?"

Man 2 said, "Bitch! Say that shit to Rocky, nigga."

Man 1 said, "Shut up! That's them, and we're getting their ass real soon."

*****

That next morning Merch met up with Isaiah, Ax, and Tee at Cupid. He made sure to call Swen as well since no one else was going to be there.

Isaiah said, "Baby, go to the bar and wait for me."

Samaya said, "Okay. What are you looking at?"

Merch said, "What's up, Saria?"

Samaya sighed hard as hell and walked off, swishing.

Ax said, "On club nights, we open the back portion of the building, then capacity will be five hundred. On dancing nights, we close it back up."

Tee said, "I need all these females working as waitresses the night of my event. They fine as hell."

Isaiah said, "What did the marshal say this morning?"

Ax said, "The dancers come with the territory, fam. The marshal already came through and cleared everything."

Merch said, "Were going to need more security for the nights you hold your events, so you'll be responsible for hiring or finding more staff."

Tee said, "Glad you mentioned that. I was thinking of starting my own security business."

Ax said, "We will keep our security as well and pay them all, so you don't have to worry about that."

Merch said, "With that said, I have the contract written up, and all we need is your signature, fam."

Isaiah said, "If you write up a business plan, bring it to us, fam. I'll look into it for you."

Tee said, "Thanks, fam. I'll get right on it."

Ax said, "You'll keep the door profit, bro, and we'll keep the bar?"

Tee said, "Yes, indeed."

Isaiah said, "Unc is here."

Swen walked in and waved at Merch, then stopped at the bar, trying to spit game at the bartender.

Merch said, "I'll be back. Let me holla at fam real quick."

Swen said, "What's up, nephew? This place is looking good. I might have a few vets that need to jiggle in this piece."

Merch said, "Unc, you a fool! Send them over, Unc, and we'll find something for them to do. Let's go to the back and handle this shit."

*****

Man 2 said, "Wake up, nigga! They back at this bitch again."

Man 1 said, "I'm sleepy as hell following these niggas. They don't stop moving."

Man 2 said, "We need to catch them on the move. That way, nobody will suspect shit when we hit that house."

Man 1 said, "Following Queen we know where everybody lives. Let us hit the storage unit, as you said."

*****

Swen handed the flame to Merch, then Ax, and Isaiah walked in.

Swen said, "Look at my nephews. Got damn, boy! Give me some of that basketball money? Unc needs to retire. Where my other nephews at?"

Isaiah said, "They're coming, Unc. Glad you're here. You know our moms handle all the basketball money."

Merch said, "We have that realtor money on the side, though."

Ax said, "Unc, looking good. We have a proposition for you."

When they told Swen about their plan to get him out of the game before Pops got home, he was all in.

Swen said, "I'm still bringing a few of my vets down here to show these young girls how to jiggle that ass. You hear me, nephew?"

Merch said, "We need a variety. Unc, you are crazy."

*****

Man 2 was trying hard to get his friend to join their plan, as he sat outside the club watching everything they were doing.

Man 2 said, "Just come the fuck up here. We're in the car."

The girl on the phone said, "I'll come up later for auditions or amateur night."

Man 2 said, "I need you right now."

The girl on the phone said, "I can't walk off my job, fool. I'll call you later."

Man 2 said, "I'm going to pay you. Damn!"

The girl on the phone said, "How much with yo crazy ass? And send me their info."

Man 2 said, "I got a band for you right now. I'll tell you in person. I'm not about to do this phone shit."

The girl on the phone said, "I'm on my way! If you don't have it when I get there, I'm leaving."

Man 1 said, "Hang up on her thirsty ass. Knowing damn well she doesn't have a job."

Man 2 said, "She's coming with her punk ass."

Jez
Exploring

The other night when she left Cupid, she sat in her car and noticed a flyer on her windshield. She grabbed the brochure, then threw it in the passenger seat, feeling ashamed and disgusted with herself for coming out of her shell.

She went back in the club looking for this fine-ass man, knowing this moment of courage was about to change her life.

For that same reason, she should have stayed in the damn car, and that shit played over and over in her head. Her body wanted him, and she couldn't control it.

She walked upon the man getting a lap dance, standing there as if she was reading his business card while trying to get his attention, and it worked. When he looked at her, she leaned over. "*My name is Jez*," she said.

Ishmael stood up and tipped the stripper then grabbed Jez's hand, and led her to a quieter area in the building. "Repeat your name, please," Ishmael asked.

Jez said, "Hi, Ishmael. My name is Jez. Sorrrrr—"

Before she could finish her sentence, he placed his finger over her lips softly, looking her straight in the eyes.

Ishmael said, "Nice to meet you, Jez. You don't have to be sorry, baby girl. Let me walk you to the door."

Jez said, "Thank you, Ish."

That little conversation played over and over again in her head. She couldn't believe she went looking for him. He was too handsome to pass up and let another female acquire him.

*****

The next morning, she pulled into her parents' garage, grabbing everything out her front seat and putting it in her bag. Before she could get halfway upstairs, she heard her mother's laughter in the kitchen.

John said, "Hello, Jez."

Jennifer said, "Jez? Have some lunch with us? We haven't seen you since yesterday."

Jez said, "*I'll be down when I freshen up.*"

She showered then went down to have a bite with her parents as usual and still thought of his smell.

John said, "Did you stay at your sister's house last night?"

Jez said, "Yes. Didn't feel like driving in the rain."

Jennifer said, "No phone call either? Huh. We were worried about you. Your sister didn't answer her phone, either."

Jez said, "Thanks for lunch. I'll be upstairs looking over my classes if you need me."

She wanted to have a life outside her parents' house like her sister, just not as wild to get away from the questioning.

She sat and rambled over the papers looking at his business card, thinking about calling. She went over her classes for her first trimester, but he was on her mind though, feeling as if she met her prince in his shining armor.

When she picked up the rest of her folders, a flyer dropped out. She picked up the brochures and threw in the trash, and noticed writing on the back.

You're going to be mines real soon, beautiful.

"*What the hell! Mom? Dad?*" Jez screamed, rushing downstairs, crying to her parents with all the notes left on her car. While she shoved the letters in her father's chest, he had to grab and hold her up.

Jez said, "I can't take it anymore. Does this bastard know where we live? This flyer was in my car after I left the strip club. I dropped some clothes off for Jai. I went straight to her house afterward."

Jennifer said, "*Oh, hell no! We're going to the police.*"

John said, "Honey. Why didn't you tell us when you got the first note? I'm sorry. Come here, dear. Don't cry."

Jennifer said, "Dropping off clothes for her where? That figures! Damn it, Jai!"

Jez couldn't stop crying for anything, but she saw the anger in her parents' faces, but she still wanted to move out.

Jennifer said, "*Do your sister know about this shit?*"

John said, "Jennifer, stop with the badgering. Does your sister know about this, dear?"

Jez said, "*Yes. Yes.* I told her, Mom."

John said, "We need to talk with her because this is serious."

Jez said, "It's not her fault. She told me to tell you. I refused."

Jennifer said, "Why the hell didn't you girls tell us?"

Jez said, "*I don't know who this is. I went to the police.* They said they'll call me when they get some leads, and that was two weeks ago."

Jennifer said, "I'm upset. What do they mean they'll call."

John said, "Let me take care of this. I'll make a few phone calls."

*****

As she dialed the numbers on the phone, her stomach balled up in a tight knot, feeling as if she had to throw up.

With all the notes and her parents getting on her nerves, calling him would be a breath of fresh air.

Ishmael said, "Hello…"

Jez said, "Hello. It's Jez. How are you?"

Ishmael said, "I'm good, baby girl. Glad you had time to call. What have you been up to?"

Jez said, "Yes, I have time…Going to school and work."

Ishmael said, "What's funny? What are you majoring in?"

Jez said, "I received my cosmetology license this month. When school starts back, I'm going for my master's in accounting. How long have you been a lawyer? You look very young?"

Ishmael said, "Cosmetologist, huh? Accounting is good. Well. I graduated high school at fifteen, went straight to college, and graduated law school this year."

Jennifer walked past Jez's room, noticing her on the phone smiling. Jez lay across her bed, all into the conversation, playing with her hair. *Acting like the notes didn't mean shit*, Jennifer thought, and it pissed her off.

Jez said, "You are smart? Nice…"

Ishmael said, "My father made sure of it. Accounting is not easy, baby girl."

Smiling from ear to ear, loving the way he called her baby girl. Her father was the only man that ever called her that.

Jennifer said, "Jez? Did you sign up for your classes? Who are you talking to? Is it the police again?"

Jez said, "*Mom*…when I get off the phone, I'll come to talk to you."

Ishmael said, "Do you want me to call you back?"

Jez said, "Well, my mom wants to use the phone."

Ishmael tried not to laugh at her innocence, but he's been waiting for someone like Jez for a long time. Beautiful, no street smarts, clueless, no cell phone, and probably used the school library for their computers.

Ishmael said, "The house phone?"

Jez said, "Yes…I'll call you back. Bye!"

Ishmael said, "Bye."

She was so excited that she just made a big step by calling. Her face frowned when she heard her noisy mom pick up the phone right before she hung up.

*****

When Tara pulled up, Jez ran straight out the front door and jumped in the car.

Tara said, "Hey, girl. Who are you running from?"

Jez said, "Hey. My mom was asking me all these questions. You ready for this last test?"

*****

Tara pulled up to the school to see a few walk-ins waiting for their free cut, standing outside, smoking.

A lot of people came on testing days because everything was free, and each student had a limit of three.

It was "first come, first served," "come to get some free" type shit. Some choose to tip, and some didn't have the audacity.

A few beauticians came in to check out the newbies to see whom they could hire, but Jez didn't like any of them.

Teacher said, "Hello. I'll have Ms. Jez take you, and Ms. Tara can slay you today. I'll come to check the cuts when they're finished."

Jez said, "Hello…my name is Jez. What kind of cut would you like today?"

Jill said, "Hi. My name is Susan. I would like it layered, starting at my shoulders. Thank you."

Tara said, "Hi, my name is Tara. How can I help you today?"

Kala said, "*Hello. They call me Princess.*"

Tara looked straight at Jez and held her laugh, and she sounded like Sunshine with the loud talking, but better looking.

Jill said, "Do you have any plans after school?"

Student 2 said, "You're talking to the wrong one."

Jez said, "I wouldn't be here if I didn't. You sure you want all this brought up to your shoulders?"

Jill said, "Wouldn't have said it if I didn't."

Student 1 said, "*Bam!* Straight comeback."

Jez said, "*Bam.* That's why y'all sidelining with no customer yet."

Tara said, "*Bam.* Straight checked!"

Tara glanced at Jez, hoping she didn't cut her with the scissors and walk off.

Jill said, "*Ouch.*"

Jez said, "Damn. I didn't mean to comb your scalp that hard. Sorry. Is it Susan?"

Jill said, "Yes! *Can someone else do my cut?*"

Teacher said, "What's the problem? Never mind, Student 1 will do you."

Student 1 said, "Come on, girl, I got you."

Kala said, "Tara? What're your plans after school."

Tara said, "Haven't thought about it yet. What do you do for a living? Why do they call you COE?"

When Jez chuckled, Kala rolled her eyes at her. "Tara, you're silly for that," Jez whispered softly so that the teacher couldn't hear her.

Kala said, "*I'm spoiled. My daddy has a lot of coiii, coinssss.*"

Tara said, "What made you come here if your daddy has a lot of money?"

Kala said, "My friend told me about you. You slayed her, girl."

The teacher talked to Jez and sent her the next person in line. The teacher stood between her, and Tara watched them for a few minutes, as she wrote on this piece of paper, then walked off with a smile.

Teacher said, "When you finish up, Jez, your mother is here waiting."

Jennifer walked over, smiling from ear to ear, feeling twenty years younger and free.

Jennifer said, "Hello, everyone."

Tara said, "Hi, Ms. Jennifer. You're as beautiful as always."

Jennifer said, "Hi, baby…Thanks."

All the ladies spoke, and Jez eyeballed Kala, hoping they didn't say shit or talk to her in front of her mom. Little did they know she would still politely check or ignore they ass.

Jez said, "H, Mom. Glad you could make it. I'll be done in fifteen minutes, Mom."

Kala said, "*I see you over there, Jez. You are slaying that.*"

Jez said, "Thank you, Coinless."

Tara chuckled loud as hell to piss her off. "It's Princess," Kala said. Out of nowhere, Jill jumped up, spazzing out and grabbing her hair.

Jill said, "*What the fuck is you doing? I said layered from the shoulders. You cutting my shit up too high. Fuck!*"

Student 1 said, "*Wait! I can fix it.*"

Jill said, "*Are you serious? Bitch, please.*"

Jez and Tara laughed until the teacher came running over with a confused look on her face, but she knew Student 1 was going to fuck her up. The teacher rushed over, trying to hide her smile, still trying to offer assistance, yet Jill even stormed off.

CHAPTER 14

Tara
Going as Planned

Tara and Jez interviewed all day for beauticians, receptionists willing to do light cleaning, and maintenance. They chose a vendor for hair products, and ordered more custom towels and business cards.

Tara went shopping for receipt books, stationery items, and finally paid for some radio time. Then she invited Jez for lunch at the bar and grill on the waterfront.

Tara spotted Princess walking up to the entrance and put the menu over her face so that she wouldn't see them. "Bitch! Don't turn around. Don't turn around. It's Princess loud ass," Tara said. "Damn...I just had to look. Fuck it! Here she comes," Jez muttered.

Kala said, "*Hey, ladies. How are you doing today?*"

Tara said, "Why are you so fucking loud? We can hear *you*. Damn!"

Jez spit her water out across the table, trying not to choke. She looked at Tara in disbelief, because she never heard her talk like that.

Kala said, "*Excuse me?*"

Tara said, "Naw, excuse you! I was trying to be helpful, but that loud shit is irritating as fuck. Go on somewhere with that shit."

Jez said, "That means kick rocks. Go now!"

Kala said, "How about I take this water and serve you..."

Kala picked up the glass of water and doused it in Tara's face, and before Jez could get up, Tara tackled Kala's ass onto the ground. The waitresses rushed over and tried to break them up, but Tara was swinging too fast.

Kala started pulling Tara's hair; then Tara lifted her body and kneed Kala in the stomach. Jez pulled Kala's hands loose from Tara's hair.

One of the waitresses pulled Kala, and Jez jumped in front of Tara. Tara reached over Jez's shoulders, grabbing Kala back toward her, and they were pulling each other's hair again.

The waitress tried to grab Tara, but she socked the waitress in the face, knocking her out her way. Jez jumped in front of the waitress. "Don't even try it, bitch," Jez said.

Tara struck Kala, and they rolled on the floor for a few minutes until management came.

Tara was swinging like a professional female boxer and knocked Kala on her ass again. All the staff had to break them up, and as soon as they put them all out, Kala ran back to her truck, immediately talking shit.

Kala said, "*Bitch...why didn't you come to help me? What the fuck.*"

Jill said, "They wouldn't have known we were together. Besides, it was a one-on-one anyway."

Kala said, "*What they got you riding with me for anyway?*"

Jill said, "Look! You jumped out the fucking car starting shit, and we were supposed to follow their ass...And what she wants?"

Knock. Knock.

Kala said, "*What the fuck you want?*"

Jill said, "Roll the window down, so you can hear her...Duh!"

The lady said, "You dropped your phone. Here you go! I'm sorry about that!"

Kala said, "She hit you too? I should go back over there and fight this bitch again."

The lady said, "My job description says we cannot fight customers, but she was out of pocket."

Jill said, "What's your name?"

The lady said, "Hey. My name is Rachel."

Jill said, "When do you get off?"

Rachel said, "I get off at four, but I work my second job today."

Jill said, "Let me get your number?"

Tara paid Jez for her services, and Jez sat there staring at her in a daze. Jez wanted to talk with Tara about what she saw because she'd never seen a woman fight like that, with structure and poise.

Jez said, "Thanks for my pay, girl. I can't believe this bitch grabbed that glass. Girl, you can fight, like, for real, for real."

Tara said, "Long as you help me, Skunk will pay for your services. Don't take it the wrong way. I love him, and he loves me. I know you hate people that use other people, but, Jez, when you're in a committed relationship or having relations with people, doing for each other is an act of appreciation."

Jez said, "I only think like that because I've never been in relations, period. I met somebody the other night. Seriously, how did you learn how to fight, though?"

Tara said, "I don't know! The anger made me do it."

Jez said, "You could be a boxer. Throw a little water at your ass...she activated."

Tara said, "Girl, please! Anyways. What's his name? How does he look? Where'd you meet him? Does he have money? Oops! I forgot you don't care about the money."

Jez looked at Tara, and they chuckled. "When did you start flaming?" Tara asked.

Jez said, "Ishmael. He's fine, skin tone looking like a piece of caramel, tall, and he smelt good."

Tara said, "So, you're gonna ignore the question. Let me hit that shit."

Tara didn't spoil it for her, but she knew who he was. Skunk was supposed to hook her up. Besides, she'd tell her sooner or later after Ishmael tamed her ass.

After, Tara left the shop, and she went straight home. She walked straight to the bathroom for a hot shower, feeling blessed for everything that has been given to her and everything that she earned.

*****

Kala said, "The bitch lied...This bitch got a shop, and they both were in that bitch together. I got something for this bitch."

Jill said, "Rachel called and gave me the bitch information off her ID card she dropped."

Kala said, "This bitch got money. If that's her man that walked in there, he fine as fuck."

Jill said, "I know exactly how to get you close up and with their ass. Can you dance?"

Kala said, "You mean strip? I'll make this muthafucka twerk for some cash and to get this bitch."

Jill said, "It's a done deal...Don't ever mention this shit to anyone, and this stays between us."

*****

Skunk walked in and saw Tara sleeping like a baby, so he climbed into bed, trying not to wake her.

He tried sleeping, but her phone kept vibrating, so he picked the phone up and noticed she had a lock on it. He put the phone under her pillow and went straight to sleep with her.

*****

Skunk loved waking up to Tara's warmth, which he always thought could be a little better. This morning, he couldn't keep his mind off the fact she put a lock on her phone.

Tara said, "Hmm...you like that, hubby?"

Skunk said, "Hell yeah, baby. Do you?"

Tara caressed his body, but in her mind, she kept seeing him grab that Chaste bitch's cheeks and prayed he wasn't sliding in that bitch that walked out the club.

Skunk said, "Damn, Tara...hmm, baby!"

I should have proposed a long time ago—a matter of fact. Who the fuck is teaching baby this shit, Skunk thought to himself as her head went up and down.

Skunk said, "Oh, shit...Got damn, baby girl!"

Tara pulled back and started caressing his body from top to bottom like a sucker from the got damn corner store. Skunk grabbed her head, holding on, looking like she had turned into a possessed horse.

Tara said, "This what you want? Like this, Daddy? Hmm, like this?"

Skunk said, "Do you, baby!"

*****

He lay in the bed, letting his baby do her, gripping her softly. When she exhaled a soft moan, he looked at her. "Why is there a PIN on your phone," Skunk said. When she lay facedown arching her ass up, he looked at her and went in, forgetting all about the notifications.

Skunk said, "Got damn, baby girl!"

Tara said, "Are you okay?

Tara was showering and didn't hear the doorbell. Marjorie handed Skunk some flowers that were just delivered.

Skunk said, "Who brought this here, Ms. Marjorie?"

Marjorie said, "The delivery man, sir. I didn't read the card."

Skunk said, *"What the fuck! My dearest...Love, my ass."*

My dearest Tara,

I enjoyed your time the other night. Let's meet again.

Love, Donald

He got dressed and sat on the bed, waiting for her to come out of the bathroom. When she saw the flowers, she was all excited.

Tara said, "Baby, you went and had flowers delivered? They're pretty. Maybe I should perform like that more often. Thank you."

He crumpled the card up and put it in his pocket. "I'm going to fuck Tara and him up," Skunk whispered to himself. "Zaddy, are you okay" Tara whispered in his ear.

Skunk said, "You're welcome! Anything for my baby. What are your plans for today?"

Tara said, "Why are you holding your pistol like that? Put that thing up. I'm going to the shop to catch up on some paperwork. What're your plans?"

Skunk said, "My dear, I enjoyed last night so much. I might come to help you today."

Tara said, "Oh, that'll be nice. You don't have to, because Jez will be there. But thanks."

Skunk said, "Well, let's meet up tonight, okay, love?"

Tara said, "Of course. Thanks for the flowers. I need to get dressed, so I'm not late meeting up with her."

Skunk said, "Lay down."

When she lay down, He devoured her body, watching her squirming like a caterpillar. *Whoever the fuck Donald was, he was gonna have sloppy seconds*, he kept thinking.

*****

Tara strutted into the shop late with all smiles from ear to ear, "Hello, everyone," shouting as she walked in, knowing her plan was working.

Jez was there early getting caught up on the books, meeting with the new employees, and had the three models finished up already.

Tara was so pleased with Jez, and she let her decide on what employees to keep. After everyone left, Tara locked up. She and Jez stayed arranging their work and putting everything in order.

Tara said, "Girl. I'm glad you went to the police, but I got a surprise for you."

Jez said, "My heart just jumped out of my body. It's shiny and heavy, but my parents would kill me if they saw me with this. What should I do with this? Where would I put it?"

Tara said, "It's okay! Breathe, girl! While the twelve looking for whoever leaving notes, this is going to be your new best friend. Jez, meet 9-millimeter. Nine, meet Jez."

Jez said, "Thank you so much, Tara. Seriously, I don't know how to use this thing."

Tara said, "Well, I'll take you to the gun range. Until then, take the safety off like this. Lift, aim, point it like this, and shoot. Let me show you how to put the clip in."

Jez said, "You mentioned something about relationships to me before. I've never been in any relations. So, where do I begin?"

Tara said, "OMG, Jez! You've never dated or fucked?"

Jez said, "No, nothing at all. My first phone call was yesterday. My mama was snooping around, picking up phones."

Tara said, "Nooo...Bitch, I know an Ishmael. Where'd you meet him?"

Jez said, "At the strip club by the airport. Before you say anything, I was dropping clothes off for my sister. He followed me to the back and gave me this business card."

Tara said, "I know him. That's Skunk's brother. Do you know who he is?"

Jez said, "A lawyer. Did you lock the back door? Let me call my sister before we leave. She can run her own business today. I need to move around."

Tara said, "Listen to you getting some wings, but I'll tell you later. Let's go shoot some shit."

When they pulled up to the range, Jez was shaking and looking all nervous, so Tara handed her the flame. Tara called Samaya to meet up with them. She was already in traffic, so she got dropped off to them.

*****

Kala said, "Aw...These bitches learning how to shoot and shit."

Jill said, "That's okay. All we're doing is following them."

Kala said, "Bitch, please! I'm upping my game."

Tara got out of the car, greeting Samaya with hugs and kisses. When Isaiah rolled his window down to speak, he didn't notice them watching him.

Rachel said, "I know that dude. He comes into the restaurant all the time."

Kala said, "He's looking good in that truck. Damn! Why Rocky fucking with them?"

Jill said, "I've seen him at Ishmael's house before. I believe that's one of his brothers."

Kala said, "I should follow his fine ass. His bitch cute though."

Rachel said, "His name is Isaiah. It's like four or five of them. They leave decent tips."

Kala said, "Where the rest of their ass at?"

Jill said, "I told you to come to the club for amateur night. They are in that bitch deep."

Rachel said, "He got a big dick. And don't ask me how I know."

Kala said, "We know how! How you get to see the muthafucka is the question?"

Jill said, "Bitch, you silly. The question is did you get paid?"

Rachel said, "Fuck yeah. Y'all laughing, but he paid well each time."

Kala turned around, looked her up and down real slow then shook her head. Jill tried not to laugh because she knew Kala was petty, trying to piss her off. "If she were smart, she'd use Rachel to get the information she could use," Jill thought. "I don't see it," Kala smirked, and turned back around in disgust.

Rachel said, "What? You're tripping."

Kala said, "Well...what the other ones look like?"

Jill said, "She had him. I had Ishmael. Then it's two left. Merch chocolate fine ass and Skunk sexy caramel ass."

Kala said, "What y'all got to do with me and how I move? I saw Skunk sexy ass already."

Rachel said, "She said 'y'all' like I care what or how you move. Remember, you asked me to roll with you."

*****

Samaya watched Jez try to shoot the gun. "She's getting on my nerves with all that jerking," Samaya shouted.

Samaya said, "Let me help you. First, relax and look at the target. Close one eye and focus on the red dot. Hold your arms up, and aim…Now think of the bitch leaving them notes on the windshield. Relax and squeeze."

Bang. Bang. Bang. Bang. Bang.

Tara said, "*Damn!* There you go. Keep doing that shit. Told you, sis got that touch."

*****

Tara went to the mall to grab some lingerie and perfume. After she grabbed a gift bag, she put everything in it and dropped it off at home.

Skunk
Decisions

Skunk went to the mall to pick up some jewelry, his suit, and some last-minute gifts for his family.

He watched the lady bending over in front of him, so he went to help her. "Excuse me, miss? Let me help you pick this up," Skunk said.

The lady said, "No, thank you. I'm okay."

Skunk said, "Miss, this is a lot of papers. I don't mind."

The lady said, "Thank you. I appreciate your help."

Skunk said, "You're welcome, and I see you're studying math here. What's your major?"

The lady said, "Excuse me? I'm Kala. Nice meeting you, and thanks again."

Skunk said, "I'm sorry, my name is Skunk. I see some homework here. Do you need some help?"

Kala said, "I'll manage unless you want to do it all."

Skunk said, "What are you doing in the mall with all your homework? You're supposed to be at a library, not shopping."

Kala said, "I like studying here. Besides, I'm looking for a part-time job to pay for school. No shopping for me."

Skunk said, "What type of work?"

Kala said, "I normally don't tell people, but I've been dancing for a quick buck or sales."

Skunk said, "I'll have my guy give you a call. He just opened a gentlemen's club. He might have something for you."

Kala said, "I met you, Skunk. Therefore, let's exchange numbers."

Skunk said, "You're right. Have a nice day, beautiful."

Kala said, "Thank you. Do I need to audition for you?"

Skunk said, "Straightforward, huh? I'll call you."

Kala said, "Forward as it comes. No point in going backward. Won't get me anywhere."

Skunk said, "You're right about that. I'll arrange it as soon as possible."

*****

Skunk went to his mother's house to discuss his graduation party and to meet up with his friend Terrence.

When he got there, his mothers were discussing and looking at properties in the gated community.

Skunk said, "Mothers. Terrence is here."

Marsha said, "Hello. How's the family?"

Jean said, "Hey, Terrence. How are you doing?"

Terrence said, "Hello, ladies. We've been well. How about you?"

Marsha said, "We're good, son. I hear business is well for you. Make sure to tell your family hi. We're going to look at this house. We'll see you later."

Skunk said, "Mom. Thanks for picking up my suit. Did you both get the dresses you wanted?"

Marsha said, "*Yes.* I hope you are not bringing that girl. What are you doing for your graduation besides the party?"

Terrence and Skunk chuckled, because telling your mother that you might be getting topped off was out of the question.

Jean said, "Yasss. I can't wait to see my babies all suited up and looking good. We found a nice house that's big enough for us. Ishmael and Merch on their way over."

Skunk said, "We kicked it the other night, did a little something at the new club."

Marsha said, "Well, Jean and I have something nice set up. Terrence, I'll see you there."

Terrence said, "I have a business meeting in Minneapolis, but I'll try, Ms. Marsha."

Skunk said, "Mom, I'm not bringing nobody. Long as I walk across the stage with my family there, I'm good. Why don't you like her?"

Marsha said, "Heard she take her clothes off for a living, son?"

Skunk said, "She used to, and that doesn't make her a bad person, Mom. See you later. Love you."

When Merch and Ishmael walked in Terrence shared the information he gathered for the females.

*****

Rocky was on the phone talking to the other men, as he sat and watched the brothers enter this big-ass house. He saw the man come in with a briefcase, but it was different from the one he saw Samaya carrying into the bank.

He was mad as fuck because he didn't know if they were switching shit from case to case, or gave his shit to the five O.

Rocky said, "Stay at his house until I tell you to make a move."

Man 1 said, "We're still following dude and ol' girl tonight."

Man 2 said, "Soon as they go back to the house, it's time. I'm not waiting anymore."

Rocky said, "Tell that motherfucker I said wait with his anxious ass."

When Rocky hung up, they immediately went into beast mode and went along with their plan.

Man 3 said, "You told me Rocky knew about this. I hope they got bread because I'm not going on a blank mission."

Man 2 said, "Man...all Rocky is worried about is a briefcase and box."

Man 1 said, "We've been following them for a minute now. And I got my friend following them."

Man 2 said, "He thinks we're at the club looking for his shit. That's a dead-end job."

*****

Terrence went over all his findings of the things they found in the club after they bought it.

Terrence said, "This is some disturbing shit. This man has been watching women for a while, raping, and selling them. I destroyed pictures and deleted videos because your brother and a few of his friends were handling business."

Merch chuckled, knowing damn well he was on them.

Merch said, "Thanks. I don't want to be on the five o'clock news."

Skunk said, "Thank you. What's the deal with all the guns? Sad part, he came back looking for the shit."

Ishmael said, "I would have come back for this shit."

Terrence said, "I have a friend downtown that told me they already have a case going but needed more solid evidence on the trafficking. I gave them a few guns and a few of the tapes that I had already looked over. I didn't tell them where I got it from, so they don't know anything about him selling the club until I informed them of it."

Ishmael said, "We need to hurry up and get this out of our possession. Shit is sickening."

Skunk said, "If they come looking, his ass might run."

Ishmael said, "We don't need the people coming to Cupid looking for him either."

Terrence said, "We don't want to give them all the information yet. I need to finish reviewing the rest. Let them make their case because we might need it in the long run."

Merch said, "What are we going to need it for?"

Terrence said, "In case Mr. Rocky comes back again. Trust the process. The people know he sold the club already."

*****

Skunk looked at his phone, noticing Kala had texted him already. He usually didn't like the pushy girls, but a change was something he needed. He got the club keys from his brother and met up with her there.

Skunk said, "What's up, Ms. Kala?"

Kala said, "There's nobody here. I feel special."

Skunk said, "The owners are attending a family function tonight, so I have a few hours before I have to go. Hold on, before you start. Let me see your ID?"

Kala said, "I'm old enough. Here, take a look."

Skunk said, "Let me see what you're working with."

Skunk finished at the club and headed home to check in on Tara before going to the party. When he opened the door, Marjorie was on her way out. "Good day, sir. A package came for Ms. Tara today," Marjorie said as she walked out.

Skunk said, "Hold on, Marjorie. Who brought this here?"

Marjorie said, "Don't open, Mr. Skunk. It's for Tara, sir."

Skunk said, "See you later! Thanks for your services today... *Here!*"

Marjorie said, "Thanks, Mr. Skunk!"

Marjorie said everything Tara said to say and nothing more. He opened the box then put the items on her bed and placed the perfume bottle on top of it. He ripped up Donald's love note. "He knows what perfume she likes," he whispered as he got up to leave.

*****

Skunk was standing with Merch and Ishmael sipping on some fine champagne, looking around at family, college students, and childhood friends. Everyone was waiting for Isaiah to show so they could all take a family picture.

Skunk smiled from ear to ear when he saw Adana's fine ass walking up with her sister Anema. He nudged Merch to look.

Skunk said, "*Damn!* She looks good as fuck with that white dress on."

Merch said, "Look at *Anema's* fine ass. I'm about to chop it up with her. Did you know Moms invited them?"

Skunk said, "*Hell no. Happy she did.*"

Merch said, "Anema grew up."

Skunk looked at his phone and sent Tara's ass straight to voice mail. "She can call Donald," Skunk said.

Merch said, "I see you're not on that marriage shit tonight."

Ishmael said, "Bro ass always late. How much you bet he comes in looking like a model?"

*****

Rocky got back in the car, looked at Jill, then slapped the fuck out of her. She reached for the door, and he grabbed her by the hair.

Rocky said, "What made y'all follow him to a motherfucking party? Who told y'all to follow the ladies? Them bitches didn't buy the club."

Jill said, "They told us you said to follow them and to look for a briefcase and box."

Rocky said, "*Who the fuck is they?*"

Kala said, "I was told the ladies would lead us to the men. We already know where the women stay, so we started following the men."

Rocky said, "What the fuck is she doing here? Who are you? How old are you?"

The lady said, "I'm Rachel. I gave them her information off her ID. What does my age has to do with anything? I'm grown."

Rocky said, "It's got a lot to do with it, and you in my shit."

Kala said, "Plus, she was fucking on Isaiah. Right?"

Rocky said, "You followed him around to see them partying? Stop all that fake crying shit, Jill."

Jill said, "Man 2 told me they were watching the other brother tonight. I don't see him here yet."

Kala said, "Actually, Skunk told me they were going to all be here."

Rocky said, "So, all you bitches just fucking and following them? Do you even know for what?"

Kala and Rachel jumped out his shit, but Jill had a stuck look on her face.

Rocky said, "They're not answering. Where the fuck he live?"

*****

Teresa tried to hand the flame to Queen, but she was too pissed at what she was seeing and pushed it away, but Tara grabbed it fast as hell.

Queen said, "I just bought this nigga a motorcycle, and he couldn't invite me to the party?"

Teresa chuckled hard as hell, choking off the flame.

Tara said, "I said get him something for his birthday, not a motorcycle. Damn!"

Teresa said, "You mean, he just bought himself a motorcycle? Take it back! Buying him shit isn't going to make his ass love you. Maybe appreciate you for a minute. From the looks of it, he ready to fuck on that girl. We haven't seen her yet, matter of fact. She wasn't the one walking in the club the other night either."

Queen said, "*Auntie, stop! Damn, I know.*"

Tara said, "I would get tested and leave him alone."

Teresa said, "What we need to be doing is making money and stop following this man like he a damn puppy on the loose. Another thang, stop fucking this nigga or make him use protection. I don't want you jumping in my shit all bumpy next week."

Queen said, "True. Let's go!"

Tara said, "Naw, fuck that, I see my fiancé having fun also. That's the same bitch from the club. If he's eating her ass like he did mines this morning, I see why the bitch all on him."

Queen said, "*Damn!* I saw Rocky over there. I didn't know they were that cool."

Teresa said, "*Way too much information!* If y'all fucking them raw, we need to make some protective shields and shit. They fucking bitches that look like tadpoles, da fuck!"

Queen said, "Auntie, stop! We're mad right now."

Teresa said, "Keep laughing. Gonna come y'all ass out in the sun, and start melting, and looking like you're in the larval stage."

Tara said, "What the fuck? Aw, he done blocked my number. This what he meant when he said, 'I want you busy and happy,' motherfucker wanted me to keep my eyes shut."

Teresa said, "Look it up. Look it up. Let's go, because I can't chase both y'all ass. And big as they are, they'll throw all our asses in the ocean."

*****

Marsha was all in Adana's face giggling then Skunk stepped to the side to check up on Isaiah.

Teresa convinced Tara to put her pistol back in her purse and pulled off.

Skunk said, "I'm going to call my bro. He should have been here by now."

Merch said, "He's with Samaya now. She's making him slower than what he already was."

CHAPTER 15

Isaiah
Trying the Real

As soon as he went to open the door to his ride, everything went dark.

Man 1 said, "Bitch, where the fuck is the money?"

Man 2 said, "I don't give a fuck about her crying. Shoot that bitch if she doesn't show you."

The girl said, "I don't know what you're talking about."

Man 2 said, "Where the fuck is the briefcase? Did you kill this nigga? Damn!"

Man 1 slapped her so hard, blood came out of her mouth, and her scream started waking Isaiah up. Isaiah tried figuring out what the fuck was going on, but the pain from his head made him realize quickly what was going on.

Everything was black when he opened his eyes. Noticing he couldn't move his hands or feet, he tried to stay still so they wouldn't see him moving. He kept holding his head to the side, trying to act as if he was knocked out. It was difficult trying to see through the mask, but the blood was rushing into his eyes. As the men got closer he tried to make the voices out but didn't recognize them.

Man 2 said, "Take this bitch upstairs while we look down here. Make her find that goddamn briefcase."

The girl said, "Stop pulling my hair. I don't know what you are talking about."

Man 1 said, "Fuck you, bitch!"

Man 1 was dragging her by the hair across the floor then up the stairs. When he made it to the bathroom, he pushed her onto the floor and jumped on top of her. He forced his way with her, gagging her mouth, so she couldn't cry out, letting the other men hear him.

At this moment, she knew all the shooting practice and her pistol being downstairs in her purse couldn't keep this crazy fucker from doing him.

As the girl was sobbing, Man 1 was enjoying every moment of taking something that wasn't granted permission.

Man 1 said, "Yeah. You think you all that, huh? You got some good, good. Now where the money at, bitch?"

Man 1 stood up and punched her in the face when she didn't respond. He fixed up his clothes and snatched her up by the hair, and dragged her down the hallway into a different room, checking for shit.

When he couldn't convince her to tell him shit, he went back downstairs with her peeping how Man 3 was looking at her beat-up face.

Man 2 said, "Wake up! Punk bitch-ass mothafucker. I told you not to hit the nigga that hard."

Man 3 said, "This nigga big as hell, and I'm not getting caught slipping. It's some expensive shit in here, though. What does this box have in it that I'm supposed to find?"

Man 2 said, "Fuck all that box shit. Find the money."

Isaiah still pretended to be knocked out. *Who the fuck is these bitches? And, how the fuck they know about me*, Isaiah thought. His mind went to wandering. *This bitch Samaya set me up*, knowing she was the only female that knew where his house was. He heard them say briefcase and box but didn't get what the fuck they were looking to find.

Man 3 said, "Fuck him. Wake his ass up so we can get the money, this mystery box, and get the fuck out of here."

Man 2 said, "Quit talking and go look for something of value. I'm not leaving empty-handed. This nigga was up there killing the bitch."

Man 1 said, "Bitch, where is the money? I saw you leave the bank with the briefcase, ho."

He punched her in the stomach, and the girl moaned in a soft cry, holding her stomach.

The girl said, "I don't know!"

Man 1 dragged her ass into the living room, tied her up, and she passed out. When he went to look in the closet by the front door, he noticed some mail on the table. He started going through it and opening it to make sure he was reading it right.

Man 2 took off Isaiah's mask and threw some cold water on his face. That's when it hit Man 2. He saw Isaiah playing basketball on TV, but he didn't say shit, because he knew they were in over their head. Now he knew Rocky was on some bullshit, because these aren't some street gangbangers like he portrayed them to be.

Man 2 said, "Wake up, nigga! I know this nigga got some money in this bitch."

Man 3 said, "I got all the jewelry, but I can't find a safe, and all this shit looks like a nigga shit. Thought they said this bitch had the bag. This some bullshit."

Man 1 said, "Look at this mail! His name on all of it. This his crib."

Man 2 said, "Let's get what the fuck we can and bounce, fam."

Man 1 said, "He's going to be a good boy and tell us where the money at, or I'm going to shoot his bitch in the face. Ain't you fool?"

Man 3 said, "Boy...you sound stupid. This nigga done went back sixty years and shit."

Man 1 said, "Fuck you, nigga. This house got some expensive shit in it. Should've brought a moving truck. Man 2, what the fuck are you laughing at?"

Man 2 said, "Only moving you're doing is moving that bitch back in here before she wakes up and try some shit."

Man 3 covered Isaiah's face again. He saw three men with masks on wearing all black, but the blood dripped into his eyes, clouding his vision. He saw one of the men drag Samaya into the kitchen looking helpless, covered in vomit and blood. He looked around, trying to see everything when Man 3 pulled the mask off again and punched him in the face with his gun.

Man 3 said, "Nigga...where the money? I don't have time for a box hunt. Where's the briefcase and shit!"

Man 1 said, "He passed out again, punk bitch! Quit hitting his ass so he can talk. I'm not trying to be here all night."

Man 2 said, "Let's find the money. Damn!"

Isaiah let his head lie to the side as he pretended to be passed out, watching the three men search his house, rambling around through his closets.

Man 1 read a bank statement and yelled out for the other men to hear, "The wrong house. Ain't shit here."

Isaiah saw their shadows in the living room, moving on the walls, so he tried to jump over to kick Samaya, but he was tied too tight to the damn chair.

Isaiah said, "Samaya...wake up."

After hearing the men talk, he knew she didn't have anything to do with this shit. They thought they were robbing her and looking for a damn box.

Isaiah heard a phone ringing when he realized it was his phone in his pocket. He told his phone, "Answer," so he started talking loud enough for them to hear.

Merch said, "Where you—"

Before he could finish saying anything, he heard Isaiah mumbling in a low tone.

Isaiah said, "Help, bro! Help! Hurry! They got us at the house."

He heard footsteps coming down the stairs, so he tried to hang his head back to the side. Man 3 walked back in the room where they were tied up and saw Isaiah's head moving slightly.

Man 1 said, "*Fuck! This motherfucker full of hundreds, nigga.*"

Man 1 looked at his phone and saw the missed calls and texts from Rocky. He sent Jill on a mission to follow the other brothers so they wouldn't know what they were doing. Hopefully, she followed the plan and didn't tell Rocky.

Man 2 said, "Don't let Man 3 see this. Fuck him! He got all the jewelry."

Man 1 said, "Fuck that gorilla-face muthafucka."

The men were chuckling about their discovery when they walked in on Man 3 pointing the gun at the girl's head, yelling.

They didn't say shit about the money they found in the briefcase. Man 1 set it by the front door closet and walked back into the kitchen with them. Man 3 dragged Samaya over to Isaiah, pulling her by the hair. He held her face up so he could see her in pain.

Man 3 said, "Where is the fucking money? Before I shoot this bitch."

Man 1 said, "This nigga done got a burst of whoop-ass energy."

Man 2 said, "Well, he needs to burst some info out they ass so that we can bounce."

Samaya said, "Please stop! Please leave us alone."

Man 2 said, "I never thought of you as the begging type. *Shut the fuck up!*"

Merch was driving fast, listening to this shit on speaker while the three men carried on with their plan.

Man 3 was too busy talking shit, and the other two men were too busy looking through the house.

Skunk said, "Hurry, bro, before these pussy-ass fuckers kill my brother."

Merch said, "That's my brother too! What the fuck is going on?"

Ishmael just sat there quiet as hell in the back seat, thinking in his head what he was about to do. He sat in the car, ready to squeeze, and let his pipe off any means necessary.

Merch said, "Bro, give them the money. Damn!"

Skunk said, "Y'all know bro don't keep money in his house."

Ishmael said, "Give them the money. Don't let them kill you over some petty money, bro."

*****

Isaiah knew his brothers were coming, so he tried stalling the bitch-ass fuckers.

Isaiah said, "Leave her alone. The safe is upstairs."

Man 3 said, "Come on, nigga? If you try anything, this bitch dead."

Man 1 wasn't trying to go because he had found enough, so he started passing the time, looking around for little shit.

*****

Skunk said, "Make sure y'all shoot before they do. No sympathy tonight."

Skunk looked through the front window, motioning to his brothers when to go in. He could see Samaya lying on the floor. Man 2 and 3 passed by the window, following Isaiah upstairs.

Merch said, "Look at these bitches! How many do you see?"

Skunk said, "I can't tell! Wait for my signal."

Skunk motioned to his brothers, holding up three fingers to let them know everything was clear to go in the front door. He had ran to the back door, which was closer to Man 1.

Skunk punched in the code for the back door. Man 1 heard the sound on the door alarm, so he headed to the back door. As soon as he opened the door, Skunk snatched his ass out the door. Before Man 1 could do anything, Skunk hit him over the head with his pistol a few times and pulled him back inside the house.

Ishmael and Merch came through the front door creeping. When Skunk was pulling Man 1 under the stairs, he motioned for them to move in. They went upstairs while he stood there watching dude and the entrances.

Isaiah led Man 3 to the safe inside his walk-in closet. He knew they were going to kill him after they got the money, so he started fidgeting around with the safe.

Man 3 stood at the entry of the closet door, and Man 2 was positioned at the bedroom door. Isaiah put in the wrong code again, and it made a beeping sound.

Man 3 said, "What's taking so long, nigga?"

As soon as the safe opened, Isaiah grabbed some of the money and gave it to Man 3. As soon as he turned his head, Isaiah put his pistol underneath his shirt on the side.

Before he handed Man 3 all the money, he had to think up something quick, because he didn't have space to run with them so close.

Isaiah said, "There's another safe in the other bedroom down the hall to the right with more money and jewels in it. It's behind the big picture."

Man 2 said, "I'll go check!"

Man 3 said, "Come on, nigga, you going too. Don't try any stupid shit. *Go!*"

Merch and Ishmael crept up the circle-shaped stairs. When Man 2 turned around and started talking to Man 3, Merch came up and went around the corner first.

Man 3 was pushing Isaiah out the closet, then Man 2 turned and walked down the hall. They walked right past Merch and went into the room.

Merch rushed behind Man 2 and hit him over the head hard as fuck, knocking him out cold. He pulled him out the way so Man 3 couldn't see him in the hallway.

Man 3 said, "*Man 2. What you find?*"

When Isaiah came out of the room, Man 3 was pushing him toward the stairs. Ishmael went and stood by the door, waiting for the other man to enter.

Man 3 said, "Man 2, where you at, nigga?"

As soon as Isaiah walked past the stairs, Man 3 was right behind him. Before Man 3 could even blink, Ishmael stepped right behind him. He didn't want him to see Man 2 on the floor, so Ishmael put the pistol up to his head.

Ishmael said, "*Motherfucker, drop it now! Before I blow your goddamn brains out. Bitch!*"

As soon as he dropped the pistol, Merch ran over and hit his ass over the head a few times, knocking him out, and then they carried them downstairs.

Isaiah said, "Bro, what the fuck? That was close as fuck."

They had two of the men lying in the hallway downstairs. When they went to get the other man Skunk knocked out, Merch saw his hand rising. *Bang, bang, bang, bang.*

Skunk said, "What the fuck, bro!"

Merch said, "He was raising his hand."

Bang, bang, bang, bang, bang.

Ishmael said, "*What the fuck!*"

When they ran into the hallway, Samaya was standing over their bodies, crying.

Merch said, "Get the gun from your girl, bro. Check to see if they have phones."

Ishmael said, "Where are their guns? We need to put them in these niggas' hands or something."

Skunk said, "Let's check their ass. Take the last five numbers they called and put the phones back in their pockets."

Isaiah went to grab the gun from Samaya, and she passed out right into his arms.

Merch said, "Who is these muthafuckas?"

Ishmael started taking the mask off Man 1. Right before he touched his mask, Man 1 went to grab at him. *Bang, bang, bang, bang.*

Ishmael
Nothing Matters

Ishmael said, "Why y'all looking at me? He went to moving and shit after I was putting the gun in his hand."

Isaiah said, "Shoot or be killed! Fuck him! Go get me some Q-tips and plastic baggies, bro."

They stood watching Isaiah swab their mouths like he was an agent, then put the Q-tips in a separate baggie like he took classes or something.

When he checked their pockets, they didn't have anything but a parking pass from the beach. Only one of them had a phone, and he checked it thoroughly.

Ishmael said, "What the fuck is that?"

Isaiah said, "We know where this is. Look at this shit! They have been following us."

Ishmael said, "Let me see! Take a picture, and put that shit back in his pocket."

Merch said, "Come on, bro, and let the fucking people do their job."

Ishmael said, "I need to know who they are. Do your thang, bro."

Isaiah said, "You know they are not going to tell us who they are, until they are ready."

Skunk said, "I've seen them before, but I can't remember from where."

Ishmael said, "Wake up, before we fuck you up, bitch."

Isaiah said, "Chill the fuck out! She didn't have anything to do with this."

They started shaking Samaya like a rag doll until Skunk told them to back off. She cried out, "Please stop," like it was her last breath.

Merch said, "*Fuck that!* Samaya, did you set my brother up?"

Skunk picked her up and carried her over to the couch, laying her next to Isaiah. He sat with his hands over his face in disbelief; this pussy shit happened to him.

Ishmael said, "Now, y'all want to appease her ass? Hurry up and lay her ass down, before them people get here."

Skunk said, "Bro, did this bitch have something to do with this shit?"

Ishmael held the pistol over her head, hearing the moans of pain she was in trying to say no, but before he pulled the trigger, Isaiah grabbed his hand. "No, bro," he said.

Isaiah said, "They thought it was her crib, bro. I heard their stupid asses talking about a briefcase and box."

Samaya started crying softly, pointing at the man on the floor. "I've seen him at the club, Sai," Samaya said.

Ishmael said, "Bro, I bet' not find out she had anything to do with this."

Merch said, "Now she done seen the mufuckers before. Come on! What a coincidence."

Isaiah went to get three clean glasses so he could get their fingerprints before the people arrived. He put them back in the cabinet until the shit died down.

Isaiah said, "Samaya, is this you?"

Skunk said, "They're sleeping now! Just tell the truth, Saria."

Samaya said, "I didn't have anything to do with this. I don't know them. *Da fuck!*"

Ishmael said, "You got some strength all of a sudden, I see."

Isaiah could see the tears run down Ishmael's face, and he prayed that Samaya didn't have anything to do with this shit.

Samaya and Isaiah went to the hospital. Ishmael stayed with the people while their lawyers talked to them.

*****

Rocky said, "Are you sure this the house? What the fuck is all these ambulance and pos here? Could you see who was on the stretchers?"

Jill said, "I really can't see that far in the dark. We followed Isaiah and Samaya here a few times."

Rocky said, "*Damn! That's the car over there. Did you know they were coming here?*"

Jill said, "*Oh my gosh!* They're carrying body bags out now."

Rocky said, "Why the fuck are you crying? You fucking one of them niggas? Fix yo shit. Why is it three bags? I need to know who's in them, right now."

Jill said, "You want me to go up there and see?"

Rocky said, "Hell naw, bitch! Fuck around and get us both locked the fuck up. I'm gone!"

*****

Ishmael's mind was speeding, and he couldn't control his thoughts of wanting to harm Samaya. Before the man lying on the floor could speak, he saw her facial expression, looking as if she didn't want him to say anything.

Ishmael said, "You're leaving with the rest of them, right?"

Detective Thomas said, "Yes. I'm sorry this happened to your family. Are you aware of who these men are?"

Ishmael said, "I'm going to find out, just like you. Have a good night, sir!"

Detective Thomas said, "Congratulations, young man. Again, I'm sorry!"

Ishmael said, "That's real, thanks! You don't have to be sorry. No mercy over here!"

*****

Ishmael went straight to the club, went upstairs, and locked himself in the office. He met Terrence on the way there so that he could grab the videos from him. He informed Ax on what had happened, and not to let anyone know he was there.

He sat up all night looking over their video surveillance, Rocky's videos, drinking, and flaming. The faces he even thought looked like them, all the men, plus the women that were coming and going, and the employees, he made sure he printed them all.

*****

Coral said, "I can't give out tenant's information, sir."

Ishmael said, "Look at the picture again. I know she stays here. Look, I'm here for her best intere—Mr. Coral!"

Coral said, "I really can't say anything, sir. What's this?"

Ishmael said, "Do you know her? Why are you tearing up? Take my card and let them know I stopped by."

*****

"Stop yelling, the fuck," Queen shouted. "He was here looking for you," Coral explained.

Queen said, "What the card say? Quit crying, damn! Samaya is okay. She's at the hospital, not seeing anyone."

Coral said, "He had both y'all pictures, and said something about contact him, for him to help y'all. Oh, Lort! They about to get my babies. *Hello. Hello. Hello.*"

Coral almost fainted when the man came back in the building. "Sorry, I forgot my phone on the counter. Good day," Ishmael said softly, as he walked off with a smirk on his face. *Lying ass*, Ishmael thought. He called his other phone and left it on the counter so he could hear everything Coral had said.

*****

Ishmael went back to his office and called Lia to meet him. He closed Cupid until he figured out what they wanted.

Ishmael said, "I need you to take these pictures and get back to me when you find out who they are."

Lia said, "Excuse me?"

Ishmael said, "Look! I know you are the police, but I haven't told my family yet. You are not investigating us. I knew before you stepped foot in my circle. Now, take these pictures and get back at me."

Lia said, "Wow! I met you the night I was doing an investigation on the previous owner. How'd you find out so fast?"

Ishmael said, "What do I look like, telling on my connects? I met my brother here that night you walked in. Listen, I don't care about that right now. Go do what I said."

Lia said, "I will, Ishmael, but I need him off the streets. I'm so sorry about your brother and that innocent lady."

Ishmael said, "Innocent until proven guilty, right? Get me what I need, and you'll have a promotion in no time."

Lia said, "Who else knows about who I am?"

Ishmael said, "Don't come at me with this who shit. Call me when you're outside with the info. Thanks."

Lia said, "That's part of my job. I was coming here for Rocky. That's it!"

Ishmael said, "I own it now, and you've known about him, and he's running loose now. What's your job description again?"

Lia said, "I'm sorry about your brother, again. I do believe Rocky had something to do with it. Please let me do my job because I don't want you mixed up in this nonsense."

Ishmael said, "The nonsense started when they tried my brother. Thanks for the information."

*****

Ishmael looked over the information that Lia dropped off and went over it, word for word. He had enough information to go on another mission.

*****

He sat there watching Rocky storm back and forth into the house with duffel bags and suitcases. When he saw the other men from the pictures, he felt like his mind left his body. "These mutha-fuckas know each other," Ishmael said out loud in anger to himself.

Bang, bang, bang, bang, bang. It continued to ring out.

Rocky said, "*Get down!*"

Bang, bang, bang, bang, bang. As the car pulled off, the man with Rocky stood up and started shooting back, but the car was long gone.

Rocky said, "What the fuck you shooting? The air?"

The man said, "Long as he heard the shots, he knows we're packing, too, nigga!"

*****

Ishmael arrived at the hospital. He already knew the questions were coming, and he wasn't going. "You good, bro? I was worried about you. Were you able to get my phone?" Isaiah said.

Ishmael said, "I'm good! Had to make a few runs before I came. They stitched you up, I see, and these females had something to do with this."

Isaiah said, "How? I heard them talking. They thought it was her house. She just that crazy to let them fuck her up?"

Ishmael said, "I went to talk with Queen, and she was hitting corners in a damn hospital. Rocky is behind this, I know it."

PART 4

Where Did They Come From

CHAPTER 16

Samaya
Why

Samaya didn't want anyone seeing her all fucked up while she was in the hospital. She felt guilty that one of her customers tried to rob and kill them.

Detective Phillips waited for the doctor to come so he could coach him on what to ask Samaya before he came in.

Detective Phillips said, "Doc? I need to know if some people got away? What made some locals go that far?"

Dr. Tucker said, "It's Dr. Tucker. This woman was raped and beaten. You think I'm about to ask all these questions, and I have to deliver bad news. Give the woman some time to recover. I heard the crooks are over at the morgue on Seventh. Go ask them some questions."

Detective Phillips said, "Can you at least ask her, does she know them?"

As soon as the doctor turned around from Phillips, Tamyra and Tara were right in his face. Queen sat off to the side with her phone glued to her face, waiting for Samaya to say something.

Tamyra said, "Dr. Tucker? Doctor! Can you please convince my daughter to let us in."

Tara said, "Is she okay? *Oh my gosh, Daddy.*"

Sammie said, "Come now! Baby girl, she's going to be fine. Your sister is a tough one."

Dr. Tucker said, "She's fine, shook up. Let me go talk to her. Maybe I can persuade her to see you."

Sammie said, "We're her parents. We should have rights."

Dr. Tucker said, "Long as the patient is in her right mind, we have to follow protocol."

When the door opened, Samaya tried to wipe her face so couldn't no one see her crying. She didn't want to be there, but the pain was excruciating.

Nurse Janice said, "Hello, Samaya. My name is Janice, and I'll be your nurse this evening. Dr. Tucker will be in shortly. He's speaking with your family. I'll get your vitals while we wait. Are you in any pain? Can I get you anything to drink?"

Samaya said, "Yes, I'm in pain. How's Isaiah doing, Nurse?"

"We can't discuss a patient's business with others. Between one and ten, what's the pain level?" Nurse Janice asked. "Ten," Samaya replied.

Samaya thought about calling the operator and realized she fell in love with a man without knowing his last name. She rolled over to cry and felt a tap on her shoulder.

Dr. Tucker said, "Hello Samaya. Samaya, I'm Dr. Tucker. We're going to take care of you. I need to talk to you. I have some bad news and good news. Sorry to tell you, we couldn't save the baby. You have a few rib fractures, a few stitches, and a minor concussion. We're going to keep you here for a while until you heal up. We got cultures from the rape kit, and we're handing it over to the police, so they'll be in shortly. Good news is you have a lot of family and friends waiting to see you."

Samaya rolled over crying, thinking, *What baby*. She didn't even know she was pregnant.

Samaya said, "I don't want to see them right now. Did you tell the father I was pregnant?"

Dr. Tucker said, "I can't discuss patient's business with others. You and your friend are lucky to be alive. I'll have your nurse get you some pain medication."

Samaya said, "I want you to tell."

As soon as Dr. Tucker opened the room door, he got confronted with a pen and pad. Tucker was used to all the people and family getting turned down, but that pushy-ass detective was still there.

Detective Phillips said, "Hello...Doctor, when you're done, I'd like to talk with Samaya?"

Dr. Tucker said, "I'm done. I'll be back, young lady. Detective, not too many questions. She needs rest."

Samaya said, "I don't want to answer any questions right now. Doctor, please make him leave with you!"

Detective Phillips said, "Can you please tell me what made them target you?"

Dr. Tucker said, "She needs her rest right now. We have the cultures back if you want to start with that? Detective Phillips...come with me please."

Detective Phillips said, "Samaya! I'll get on it and get back to you soon, and thank you for your time."

Dr. Tucker said, "Janice? Can you order some ointment, please? You can show her how to apply it as needed."

Nurse Janice said, "Okay, Mr. Tucker. Is there any other orders she needs right away."

Dr. Tucker said, "I'll wait until her blood work comes back. Thanks."

Dr. Tucker didn't get past the ICU station good before Tamyra jumped in front of him. "Hold on," she mumbled out in a cry.

Tamyra said, "See...you let that man look all in the room and ask questions. But I'm her mama, and I can't even see her? *How in da fuuuuuu—*"

Before she could finish her sentence, Sammie grabbed her mouth. "Shhh, baby. Let's go to the waiting room," Sammie said then walked off.

Sammie sat and watched his wife look at Queen as if she wanted to tear her apart. He wanted to know why Queen wasn't fucked up like his baby girl since they were rollies.

Sammie said, "Queen. What happened to my baby?"

Tamyra said, "Right! I thought y'all rolled together every day?"

Teresa said, "No, they didn't! Ignore them, Queen."

Queen said, "Hold the fuck up! Let me tell you something. Samaya has a life, besides being with me every day. I'm unaware of what's going on just like you are. I was with your sister. I think she was meeting up with Isaiah."

Tamyra said, "Did she say tell me something. Look, little girl. You might be my niece, but I will treat you like one of these females off the street. If you ever in yo life think you are checking me, you better ask yo mama who the fuck I am?"

Sammie said, "Baby. Baby. Baby. Chill, we're going to get to the bottom of this."

Queen said, "I'm sorry, Auntie. I'm just scared because I don't know what's going on. If I were with her, we'd both be in here, or they'd be dead for trying us. I'm sorry!"

Tamyra said, "Give me my purse back! I'm not about to do shit in a hospital. I'll accept your apology, but don't let your tongue loose on me again."

Sammie said, "Did she get involved with that stealing boy from years ago?"

Queen said, "I don't know! She was with Isaiah every day since they started dating."

Tamyra said, "And, you just gonna sit over there hiding behind yo sunglasses? Like you don't hear shit!"

Teresa said, "Whoa! See how you're letting your lips loose on me. I'm not Queen, sis, and Queen was with me all night. You know what? I don't have to explain myself to nobody."

Tamyra said, "You are running around with them like you're a kid, doing dumb shit. Now my daughter laid up, and all of a sudden don't nobody know shit."

Teresa said, "Remember my age, oh…I forgot! You can't even remember to pick up the phone to check on your daughters, let alone to see how they're doing."

Tamyra said, "Girl, your daughter doesn't even acknowledge your ass!"

Sammie said, "This is not the place for this, ladies. Please stop!"

Teresa said, "Naw! If she picks up the phone other than just for money, she'd know her daughter was falling in love. Now run that!"

Queen said, "*TT, Teresa, stop!*"

Tamyra said, "*Let me go, Sammie! Mama should have swallowed yo li'l evil ass!*"

Sammie said, "Y'all need to stop this nonsense. Ain't none of us perfect."

Teresa said, "Let her go! The truth hurts, doesn't it? You're only here to make sure your bills are going to continue to get paid. Huh?"

Sammie wouldn't let Tamyra go in her purse, but he let her go because Teresa said too much. As soon as Queen saw him let her auntie Tamyra go, she tried to jump in between them, but Teresa was ready.

Security had to come to break them up and made them wait in separate waiting areas.

*****

Nurse Janice said, "Here's your pain medication. Drink a little more water, please. If you need anything, let me know?"

Samaya said, "I want to talk to Isaiah."

Nurse Janice said, "He's doing okay, girl. You need to get better. You lost a lot of blood from losing the baby."

Samaya said, "I feel fine, though. I need to hear his voice."

Nurse Janice said, "If you talk to your family, they could go figure something out. I can lose my job by telling you about his business."

Samaya said, "I've never been a snitch, and we came here together. Hell, he was my baby daddy, lover, and my friend."

Nurse Janice said, "Throw this in the toilet after you read it. I'll be right back!"

As soon as Janice left, Samaya went to dial the number and hung the phone up.

*****

281

Nurse Janice said, "Please don't be mad at me, but I went upstairs and checked on Isaiah. I'm not his nurse, so I played it off like she was on break. I asked him how was he feeling just for you. He's beaten up pretty bad, but he should be able to play after a while."

Samaya said, "Why would I be mad? Thank you so much."

Nurse Janice said, "I don't understand people these days. I guess they did all this for his money, but raping you was something new to their record. I thought all famous people lived in gated communities or had security. You're all over the news, very sad."

Samaya said, "Where is the remote? How do you know he's famous?"

Nurse Janice said, "You are in love with a rookie basketball player, with the best contract ever, and you didn't know? That's good in several ways. You're not into sports, and you are not after his money. You missed the news, Samaya, and pay attention when it comes back on."

*****

Detective Phillips was waiting by the stairwell for Nurse Janice to come out.

Detective Phillips said, "What's the deal, Janice? I need to help this woman and her family."

Nurse Janice said, "If I help you, this better be for her and not a promotion. I heard something about you and your presence around this hospital."

Detective Phillips said, "What did she say? They can say what they want. I solve cases."

Nurse Janice said, "If Dr. Tucker finds out I'm talking with you, I'll get fired. Phillips, she doesn't even know who she dealing with, and I'll call you when I get more information. What do you need?"

Detective Phillips said, "If she knows Rocky's whereabouts? What made them target a basketball player? I know about the hood robberies, but this is way over their head. She worked for Rocky at his strip club, and he's been on the radar for a minute. Hopefully, he's not behind all this."

Nurse Janice said, "That's a lot of shit for a victim, even for me, Detective."

Detective Phillips said, "I'm trying to catch a local robber turned to rapist before he does this to someone else's family. If it was your daughter, what would you do?"

Nurse Janice said, "Go on, Detective, let me do my job, and you go do yours over at the morgue. When I find out something that you should know that will help her, I'll let you know."

*****

Samaya sat looking out the window sipping green tea when the nurse came in. She was sitting with her back toward the door, so she didn't see her come in. When the nurse spoke to her, the voice sounded familiar, and she jumped up so quick, you would have thought she saw a ghost.

Queen said, "What? I was getting in one way or the other."

Samaya said, "Queen, how'd you get in here? You dressed up like a fucking nurse? I guess you went and seen Evie, right? You're looking good all covered up."

Queen said, "What the fuck is wrong with you? I would never do you like this. Who did this to your face? Why are they fucking with you?"

Queen was panicking like she saw someone following her. "Why are you looking like you saw a ghost," Samaya said.

Queen said, "Why did they do this to you? I'm scared, Samaya. What should I do? I think they're after me. I swear Merch brother was following me."

Samaya said, "They are crazy! But why would they be messing with you?"

Queen said, "I don't know! I swear he said, 'Come here,' all strongly, so I kept walking. Bitch! I almost ran."

Samaya said, "They kept asking me for a briefcase, and they were looking for a box. They kept asking me for money like it was my house. The shit I went through, I wouldn't wish on anybody. You should leave, Kya."

Queen said, "You are using government names. That means you're scared. What the fuck is going on? Should I follow our plans for emergencies or what? Look at your face, baby. They fucked you up."

Samaya said, "Who's to say they're not more of these fuckers. What's up with Merch and his brothers? I know for a fact that one of the robbers used to tip me at the club that did this shit. I need you to go upstairs and give this note to Isaiah."

Queen said, "I'm scared, bitch! This shit might not work again. Everyone keeps asking me, 'Are you new here,' and shit. Matter of fact, let me take this shit off before these people arrest my punk ass."

Samaya said, "Isaiah didn't have nothing to do with this, so why would his family. If anything, they think we set this shit up."

Queen said, "Where this we, we shit coming from? Samaya, your mom and TT out there fighting. Then your dad mentioning Chad. I don't know what the fuck is going on."

Samaya said, "When don't they fight? Hell, they fought in the church at my mama's wedding and Toonie's graduation."

Queen said, "TT was saying some shit, though."

Samaya said, "I need my shit from his house."

*****

When she pulled up, they turned the headlights off and continued to flame for a few while they watched the house. Queen knew Teresa was high as hell because she kept looking behind them, and she barely blazed.

Queen said, "*Stop, TT!* Make sure ain't nobody up there moving around, da fuck. You are just pulling up all gangsta style and shit."

Teresa said, "Bitch, please! You need to stop acting all scared and shit. You are blowing my mothafucking high. They all at the hospital with him. Ain't nobody here with the yellow tape up. Now let's see how them niggas got in so that we can get her stuff."

Queen said, "They probably locked the doors after the people left. Wonder if it's all locked up? You think somebody in there? Auntie? What's the plan?"

Teresa said, "See, I just felt bad about calling you a bitch, but all these questions need to stop with yo scary ass."

Teresa chuckled, knowing damn well what to do.

Queen said, "What's funny? They laid all these people out. We're not exempt. If we got to bust windows and shit, I'm not going. Fuck that purse!"

Teresa said, "Keep this shit running. I'll be right back, scary ass. What the bag look like again, and where is it? Get in the driver's seat, and be ready."

Queen said, "What the fuck is that, TT?"

Teresa said, "Are you coming? If not, mind ya business."

Teresa ran to the back door. When she went to break the lock, she noticed the door was already propped open. She crept toward the stairs, went under the yellow tape, and heard some people walking around upstairs.

"The purse was on the side of the couch," Teresa kept repeating. When she saw the flashlight moving around on the walls, she ran toward the front door instead of the back and ran straight into a briefcase by the front closet, making noises. As soon as she heard the people coming down the stairs, she grabbed the case and ran to the car.

Teresa said, "*Go. Go. Go. Don't turn the lights on yet.*"

As soon as Queen came to light, she could see a few cars pull up at the stop sign a block behind her. The other car put there lights on and hit that right from the way they came from leaving his house, and she sped off.

Queen said, "What the fuck you do, TT?"

Teresa said, "Girl, it was some other people in there. I got her shit and dipped."

Queen said, "What the fuck is that?"

Teresa said, "I ran into it at the front door. When I opened the front door, a light started flashing on the alarm box. They about to get them niggas, or whoever killed who."

Queen said, "*Who about to get who? What niggas, TT? You just saying shit!*"

Teresa said, "Girl, I don't know! They didn't see me, and I saw shadows."

Queen said, "I'm about to drop you off and take this car back. I'm going to see Samaya later. TT, open it! Let's see what's in it, with yo paranoid ass."

Teresa said, "*Oh my gosh!* We hit a lick. We can't tell Samaya until she leaves the hospital."

Queen said, "Hopefully, it's not hers."

Teresa said, "I know for a fact that this is not my niece case..."

Queen said, "Them men were looking for a briefcase and a box, I heard."

Teresa said, "And...I heard they were looking for the yellow brick road. Da fuck!"

Queen said, "Bricks and roads can get broken..."

*****

Samaya wasn't feeling the hospital shower or clothes, so she had Queen get her something from her house and drop it off with her purse.

All she thought about was Isaiah and why he hadn't tried to contact her. When she finally watched the news, it seemed like they were the main story, and they damn near made the front page. They didn't say her name or show her face.

Nurse Janice said, "Queen is here to see you. Why don't you want to see anyone else? If you don't mind me asking."

Samaya said, "She can come in, and I don't have time for all the questions, crying, and for the people that weren't there from the beginning. I hope everyone left?"

Nurse Janice said, "This is your pain medication, and Dr. Tucker will be in shortly. Your family left, but why not let your mother see you? We only get one."

Samaya said, "Long story. How long have you liked Dr. Tucker? If you don't mind me asking."

Nurse Janice said, "Good question, but long story."

Samaya said, "I see you play too much. He is fine, though."

Nurse Janice said, "He wouldn't leave his main chick, so I stopped dealing with him. Good sex, though."

Samaya said, "Ms. Janice…it's good dick! Saying sex is corny."

Nurse Janice said, "I'll be corny then. That man is here again to ask you questions. I told him I'll see how you feel first. You can always talk to me if you feel more comfortable."

Samaya said, "I was raped, then beat up by someone I don't know, asking about a damn briefcase and box. I don't want no one knowing about this embarrassing shit."

Nurse Janice said, "We couldn't even tell your family what had happened. Let alone mention it outside the hospital walls. Your friend is doing well."

Samaya said, "Whatever! I don't even care anymore…He could have checked on me."

Nurse Janice said, "Well…he must care enough because he lawyered you up. I would ask him, but a girl needs her job!"

Samaya said, "I guess I could have done that myself, and why do I need a lawyer? I didn't do shit!"

When Dr. Tucker was walking up to Samaya's room, he noticed Detective Phillips pacing back and forth, looking anxious as hell. Before the doctor could even speak, Detective Phillips rushed to him quickly.

Detective Phillips said, "Doc? I need to speak with Samaya about what happened. Janice is in with her right now, but I'm in a hurry, so can you go ask her a few questions?"

Nurse Janice said, "Sorry, I was leaving. She's waiting for you, Dr. Tucker."

Dr. Tucker said, "Thanks. I'll let you know if she's ready to talk. Give me a few minutes."

Detective Phillips said, "Let her know we found out who the perps were. Maybe she'll talk then."

Dr. Tucker said, "I gave Samaya your number. When she's ready to talk, you'll receive a call from her lawyer. Please don't put your workload on us. Good day, Phillips."

Detective Phillips went straight to the stairwell when he met eyes with Janice, thinking she was about to follow him. Little did he know, Dr. Tucker told her to go to the desk and not talk with him about the patients.

He stood there looking dumbfounded when she went behind the desk, so he went to talk with Isaiah.

When he saw Isaiah's lawyer, he already knew what time it was. The lawyer stopped Detective Phillips immediately, then advised him that Samaya was his client as well, and any questions had to come through him.

Jai
Accepting It

Jai called the hospital every day, checking to see if Samaya wanted visitors. She had flowers delivered to Samaya every day she spent in the hospital.

My dear Samaya,

We're all here waiting for you.
Everything will be okay.
Please call me.

Jai and Jez

On the other hand, Jez was happy that her sister was around more, focused back on her and the business.

Kimberly said, "Sorry about your friend. I know she was your bestie."

Jai said, "Thanks, Kim. Oh, we have a customer."

Kimberly said, "Hello. How are you today, sir? Let me know if you need help with anything?"

Rocky said, "Which one is it?"

Kimberly said, "Excuse me, sir?"

Kala said, "Clearly he's not talking to yo dumb ass."

Jai said, "*What the fuck is going on?*"

Jez said, "Why the fuck are you in here? Bitch! I don't like you, period."

Kala said, "*Bitch! You ain't nobody.* I didn't know it was two of them. I know one of them was with her all the time."

Jai said, "*Leave now!*"

Rocky said, "*One of you hos going to tell me where them bitches live?*"

Jez said, "We must be something if your bitch ass is here trying to get information."

Kimberly said, "Obviously, we can't help you, so please leave."

Rocky said, "Shut up! With yo frog-looking ass, bitch. Which one you think it is?"

Jai said, "Kimberly, call the people! I don't have time for this."

Kimberly picked up the phone, and before she could dial a number, Rocky had his pistol right to her temple. She politely put the phone down, and Rocky snatched the cord out the wall. "Dumb ass," Rocky mumbled. "I should beat yo ass as Tara did," Jez said.

Kala walked up to some clothes on the shelf and pushed them on the floor. Before Kala could make it to the other rack, Jez ran over to her and snatched her up. Kala tried to square up and swing back, but Jez was too fast copying what Tara was doing. Jez was punching fast as hell, hitting Kala all in the head until Rocky snatched Jez by the hair and pulled her back. "Where Queen at, bitch?" Rocky shouted.

Before Jai could get to Jez, Rocky waved his pistol at her. "Step yo ass back," Rocky said with a weird grin on his face.

Kimberly tried breaking it up, but Kala knocked her in the nose so hard, she stumbled over some clothes and came back swinging.

Jez said, "Don't be using my sister shit for your nose. The fuck!"

Kala said, "*Fuck you! You banana-body-shape-ass bitch!*"

Rocky said, "*Shut up! Damn! I know you know where Saria and Queen live? Now, one of you double motherfuckers going to tell me where she lives?*"

Jai said, "They're my associates. We've hung out at the club a few times, but I've never been to their home. Now, please leave."

Rocky said, "Bitch! Quit lying!"

Jez said, "My sister don't fuck with them like that. They're some bums."

Rocky said, "Yeah, you bitches don't know who y'all fucking with, if you think they're some bums. Let's bounce, K."

Kala said, "Bitch! I'll see you again!"

Jez said, "Whatever, donkey!"

Kimberly said, "What type of gangsta shit was that?"

Jai said, "I'm going to get to the bottom of this. What has she got herself mixed up in?"

Jez said, "Told you to leave them alone, twin. *This shit is way too much!*"

Jai said, "Watch your tone, sis! I'll handle it."

Jai went straight to the hospital to talk with Samaya, but she still didn't want any visitors. Jai stood looking at her phone, waiting for a response from Samaya, but her calls kept going straight to voice mail.

Jez pressed the elevator button, and she could see a group of men approaching from behind her on the mirror door, talking loudly. When the door opened, they all got on together, continuing to speak loud in an angry tone, not caring about their presence.

When the doors closed, she went to press four, trying not to notice the guns they had under their shirts and jackets.

Jez said, "What floor would you like?"

Merch said, "What's up, Jai?"

Jai said, "Hello, Merch!"

By now all the guys were looking at their fine ass, especially Ishmael noticing Jez looking at him, but the way he was feeling right now, he felt numb to speak.

When the door opened, the men moved and let them exit the elevator first. Ishmael grazed Jez's hand softly when she passed him, but the questioning from Detective Phillips, his brother in the hospital was too much for him, and he couldn't talk to her.

Jai said, "Samaya still doesn't want any visitors so we can leave, sis. We need to get back to the shop and help Kimberly clean up."

Jez said, "I wouldn't want any visitors either. Especially if people like that are looking for her."

Jai said, "Mom wants you to call her. She's still nervous from all the notes."

Jez said, "We took all the notes to the people. We're waiting for fingerprints and video surveillance to come back. Tara gave me this for protection."

Jai said, "*What the hell? Put that back in your purse.*"

Jai noticed Queen walking fast in the hallway like she was in a hurry, so she tried to wave her down, but she dashed onto the elevator to quick.

*****

That next morning, she handled her business before going to the shop. She prayed that didn't anyone see her leave that building that she knew.

As soon as she jumped in the car, tears ran down her face like a waterfall. When she sat down, she started cramping immediately and popped some pills. Before she got out of the car to get some coffee, she dried her face.

Chuck said, "Hey, sweetheart. How's it going?"

Jai was in her own world, not hearing shit Chuck said, so she kept walking. When he stepped in front of her, she pushed him real hard. "Move out the way," she shouted.

Chuck said, "What's up with you?"

Jai gave him a half smile, not feeling or hearing shit he had to say. He placed his hand softly on her chin, lifting her head. She wanted to ask him, "What the fuck are you doing," but she held her composure.

Chuck said, "Baby? What's bothering you? I'm here if you need to talk. Come sit for a minute and relax."

Jai said, "I'm not feeling well right now. Let's do this another time, because the shop opens shortly, and my sis is waiting for me."

He noticed she was rambling on, so he grabbed her hand and led her to the table.

Before sitting, he hugged her tightly as he pushed her head softly into his chest. Jai looked up at Chuck, then pushed herself away. "I need to go get things done this morning," Jai said softly.

Chuck just stood there watching her walk off, knowing well he was just a fuck from the start when they hooked up. She made it known shit didn't change.

*****

When she walked in the shop, her sister and Kimberly were cleaning up the rest of the mess from Kala's punk ass.

Kala walked out of the shop, and pulled over a few racks of clothes, then knocked some sample fabrics off the counter. Jai wanted to rush her, but she knew if they had whopped her too severely, he would have used the gun.

Jai said, "Hello, ladies! I'll be in my office for a bit. Let me know when Daisy gets here. Thanks."

Jez said, "Good morning. Are you okay?"

Jai said, "The alarm company should be here to put the new lock on the door this morning. Thanks for cleaning this mess up. I like how you ladies switched everything up. I need to go to the back for a while…I'll be back out to help in a minute."

Jez said, "Slow down, sis, you're repeating shit! Hello, how are you this morning?"

Kimberly said, "Hey, Jai! Your mail is in your office, and your flowers are in the water."

Jai said, "I'm sorry! I need to make out these bonus checks for my helpful staff and order the new fabrics for my upcoming show."

Jez said, "Hey…that's what I'm talking about, handle your business, girl. Thanks for the coffee."

Kimberly said, "A bonus? I've never gotten a bonus before. *Okay!*"

Jez said, "Girl, please. My sister gives bonuses every week if you treat her right."

*****

She looked at the instructions again, but she had the gun shop put the bullets in the shotgun before she left their shop. They showed her how to use it, and she was about to make sure her staff knew as well.

Jez looked at her twin walking from the back, swinging the shotgun in her hand like she was about to raid some fucking body.

Kimberly said, "Whoa…they done let the damn crow out."

Jez said, "They let Ja'Quesha out! Looking like she's about to swing on some vines."

Jai said, "Both you ladies can join in the letting Quesha out. Let me show you how to use this. It's effortless."

Kimberly said, "Were you able to talk with Samaya? And that fat motherfucker better not come back, and that female was out of pocket."

Jai said, "Fuck them! Samaya is not seeing anyone, and Queen is not answering."

Kimberly said, "I feel so bad for her. I saw that shit on the news."

Jez said, "I can't wait to see that bitch Princess again. Tara already whipped her ass, and she got her hair done at the school on a free day."

Kimberly said, "Sounds to me like, she's playing his fat ass. She knows something."

Jai said, "We shouldn't go home until everything calms down. Let's stay at the hotel again. Oh, the alarm guy is here!"

Kimberly said, "Damn! He's fine as fuck."

Alarm man said, "Hello, ladies. I'm Danny. Is Jai available?"

Jai said, "Hello Danny. I'm Jai."

Kimberly and Jez said, "*Hello, Danny!*"

Danny said, "Let me look around, then see what we have here. It shouldn't take me more than two hours. If so, you'll get 10 percent off your bill."

Jai said, "We'll just finish up while you handle your business, and thank you."

Danny finished up with the alarm system. He showed them how to buzz people in, set the alarm when coming and going, and how to use the shotgun properly.

Danny said, "I put the camera monitor in the back office. Come let me show you, ladies, how to rewind, fast-forward, and all the good stuff."

*****

294

After everyone left for home, Jai sat around doing her books. She noticed that her clientele was climbing fast, and she'd need another building.

She could see the main entrance and lobby from the cameras. When she saw Danny's company truck had pulled up, she watched him walk up and ring the bell on the door.

He could see her walk from the back swishing like a runway model, and he was so ecstatic to see such beauty. Before she buzzed him in, she used the intercom system to show him that she knew how to use it.

Jai said, "How can I help you, Danny?"

Danny said, "I left my equipment behind the desk in your office. It's in a small red metal case. It has screwdrivers in it. I can wait outside until you come back."

Jai said, "Hold on! Your boss told me you were coming back."

He watched her ass as she walked to the back, wishing she'd sit on his face. As soon as she came back, he had to regain his composure.

Danny said, "Thank you for lunch earlier. Ms. Jai, that's my company. I'm my own boss. Thank you again for your business, and your generous tip. Here are a few business cards for customers if you don't mind."

Jai said, "Networking, I can do, and you're welcome."

Danny said, "I know this is out of the ordinary. Would you like to have a late drink or bite with me? I still have my work clothes on so that it wouldn't be anything fancy."

Jai said, "Sure, Danny. I'll follow you once I lock up."

CHAPTER 17

Queen
I'm Gone

Queen was soaking in the tub, crying as she thought about all the females Merch was messing with, hoping he was safe. *Glad my pussy checked out okay*, Queen thought.

Every time she thought about the situation with Samaya and Isaiah, she made sure her pistol was in hand's reach and the safety was off.

The music was on, the flame in the air as she packed three suitcases. One had money, and the other two had clothes.

Her trip to the doctor cleared her for a quick getaway from all the bullshit, so she finished organizing, locking up everything, including the windows, and turned the alarm on. She was trying to make her exit quick while watching her surroundings, praying hard that she didn't have to merk anyone.

When the garage door opened, the lights on the truck went off, and Queen pulled her pipe off her hip and proceeded to leave. Since it was down the street away, she pretended to pay it no mind.

*****

Rocky said, "There the bitch go! Go, run up on that bitch before the garage door close."

Kala said, "*And...say what? Where's his box of tools?*"

Rocky said, "I haven't told you shit about anything. Tell her, 'Rocky's looking for you,' and see what she says."

Queen saw a shadow approaching at a fast pace coming from where the truck was parked, and she let that thang go.

Bang, bang, bang, bang.

Kala said, "*What the fuck!*"

Bang, bang, bang, bang. Queen had the whole block whistling and didn't give a fuck if the neighbors heard or saw.

Kala started running back to the truck so fast in a panic, screaming. Before she could stop in time, she slid under the truck, scraping her legs. She yelled for Rocky to open the door, but he started reversing with her barely holding on.

Rocky said, "*Come on, bitch! Is she coming? Get in.*"

Kala said, "*Shoot back! Shoot...*"

Rocky started shooting in the air to slow her down. *Pop. Pop. Pop.* Then Queen stopped and stood her ground and finished her clip at their asses as they pulled off. *Bang. Bang. Bang. Bang.*

Rocky said, "This bitch done reloaded some shit. I'll find her ass."

Kala said, "I'm not going out like that with this chubby-booty bitch. She got it coming."

Rocky said, "She probably going back to the hospital. Chill out, and I'll handle this shit."

Kala said, "I'm just saying. Why the bitch so nervous?"

Rocky said, "Want me to take you back so that you can ask her?"

Kala said, "*Hold on! Mr. She's Coming, drop me off, Rocky!*"

Rocky said, "Yo punk ass ran! Just like I told them, y'all don't know who y'all fucking with now. Get out my shit!"

Kala said, "Fuck you! And I'm telling my daddy!"

Rocky said, "I don't give a fuck! Now get out..."

*****

Queen arrived at the hotel down the street from the airport, still deciding on which spot to go, so she texted Samaya.

They always talked about where they would meet up in case of an emergency or something awful happened.

Merch had texted her earlier asking what's up, which he never does, and he always just came through, so she ignored his ass.

She overheard him asking the nurse about Samaya which threw her off, so she stood to the side until he walked off. Then he left the hospital with a group of men that she hadn't seen before, so she didn't say anything.

She was worried because she hadn't talked to him after the incident with their family. Plus, Samaya said his brothers were asking too many questions, so she backed off.

*****

That morning Queen was on the move and watching her back at the same time, not trusting nobody because Ishmael had her nervous questioning Coral.

She went to the bank and made a deposit into her checking account, got a cashier's check, wired her granny some cash, and booked a flight.

*****

Queen finally touched down and checked into her room, so she made all the necessary calls for the house and cars to get sold. She didn't even think about going to Cupid for her belongings or having it sent to her, because nobody knew her real name.

Queen wasn't about to get caught up with questions or conversations, period, knowing she'd never snitch, but Samaya had too much money to go back to the hungry ways. She was hoping and praying her cousin wasn't up to her old ways again, trying to have this man robbed with Chad's punk ass.

Merch texted again, again, and again, which was weird because he's not the stalking type. *I should have ignored his ass a long time ago to get this much attention,* Queen thought. Then Ax texted to see if she was coming in to work. "This little punk motherfucker." So she changed her number. She called and gave it to Teresa, because she knew the necessary people would get it.

As the warm water hit her body, she turned the vibrator on, hoping it would release some tension. *I need a body with this shit,* Queen thought.

With all the shooting, crying, fighting, and having a baby wouldn't make him stay or love her, how she loved him. After watching Merch deal with all of them females, it hurt her deeply, but deep as she went into his pockets, she felt even.

*****

Merch tried several times to make the house key fit to realize that the lock was changed, which made him furious. He tried calling Queen several times, but he kept getting the operator.

The lady said, "Hello…how may I help you, young man?"

Merch turned and looked at the woman approaching with what seemed to be a couple to look at the house with confusion.

Merch said, "Well, I came to make sure all our mail was getting forwarded to the correct address. I must have missed the mailman."

The lady said, "Yes. Everything got moved out early this morning. You can always do the address change at the post office."

Merch said, "Thanks!"

Merch looked at his phone and hoped it was Queen calling back. He was so livid that he wasn't prepared for this shit, nor did he see it coming, and he was ready to find her ass.

Merch said, "What's up, bro? How are you feeling?"

Isaiah said, "I'm okay, bro. I am checking out this new pad in this gated community. I'm meeting up with Ishmael later. Are you coming out?"

Merch said, "I'm sliding through."

Merch
Issues

Merch made a few calls for India, dropped off a few packages to Nyala, then went to relax at his hotel. He reserved a suite on the top floor with the best view over the city and ocean for the whole week.

Merch invited Anema to his birthday party because everyone knew how his mother took a liking to her. He hated Anema when she left him after high school, after making plans on getting married, having children, and moving into their own home. When he met the streets, all the feelings vanished until she recently came home.

He wanted to relax before he celebrated his birthday this weekend, yet Merch underestimated Queen getting another realtor company to sell some shit he bought for her. What made him mad was he didn't even know her real name until she did this shit.

Not wanting to be bothered with no one until everything had settled down with his brother, then Queen pulling this shit off had him second-guessing all the females he trusted. He thought Queen was his main female he dealt with, and he trusted her more than anyone.

After he put the forwarding address in his search, he called the number and asked the lady for the exact address for their building.

The lady said, *"Hello, Yans Suites! How may I help you?"*

Merch said, "Hello. Quick question. Where are you located?"

The lady said, "We're right down the street from the airport."

Merch said, "My friend gave me this address to send them an invitation. Sorry, must be the wrong address. Thanks."

The lady said, "Yes…it's easier for travelers to get a PO box here than to travel downtown. We're open until five thirty if you need to stop by, or you can send it."

Merch said, "Thank you, miss."

Anema waited for the elevator door to open so she could see her only love that she left as a boy who matured to be one of the most handsome men she's ever met.

Her stomach tightened up as the door opened, then this handsome man stood there with his hand out.

When she placed her hand in his, her whole body felt the excitement, and it felt like her legs went limp. She allowed him to lead her to the balcony, just how she wanted him to walk her down the aisle for better or worse.

They sat next to the fireplace gazing at each other for a while, and he handed her sparkling water with lemon and poured himself some champagne.

Anema said, "I'm so sorry about your brother. Glad everyone is okay."

Merch said, "Thank you."

Anema said, "Thanks for the drink. I see you remember what I like?"

Merch said, "Always! My pleasure, Anema. I want to know everything. When are you done with school? Do you have any kids? Are you planning on coming back home?"

Anema said, "If you haven't heard it from my mom, then no."

They both chuckled, gazing into each other's eyes as the light from the fire glared across their faces, making the moment so romantic.

Anema said, "Just finished my third year of law school, no kids, and I'm coming home after I finish school. How's everything going for you?"

Merch said, "Move home, and finish school here!"

Anema said, "Heard you finished your business management course, a successful business partner with your brothers, no kids, or wife yet."

Merch said, "I'm doing swell, beautiful. Everything my mother told you is accurate. What spells do you have on my mom?"

Anema walked over to the balcony looking at the fantastic view. Merch placed his arms around her waist as they stared at the water for a few minutes before his manhood pressed against her butt. She turned around slowly to face him, smiling from ear to ear.

Anema said, "Merch. I'm still a vir... And what you keep chuckling for?"

Before she could get the whole word out her mouth, Merch grabbed her chin and kissed her for all the years she had left. He picked her up and carried her to the couch, then poured her some champagne. She was hesitant at first, but she sipped it, thinking about the verse "Love, honor, and obey."

Merch said, "Baby girl. I'd never rush you into something you didn't want to do."

Anema said, "Shut up, Merch! I've always loved you, and always will. Come here!"

When she said, "Shut up," then "Come here," his dick got hard as hell. He tried not to let her see, in case she got nervous. She jumped on top of his lap, looking him straight in the face, thinking, *For richer, for poorer.* When she felt his manhood, her body was reacting in a way she's never felt before, and she liked it.

They kissed for minutes, and he couldn't take it anymore and slid his hand under her dress and pushed her panties to the side. He started fingering her to the beat of the music, and as her moans started getting louder, he stroked faster, then he felt her insides tighten up.

She lifted enough to unzip his pants, then she lay back onto the couch, hoping to hear one day, "In sickness and in health." He stood up over her, looking at her beautiful innocent body, her wanting him in a way that he's never felt from anyone.

He knelt, kissed her navel, squeezing her nipple softly as her body squirm in a wanting motion. When he started sucking her nipple, she moaned out loud, holding his head. "More," she moaned softly.

She watched as this handsome chocolate man levitated over her body with warmth and comfort. He lifted her leg over his forearm, slid the tip of his manhood in slowly, and she screamed out in enjoyment of pain and pleasure.

Merch said, "You okay? We can wait!"

Anema said, "I'm okay. It's too late! Kiss me, Merch. Shhh!"

Merch said, "Damn, Anema!"

*****

Merch flamed while watching Anema dance around to the music as if she was a cheerleader with no rhythm, swinging her arms.

She made her way over to him, trying to get him up to dance with her, but he wouldn't budge. "Give me a minute, Nema," Merch said.

Anema said, "Get up and dance with me, Milan. Live a little. Quit being so tense all the time."

Merch said, "Nema? I don't know how to dance. Hit this!"

Anema said, "I don't smoke! It's not good for you, Milan."

Merch said, "It'll loosen you up because yo ass has no rhythm."

Anema said, "Did I have some rhythm when we were just sexing each other?"

Merch said, "Truthfully...no, you didn't, but the pussy bomb and tight as fuck."

Anema chuckled and snatched the flame out his hand. Before he could tell her how to hit it, she was choking and handing it back to him. When she downed the champagne, he knew she was going to be ready for round two.

Merch said, "Baby lungs! That's how you get the esophagus ready."

Anema said, "Ugh, nasty ass. What's funny?"

Merch said, "We got all night to train you how I like it. When you finish school, you can come back for your evaluation."

Anema said, "Training, huh? Evaluation to see if I can be one of your girls?"

Merch said, "Quit playing, baby lungs. I want nothing but the best for you, even if you are across the country. Here, hit this again."

Anema said, "My mother wants me to transfer to the university here, but all that packing, transferring, and living with her will be way too much. Milan, when I become your only baby, my esophagus will be all yours."

Merch said, "Who said I have a woman? I have friends. Remember you left me and moved to Minnesota. Anema, can't no one take your place. I'll get you a place."

Anema said, "Really, Milan? What about Queen? And don't lie."

Merch said, "What about the bitch? You would never have to question me about another female. Look, all my friends don't ever ask questions about relationships. They always want something for something, and always have they hands out."

Anema said, "What about that model chick? You seem to support her a lot."

Merch said, "Okay…you heard about her, and? I support all my friends following their dreams, or to make money. What's wrong with that, Anema?"

Anema said, "Nothing, I guess. I've always loved you. If I transfer, I'm going to stay focused on school. You said, 'Get you a place' What about you?"

Merch said, "What about me? I have a place, baby lung. Come yo pretty ass here!"

Anema said, "I want you to come also! Not saying we have to rush things…"

Merch said, "Let's give it some time before we move together."

She stood up and sat on his lap, kissing him before he could hit the flame again. When she leaned back, he hit the flame and blew the smoke in her face. They looked at each other for a few minutes, passing the flame back and forth. She was so high that all these feelings were taking over her mind and tongue.

Anema said, "Milan? I don't want to live like your mom. I'm sorry, oh, my gosh! I can't believe I just said that. I'm sorry, Milan."

Merch chuckled because he knew it was coming, but he always planned on being like his father. If that meant it would be without her, oh well.

Merch said, "Don't knock it until you try it. Back up some, and squat in front of me."

Anema said, "What the fuck, Milan! Take this. I'm too high."

Merch said, "Drink some of this, and get your mouth wet."

Anema said, "Yo ass nasty."

Merch said, "You're mines, right?"

Anema said, "Yes."

Merch said, "Grab it and kiss it like, yup…There you go! Then open your mouth. Hmmm, wait a minute. Go a little bit slower, Anema."

Anema said, "I can't, I don't know what I'm doing…Like this?"

Merch said, "Quit thinking so hard. Now close your eyes and think about a sucker or something…Just like that! Damn! No teeth, baby lungs. Let me show you a video or something."

He grabbed her head, wrapped his hands in her hair, and guided her to the rhythm he wanted. He gently pulled her up until she was sitting on top of him. She didn't have much rhythm, so he guided her hips, showing her how to ride.

Anema said, "I love you, Milan."

Merch said, "I love you too."

CHAPTER 18

The Club
The Digging Begins

Ishmael called one of his frat brothers to meet him at the club along with Skunk, Swen, Ax, and Tee.

Terrence walked in the club, noticing the changes since the last time he came through on his wild college days.

Ax and Tee stayed downstairs, evaluating how much they could profit after the renovations if their fam decided on selling.

Skunk and Terence walked upstairs to the primary office greeting Ishmael as he sat looking at the glasses in the plastic bags.

Terrence said, "What's up, Ishmael? Damn! My friend went pro on us."

Ishmael said, "I've been trying to catch up to you."

Terrence said, "I heard about what happened. I made sure they laid off the family with all the questions, but they won't release any information yet. Did you get any pictures of these fucks?"

The guys flamed and took shots while Ishmael told Terrence what happened that night of the robbery. Then Skunk finished the story after taking another shot of vodka as if he was the victim.

Ishmael handed the glasses with the fingerprints and the cotton swabs to Terrence along with some pictures and numbers from Isaiah's phone he took from the men.

Skunk said, "Their fingerprints are on them, and we need to know who, what, where, and why they came for my brother? I want to know who they were born to? Who sent them? Why they came? Where were they born, plus been?"

Terrence said, "Will do!"

Ishmael and Terrence chuckled because they knew Skunk was drunk and very serious.

Terrence said, "I already know the deal, fam. I'm going to handle this shit myself and get back to you. Meanwhile, it's some badass females downstairs. Let's go see the performance."

*****

Merch came looking for one of Queen's coworkers that she talked to, which was rare. He waited for Sunshine to exit the stage and met her in the back.

Sunshine said, "Hey, Merch? I've been trying to get a package from Queen for the last two days. Did she send it with you?"

Merch said, "Yes. She did! I forgot what you wanted? When's the last time you talked to her?"

Sunshine said, "Shit, I don't know! Let me get my bag so that I can go."

He knew that Queen was running from something, but disappearing while her favorite cousin was in the hospital didn't fit right with him.

*****

Merch watched the females dance for the amateur night, reminding him of Queen when she first started. He didn't like the advanced females because they wanted too much. He always wanted the amateurs, so he could train and teach them the way he pleased.

DJ introduced the last amateur for the night, and he noticed not too many regular customers were into her. Beautiful as she was, he gave an introduction that made everyone think she was a pro.

The amateur moved slowly to the music, trying not to pass out from being so nervous, but Merch and the other men noticed how she got loose after being on the stage for a few minutes.

Merch approached the stage and stood there to see what she'd do for the money he pulled out his pocket.

The amateur didn't know what to do with her body seeing all this money hit the stage. She dropped to all fours, making sure her ass was facing him and started moving it. She couldn't make that bitch twerk for shit, so she moved it like she was throwing it on the dick.

He was impressed with her motivation for the money and started making it rain with nothing but twenty-dollar bills. A few of the other men came and followed his lead as if they were trying to get her attention as well.

She did the splits like she's been doing this shit for years, trying to make her ass cheeks move up and down to the music. *I hope I can get the fuck up*, the amateur thought. They wouldn't move how she wanted, so she made her way to the pole and pulled herself up, and started bouncing as the money fell.

DJ already knew Merch was about to cuff her, seeing that he got Queen the same way, and that shit pissed him off.

Ax watched Merch, knowing his fam didn't throw money on shit he couldn't invest in, or profit off the street game. Ax knew his brothers didn't like it, but Merch has always been the hardheaded one, and he was right by his side.

DJ said, "That was Ms. K, gentlemen. Nice job!"

Ms. K picked up her money while giving Merch a quick eye contact before racing to the back with excitement.

She was in the dressing room, counting her money, when the manager came in and asked the amateur dancers which girls would like to join Cupid. Then she pulled Ms. K to the side and told her one of the bosses would like to meet her. *This bitch said it would work*, Ms. K thought.

Ms. K stood at five feet eight with the three-inch heels on; light pale skin tone; long thirty-inch blonde wig on, so you couldn't see her pretty sandy brown hair; dark brown dreamy eyes covered with cheap makeup; 36Ds sitting straight up and perky nipples; thirty-two-inch waist; and ass sitting high, complementing her thick thighs and hips.

Merch noticed Ms. K's cheap attire, hoping she was old enough to be in their establishment.

Jill said, "Boss…is this the young lady you were talking about?"

Merch said, "Yes! Thanks, Jill. Have a seat, Ms. K."

Ms. K sat next to Merch, hoping her stomach would stop bubbling from nervousness. She was hoping Queen didn't see her the other night to tell him anything. They followed her from her house and lost her at the airport hotel parking garage.

Merch said, "Hello, Ms. K! Are you old enough to be in here? I don't need no fake IDs getting my establishment fined or closed. If you plan on working here, I need some information from you."

Ms. K said, "My birthday was last month, and I'm twenty-one, boss. No fakeness over here. I'm not going to jeopardize myself, or the business, never been my forte."

Merch liked her jazziness, but she needed a makeover badly, and he knew just the person to help.

He motioned for her to get up and give him a lap dance. He wanted to see if she hesitated, or how fast she moved to demand.

He flamed, watching her rhythmless body dance to the music, so he tapped her. When she turned around to face him, she was rubbing her body slowly up and down.

Ms. K saw him trying to hand her the flame, so she turned back around fast. Before she could even blink, Merch stood up, grabbed her waist, turning her back around toward him.

Ms. K said, "Oh, shit! You're fine as fuck!"

She looked at this chocolate man standing at least six feet five, hovering over her, muscles popping through everything, juicy pussy-eating lips surrounded by a nice beard, and smelling like money. His whole outfit was crisp, plus, he was the boss, and that shit turned her on.

Merch said, "I'm here to make it better. I got you, K. Why are you here?"

Ms. K thought he knew about Rocky and Jill. When he said that, her heart dropped into her stomach. In her mind, her legs were running, but she stood there in shock. Her mind was racing fast, and she heard her mind say, *Run bitch*.

Merch said, "Are you okay? What made you want to dance?"

Ms. K said, "*Oh*...aw, shit! I need some quick money."

Merch said, "Did you graduate? How's your family going to feel about you being here? I don't want problems with your father, brothers, or uncles snatching you out my establishment."

Ms. K said, "I've been doing me for a long time. The only time they give a fuck is if it's benefiting they monkey asses. They don't know my business anyway."

Merch said, "Most women ask their immediate men in their family first. I don't want you coming down on the pole twerking, and your father right there. At least give them a heads-up, Ms. K."

Merch said, "I'm serious...We don't need cases in my establishment."

After hearing his deep voice, spit some shit she never understood, made her pussy jump, and some more shit. The inner bitch said, *Fuck it*. She hit the flame like a professional and took some shots.

Ms. K said, "I'll tell their asses!"

Jez
Stepping Outside the Box

Ishmael said, "Give me the address so that I can meet you there?"

As Ishmael walked in the door, he noticed her shyness, and he was amazed at her beauty and innocence.

Tara said, "Hello, Ishmael. What brings you here today?"

Ishmael said, "Her."

Jez smiled hard as hell when he handed her the box, not even knowing what was in it.

Tara said, "Shit! This who you met? Girl, welcome to the family."

Ishmael said, "Now you can call me off your phone. I'm gone, Tara."

Jez came running from around the desk and gave Ishmael a big hug. Tara leaned back, smiling, then Ishmael smirked at Jez's boldness.

Jez said, "Thank you, Ishmael."

Ishmael said, "No problem, baby girl. I'm gone, ladies."

Tara said, "Jez…you didn't tell me it was Skunk's brother bringing phones to you already. What else has he bought?"

Jez said, "I didn't know! Then they found the fucker that was leaving the notes. A got damn janitor that got fired from the gym."

Tara said, "The gym you left? Don't try to ignore me, bitch."

Jez said, "Yes. I'm not a bitch to kiss and tell, Tara.

Tara said, "That's why you called Ishmael? Why didn't you have a cell phone, bitch? I need to catch you up."

Jez said, "He wanted to know when they caught him. I don't need all this new technology. Who's going to call me anyway? Well, I'm going to check on my sister before it gets too late. Thanks for setting my phone up."

Tara said, "Girl, whatever! Give me the phone!"

*****

Jez left out and went to get in her car, and before she could get in her car, she was being snatched up.

Jez said, "*Stop pulling my fucken' hair, bitch.*"

Man 1 said, "Shut the fuck up! Where is that nigga going?"

Jez said, "*I don't know! Hellll!*"

Man 2 slapped the fuck out of her before she could call for help. Man 1 threw her ass in the trunk hard as hell, knocking her out, and took her phone before he closed the car trunk.

Man 1 said, "You mean to tell me we drove around with the bitch to bring her back here?"

Man 3 said, "He shouldn't have knocked the bitch out. How is she going to tell us where he lives if she's passed out?"

Man 1 said, "Get the bitch! Let's make an example out of these hos."

Man 2 said, "I saw her with the other bitch coming and going. I know she works here. Get your ass out this trunk, bitch. We're home."

Man 1 said, "Give me the code, bitch, before he snaps your fucken' neck."

She whispered some numbers out vaguely, as Man 2 held her up from falling by her throat.

Man 2 said, "Let's go! The bitch gave me the right code."

Man 3 snatched Jez from Man 2. "Show me where the money is, bitch?" Man 3 shouted.

Jez said, "I don't know."

Jez tried to yell out Tara's name, but Man 3 punched her so hard, she fell to the ground and passed out. "Damn, she's leaking, dude. What the fuck," Man 4 said in disappointment.

Man 1 and Man 2 started creeping upstairs to make sure Tara didn't hear anything.

Man 1 said, "That bitch up here, my nigga."

Tara said, "*Skunk? Jez? Who is that?*"

Man 2 said, "Bitch calling out Skunk. He's not here, whore."

Man 1 stood and listened to her speak on the phone, making sure it wasn't one time. When he heard her say, "Mom," he motioned for Man 2 to come up all the way.

Man 3 said, "Take that bitch to the back, Man 4! Do something than just standing there."

Jez said, "What do you want? Leave me alone, please."

Man 4 said, "Where the money at, bitch?"

Jez said, "I don't have any money."

Man 3 said, "Call that nigga before we kill you, bitch."

Man 4 said, "Where the money you made today, bitch?"

Man 3 said, "Let's go upstairs with them, dude. The other bitch upstairs."

Man 4 said, "Be careful, nigga, these bitches be at the gun range."

Man 3 said, "I can hear the bitch."

CHAPTER 19

Tara
Damn

Jez had Tara's appointments set for the whole week, so she's been busy trying not to stress about her sister, hoping she comes around and let the family visit her.

After work, Tara stayed in her office looking over her books and checking her phone constantly for a text or call from Samaya or Skunk. She understood why Samaya didn't want to see anyone or talk, but Skunk has just been MIA for the last few weeks.

Tara answered the phone for her mother, hoping she got some news from Samaya as she told her everything because she knew her mom wasn't going to let up.

Tara said, "Mom, everything is going as planned. I told Jez to leave. She done came back."

Tamyra said, "Yeah, she needs a break if she did all that for you, and she works with her sister."

Tara said, "They found the person who was harassing her. Then Rocky went to her sister shop, acting a fool."

Tamyra said, "Told Samaya that man was crazy. How are you? Did you hear from your sister yet? Has anybody called you? What do you think happened? I don't know why she hasn't called me?"

Tara had to cut her mother off because she wouldn't stop with all the questions.

Tara said, "You know why she doesn't want to see anyone. Face probably all messed up, and from what the doctor said, she's confused."

Tamyra said, "I'm her mother. It shouldn't be that way."

Tara said, "Give her some time to rest. She'll come around to call."

Tamyra said, "I'm happy for you, then this happened to your sister. All these mixed feelings are driving me crazy. I can't take this right now."

Tara said, "Mom, I know it's hard, but I'll come over when I am finished here."

Tamyra said, "Your father is here for me, so I'll be all right. We're on our way back to the hospital. I heard you called Skunk's name. Tell him hi."

Tara said, "He hasn't come up. It could be Jez!"

Tamyra said, "Well, when is the big date?"

Tara said, "Mom, Jez left you a spot open on every Tuesday."

Tamyra said, "What color did you guys choose?"

Tara said, "Mom, we didn't do anything yet!"

Man 2 stood at the top stair waiting to rush her, as soon as she hung the phone up. When Man 3 made the stairs crack, Man1 knew they had to go.

Tara said, "Hold on, Mom. I think that's Skunk or Jez. Excuse me? Who the fuck are you? How did you get in my shop?"

Man 4 said, "Shut the fuck up, bitch! Where is the money?"

Man 4 pressed the gun into her forehead hard as hell, snatched the phone from her, then hung it up. Man 3 searched the other empty rooms, making sure no one else was there.

Man 4 said, "Give me that motherfucken' phone, *bitch*."

Man 3 said, "Did you get the bitch phone? Not trying to fuck up as them dudes did."

Man 4 said, "I already took it from her and hung up on who-ever she was talking to."

Man 3 grabbed her by the hair, slung her to the ground, kicked her in the back, then her ribs, until she cried out. Before Man 4 could hit her with the pistol, Man 2 slapped his gun to the side. "What the fuck, nigga," Man 2 shouted.

Tara said, "Stop. Stop. Please, stop! What do you want?"

Man 3 said, "Shut up! You know what we want?"

Man 2 said, "This bitch was on the phone. Let's get the fuck out of here now. I'll be back, *bitch*!"

Sammie and Tamyra jumped in their car with a 9-millimeter on their hips, ready to blow any bitch in their way, driving fast as hell. She had already called 911, then tried calling Skunk several times with no answer. When Skunk's voice mail came on, Tamyra went crazy.

*****

Tamyra said, "*Skunk. Skunk. Skunk. They got my baby!*"

Sammie said, "Keep calling, Tam!"

Tamyra said, "*Skunk…they at the shop holding my baby hostage.*"

Sammie said, "Did he answer? Call him again!"

Tamyra said, "*Help…Help…Skunk…Please pick up!*"

Skunk went to turn his phone off, but Tamyra had left three voice mails back-to-back, so he checked them. When he listened to the first one, he couldn't believe what he heard. He ran out the door calling Merch.

Skunk told him what he heard on the voice mail and told him to round up and meet him at the shop.

Merch told the other brothers to meet them at the shop. Then the homeys he was already driving around with had them thangs, so he called a few homeys that were ready to ride through.

*****

Tamyra said, "*No, no, no…*not my baby!"

The people were pushing Tamyra away so the EMTs could do their job as they put Tara in the ambulance. Skunk and Merch pulled up at the same time.

Skunk jumped out the car, running over to the ambulance, noticing that Terrence was handling his business while they tried to hold Sammie and Tamyra back.

Skunk said, "Is she okay, sir? Please let me know if she's okay?"

Police 1 said, "She's okay, son."

Merch said, "He's not your fucking son."

Police 1 said, "Calm your nerves, young man. *Let me get everyone to move back, please.*"

Merch said, "Well, calm your nerves with that son shit."

Skunk said, "Come on, bro. Come on. Let these people do their job."

Skunk already knew what the deal was, and somebody fucking with these females was trying to fuck with them. He followed them to the hospital so he could talk with Tara and get her side before the people came.

Skunk left the password for the backup camera that he had installed in Tara's office closet. Isaiah, Merch, and Terrence waited for the cops to leave so that they could look at the footage for themselves.

Terrence gathered much information as he could before the commotion died down, and the ambulance pulled off.

*****

Kala said, "Them some stupid muthafuckas. They didn't get no money, so what's the fucking point of this shit?"

Rocky said, "They running out like they hit a lick. Dumb shit!"

Kala said, "Which one of them did that shit? Ain't nobody getting away with murder."

Rocky said, "I know it's one of them. Go run up and ask them, like you did Queen."

Kala said, "Fuck you! You didn't get out the car either. Scary ass!"

Rocky said, "Which one haven't you fucked yet is the question. Whoever fucking Samaya did it!"

Kala said, "Wow. Don't believe everything Jill tells your old ass. *Look, that's him! The one with the tight suit.* They called the whole fucking family to this bitch!"

Jill said, "First of all! Don't speak on what I said."

Rocky said, "Why the fuck you yelling? How the fuck would Jill know anything?"

Kala said, "Anyways, I've seen them together before. Matter of fact, at the gun range."

Rocky said, "So, who threw the money on you?"

Kala said, "Motherfucker, please! I hope you are not being funny, because I got something for not hurting anyone, but my fucking self-pride."

Rocky said, "Bitch! Jill said you liked it. Dirty ass!"

Kala said, "*Nasty? What are we looking for again? Seriously, mothafucker! What are they looking for, Mr. Rocky? Huh? Nasty who?*"

Jill said, "Please stop!"

Rocky said, "Lil girl, if yo daddy wasn't the plug."

Kala said, "You don't know shit about me...Now take me to my car!"

Rocky said, "Bitch, you can get out!"

*****

When the detectives took the drives out of the security system DVR, Terrence didn't care because they were looking over the backup system before they left the parking lot.

They saw everything from the outside until they came in the building creeping. They yelled at the monitor for Tara to turn around, like she could hear them.

The other homeys stood ground downstairs, ready to shoot anything that came through the fucken' door, and some stood outside surrounding the building.

Skunk
Problems

Skunk and his brothers had an apartment that nobody knew of, so he went there to get away from everyone. He kept ignoring Tara's phone calls and texts, then this shit happens.

He was at the point he questioned about marrying her, especially if her family had something to do with this fluky shit, and now he second-guessed everything.

Somebody tried to rob his brother and fiancée, which made him want to know who was behind the madness. He hoped that Samaya and Queen weren't into something and it backfired on them.

Not knowing who had done it made his nerves bad. He was taking shot after shot, and flaming back-to-back had his mind wandering, rewinding the video over and over.

*****

Sammie just sat there with his head in Tara's hand, as she lay there helpless. Skunk bent over behind him and whispered in his ear.

Skunk said, "Pops, I'm going to get the mothafucker who did this to our baby."

She was thinking about asking Tara if her sister knew them bastards, or if she saw them before. He didn't want to interfere with Terrence's investigation or bother her while she was in the hospital. There was too much family there for her to be honest about her sister or her feelings.

They had to give Tamyra sedation to calm her down because she had a panic attack.

When Skunk saw the rest of her family coming, he left because he heard them asking too many questions.

As he pulled off, he thought Samaya jumped in a cab but didn't pay it any mind because he was high as hell.

Skunk went to park on the side of the shop, making sure nobody couldn't see him strapping up when he got out of his car. Before he made it to the door, he heard a moan and cry, which made him grab the goons from the shop.

Skunk said, "*Somebody in the back dying. I heard a cry out.*"

Goon 1 said, "I've been standing here the whole time. I ain't heard nothing."

One goon stood at the front door, another at rear, while two of them surrounded the dumpster. One of the goons opened the top of the dumpster slowly, and the other goon aimed the gun in the dumpster.

Goon 1 said, "*What the fuck! Nigga…it's a zombie!*"

"You play all day, dude," Skunk said, as he called for his brothers to come downstairs to see who they pulled out the dumpster.

Terrence said, "I told y'all they didn't take her."

Isaiah said, "What the fuck is going on? Where the fuck she come from?"

Merch said, "Who did this to you?"

Ishmael said, "Where did they grab you? Do you know them, *Jez?*"

Skunk said, "I thought they took her somewhere when they dragged her out."

Terrence said, "One of your homeys can take her to the hospital. This some crazy shit!"

"They made me give them the code to the door," Jez said vaguely. "We saw everything. It's okay!" Ishmael replied in concern.

Skunk said, "She's been working with Tara. Now they got her mixed up in this shit."

Terrence said, "I see they're following everybody now."

Ishmael said, "Jez. Who did this to you? Did you see their face, baby?"

Jez said, "They grabbed me from behind, and they took the phone you gave me."

Terrence said, "Can we get a location on it, Ishmael?"

Ishmael said, "Indeed, T! Baby, before you go, can you remember anything they said that would help us? Did you see them?"

Jez said, "They kept asking for money. They kept saying, 'Where he at?' so, I didn't say anything."

None of them knew Ishmael was talking with Jez, so when he said "baby," they all looked at each other. Then she said "phone" had them perplexed. *Why didn't Ishmael say something in the elevator that day*, Skunk thought.

Merch looked confused because he never knew Jai had a twin sister, or paid attention the few times they hooked up. Jez favored Jai that day in the elevator, but the way she dressed, you wouldn't know unless you stared hard. Jai carried herself more freely, and that made her look different from Jez's purity in how she carried herself.

Merch never had a conversation about anything with Jai, just strictly sex. Listening to Ishmael say Jez's name let him know they had relations. He didn't want everyone knowing he was smashing Jai, so he stayed quiet.

Merch said, "Something ain't right!"

Ishmael said, "Let me carry her to the car. Where is your sister?"

Jez said, "Call my mom! Please…"

Terrence said, "It's okay, baby girl. We're going to get you some help."

Isaiah said, "Ishmael, let Terrence find out who the fuck is sending these dudes."

Skunk said, "I see that look also…"

Ishmael said, "If they're looking for me, I'll find them."

Merch said, "I need to see this tape again. One of you can take her to the hospital, please. Goon can stay guard at the front door?"

Goon 2 said, "*We got it, fam!*"

*****

Kala said, "You seeing all this shit?"

Rocky said, "I'm sitting right here with yo ass. I don't give a fuck about none of them niggas or bitches. I need my shit and whoever pulled the trigger? Fuck them!"

Kala said, "Never knew they had something of yours. What they got again?"

Rocky said, "What's not known is not to be understood. Bighead ass!"

Jill said, "I'm ready to go! If the people find out we're behind all this, we're so fucked!"

Rocky said, "You can't go to jail for following people. Dumb ass!"

Kala said, "Why did we come back here? I said drop me off, not pick up Jill and come back. Do you see all them goons? They're ready to kill somebody!"

Jill said, "*Girl! Stop with all the questions. Damn!*"

Rocky said, "When did you start talking out of line? Shut up!"

Kala said, "*Look! You're the one that told me about a damn briefcase and guns! Da fuck.*"

Rocky said, "She doesn't know shit her damn self! Inform me, Jill?"

Jill said, "Nothing at all…"

Rocky pulled off and immediately dropped Kala off, and Jill tried to jump out of the car with her. Rocky snatched her by the hair, pulling her back in the car. "Stop, Rocky!" Jill shouted out in fear.

Kala pulled her hand out of her purse, and she sprayed Mace right in Rocky's eyes. She grabbed Jill by the arm and helped her out. They both ran away watching him squirm and trying to unbuckle himself, screaming.

Kala said, "Run, bitch! Get in."

Jill said, "Oh my gosh, girl! He's going to kill me!"

Kala said, "He has to catch us first…Fuck him!"

Jill said, "That's easy for you to say. You don't live with him. I've never seen anyone stand up to him."

Kala said, "Bitch, please! He's human just like us…We all bleed the same, and his fat ass isn't exempt. Da fuck he thought this was?"

Jill said, "No, girl! He's going to kill me. I'm so scared! Then you told him what I said."

Kala said, "Not if you kill him first! All that scary shit can make a plan come up. You're coming with me."

Jill said, "Where we going? I don't have time for this."

Kala said, "Yes, I told him, because he's a liar. I'm going to tell you what to say and who to talk to. I have a plan, chill out! Or, go back to fatty and die."

Jill said, "This is not funny."

*****

They went back to when Tara first came on that day so they could see everything. They watched the video over, and over, trying to see anything they could use, and even body language.

They saw the car shadow but couldn't make the model. They saw how they jumped Jez and threw her in the trunk and dumpster after watching it over.

Ishmael said, "I need to see them...They're out of pocket..."

Terrence said, "Hold on. Turn the volume up? I need to hear everything they say, so I can piece it back together with what she said."

Skunk said, "*Damn!* They have been following everybody."

They heard everything but couldn't see who was saying it because the masks were covering their entire faces. The men kept rewinding one part over and listening to one of the masked men say, "Don't fuck up like them punks did," and that confirmed they were all affiliated.

Isaiah said, "That means the same organization sent them?"

Skunk said, "What did you find out, Terrence?"

Terrence said, "All my leads led me back to the club you just purchased, Cupid, and hopefully the last names ring a bell. Thomas, Abraham, and Simms. I'm waiting for their backgrounds now."

Merch said, "Hold the fuck on. Simms is the last name of that bitch Rocky. If his bitch ass got something to do with this shit, he's easy as found."

Ishmael said, "He must know we found his shit. Dirty ass!"

Terrence said, "I'm on top of it. Meanwhile, I need you to put the club back on the market. I need for you to stay strapped and safe until I get his ass off the street. Please don't go looking for him."

CHAPTER 20

Isaiah
The Circle

Isaiah said, "He seemed all shaky Monday when I saw him at the bank. I had to sign and give him the last check for the club. Why he fucking with the ladies and we're the ones who bought the club?"

Terrence said, "That's what I'm trying to find out now. I talked to a few of the girls at the club, and they told me he had a main chick that scoped out who had money, but not no robbery type shit."

Terrence pulled out the picture and set it on the desk for them to look at, and all their faces looked as if they were displeased.

Terrence said, "I'm waiting for her real name to come back, but the ladies at the club says she goes by Jill. She was seen putting notes on this car. The information to the owner hasn't come back yet."

Skunk said, *"Bitch is on our payroll!"*

Terrence said, "Don't say anything to her. She was on the tapes getting violated, and we can use her for our advantage."

Ishmael said, "Dirty ass bitch! Been around me all this time, and never would have thought this bitch would set me up, and that's Jez car. What the fuck is this bitch on some jealousy type shit?"

Isaiah said, "I've never known for jealousy to rob and snatch people. Damn!"

Terrence said, "Well, don't let her know that you're on to her yet. Keep a distance from her, but answer her calls, Ishmael. I'm going to find out how they're all tied together, and who is initiating this shit. Don't go on a killing spree. Please, let me find out what's going on first."

Terrence got the fingerprints off the alarm system before the commotion died down. He took Tara's phone to get the prints off it. When he left the shop, he made sure to pull his jacket back. If one of them were still watching, they would see his holster holding his pipe with the safety off.

Isaiah started thinking about Samaya getting caught up in this mess over a fat thirsty bitch, and his bitch. Isaiah told Skunk everything he heard them say that day, word for word.

Skunk said, "I thought these females of ours had something to do with this shit. They did work for the nigga."

Ishmael said, "I still do! They worked for him. They could have done this to other people, and in this case, it backfired."

Skunk said, "Bro, I just started feeling bad for they ass. I don't want to believe that."

Isaiah said, "If Rocky got something to do with this, he knows our females very well."

Merch said, "Well, I don't trust none of these bitches. Queen's been missing since this shit started, and they're all related, so hopefully, Terrence finds this bitch. I need to know what the fuck is going on before I hurt all their asses."

Isaiah said, "What the fuck was he looking for that day, lying fucker."

Ishmael said, "His box and videos I hear started all this shit."

Skunk said, "Hold up! How do you know she's missing, bro?"

Isaiah said, "He went to the house, it was empty, and the locks were changed. She's not answering his calls nor responding to his text."

Skunk said, "*Damn!* That was your right hand."

Isaiah said, "And to think I'm fucking the cousin."

Merch said, "I wouldn't give a fuck if she was my left hand. If the bitch got something to do with this shit, she's fucked!"

Ishmael said, "Sounds suspect to me. We need to find Queen. Question Tara, Samaya, and the damn double twins."

Isaiah said, "*This shit right here! This why I don't trust bitches.*"

*****

Ishmael, Isaiah, and Merch went back to their apartment for the night to get some sleep. Skunk went back to the hospital with Tara.

*****

The next day they made phone calls to their family and riders to meet up in a few days at Ishmael's house.

All his brothers, four cousins, two uncles, Terrence, three frat guys, and some of Merch's goons were there all strapped waiting for a bitch-ass nigga to try some fluky shit. They had them dropped off so no one could see how many people were inside his house.

Ishmael said, "Let me hit the flame, Unc?"

When Terrence arrived, he pulled the brothers to one of Ishmael's rooms so they could talk about the new information he found.

Terrence said, "I do know that Rocky and Jill didn't leave the States yet. We've been following them to this house right here. These other four going in and out are the stick-up guys."

Merch said, "They been in the club before, and that's Kala's punk ass."

Terrence said, "Hold on a minute, Merch! Tee, can you go let my friend in, please?"

Merch said, "These people have taken too many minutes already. I'm tired of this shit."

She walked in the room boldly, then Merch's and Skunk's mouths dropped wide open, because they didn't know she was working with Terrence.

Skunk said, "Ms. Kala!"

Merch said, "What the fuck is going on here?"

Kala said, "Hello, fellas. Hi, Terrence. I have a lot of information that I need to share."

Terrence said, "Is everyone okay? I had to do what I saw fit to get to the bottom of this."

326

Ishmael said, "Continue, please! We need to know what's going on. My bad, how are you doing, miss?"

Kala ignored Ishmael, knowing damn well he acted all reserved when she tried to holler at him. Merch and Skunk let her have her way, and she didn't care with the way they tipped.

Terrence knew she could get information from anybody from the way she looked, talked, and sucked the life out of a nigga's dick.

Terrence said, "Hello, Kala. Back to business. The sad part of this shit is two of these boys is Rocky's sons. The other one is Jill's punk ass brother."

Ishmael said, "What the fuck! You mean to tell me I let this bitch in?"

Terrence said, "Hold on, bro! Jill's real name is Jillian Abraham. One of the dead niggas that was in Isaiah's crib was her baby brother Chad. The other two were Rocky's oldest son's Ricardo and Ricky Simms."

Merch said, "What? These mothafuckers from an island or something?"

Terrence said, "Let me finish! Charles is Jill's oldest brother, who left his handprint on the alarm at Tara's place. Rocky's other two sons are Reggie and Roger. I believe they're the other two mystery guys at Tara's shop. Now we know they're pissed off that their family is dead, so they're coming full force."

Terrence pointed out everyone, told each detail on when they came, left, whom they were born to, all their exes, and where they worked.

He pulled the picture out of Charles at the coffee shop hugging Jai. Merch couldn't believe what he was seeing. Then Ishmael took a double take to make sure it wasn't Jez.

Isaiah said, "Which twin is that? Knowing when they started dating would be nice."

Merch said, "Bro, that's Jai! She hangs with Samaya and owns a clothing shop."

Terrence said, "Her name is Jai! She doesn't know who's she fucking with."

Ishmael said, "We need to find Rocky and his punk-ass off-springs because the whole family fucked up. We need Jillie, Queenie, and whoever the fuck else in these pictures. *Fuck all of them!* Jai does look different from her twin. Wow!"

Isaiah said, "Terrence? What else did you find out?"

Terrence placed three more pictures down from his pile, giving them a little bit at a time.

Terrence said, "This young lady used to be a stick-up girl back in the day with her brothers Osseo and Oswell. We tracked her down at work, and unfortunately, the investigator I had following her lost an eye when she slipped out the back door."

Isaiah looked like his heart stopped because his brothers didn't know about his situation with her. Then Kala looked like she had seen a ghost because she didn't give him that picture.

Isaiah said, "I've seen her before, bro!"

Ishmael said, "*Yeah*, we all seen this bitch!"

Merch said, "This bitch shouldn't know anything about my got *damn* family."

Terrence said, "She might have left out the back door, but she ran and uses her mouth well, right, Isa—"

Before Terrence could get Isaiah's name out his mouth, he spoke up, hating the fact that he had to tell his business.

Isaiah said, "She gives me brains at our meetings. I'd probably went a few times other than that, but I only nut and left. She knows about the W shit, so we don't even talk. The few conversations we had, I never said anything to the bitch. She doesn't even know my name or have my number."

Merch said, "You don't have to explain shit. It is what it is, big pimp."

Ishmael said, "My bro been getting sucked at the meetings. *Damn*...Why didn't you tell us? Do they all know each other or something? All these bitches are trying to get a piece of the pie like we some pussies running up on my brother's females."

Kala said, "I thought that weird-looking bitch was lying."

Terrence said, "Chill out, Kala! Glad you asked, Ishmael. Look at this picture of Mr. Rocky pulling her by the hair out the back door of Cupid."

Kala said, "Rocky wants his shit back. He doesn't give a fuck about what happened. Then he's pimping Jill and that other girl, so they don't have a clue of what's going on."

Merch said, "Fuck him! It's too late for that."

Isaiah said, "Him pimping don't have shit to do with running up in my shit!"

Ishmael said, "He wants his shit back, but don't give a fuck about his kids? He doesn't want to do no jail time. That's it."

Terrence said, "Well, it's too late for all that. He ain't getting shit back."

Merch said, "I can't believe they worked for him all that time not knowing what he did."

Kala said, "What's up with Queen? She didn't even see my face and started shooting at me the other night."

All the men chuckled because they knew Queen didn't give a fuck about shooting a bitch. Merch had to provide Samaya with money to bail Queen out for a gun charge and a few assault and battery.

Merch said, "Where? Only way Q will shoot is if you have a problem with her."

Kala said, "Rocky thought she knew where you guys lived, so he took me to her house. He wanted to ask her. I need to go, Terrence. I'll see you guys later."

Merch said, "Hold on! How did he know where she lived?"

Kala said, "I didn't ask. I went to tell her to be careful…"

Terrence said, "Ms. Kala, I'll see you later. Thanks for your input."

Skunk said, "Thanks for your input, but don't give Rocky no input on us."

Merch said, "Hold on, Kala. Where did you last see her?"

Kala said, "When she shot at me, nigga!"

Merch wanted to leave so bad after Kala told him. He didn't want anyone thinking that he cared for Queen.

Terrence said, "I know you want to find her, Merch, but I'll have my guys look for her. Look, trust none of these females either, and I most definitely don't want anything happening to you guys. Now I need you to be careful with Kala also because she can suck the skin off your shit like a run along sentence."

The men chuckled and choked off the flame.

Ishmael said, "Damn! This nigga said she doesn't breathe and you mean to tell me she doesn't use commas?"

Merch said, "Nope! She keeps going and going…"

Skunk said, "Man…and she goes all the way down without choking."

Isaiah said, "She did both of y'all? Damn, Kala."

Ishmael said, "Gots to be more careful with the throat. She's topping family off and doesn't even care. Let me go and make sure she didn't use any of my glasses."

Merch said, "Yo ass funny, bro…"

Terrence said, "You mean, three? I met Kala at the club one night she was about to quit. I paid her to find out about Rocky and all these females. Not to be sucking and fucking on everybody."

Merch said, "So, none of us know her?"

Skunk said, "I sent her to the club, and I met her ass in the mall."

Isaiah said, "I think that shit's nasty! Then y'all bragging…"

Ishmael
Not the Family

Ishmael kept in contact with Jez but didn't answer any calls from his other chicks. He wasn't trusting any of them until he found out his truths and facts.

He couldn't wait to set Jill straight. Terrence gave him specifics on what to do when she called.

After everybody arrived, Terrence made sure everything was set up as planned in case the juke boys came.

Terrence knew Kala was money hungry and could switch just like the next bitch. He gave her a schedule to keep her busy while he handled business with his boys.

Terrence said, "I know your father would be pissed about this whole situation. I'm going to bring this to an end as soon as possible. We need you guys to handle business accordingly. I'm not saying don't stay strapped, but you're famous now, and we don't need all this juke boy attention brought to the family. Let me deal with this nasty video recording, wannabe pimp, and his family my way."

Merch said, "My father doesn't have anything to do with this. Bro ass giving us this long speech is not going to keep them juke ass niggas from running up."

Tee said, "They don't know who your father is? Who's the juke boys?"

Ishmael said, "That's some shit they just made up, fam.

Merch said, "Come on, fam, stop smoking that over-the-counter shit."

Tee said, "Man….all this shit flame the same, fam. Here, try this shit!"

They all laughed so hard. "I'm good, fam," Ishmael politely whispered.

Isaiah said, "Pops has everything to do with this. He's the truth. I'm not trying to be mixed up with the zigzag boys, jukebox ass, or whatever you call them. My career has just started. I'm going to training with a clear mind."

Tee said, "Hold up! I'm not that high…Who the fuck are the zigzag boys?"

Merch said, "Fam! Give me that shit! Yo ass funny as hell…"

Ishmael said, "Seriously, fam, that's not flame…Bro, training is hard, but them checks look nice before Moms Dukes get their hands on them."

Tee said, "Fam! These his sons we're talking about, right?"

Terrence said, "Seriously! Merch, hand Tee some real shit to flush that shit out his system. It's his sons doing this shit! We don't know what they go by…"

Tee said, "Come on, Terrence. Tight ass that shirt is, he needs to pass you some, *sir*…"

Terrence said, "Aw, man…My boys are laughing at me…"

Skunk said, "Ishmael? Our mothers manages very well. Why not pay her top dollar? She got y'all monkey asses signed with the best NBA teams. Four sons through college, and she lives with her husband's mistress. Hell, they can have whatever the fuck they want in my book."

Ishmael said, "Well, damn! I was kidding, bro. I would never think to underpay Moms. Wish I could find a woman that is half as good as her."

Merch said, "A bro just called us some monkeys. Hell naw! I'm not knocking Pops or her with their arrangement. What's up with the flame? Let's roll this shit up and bring Tee back to life."

Beep, beep.

Ishmael said, "Got dammit! This bitch text me. It's on!"

*****

Ishmael opened the door for Jill with a big smile as usual. He slapped her on the ass as she walked past him. "Hey, Daddy, how's it going?" Jill said. "I'm all right. Needing some of that good pussy and head from my homegirl," Ishmael replied.

Jill said, "You play too much. Ugh!"

Jill was laughing hard until she saw all his goons at the house playing pool, shooting crap, and watching the game. She passed two females on the pole that she'd never seen before twerking hard as hell.

Jill continued to walk past everyone with a fake smile, trying not to show her nervousness because there's been people there before, but not this many.

Ishmael said, "Let's go upstairs so that we can have some privacy. Don't want everyone in our business."

Jill said, "Are you having a party for your graduation? It's so many people here, Ishmael."

Ishmael said, "Nope! That was last week. What have you've been up to?"

He noticed her facial expression had changed from when he let her in to when she saw the goons. Now he knew a bitch couldn't come in without an army and try him like they did Samaya or Tara.

Jill said, "Daddy, where are the other girls?"

Ishmael said, "It's just Jill and I tonight. Did I tell you I graduated?"

Jill said, "I heard one of the other girls say it…You mean, I get you all to myself?"

Ishmael said, "I've been seeing you for a few months, and I like how you take the initiative around the house, and how you check the other girls. I wanted you for myself tonight."

They smoked like three flames, and he watched her take shot after shot until her speech got slurred.

He started kissing her nipples through her shirt. When feeling her nipple get hard, he pressed his tongue against it harder. He watched her eyes roll up, then palmed his head. She started rubbing his head in a circular motion, moaning, and tried not to get louder than the music.

She started taking his shirt off with her other hand, trying to pull it up over his head. He stepped back and looked at this pretty woman up and down mad as hell she worked for Rocky.

He started walking to the bathroom, and she followed him with pleasure. *I guess she's used to following me,* Ishmael thought. "Take your clothes off, so we can get in the shower," Ishmael demanded. He stood there watching this snake bitch washing her ass in his shower, which disgusted him even more.

"Go on and do you," Ishmael said as he pushed her head down to his hard dick. The water splashed over her head while she sucked, trying to breathe through the water.

Ishmael said, "Don't drown trying to show out."

Jill said, "You play too much. Why are you talking to me like that?"

Ishmael said, "Quit acting all sensitive gang, gang. Did you bring the Backwoods as I asked?"

Jill said, "Yes. I enjoy pleasing you, Ishmael. I don't know what showing out is?"

Jill squatted down, grabbing his dick with her lips, loving the force he was using. Knowing it was all hers for the night made her excited than a mothafucka.

Still not losing focus on why she was there, but she was falling for him even more. Her tears washed away with the water that was hitting her face as she thought about everything this girl told her to say.

Her face pressed in the pillow with her ass arched like the Cotter Bridge with dimples. She was throwing her ass in a circular motion, trying to go with his rhythm. When he grabbed her hair, he pulled it enough to make her squirm like a sneaky snake that she was.

He let go of her hair, got up, and walked over to the chair knowing she was about to bust one, and he didn't want to give her the pleasure anymore. "Why did you stop?" Jill whispered as she sat up on the edge of the bed, faulty.

Ishmael started flaming again to take his mind off this disgusting woman that he thought was his homey. "Why did you stop" kept playing over in his mind. Not trying to lose track of what this bitch was here for in the first place, he passed her the flame.

Jill said, "What's the matter, Daddy?"

Ishmael said, "That pussy juicy. It's gripping my dick, and I don't want to nut yet."

She started playing with herself, while she watched this muscular, lean caramel brown skin, six foot three, with a man bun, Chinese light brown eyes, sweet medium lips, and dick big enough for two to three more bitches to join, watch her.

He handed her the flame again. When she hit the flame, she looked in his eyes, trying to keep her feelings in check and wishing he was hers.

Ishmael said, "Stop doing that!!"

Jill started laughing but did what he said. "Ain't shit funny," Ishmael said. Ishmael motioned for her to come to the edge of the bed. She was enjoying this new personality that he had, and then it was just the two of them alone.

Ishmael said, "Now, what's so funny? Turn around!"

Ishmael lay down on her, putting her legs onto his shoulders stroking fast, then slow, then he whispered in her ear.

Ishmael said, "Jillian, you're not leaving here."

She moaned, taking his words as if he loved her, but she knew Rocky would come looking for her eventually and get fucked up.

Ishmael said, "Get up and get dressed."

*****

Ishmael arrived at the club that morning, so he called for his brother to meet him there along with Ax and Tee. He wanted to come up with a plan for safety, as far as being robbed by the juke boys.

They didn't know what to do with the club anymore, so they talked about selling it, but Ax and Tee were trying to convince them to let them run it until everything died down.

*****

Kala sat out in the front with Rocky and his sons arguing about Jill, the box, and briefcase takers. She texted Terrence and told him what they were doing, so he could give them heads-up on what was going on there, making sure they weren't at the club.

Rocky said, "Where the fuck is Jill? I know she's with you or them fuckers."

Reggie said, "Chill the fuck out!"

Rocky said, "This bitch sprayed me with Mace and ran off with Jill. Now, where is she?"

Kala said, "You walk in there and ask them. What the fuck I look like?"

Rocky said, "You in all their faces, and probably sucking them off, and you don't know shit? Where the fuck is Jill?"

Reggie said, "Which one killed my brothers? Fuck Jill and these boxes you were looking for."

Kala said, "I wasn't there. Ask Jill. She's been around them longer. She probably heard or seen something. And fuck you, Rocky."

Roger said, "*Right! Fuck the suitcase and boxes. What about my family?*"

Rocky said, "*Fuck you! Who y'all think you're talking to? I'm y'all got damn daddy.*"

Charles said, "Whoa...I'm here for the paper. This family shit too much! I'm gone."

As soon as Charles opened the door, the door to the club opened at the same time. Kala was hoping that Terrence got her text in time to warn them.

Boom. Boom. Boom. Ax saw his face and didn't hesitate one bit. *Bang. Bang, bang. Bang. Bang. Poop. Poop.*

Tee said, "*Get down...fam!*"

Pop, pop, bang, bang, pop, pop. Tee was letting his shit go. He didn't give a fuck about who was in the car. When Rocky saw that they all started shooting back, he jumped in the passenger seat and climbed out the door, then started shooting over the hood of the car.

Isaiah said, "*Bro, get down!*"

Pop, pop, pop, pop, bang, bang. Kala ducked down and managed to get out of the side passenger back door and rolled across to the next car to get out of the path of the firing.

Merch said, "*Bro, hit!*"

Kala saw Charles jump in the driver's seat and start the car. Everybody managed to get back in the car, and he pulled off. "What the fuck," Charles shouted.

Merch started chasing the car down the street, shooting all their windows out, and Tee was right on his side running, letting their pipes ring. "Look at these fuckers galloping, get down," Rocky shouted.

Kala was so scared to come out because she knew Ishmael and his family would think she had something to do with it. When she saw one of the men lying on the ground holding his leg, she texted Terrence, "911."

Roger said, "I'm getting them, niggas. Take me to the hospital. They shot me in the shoulder. *Fuck!*"

Charles said, "One time is going to be all over that bitch. Did it go through?"

Roger said, "Do I look like a fucken' surgeon, nigga? This shit stinging…"

Rocky said, "You're shooting at these fucks in an open area. What the fuck you think going to happen? Now, y'all bleeding all in my shit."

Charles said, "They shot first! That means they know who we are."

Reggie said, "I see Kala got away. Sneaky ass bitch! I told y'all, she's chasing the money."

Rocky said, "Y'all brought this bitch in the mix. Crazy bitch leaving notes, and shit on people shit."

Charles said, "I didn't bring shit in."

Rocky said, "*I told y'all to leave my girls alone! And, nigga, don't think I don't know about my boys telling you about them a long time ago. You and yo punk ass brother.*"

Charles said, "I'm not a punk, nasty ass! What are we looking for?"

Rocky said, "*We're looking for my money, bitch!*"

Charles said, "Man…Reggie? Tell him what these goofy-ass broads are saying."

Reggie said, "That's not what Jill told Kala. If you weren't so in love with Saria and Queen, I could have been got they ass before these niggas came into play."

Rocky said, "*What the fuck! They made me more money than all my other girls. So, why would I let you fuck that up?*"

Reggie said, "Dad? What are we looking for, and quit going around the question?"

Roger said, "Can y'all shut up! I'm back here losing blood about to die, and y'all questioning each other like some detectives."

*****

He kept banging on the door until she opened it. When she saw them all out the peephole, she got scared as hell.

Rocky said, "*Open the fucking door!* Before I shoot this bitch down."

Rachel said, "Sorry, I was sleeping. Oh my gosh! What's going on?"

Rocky said, "Shut the fuck up! Get some rags, warm water, and alcohol."

She stitched up Roger's shoulder and watched him down the tequila out the bottle like some water. *Why the fuck is he is touching my leg*, Rachel thought.

She got ready to do Charles's left arm, and he moaned vaguely as the flame came out his mouth. "Are you okay," Rachel asked.

Charles said, "I'm good! Just hurry up, please…I need to get the fuck from around them."

As she cleaned the glass from Rocky's hair, she wondered why the evil ones never got hurt.

Rachel was pissed when Jill picked her up with Rocky in the car one day because she didn't like how he treated them.

That day she pulled Jill to the side and asked her, "Why did you tell him where I live?" and Jill didn't say anything. She knew Jill was terrified of him, so from that day on, she stopped messing with her.

*****

They arrived at the hospital. Jean, Marsha, Terrence, and Swen were there waiting for them in the emergency room.

They had to sedate Jean and Marsha because they were going off to the point of having a nervous breakdown.

*****

When he opened his eyes, everyone was staring at him. "Why everybody looking at me like that? It's just a leg, damn," Ishmael said.

Marsha started crying again. "*My baby*," she shouted as she ran into the bathroom. Jean held his hand sobbing, trying to talk, but the words wouldn't come out.

Merch said, "Bro, you are not going to be able to play basketball again. They hit close to a nerve, and…"

Merch couldn't even finish his sentence. He placed his hands over his face in disbelief. Ishmael couldn't believe what he heard. "Isaiah? Did they cut my leg off or something?" Ishmael asked.

Isaiah said, "No, bro! You're going to get better with some physical therapy."

Ishmael said, "Then…what is y'all crying for?"

Jean said, "Boy…shut up! The hell you mean? We're sad, which is a got damn feeling. You're blessed that you didn't get hit anywhere else."

Isaiah said, "Whoa…Come on, Mom. Let's go get some fresh air."

Swen said, "Who did this to you, nephew?"

Ishmael said, "I didn't see them."

Terrence said, "I know who did it. I got a 911 text from Kala. I didn't get the shit in time unless I could have prevented this shit. I'm so sorry, fam."

Ishmael said, "This shit isn't your fault. Who did it?"

Terrence said, "Rocky, Roger, Reggie, and Charles did this shit. Kala met them at the club. They asked her about the killings and Jill, so she told them to ask for themselves. Before y'all came out, she texted me, informing me of what they were doing. If I had seen the text, I could have warned you guys."

Isaiah said, "Bro…we're glad you're okay."

Ishmael said, "Why didn't she come in Cupid and tell us they were outside? We could have come up with something to say to her. Where is she now?"

Terrence said, "I thought about the same shit. She's with one of my partners until I figure this shit out."

Swen said, "I need to be filled in on what the fuck is going on immediately. Who are these rollow rogie muthafuckas? Where they live? And why the fuck haven't I heard about this shit? Where these pig nose bitches? They know something, got dammit!"

Merch said, "Let's go get the bitch, Terrence. Ax and Tee are downstairs waiting."

PART 5

Why Us

CHAPTER 21

Samaya

?

Samaya kept applying the ointment to her face, and looking at her small bald spots and bruises over money were unbelievable.

When Nurse 1 came in to take her to X-rays, she noticed that Samaya got dressed like she was going somewhere.

Nurse 1 said, "Hello, Samaya. You are moving around swell, I see."

Samaya said, "When you have time, may I get some more ointment? Thanks!"

Nurse 1 said, "Yes. Here's your pain medication before we go. Thanks."

They walked down the hall, passing security as he walked back toward her room. When she saw all the security, she started sweating from all areas of the pits like everyone knew her plan.

The X-ray technician said, "Hello, Samaya. You can take your clothes off and put the gown on. Then come back to room two, please. The bathroom is down the hall to your left."

Samaya said, "Okay!"

Nurse 1 said, "I'll be back to get you, Samaya. Let me know if you need anything else."

Samaya said, "I guess!"

Samaya grabbed a long white jacket from off the hook when she passed the door in the office, knowing she wasn't about to do shit, they said.

She pulled her hair down over her face to hide the scars and pushed the other piece of hair over the stitch on her ear and brushed it accidently. That feeling of pain alone made her think about getting the motherfuckers who killed her baby.

Opening the door slowly, she crept out trying to see where the X-ray technician was standing, so she hurried out as soon as she saw he was behind the desk.

He was waiting for her to come out of the bathroom, so she crept in the hallway and saw the HUC approaching her room down the hall.

She grabbed the clipboard off the wall and covered her face like she was reading a chart and went the opposite way toward the exit sign leading to the stairs.

The HUC was talking to the security guard, then Nurse 1 went into the room next to the reception desk, and she dashed off, not looking back.

Samaya started walking fast as hell because she noticed Isaiah from the side, so she ran down the stairs with tears running down her face.

Samaya hoped no one seen her, but her heart wanted to go back to him.

HUC said, "Hi, security. Her husband is here to see her."

Nurse 1 said, "She's not married, miss. Let me double-check and see if they're finished with the X-ray. The detectives are here to see her also."

*****

Samaya jumped right in the cab at the front entrance and headed home. She texted Queen and her parents, and that's it. When Queen didn't text back right away, she called her.

The cabman said, "Where to, miss?"

When she thought about all the questions Nurse 1 was asking about Isaiah, she knew something wasn't right.

She gave the cabman the address to the corner building by her condo, because everyone was suspect until she got to the bottom of this shit.

*****

Coral said, "Baby girl. What are you doing here? It's been a few people here asking about and for you. Make sure you stay safe, bitch."

Samaya said, "The people? I'll call you upstairs if I need you."

Coral said, "No, bitch…A bunch of thugs and some chick I haven't seen before."

Samaya said, "Did they change the locks yet?"

Coral said, "No. I wouldn't let them do that until I saw you first. The fuck! Queen did her thang. What are you doing here? Baby, you don't look okay…"

Samaya said, "I forgot one spot to tell her, and I'm not walking around without my pipe."

Samaya got the rest of her money and the pipe out of the hiding compartment that she forgot to mention to Queen.

Queen had the same realtor sell all Samaya's belongings, and she moved her money to their storage unit. She left enough money for her at the hotel room she had reserved in another fake name for her to move around.

*****

Zach said, "I followed one of them from the hospital, and she jumped in a cab with a hospital gown on, and I followed her to these condos off the view."

Terrence said, *"Follow her! Don't take your eyes off her. If she gets on a flight, train, or bus, follow her. Don't lose her."*

Zach said, "The way she stumbled in there, she might not make it out."

345

Terrence already knew she was running to Queen, but what the fuck were they running from was the question. He didn't know if they were in on the shit with Rocky, and pretending to get their ass beat for a penny, or just running from being scared.

Isaiah said, "I thought they were lying to me when they said she left."

Terrence said, "Brother, you need to tell me everything you heard that night."

Isaiah said, "Where is she? I need to talk to her. Where is she at, Terrence?"

Terrence said, "My private investigator is going to make sure don't nobody fuck with her. She went to her apartment first. I'll tell you when she gets to where she's going. She's taking us to Queen, watch."

Isaiah said, "Why leave the hospital all fucked up if you didn't have anything to do with this shit?"

Swen said, "I've been waiting for you to say that. Thought you were pussy whipped, nephew."

Isaiah said, "She lost a lot of blood. I don't want her to die over this fat fucker."

Merch said, "Right now, I don't give a fuck, and my brother is laying up in a hospital. Then they did this shit to you, bro. Fuck these females!"

Swen said, "My nigga…that's what the fuck I'm saying. Fuck a bitch and a bitch-ass nigga fucking with mines!"

Skunk said, "I don't know what the fuck is going on. Tara monkey ass leaving the hospital tomorrow, and she needs to start talking also."

*****

Samaya had Coral call her a cab, and make sure the instructions were to meet her in the garage. She waited in the office and talked with him until they came.

Samaya said, "Did they leave names?"

346

Coral said, "No, bitch! These niggas were thugs. They had guns all visible, with rags all tied around their heads, and some more shit. I'm off this weekend if you need me to go with you, girl?"

Coral walked out first with Samaya behind him, and they waited for the gate to open. She had her pipe on her waist, and her hand right on trigger, wishing a bitch would run up. Before Coral opened his door, he saw a girl pointing at them parked across the street, looking directly at them.

*****

Rocky said, "That's her. We about to follow this bitch."

Kala said, "I knew that bitch would come back here."

*****

Coral said, "Uh-uh, bitch! That's the bitch! She was with them thugs in that black truck, right there."

When Samaya looked at the black truck he pointed at, she found the strength to lift her arm and squeeze that thang. It sounded like World War I in the burbs.

Coral screamed, and Samaya was shooting, but she was surprised that Coral pulled out a gun from his fanny pack, letting loose on their asses as they tried to pull off. *Bang, bang, bang, bang.*

Rocky said, "*What the fuck! I'm hit!*"

Kala said, "*Go, motherfucker! This bitch crazy!*"

Boop, boop, boop, boop, boop.

Kala said, "Where is your gun? Why didn't you shoot back?"

Rocky said, "Fuck you! Why didn't you shoot back? *And where the fuck is my bitch?*"

Kala said, "I don't know! I heard she was at that club again."

*****

Sitting in the hotel room wondering who the fuck killed her baby was the only revenge she wanted. Continuing to drink shot

347

after shot, she placed a wet towel over the door crack and flamed until she fell asleep, thinking about Lovely Vines.

Coral said, "Come on, drunk ass, before we miss our flight. Can't leave my Queen waiting."

Samaya said, "I'm tired."

Coral said, "You look like you need a facial and plenty of water…Seriously!"

*****

As soon as they touched down, Queen read the text and smiled liked she saw an angel. Samaya and Queen always had each other's back, and they made a vow to never let anybody come in between their bond from the beginning.

*****

Terrence said, "What's up?"

Zach said, "We just landed in Vegas, bro. *Got damn, they running for real.*"

Terrence said, "I'm going to send some help out there with you until we touch down. *Make sure you follow them everywhere!* These some smart-ass women."

Zach said, "I'm on it! They were just in a shoot-out. She's good, though!"

Terrence said, "Damn! I heard she has an arm, so stay safe."

*****

The bartender said, "Hello, beautiful! What can I get for you this evening?"

Samaya said, "I'd like ice water and a double shot of tequila, please."

Coral said, "Bitch, please! Hold the tequila, sir. Thank you!"

The bartender said, "We also have some nice appetizers. Would you like to see our menu?"

Samaya said, "No, thank you!"

Coral said, "Come on, we gotta go! I know that's the same man. Who y'all piss off? Did we kill one of their ass and the police following us? Bitch, I know that's him, and call Queen. Fuck all that texting shit."

Samaya said, "Here you go with all this paranoid shit. Where is he? Queen's coming, damn!"

Coral said, "Damn, my ass! We left the guns at home, and I'm not about to get caught slipping. Fuck that!"

Samaya said, "Has anyone ever told you that you curse too much?"

*****

As Queen read the message, she knew what was going on. She looked in the hallway before going out of the room.

Samaya saw her approaching quickly with the bags, so they all started walking toward the exit. They all jumped in the cab together and told him to drive.

The cabman said, "Where to, ladies?"

Coral said, *"Drive fast! This shit got my blood pressure up."*

Queen said, "What are you doing here, bro?"

Coral said, "I just let a clip off! Now I'm being followed by some man in black look-alike."

Samaya said, "Coral? You let off a pocket protector."

Queen said, "Did he scream too?"

Coral said, *"Fuck y'all!"*

*****

Mint said, "What's up, T? I see your girls jumping in a cab as we speak. It looks like they're in a rush or something. I'll keep an eye on them."

Terrence said, "We on our way!"

Mint said, "Let me see where they lead us to."

*****

Queen stared at Samaya for a while before saying anything. She was glad she let loose on whoever walked up because she was next.

Queen said, "Girl, I missed you so much. Oh my gosh! Look at what they did to my baby face?"

Coral said, "That girl with the thugs that came looking for y'all. I'm trying to tell you, I saw that man following us."

Queen said, "Boy, please. Everybody is not a thug. You are a trip, for real."

Samaya just laid her head on Queen's chest, sobbing like a baby, and all Queen's tears ran down her face into Samaya's hair. "Oh my gosh! I love both my babies," Coral said as he tried to hug them both.

Samaya said, "Queen. I lost my baby. I need to find the people who sent them to do this shit to me."

Queen said, "Maya, you were pregnant?"

Coral said, "*Oh no, bitch! Why didn't you tell me? I can't take no more stress right now. Oh, Lawd.*"

Samaya said, "Yes, they killed my baby. I saw that man on the airplane watching us and shit. I didn't think nothing of it until Coral saw him again at the hotel."

They both looked at Coral throwing himself side to side, back and forth, squirming, holding his chest, and crying as Samaya told them the news.

Queen said, "I see why y'all let loose. Better safe than sorry. I had to let loose on somebody running up on me when I was leaving."

Coral said, "*Why am I just finding out about all this shit?*"

Queen said, "Quit crying before you have an asthma attack, Coral."

The cabman said, "Are you okay? Should I get off the highway now and go to the hospital?"

Coral said, "Keep driving! Let me pull it together and see if anyone is following us. You all wanted by the people, some rugby thugs, and the bro crew. I need to flame as soon as possible."

Queen said, "Take us to the closest hotel. Thanks."

Samaya said, "Who did this to me and Tara?"

Queen said, "*What do you mean Tara?* Is she okay? Samaya, is she okay?"

Samaya told them everything and how she left the hospital. Queen had to hold Coral because he was being overdramatic and shaking.

When they arrived at the hotel, they rushed in, trying not to let anyone see them. The cab driver went around the block a few times listening to their demands, and he didn't care as long as the meter went up.

Samaya said, "After you left, I didn't know what to think. I stopped by Tara's room, and she was too shook up to leave."

Queen said, "You know, she's not leaving Skunk."

Coral said, "I wouldn't either. With his fine ass…"

Samaya said, "Should I love Isaiah with all my heart? He always made sure I was happy. Who should we trust?"

Queen said, "I miss Merch. He was my first love. I just kept thinking they were coming for me next, so I bounced. I love hard, but trusting is hard in this type of situation."

Coral said, "My girls…in love. All the men are fine with money. *And trying to kill y'all!*"

Queen said, "I see you're done acting and falling out. You scared the damn cab driver."

Coral said, "Fuck you, Queen! Hand me the flame."

Samaya said, "I hope Jez okay. I didn't have time to stop and see her."

Queen said, "Hmm. They found her in a dumpster? That's fucked up! Smartmouth-ass bitch was probably getting jazzy."

Samaya said, "You are so wrong! I don't wish this shit on nobody innocent."

Coral said, "I'm good at diagnosing, but she was something else, girl. I wanted to choke her my damn self. I didn't tell y'all, the bitch asks me if I was funny. It took every ounce of that five thousand not to punch that bitch in her esophagus."

Samaya said, "Y'all wrong. What five thousand?"

Coral said, "Somebody gave me money to keep her at the mall longer, so they could."

Queen said, "Shut the fuck up, Coral. You're always telling shit."

Samaya said, "He has to tell me because I'm the one always getting y'all ass out the slammer."

*****

Detective Thomas kept looking over the information, trying to make sense of what was going on with Samaya leaving the hospital and all the robberies.

Detective Phillips said, "I thought they were robbing them for money, but why involve Tara?"

Detective Thomas said, "Hope these girls didn't get involved with setting people up and it backfired on them. Think about it! How'd they got their address? They were supposed to come out with a lot of money, and the men were supposed to get killed. The plan didn't go accordingly, so they're coming for the girls. Now, she's running from the robbers, or the victim's figured it out, and she's running from them."

Detective Phillips said, "Right…we need to find them before Mr. Simms or the brothers."

Detective Thomas said, "They want revenge for some shit they started. It was some calls that came in, reports of shootings by this address and the club."

Jai
Way Too Much

Jai closed the shop down and stayed at the hospital with Jez. Their parents went to work and back to the hospital every day.

She already knew her mother wished it was her in the hospital bed instead of Jez, with the sarcastic remarks. Her father loved them both equally.

Dr. Miller said, "Your daughter is doing much better, so we're going to let her go home soon. There are a few detectives here to see her."

Jennifer said, "I need to know if they found the people responsible for this before she leaves?"

John said, "Honey, let's go in and see her."

Detective Thomas said, "Hi, Jez! I'm Detective Thomas, and this is my partner Detective Phillips."

Detective Phillips said, "We have some questions for you, Jez. We're going to ask the family to leave for a few moments, if you don't mind?"

Jai said, "*Why?*"

Jennifer said, "*I'm not going nowhere!*"

John said, "We're her parents, *Detectives.*"

Detective Phillips said, "Is it okay, Ms. Solomon, if they stay?"

Jez said, "Yes, they can stay. And Jez is fine."

Detective Thomas said, "Jez? Do you remember what you were doing or anything unusual that day before the assault?"

Jez said, "I went to the gym, school to pay for my classes, stopped at home, and went to work with Tara."

Jennifer said, "Who's Tara? I thought you worked with your sister only?"

Detective Thomas said, "Miss, please let her finish."

Jez said, "I went to pick up our packages from the north side post office around five PM. I, I, I felt something hit my head and woke up in a trunk being grabbed out. They told me to put the code in for them so that they could get in the beauty shop."

Jai couldn't stop crying after hearing her sister was in a trunk, knowing this wouldn't have happened if she'd never introduced her to them.

Detective Phillips said, "How did you meet Tara? Before you got hit, did you hear them say anything? When they told you to put the code in, did you recognize the voice?"

Jez didn't want her parents coming down on Jai, so she lied. After Jai introduced them, Tara convinced Jez to attend cosmetology school with her.

Jez said, "We met at school...I work at her shop part-time, and we hang out occasionally. I didn't see anyone or recognize a voice. At the time, I was scared."

Detective Thomas said, "Jez? Do you know Samaya?"

Jez said, "Not really!"

Detective Phillips said, "I'm going to show you some pictures, so don't rush. Just take your time, and let me know if you see any faces you recognize. Did you see anyone sneak up on you? What about the make and color of the car?"

Detective Thomas said, "Jai? We know you're friends with the family. Is there anything you could tell us about the attacks?"

Jai said, "*Ask them! The fuck. Your here about my sister? Right?*"

John said, "Watch your mouth! What do they mean you know the family?"

Jennifer said, "What do you have your sister mixed up in? I knew it!"

Jai said, "I don't! I don't know anything."

Detective Thomas said, "Now, now, everyone. Let's not jump to conclusions."

Detective Phillips said, "So, Jai...how well do you know Merch?"

Jai said, "*Why the fuck you keep asking me questions?*"

Detective Phillips said, "We're just trying to find out how Jez got mixed up in the robberies."

Jai said, "*Your job is to find out who did this to my sister.*"

John said, "Who's Merch, Jai?"

Jennifer said, "You need to watch your mouth in front of your parents. *Who's the family? If they have something to do with your sister getting hurt, speak up.*"

Jez said, "I'm going to be okay. I just suffered some bad bruising and a busted lip. Detectives, I need to know who did this to me, instead of you questioning my sister. I didn't see who grabbed me, the car was red, don't know the make or model, and never heard their voices before, period."

Jai said, "Father, I'd never put my sister or you in jeopardy. Mama, I'm grown. They're standing their asses here questioning me like I did the shit. *Get the fuck out of here, and go find these motherfuckers before they grab or rob someone else.*"

Jennifer jumped up, leaped over John's legs, and slapped the shit out of Jai. When she noticed her lip was busted, she knew she had pushed a button.

Detective Thomas said, "*stop!* This is not the place for this."

John said, "*Dear, get off her…now!*"

Jai folded up and let her mother swing until the detectives pulled her off. John took Jennifer to the waiting area until everything calmed down.

Detective Thomas said, "Put this ice on your lip, Jai. I need to know if you heard or noticed anything suspicious when you were around them? Queen and Samaya are missing now."

Jai said, "How? When? Samaya's in the hospital, right?"

Detective Thomas said, "Samaya checked herself out of the hospital, after her sister Tara was admitted. What's your relations with Merch and Queen? Do you know Ricardo? He goes by Rocky."

Jez said, "I don't know these muthafuckers. I'm tired of all these questions. I do know that."

Detective Thomas said, "I'm asking, Jai. Do you think they have mistaken you two?"

Jai said, "What would they want with me?"

Detective Phillips said, "Someone has it out for your friends. Now, they're all disappearing. *And, you just don't know shit, Jai?*"

Jai said, "*Fuck off!*"

Detective Phillips said, "You're sleeping with both sides, right?"

Jai said, "Fuck this! I do as I please. Now go solve a case, *Detective Phillips.*"

Detective Thomas said, "Phillips? Can you leave for a moment and give me a few minutes with the ladies, *please*? Go see if their parents know anything."

Jai said, "Yeah! Go find a 'side,' Phillips."

Jez said, "Detective Thomas? Far as their business with robberies, me getting grabbed, and them disappearing, I don't know unless you fill us in. Maybe they're running from someone. Did you ever think of that?"

Detective Thomas said, "Jai? We both know you've seen a lot with this family. Whatever you've seen would be helpful. Maybe you know why they're running, or to?"

Jai said, "See...I was nice to you, Thomas. *Now quit asking me shit I don't know nothing about.*"

Jez said, "Hold on, sis! My sister sells clothes to one of them, and I work with one of them, doing hair. If you can't tell me who the fuck grabbed me, then move on and find your missing link. We don't know shit! *Good day, Thomas.*"

Detective Thomas said, "We're speaking with your parents about protective custody or having a car at your house. Until then, here's my card if you remember anything, twins."

Jai said, "Protect? When she came for protection the first time, they didn't help. Now you need help to solve your case? Now, you want to throw protective custody in."

Detective Thomas said, "Good day, ladies."

Jai said, "I really can't believe she left the hospital."

Jez said, "Queen said, 'I'd know if someone was following me,' but the bitch running. What did he mean by both sides, sis?"

Jai said, "Fuck Queen! Who are they running from? Why they fuck with you? I don't know about no damn sides. Them people are playing mind games."

Jez said, "Sis, they used me. They said, they'll let me live if I gave them the code for the shop. After they got the code from me, they dumped my ass in the dumpster."

Jai said, "*Oh, fuck!* Have you told anyone yet?"

Jez said, "*Hell no!* Not even Dad or Mom. *I'm scared!*"

Jai said, "Don't cry. Don't tell anyone yet. Let me find out what's going on first."

Jennifer said, "*Find out what?*"

Jai said, "Nothing! Mom…"

John said, "Dear? Let's not start arguing before they put us out."

Jennifer said, "I wouldn't give a fuck if they locked me up and threw away the key. Jai, tell us what you know *right got damn now before you're a patient in this hospital.*"

Jai said, "Mom? They're playing games with us. Trying to figure out what we know. I don't know what they're talking about Dad. *Please stop, Mom!*"

*****

Jai went straight to the strip club looking for Merch but bumped into a beautiful young lady. "I'm sorry. Let me help you pick up your things," Jai whispered in a soft worried tone.

Jai said, "I'm rushing and not looking where I'm going."

Toonie said, "It's okay! If you are trying to go there, it's closed."

Jai said, "Oh my gosh, Toonie! What are you doing here? You look different."

Toonie said, "Nothing! Who are you looking for, Merch?"

Jai was in deep thought thinking did she say, "Merch," and watching Toonie's mouth move, but she didn't hear nothing she was saying.

Toonie said, "*Bitch! Don't be shocked, dummy! I said, 'Merch.' Don't walk away now!*"

Jai said, "*I'm doing as a grown woman should do, little girl!*"

Teresa said, "What that bitch want?"

Toonie said, "Looking for Merch, I guess. She didn't say after I told her they're closed."

Teresa said, "Long as we have what we need. Fuck all they ass."

Toonie said, "Do my cousins know about this?"

Teresa said, "No! They lost right now. But TT got them."

CHAPTER 22

Queen
Truth, My Ass

Queen said, "Samaya, you need to rest. I'll order something to eat."

Queen sat there looking at her gun, hoping she wasn't going to have to use it on the man that bought it for her.

Samaya said, "Queen, I need to find out who did this to me. It couldn't have been Isaiah or his family. When they came into his house, I heard them say, 'I thought this bitch had money,' and they kept asking me, 'Where the money?' So, it's somebody we know."

Queen said, "I saw Merch and his brothers at the hospital. That shit spooked the shit out of me because you weren't talking. I didn't know who the fuck did what. Your silence to me meant to get the fuck out of dodge."

Samaya said, "I'm sorry, cousin. Didn't want anyone seeing me this way. Losing the baby hurt my heart differently. I was falling in love with that man."

Queen said, "Who are we running from, Samaya?"

Samaya said, "Good question. I don't know!"

Coral said, "*That's that—Rocky muthafucker. He set this shit up.* Q over there holding her pistol, like she's about to shoot something. Samaya is looking like a ghost smoking flame."

Queen said, "Shut up, boy. I love Merch, y'all, but this shit not adding up."

Samaya said, "Even after seeing him with all the females?"

Coral said, "What females?"

Queen said, "I followed his ass for all the wrong reasons. Once I stopped following him, I just asked for more money."

Coral said, "Following? Y'all was up to that shit again?"

Samaya said, "I'm glad you left. If they tried to rob Tara, that meant they were coming for you next. Who the fuck knows about our money and where we live?"

Coral said, "If y'all ask each other or yourself one more question about some shit you should know. Da fuck!"

Queen said, "That's what the fuck I've been thinking about all this time. Who knows?"

Coral said, "Y'all sound silly as hell. The only muthafucka that knew some shit was Rocky. Don't think he wasn't counting the money you made. You said he raised the rent now, you're acting dumb. Talking about who did dis and who the fuck you think?"

Samaya said, "What makes you say that?"

Coral said, "*Why you say that? Get this bitch some blood! She's sounding and looking sick.* Queen? Let's take my girl to the hospital?"

Queen said, "Samaya? You do look sick. Coral...I know yo ass is not talking, the way you cried over Billy for five months, and you lost some weight. Da fuck!"

Coral said, "See, bitch! You're always taking shit personal. I loved that man."

Queen and Samaya laughed so hard because he cried when Toonie broke up with him and he's the one that told her he liked men.

Samaya said, "Always coming at us. We say one thing to you, and you storm off pouting."

Coral said, "I think you should save the strength and oxygen you have left, sweetie. Keep laughing, and I might have to carry yo zombie-looking ass downstairs."

Queen said, "Boy...hit this shit! Yo ass in your feelings."

Coral said, "I see y'all ignoring me...Rocky did this shit!"

Samaya said, "He better hush before I call Toonie on his ass."

Coral said, "See, yo sick-looking ass always hitting below the belt. She was the first woman to hit or have me."

Queen said, "Did y'all ever fuck?"

Samaya said, "When? Matter of fact! How?"

Coral said, "See...if I didn't love y'all! Toonie knew before I did. That my shit only worked for...never mind! Nothing happened between us. *What the fuck is so funny?* Ugh, I can't stand you heifers."

Queen said, "Boy, stop it! You laugh at us all the time. Besides, Toonie is fine as fuck. What man wouldn't or couldn't get up for her?"

Coral said, "See, Queen, yo ass sitting here looking like you ready to go follow *somebody*. Then yo ass keep coughing, and we're gonna end up giving you CPR, Saria."

Samaya said, "Oh, he mad, mad! You know Saria has gotten us all out the below-minimum-wage omission."

Coral said, "Bitch! If you didn't look like you were about to pass out, I'd pull your hair. Queen, let her hit the flame so her lips can go numb. I'm tired of hearing her want to look like I'm sleep talking ass."

Queen said, "This shit funny! Here, Saria!"

Coral said, "Aww, you done fucked up now! Saria about to tell how she saved y'all from the hungry car."

Samaya said, "Fuck y'all! Samaya told both of y'all that my plan was going to work. Remember, Samaya made Saria..."

Queen said, "She told us!"

*****

Zach had waited outside until he saw them check in, then he went in and stood by the elevator to see what floor they got off on, so he could get a room on the same level.

Zach said, "We're still in Nevada. I just watched them switch hotels. I see Queen moving around a lot with some man. Samaya must be laying low. Mint is watching the back."

360

Terrence said, "We should be touching down soon."

*****

Samaya said, "We all fuck with that family, seriously. I've never seen what kind of business Isaiah owns or what he does for a living. His sketch on Lovely Vines say he's a business owner."

Queen said, "They own a lot of property and a few businesses. Ishmael and Skunk just went pro."

Samaya said, "If they got money, why does Merch do what he do? I don't get it."

Coral said, "But you get high off his shit. What is there to get but get high."

Samaya said, "Yo ass always saying some smart-mouth shit. Crybaby!"

Queen said, "I never asked questions. They had money before they got signed."

Samaya said, "I saw a picture of Isaiah and his brother holding up some NBA jerseys."

Coral said, "*Okay! Y'all got some rich dick.*"

Queen said, "You are silly. Merch is the only one that deals with flame, and the other brothers don't know how deep he's in."

Samaya said, "How do you know?"

Queen said, "Observing and listening very well."

Samaya said, "He's getting that shit for pleasure, and especially if they got bread like that."

Coral said, "*Duhhhh!* And, he's using it to get potheads like…"

Queen said, "Right! I'm the only one that profited off the shit. He's never taken money from me, so don't be pointing at me."

Coral said, "What about the other ladies? I'm just saying."

Queen said, "Shut up, Coral! Damn! If we even mention yo nigga having bitches pregnant or a side nigga, you get all asthmatic."

Coral said, "*Oh my gosh! You always extra.*"

Coral grabbed his fanny pack and stormed out of the room sniffling into the bathroom. "Mean asses," Coral said, cursing under his voice.

Samaya said, "Them fuckers mentioned a box and briefcase when they were trying to rob us. The only time someone saw my case was the cashier I bought it from, you, and when I took it to the bank with Isaiah."

Queen said, "That means they were watching you. What box?"

Samaya said, "I don't know, but they thought it was my house. They dragged me through the house, beat my ass, and one of them raped me."

Queen immediately started crying, then went over to hugged Samaya so tight, it felt like she gasped for air. "I'm sorry you had to go through that. We're getting their asses," Queen whispered in her ear.

Queen said, "Before I couldn't take care of myself, but now this shit going on. If something happens to Merch, then I'll be left alone. I don't want to be a single parent."

Samaya said, "Queen. I'll be here for you. You know that. You should have kept the baby. It didn't ask to be here. Wish I hadn't lost my baby, baby daddy or not."

Queen said, "Look what we went through as kids. Being shipped around, parents all on drugs, running the street, hungry as fuck, and now we're shaking ass for money."

Samaya said, "Shaking ass has been good to us. We're not all strung out, hopping on dicks, and most definitely not sloppy as our parents. We have money, Kya. At least they had us and gave us a chance to be rich. We fuck with some rich-ass men that will do anything for us. Quit trying to find a reason to kill babies, because you're mad in your feelings."

Queen said, "First of all, I'm not into shit! Let's say these muthafuckas fucking with us to get to them. How the fuck they find out where Isaiah live if they were after your money? See, you are letting your feelings blindside you from what could be happening. *Who are these niggas, Samaya? Answer that!*"

Samaya said, "First of all, we're going to keep our voices at a four in this bitch. They could have followed me there. I was going to his house every day since we've met, know that. Second, feelings don't have shit to do with me getting my ass whooped by the robbers and his brothers. Then, you are asking me like I know these bitch-ass niggas. Like I had something to do with this shit. You think I'm fucking with them niggas from my past?"

Queen said, "Are you? Tell me? This shit started right after Chad magically appeared that day."

Coral said, "*Can y'all calm down in there! You're getting loud. Thanks!*"

Samaya said, "Really, bitch? We were hungry back then sleeping in cars, so I made sure we ate any means necessary. The fuck! We have plenty of money right now to raise a baby, the right way."

Queen said, "Bitch…all the niggas that *tried* to rob y'all is dead as fuck. I don't want anybody coming for you. I don't know what to think right now."

Samaya said, "Yes. I didn't want Coral to know about the raping, so I waited to tell you. And yes, they're all dead like my baby. Fuck them!"

Queen said, "I'm sorry, cousin…Shouldn't no one have to go through that, that's fucked up. What would make a person rape you?"

Samaya said, "I'm the one who told them I saw them at the club before. I've never had to get my ass beat to hit a lick. Get the fuck out of here with this shit. *And I would have told you like I did all the other times I did dirt.*"

Queen said, "*Bitch, seriously?* Remember, let's keep it at four. Funny this shit didn't start happening until you saw Chad and did the splits for Isaiah."

Samaya said, "Girl, please! Again, I didn't hook up with Chad! Stop it."

Queen said, "Well, soon as Rocky sold the club, all this shit started happening."

Samaya said, "Sold the club to who?"

Queen said, "Merch and his family."

Samaya said, "That's why Isaiah was all up in the meeting with Merch and Rocky. He told my ass he didn't want to see me there anymore without him because he bought the bitch right from under my nose."

Queen said, "Rocky was calling my phone before I changed my number asking for large amounts of smoke and shit. Then Ax was calling me like I was coming back after all this shit happened."

Samaya said, "By us running they think we had something to do with this shit, Queen. We worked for Rocky, so, they think we set them up even if I did get my ass beat. Then, I'm the one who… never mind."

Queen said, "See, this is why I'm confused now. Rocky been a hot mess, and you holding shit back. I don't trust anybody."

Samaya said, "Now you don't trust me, Kya?"

Merch
Searching

Merch said, "We need to get them before whoever finds them."

Isaiah said, "Long as they're not working with whoever."

Terrence said, "I believe whoever he is, is coming for any and every one that had something to do with his sons' murder. We can't scare these girls off. Let's be nice and get them home first so that we can get some information from them."

*****

The stewardess said, "Hello, welcome to first class. Would you gentlemen like anything to drink?"

Merch said, "Hello, beautiful. Let me get two shots of top-shelf tequila, please. Thank you."

Terrence said, "Hello, I'll have a double shot of Hennessy. Thank you."

Isaiah said, "Hi. Yes, let me get a bottled water and some peanuts. Thank you."

Isaiah went to the restroom, so that gave Terrence time to talk with Merch alone. He only needed a few minutes to discuss some of his findings and give Merch time to think.

Terrence said, "Merch? When I was doing some digging, I found out you're still doing some flame business. I know for a fact that your brothers don't have an idea. The reason I didn't mention it to them is that your people don't have anything to do with the robberies."

Merch said, "What I'm doing isn't none of your motherfucking business, but thanks for checking."

Terrence said, "Look, Merch. You don't even have to do this. I'm looking out for the family's best interest. For the record, you hired me to be in your got damn business."

Merch said, "You nor my brothers didn't have a problem smoking the flame. Shit has to come from somewhere, right? Demand and supply, Terrence."

Terrence said, "My brother, at least buy enough for your needs. Fuck the demand!"

Merch said, "Nigga! You buy from me, so enough for your needs also?"

Terrence said, "You know what I'm saying."

Merch said, "Get the fuck out of here with that interest shit! Look at you! Your ready to smoke now!"

Terrence just looked at Merch's ass in dismay. He thought about all the deleted sex scenes and flame transactions he had to delete off the tapes they gave him. He already knew Rocky was coming for his tapes, but he also was coming for Merch thinking he was a drug dealer with a lot of money.

Terrence looked at his phone and saw Zach calling. He only answered because he wanted to stop the conversation with Merch before it got out of hand.

Terrence said, "Send me your location?"

Zach said, "We're off 613. Right now, they're still in the room. I can see both exits from where I'm sitting. Queen usually comes out around this time to pick up food."

Isaiah said, "Are they still there?"

Terrence said, "Yes."

Terrence said, "Zach? If Queen leaves, have Mint follow her. You stay there in case the other girl tries to leave."

Zach said, "Got it! They're still with that dude."

*****

Merch said, "What you go do, bro, get your dick sucked?"
Isaiah said, "Not this time."

*****

They made it to the hotel, and Mint rented out the room across the hall. It was down a few doors on the opposite side from Queen, Coral, and Samaya.

Mint waited by the exit on the stairs. Merch, Isaiah, and Terrence rotated standing at their hotel room door, slightly keeping it open. They wanted to see when one of them came out.

As soon as that door opened, Terrence rushed out like a bat out of hell. Isaiah and Merch peeked out the door and made sure Zach and Mint were in place.

Terrence said, "Excuse me, miss. I'm new here. Just wondering do you know anything about good restaurants in the area? The food here is dry as fuck."

Queen said, "Right! I've been eating from down the street at this nice Chinese spot."

Coral said, "Hey, mister. How are you? I don't do Chinese, but it's a good bar and grill down the street also."

Terrence said, "I'm good with the Chinese. Can you give the address or name please?"

*****

Merch and Isaiah were peeking out the door, waiting for Terrence's signal to come out. Once he got her to look down at his phone, they were to come out fast.

Merch said, "Bro, look at this. She's all giggly and shit."

Isaiah said, "Where's Samaya? Who is this skinny dude with her?"

*****

Terrence said, "If you don't mind, can you put it in my search for me?"

Queen was entering the name in his search. As soon as she handed him the phone back, he clicked the website and showed her his phone to distract her from looking up.

Terrence said, "Is this the location? This right down the street, good looking."

Queen said, "*Yes.* You're welcome."

Before she could look back up, Merch rushed out the room toward her.

Coral said, "*Ruuuuuuunnnn, bitch! Oh my gosh, run!*"

Terrence said, "Shut the fuck up!"

Queen thought she saw a fucking ghost. She started running toward the stairwell and ran right into Mint. He grabbed her arms until Merch was able to get right behind her and grab the pistol off her side.

Mint said, "Whoa, mama! What's the rush?"

Queen said, "Move, fucker! Let me go!"

Merch said, "Where you going, punk?"

Coral screamed so loud that he didn't realize Terrence was with Merch until he hemmed him up. Terrence didn't want to hold him, so he let him go. When Coral tried to run, he ran right into Isaiah's chest. "Get yo monkey ass over there and be still," Isaiah said.

Merch said, "What the fuck you running from, Queen? Or, should I say who?"

Queen said, "*Let me go, Merch!*"

Isaiah said, "Ay, bro, quit choking this girl."

Coral said, "*Stop, Merch.*"

Merch looked at Coral so fucked up, he turned his head. Queen was gasping for air and swinging her arms at Merch for him to let her go. Terrence stepped in between them and pushed Merch back. "Chill out, bro," Terrence said in a low tone of disappointment.

Merch said, "*Watch your mouth.* Bring your ass back down here, and open this fucking door right now."

Queen said, "Stop pushing me, Merch. What the fuck y'all doing here?"

Isaiah said, "Is Samaya okay, Queen? I need to see her."

Terrence said, "Let's calm this shit down before someone calls the people on our ass."

Merch said, "Who the fuck are you running from, Q?"

Queen said, "I don't know why the fuck I'm running. You tell me since my cousins got hurt and shit. Merch, let my arm go!"

Coral said, "Say something, Q! They're about to kill us...Oh my gosh..."

Merch said, "Shut the fuck up! Give me the key now."

Isaiah said, "If we were going to hurt you, we wouldn't be standing in your face. Now get the fuck out the way."

Merch opened the door then made Queen go in first just in case Samaya heard the commotion because they all knew she could shoot.

Samaya lay on the bed looking sick as hell until she saw Isaiah walking up behind Queen. She tried getting up, but her brain made her think she was moving fast, but her body was moving in slow motion.

Isaiah said, "Put the gun down, Samaya. We're not here to hurt you, baby girl."

Samaya said, "*Naw, fuck that!* Queen, *you okay?*"

Merch said, "Queen, you okay?"

Coral said, "*Oh my gosh! She fainted! Call the ambulance.*"

Terrence said, "Shut the fuck up!"

Queen hurried over, picked her up, and hugged her tightly. Coral fell into one of his panic attacks, grabbing his chest, squirming and shit. Merch looked at Isaiah and Terrence like, *What the fuck is he doing.*

Queen said, "It's okay, Samaya. I got you! *Let's go.*"

Isaiah said, "Move, Queen, so that I can take her downstairs."

Terrence said, "We need to get her to a hospital right away. From the looks of it, he needs to go too."

Merch said, "Your talking all this shit and your cousin losing her damn color and shit."

Queen said, "We didn't know what to do, Merch...*Coral, stop that shit! Damn!*"

Terrence said, "We're going to make sure nothing happens to you ladies, I promise."

Coral said, "*Okay...she looks dead!*"

Merch said, "Take her to the hospital. My homey looks sick as fuck."

Mint drove Terrence, Isaiah, and Samaya to the closest hospital. Merch, Zach, Queen, and Coral stayed behind packing up everything.

*****

Merch sent Zach and Coral to the room they rented so he could talk with Queen, and she wasn't about to leave all her money around with a stranger.

Queen said, "How did you find me?"

Merch said, "Queen. Queen. Queen. What's going on?"

Queen said, "Who are you? Tell me who I'm running from?"

Merch said, "I found you because I care. This same niggas shot my damn brother the other day."

Queen said, "Really? What brother? Is he okay?"

Merch said, "Does it matter? Long as I got to you before them, bums did. What made you run from me, though?"

Queen said, "I don't know, Merch! It was too much going on, and I didn't trust anybody. Shit started getting too close to home. When I saw you leaving the hospital that day, I got scared and confused."

Merch said, "Hold on! Quit rambling on. Did you run because you are pregnant?"

Queen said, "No, Merch. What the fuck! Can't I ask about your brother? *Wow!*"

Merch said, "Watch your mouth. They shot Ishmael, but he's okay."

Queen said, "I'm so sorry. They're trying to get all of us. Before I left, somebody ran up on me leaving the house, and I let loose."

Merch said, "You just skipped the question like I'm just that dumb."

Queen said, "I ran because I was scared, Merch."

Merch said, "Merch, my ass! Quit saying my damn name like you're lying."

CHAPTER 23

The Club
Mastermind

Rocky said, "Stay here! I'm going to see for myself. This bitch took all my money out my safe."

Reggie said, "You're gonna walk up there like we didn't just shoot at these muthafuckas. Shit crazy! I hope they didn't see you the other night."

Rocky said, "Fuck that! Jill said she was going to work the other day. I haven't heard from her since. Should have checked my shit before she left."

Reggie said, "Have you talked with Kala's punk ass? Funny how they disappear at the same time. Now, they're robbing you."

Rocky said, "Yeah! That bitch Kala not answering either. I had Rachel call them, and their shit went straight to voice mail."

Rocky got approached before he even got to the door by security. Ax saw him through the cameras and alerted Henry on who he was. Rocky saw security cutting him off before he could even get to the entrance, and he got nervous as hell. "Who are you here to see," Henry asked as security patted Rocky down.

They had orders not to let him in the club unless told by one of the owners.

Henry said, "I'm head of security, sir. How may I help you?"

Rocky said, "My name is Rocky! Is there a manager here or something I could speak with?"

Henry used his walkie-talkie and asked for Ax to come down.

Ax said, "How can I help you, sir?"

Rocky said, "Yes, you can! My girl works here part-time. I'm wondering is she here tonight?"

Ax said, "What's her name?"

Rocky said, "Jill."

Ax said, "Let me check with my floor manager."

Rocky said, "Appreciate it, man."

Ax said, "Teisha?"

Teisha said, "*Yes! How can I help you?*"

Ax said, "Damn, girl! Turn your volume down. The whole downtown can hear you. Check the employee sign-in list to see if a Jill signed in tonight?"

Teisha said, "*Hold on!* I don't have a Jill on my employee list or my amateur sign-up for tonight."

Ax said, "Don't know Jill work here. She didn't sign up for amateur night either. She might be under another name. You can come in and check."

Rocky said, "When I last talked to her, she said she was coming to work. I hate a sneaky bitch."

Ax said, "Let me know if you see her, and I'll have someone go get her."

Rocky said, "Can you tell me when she last signed in? You have a nice crowd in here."

Ax said, "Can't do that from here, so let me get your number. I'll call you when I check. Write your number on this flyer. You got to watch these females. They're sneaky as fuck."

Rocky said, "Thanks, man, she's been gone since last week."

Ax said, "Damn, and you are just now checking on her?"

They were standing in the corner behind the bar, and Ax got them some shots. They flamed while Rocky's punk ass scoped the room looking for Jill.

Ax went to grab his phone from his inside pocket, and Rocky saw the pistol holster under his jacket. "Hold on, man! I need to take this call. Let me know if you see her," Ax said.

Rocky said, "She's always doing this when we argue. Not for this long, though."

Rocky thought he had seen a motherfucking ghost when Kala walked in with four men escorting her to the back. He didn't pay attention to his phone vibrating. Reggie was trying to call and warn him she walked in the side door.

Rocky said, "*Dude? That's her friend!*"

Ax said, "Hold on! Which one? I'll call you back…Come on! Let's go holler at her."

Rocky said, "She just went towards the back. What the fuck is she doing in here?"

Ax said, "Let's go ask the bitch."

*****

Jai walked up to Cupid, approaching the entrance. Henry looked her up and down like he was seeing a goddess.

Detective Phillips said, "We should go in right now and get him. Look at Jai!"

Detective Thomas said, "Miss, I don't know anything. Coming to inform her friends, I see. Let's wait! I see Reggie is waiting, and we can follow them when they leave. What is he doing here if his family just died in the robbery? Something's not right?"

Detective Phillips said, "Let's take Reggie right now. That way, he'll come to bail him out, or we get Reggie to tell everything. Should we arrest Jai? She lied."

Detective Thomas said, "We're just going to arrest one of them? Doesn't make sense. People lie all the time."

Detective Phillips said, "Damn! We need to go. Lia just texted me. Fuck!"

*****

Henry said, "ID, please. Twenty dollars of door coverage is on me."

Jai said, "Thank you."

Jai walked around for like an hour in the club looking for Merch before she went to the bartender and asked if she could speak with the manager. Teisha approached her with a big smile.

Teisha said, "How can I help you, miss?"

Jai said, "My name is Jai. I'm here to speak with the owner, please."

Teisha said, "I'm the manager. Is there something I can help you with?"

Jai said, "Okay! Can I speak with the owner, please?"

Teisha said, "Hold on, Jai! *Ax...hello! Ax...there is a Ms. Jai here to see you.*"

Ax said, "Don't know a Jai. Ask her or him what they need, because I'm busy right now."

Teisha said, "*She specifically asked for the owner. She acting irritated!*"

Ax said, "Give me fifteen minutes. I'll be down."

Teisha said, "*Okay!* He'll be down in fifteen minutes, Ms. Jai."

Jai said, "Thanks! I'm not irritated...More concerned than anything."

Teisha said, "*Whateva! Whateva.*"

*****

Ax said, "Teisha? Where she at?"

Teisha said, "*Bitch at the bar, in all white.*"

Ax approached the bar, amazed at her beauty. Trying not to show he was attracted to her, "Hello, Jai. What do I owe the pleasure in meeting you?" Ax said. "Hi, Ax. I'm looking for my friend Merch. He hangs out here a lot, and I need to speak with him. I'm sorry, do you know him?" Jai replied.

Ax looked at this pretty creature like, *What the hell she asking about my fam for?* noticing Henry and Teisha approaching.

Teisha said, "*You good, boss?*"

Ax said, "I'm good, Teisha! I don't know him, Jai. I can ask around, so if you leave your number, I can get back to you."

Jai said, "I came here the other day, and you were closed, and this is important that I speak with him."

Ax said, "Closed! We're open every day, twenty-four hours a day. Your number, please?"

Jai said, "Here's my business card. Thanks, Ax!"

Henry said, "I need to speak with you when you have time."

Ax said, "She was just leaving. Goodbye...Damn! No, goodbye...Teisha, if anyone else comes, get their number and tell them we'll get back to them. *And quit yelling! We can hear you just fine.*"

Teisha said, "*Okay, boss!*"

As soon as Jai walked off, she rolled her eyes at Teisha and watched as Henry rushed off in a worried conversation with Ax.

Jai knew they were lying because she remembered Ax from the first night she went to see Saria. Then Ax came up to Merch when he was propositioning her to come with him and Queen. "Why would Toonie lie," Jai mumbled in anger.

*****

Henry said, "Them people were just outside trying snatch somebody up across the street."

Ax said, "Handle that shit, fam. Make sure the vehicle gets towed if they don't take it. I'll be down in a minute."

Henry said, "Weird shit! Then they just pulled off in a hurry, but I got it."

*****

Ax said, "What's up, fam?"

Merch said, "On my way home. We should touch down in an hour or so. What's up, fam?"

Ax said, "Jai came asking about you and left her business card. Then that one situation was handled with the employee sign-in sheets."

Merch said, "Good looking, fam!"
Ax said, "Always!"

*****

Teisha said, "*Skunk on his way up, boss!*"
Ax said, "Thanks, Ms. Lungs!"
Teisha said, "*Whatever, nigga!*"
Skunk said, "What's up, fam? I see you texted me."
Ax said, "That fat fucker came looking like Terrence said, and Jai came looking for Merch, yelling about it's important."
Skunk said, "That's ole girl's twin that got caught up at the shop with Tara."
Ax said, "Damn! They fucked her sister up if she looks like that. They fine as hell."
Skunk said, "Yeah. That's fucked up. Jez was the quiet one, so I didn't mind her working with Tara. She got fucked up, and my brother got shot, then he's coming here like shit sweet."
Ax said, "Well, the paperwork went through."
Skunk said, "That's good! That gives us a few weeks or so."

Jez
Adjusting

Jez decided to go home with her parents and let the people guard the house instead of hiding. Her parents were mad as hell because they felt as if Jez was not caring about the situation.

Jez went downstairs to visit Tara before she left the hospital. As soon as they saw each other's faces, they immediately started crying like babies and hugging each other like they were blood sisters.

Tara said, "I miss you, girl. I'm so glad you are okay, and sorry this happened to you."

Jez said, "It wasn't our fault. Them pussy-ass cowards are ignorant. When are they letting you go home?"

Tara said, "Tomorrow, and Skunk hired security for the shop. I don't expect for you to come back after this happened."

Jez said, "I still got my piece you bought me. It's convincing my parents is the problem."

Tara said, "I want to wait until they find them, but Skunk said it's okay, so I believe him. I don't have time for that type of shit. Hopefully, our customers come back."

Jez said, "Well, when you leave here, call me so we can hang out. You can come to my parents' house. At least security will be outside until they catch them."

Tara said, "Skunk left a package for you. I appreciate all that you've helped me with."

Jez said, "Damn! Thank you so much, girl. You both are so nice to me. I'm coming back to the shop, and we need to change the code. Before I leave, I need to tell you that them people were upstairs questioning my family and me about Merch."

Tara said, "What did you say?"

Jez said, "Can't say anything about something I don't know."

Both the ladies laughed so hard that they didn't notice Samaya, Queen, and Coral walk in.

Jez saw Queen's face, and she kissed Tara on the cheek and started walking out of the room. "Hello, everyone," Tara said.

Samaya said, "Hi, Jez. Damn, they fucked you up too."

Coral said, "*Hey, Tara.*"

Jez said, "Hello, Samaya. Glad to see you're doing okay. Damn! They fucked you up too. I'll see you around."

"I can't stand that bitch," Queen said low enough just for Samaya to hear.

*****

Jez sat in her room, waiting for the phone to ring, missing Ishmael's voice so bad. He gave her a feeling that no other man has ever done in her presence. She pulled out the card and stared at it for a minute before getting the guts to call him.

Ishmael said, "What's up, beautiful?"

Jez said, "Hi, Ishmael! I wanted to hear your voice."

Ishmael said, "I tried seeing you at the hospital, but your parents weren't going."

Jez said, "Sorry. They didn't tell me you came."

Ishmael said, "When will I see you?"

Jez said, "Well, the police is outside my house right now, and my parents are bugging."

Ishmael said, "Jez. If you don't mind me asking, how old are you?"

Jez chuckled, knowing where he was going with the question because Jai said it all the time.

Jez said, "Twenty. How old are you, Ishmael? If you don't mind me asking."

Ishmael said, "Twenty-one, baby girl. Anything else you'd like to know?"

Jez said, "Yes! Do you have any kids or a wife?"

Ishmael said, "Neither. Do you?"

Jez said, "No. I'd like some later on though."

Ishmael said, "Can you sneak out?"

Jez laughed so hard, it made her face hurt.

Jez said, "I don't have to sneak, but I'm scared of being hurt again."

Ishmael said, "You don't have to worry about anyone while you're with me. Whoever did this to you, I'm going to find them."

Jez said, "When should I be ready?"

Ishmael said, "I'll call you when I'm outside?"

Jez said, "Don't call, I'll be looking for you. What color is your car?"

Jez's stomach started bubbling from nervousness at the thought of seeing him again.

She dashed down the stairs out the front door, running up to an all-white 2015 Dodge Challenger SXT.

She jumped in the car, hoping that he pulled off so no one would notice her leaving. He just sat there for a few minutes looking at her face as he rubbed her softly where the bruises were. "Pull off," Jez said. "How are you doing?"

Ishmael said, "Damn! They bruised my baby face up, but you're still beautiful. I'm okay. Thanks for asking. How are you feeling?"

Jez said, "I'm nervous! But okay."

Ishmael said, "You don't have to be nervous."

Jez said, "Never dated before. Just ran out of the house without saying anything."

Ishmael handed her his phone so that she could call her parents, but she didn't want them questioning her. She was hesitant at first, noticing the brace on his leg.

*****

Jennifer said, "*Hello.*"

Jez said, "Mom...I'll be back!"

Jennifer said, "*What are you doing? Who are you with?*"

Jez said, "I'm with my friend. I'll be back in an hour or so. Quit yelling, Mom, I'm grown. I'll be okay!"

Jennifer said, "*You're starting to act like Jai.*"

Jez said, "Mom, I'm okay. I'll be home later."

*****

379

TONDRIA LEATRICE

Ishmael said, "Are you okay? Where would you like to go?"

Jez said, "I'm fine. Somewhere safe, please."

Ishmael chuckled, knowing damn well she was serious. "I see you got jokes! What do you do for fun?" Ishmael asked.

Jez said, "Go to school, work, gym, and home every day. What do you do for a living that you can afford a car like this?"

Ishmael said, "That sounds like a routine! I'm a business owner."

Jez said, "What, a drug dealer?"

Ishmael said, "No. All successful black men aren't drug dealers. I have never been a street person. Why would I want to poison people? I'm a successful business owner. Grab that bag from the back seat. That's for you. Can't have you calling off your mama's house phone."

Jez said, "Another phone. Thank you so much!"

*****

They arrived at his aunt Avery's restaurant ran by her daughters and her. Ax used to work for her until he finished business management and started working for himself.

Ishmael was having a hard time getting out of the car. Jez rushed around to help him, and she noticed he couldn't bend his leg. *This is more than a fracture*, Jez thought.

She tried to act like she didn't feel the gun on his waist. She stayed trying to help him, knowing hers was in her bag.

Jez said, "Oh my gosh! What happened, Ishmael?"

Ishmael said, "I got shot coming out that damn club. Thanks for helping me."

As soon as they sat down, one of his cousins came running up to take their order until she saw his face.

Syria said, "*My favorite cousin in the whole world! Ishmael! OMG...where you been, fool?*"

Ishmael said, "I just saw you last week, quit playing. Let me introduce you to my friend Jez. This my little cousin Syria. Syria, meet Jez."

Syria said, "She must be special, cousin? He's never brought anyone here before? *Nice to meet you, Jez.*"

380

Jez said, "Likewise."

Syria said, "Oh! You got a bougie one? What can I get you to drink, Jez?"

Ishmael said, "Syria, stop it! Lemonade, and bring us the sampler platter, please."

Jez said, "It's okay, Ishmael! I'll have bougie water with a lemon please."

They both started laughing hard as hell, which Jez didn't find funny because she was serious as hell. Syria walked off to get their drinks and winked at Ishmael as she turned.

Jez said, "Is this one of your businesses?"

Ishmael said, "No. My aunt owns this restaurant."

Jez said, "Ishmael? Are you a gangster businessman? Like, who would shoot a legit business owner?"

Ishmael said, "First, what is that? Secondly, you should quit stereotyping. Third, I don't know who shot me."

Jez said, "How don't you know? Did you see them? I mean, you're carrying a weapon."

Ishmael said, "Look, quit asking questions over and over in a different way. Then, you sound like the people. Stop it! The weapon I have is no different from the one in your purse, gangster stylist."

Jez said, "I'm sorry. I'm wandering in case I need to use this. If you see them, we're shooting. I'm not getting dumped in a dumpster no more."

Ishmael said, "What's with all the talking at people, like you're talking down on them or giving orders? I don't know what race you are, but you seem racist. Maybe you should ask questions and get to know people before making assumptions, baby girl."

Jez said, "Okay. What type of businessman are you?"

Ishmael said, "Okay. Are you talking at me, or do you want to know me? Look, I wouldn't have started talking to you if I didn't want you."

Jez said, "After I felt the gun, I assumed. Sorry if you felt disrespected. I'm just scared."

Ishmael said, "Should I accept your apology because you were scared or you assumed you jumped in a car with a thug?"

Jez said, "I don't know! I'm sorry if I'm coming off rude."

Ishmael said, "My parents made sure I finished school on top of my class early, with a basketball scholarship at one of the best colleges. I couldn't go pro because I was too young, so I finished college right on time. Now, I'm signed, and this shit happened to me, being in the wrong place at the wrong time. My family owns restaurants, business offices, homes, clubs, and more. A strong black man and woman raised me in the hood with strict rules and structure. Tell me a little about yourself?"

Jez said, "Wow! You just checked me."

Ishmael said, "See…that would be the first thing out of your mouth, a misunderstanding of communication. What about 'Congratulations, Ishmael.' I'm making conversation telling you about myself, so we can get to know each other, but your smart mind thinks I'm checking you. You've never dated, so I get it. To know if we're compatible, we ask questions to see if we can deal with each other on a friendship level or more."

Jez said, "I finished high school at seventeen, started working at my father's company as an entry-level accountant for a few years. When my sister left home, it gave me the courage to start cosmetology school, which I just finished. Dad made sure we finished on top of our class but kept his hands on top of my mom's. And, I'm truly sorry for assuming."

Ishmael said, "Don't that shit feel good to talk with someone that's not your family? You don't have to apologize for something that you are not used to. We're learning each other. Congratulations, baby girl, on finishing. Sorry to hear about your mother, and I wouldn't wish that on my worst enemy."

Jez said, "Them people came to the hospital asking a lot of questions about your family and how we know you. My sister didn't say shit but caught an attitude when they mentioned your brother and that girl."

Ishmael said, "Thanks for the heads-up, but be more specific, baby girl. What brother and girl?"

Jez said, "They asked her about her dealings with Merch and Queen? She was angry."

Ishmael said, "What happened at Tara's place shouldn't have anything to do with my family. They're fishing around for shit that's not even there. I'll have my lawyer give them a call."

Jez said, "I told them what they needed to know. I didn't see anything."

Ishmael said, "Do you know how to use that stereotyping weapon in your bag?"

Jez said, "That's funny! Not really, but I will if I have to. Aim, then shoot! Right?"

Ishmael said, "That's good, baby girl! One thing for sure, you know how to aim at people for flaws, and you come off as being rude. Just because I say I'm not a drug dealer don't mean I'm knocking anyone's hustle."

Jez said, "Didn't know I was coming off as rude. Most definitely not judging people. I've heard a lot of the women speak on their men, so maybe I put you in a category that I shouldn't have. But, I don't like users…"

*****

Charles said, "They asked me to fuck with her sister, and I didn't know she had a twin. So, they all messing with one of them dudes."

Jill said, "I don't trust none of the females. Have you talked with Rocky or told him? *Charles!* What are you looking like that for?"

Charles said, "I'm not telling him shit! I don't like his ass. Have you talked to him?"

Jill said, "Nope! I've ditched his ass. Kala let me stay with her for a few days. Why do you keep looking like that?"

Charles said, "What is this? The people gave me his property. Why did he need a storage unit? Do you know anything about this? Here, you go check it out!"

CHAPTER 24

Tara:
No

Skunk made sure Tara stayed at the hotel they owned so they could keep an eye on her. He didn't want her questioned by them people either, so he had their lawyer talk to them, thinking she'd slip up and say something stupid.

*****

Tara stepped out of the shower looking at the test again, still in disbelief. She, ran to the room like a bat out of hell, jumped on the bed bouncing, screaming, and dancing. It woke Skunk up from his nap, "*Baby, look! Look! Look!*" Tara shouted.

Skunk said, "Hush before you wake up the whole hotel and get us put out."

Tara said, "*Whatever!*"

Tara waved the test back and forth in his face with tears rolling down her face. When he saw the tears, he got nervous. "Stop jumping and show me what the hell you are so happy and crying for," Skunk said. "This the third pregnancy test I took, and all of them say we're pregnant. OMG! I'm so happy, baby," Tara said.

Skunk said, "I'm going to be a daddy? Quit jumping and take that towel off."

Skunk lay on his back, then Tara sat all that pussy on his face and rode it like she was making a chocolate mousse.

As soon as she released, he turned her over and pushed her face in the pillow. He was stroking softly, trying not to hurt her then Tara started throwing her ass back all fast and hard until he pulled out of her.

Tara said, "Why you stop, Daddy?"

Skunk said, "Damn! You are throwing that pussy. I don't want to hurt the baby."

Tara said, "You're not going to hurt the baby, crazy. Come get this pussy, boy."

Skunk let Tara ride his dick because that way if something happened, it'd be her fault. He couldn't concentrate looking at her and hoping that they had a little girl that looked like her. Then he thought about the flowers she got and got thrown off.

Tara stared into his face as he slept imagining what their baby would look like, and his phone kept beeping. On the third call, she got up and grabbed it off the nightstand, and rushed into the bathroom so that he wouldn't wake up.

Tara said, "Hello...hello."

Lady said, "Hello, I'm trying to reach Sem. Is this the right number?"

Tara said, "Yes...it is. May I ask who's calling?"

Lady said, "Oh, I'm sorry, this is Chaste. Are you his assistant or something?"

Tara said, "Oh! I'm sorry as well. I'm his fiancée, Tara. How may we help you, Chaste?"

Chaste said, "Fiancée, huh? I prefer to talk with Sem when he's available, Tara."

The first time she said his government name, Tara thought she was a bill collector or family member. Tara peeped, she didn't say a business name, so she got mad immediately then the bitch tried being funny, repeating "fiancée," like she was shocked.

Tara said, "I can take a message if you'd like? He's sleeping, baby."

Chaste said, "It's complicated. I'll wait for him to call me."

Tara said, "Well, let me uncomplicate things for you, Chase. How can I help you?"

Chaste said, "It's Chaste! You can't finance, Tara."

Chaste hung up then Tara put the number in her phone, and she remembered her feeding him.

Punk ass won't be feeding again while I'm here, Tara thought as she scrolled. She started looking at the messages and skipping the ones from his family. It was one call from Chaste, then one call from Adana.

Tara was reading the text so fast, not realizing she was hyper-ventilating. She started texting Adana's punk ass like she was Skunk to see what was going on with this bitch.

When she saw that he bought the shop building from her, for some reason, it pissed her off to the point she cried.

Tara, acting like Skunk, texted, "What's up?"

Adana texted, "It was nice seeing you the other night. The way you kissed me and sucked my nipples made me want more of you."

Tara, acting like Skunk, texted, "That's what I do baby girl."

Adana texted, "when will I see you again?"

Tara, acting like Skunk, texted, "I'm busy right now, maybe later."

Adana texted, "let's meet at your mom's later...then go from there."

Tara, acting like Skunk, texted, "Yeah I'll text you later."

Adana texted, "okay, baby!"

Tara erased all the messages from her conversation and the call from Chaste as tears ran down her cheeks. She cried at the fact this bitch knows his mama and his mama's always smiling in her face but never speaks.

She went back in the room where he lay putting his phone down softly, wanting to punch his nose through the back of his head. She stood there looking at his ass sleeping, thinking hard about the pro-posal, the baby, and him pretending to be happy. The shit didn't sit right with her, but she kept calm. *I should sock his ass*, Tara thought.

She decided to call Marsha's two-faced ass, wondering why she never spoke or invited her to anything.

Marsha said, "Hello…"

Tara said, "Hi, Marsha, it's Tara. I got your number from Skunk. I have some good news."

Marsha said, "Where is Sem? Never mind! Hello, Tara."

Tara said, "I thought that we should get together and talk about the wedding."

Marsha said, "It's Tara, right? I think Sem should be the one calling me with the good news you said, right? What marriage?"

Tara said, "Oh, that's not the good news…"

Marsha said, "Where's Sem?"

Tara wanted to curse her out so bad, but the love she had for Skunk and the fact he'd fuck her up, she kept her mouth shut. She heard a lot of giggling in the back, and she sounded standoffish, so she lied.

Tara said, "He's on his way over your house, I believe."

Marsha said, "Well, what's the good news?"

Tara said, "We found out that we're pregnant."

Marsha said, "Oh? That's a big surprise. Well, I'll talk to you later. It's Tara. I have company right now."

Tara said, "Okay, good night."

When Marsha went to hang up the phone, she heard Marsha say Adana's name before the phone hung up all the way. Tara couldn't believe this bitch was at his mama's house right now kicking it, and waiting for her fiancé to show up.

Tara wiped her face off and started grabbing all her shit, making noises. When Skunk woke up, he saw Tara grabbing her bag like she was about to leave.

Skunk said, "*Where are you going?*"

Tara said, "Downstairs to get something to eat. Maybe my mama's house for this reunion."

Skunk said, "Hold on, bae. I'll go down with you because I need to make a run."

Tara said, "What? To your mama's house?"

Skunk said, "Why? Sit your ass down and wait a minute."

Tara said, "Should I order you something for when you come back?"

Skunk said, "No! I'll eat when I'm out. Thanks, baby."

Tara said, "I need money?"

Skunk said, "What you need money for if you're going down-stairs or to your mama's house? Quit playing with me."

Tara said, "I don't want to sit here by myself. Me and the baby going with you?"

Skunk said, "Who told you that? I'll be back, and you don't need to be running around with all this shit happening right now until we handle that."

*****

Charles said, "Let's follow his ass."

Roger said, "I know for a fact he was one of them at the house."

Reggie said, "I don't give a fuck about none of their asses. You kill mines, I'm coming for that ass."

Skunk
Choosing Up

Skunk picked up the deposits from all the businesses then headed to the bank. Before going to his mom's house, he picked her up some fresh roses and shrimp.

Skunk went in the house, handing each lady a rose, then gave the rest to his mother. He kissed all the ladies on their cheek with hugs. Avery, Jean, Sofia, and Marsha were eyeing him when he went to hug Adana. He was so nervous that she was going to do something outrageous in front of them; he almost didn't greet her.

They all knew he was a lady's man, and he was their favorite, but the way Adana gave head in the pantry cabinet gave him an adrenaline rush that made him feel overrated.

Adana said, "You okay? You're looking nervous again."

Skunk said, "I'm having all types of feelings right now. Finish, before they come looking for the Grey Pou—oh, shit!"

Adana said, "You good? You are so funny! And the mustard shouldn't be in this cabinet."

Skunk said, "You go freshen up, and I'll join you'll in a few."

Adana said, "You are nervous! You'll get used to it sooner or later. They're drunk, not paying us no mind, Sem."

Skunk said, "That nigga was crazy letting you go."

Adana said, "Excuse me? I didn't do this with him."

Skunk said, "If you had, maybe he wouldn't have cheated. I'll see you later."

*****

He did not notice Tara was following him, renting a different car each time she followed his ass. She started having a car dropped off while he was sleeping so she could move around when he left.

This nigga never bought me flowers, Tara thought as she watched him carry his ass in his mama's house. So Skunk wouldn't notice she was following him, she went straight to his mama's house most of the

389

time and parked down the street, waiting for his ass to pull up or pass her watching Adana's head come up on a few occasions.

She had her pistol in the glove box because she didn't know if Adana was about that life, and Toonie had to stop her a few times from using it.

When she saw him pull up, her heart dropped each time, hardening her heart, but the love for him stayed, but her staying with him was coming to an end.

Skunk said, "I should have brought more flowers seeing all these beautiful women here."

Marsha said, "Come eat, baby."

Sofia said, "Hey, cousin! When can I come work for you?"

Avery said, "You are not leaving the restaurant."

Sofia said, "Mom, please?"

Marsha said, "The way the numbers are looking, we can sell everything and chill."

Skunk said, "That's right, Mom. I don't want my family working anymore."

Jean said, "Hey, Sem! I'm so proud of my sons."

*****

Everyone knew when Jean had too many glasses of wine because all her words slurred. Plus, anything would come out of her mouth, but she knew better when their father was around.

Skunk said, "Thanks, Mama Jean."

Everyone knew that his mothers wanted him to be with Adana, but she was always on the move and worried only about herself and swallowing. Adana followed Skunk to the porch so they could talk alone.

Skunk said, "What's up, juicy booty?"

Adana said, "I thought you were going to text me back?"

Skunk said, "I was busy. What's up with you?"

Adana said, "Let's go! I want some alone time."

Skunk said, "Adana? Where do you see yourself in five years?"

Adana said, "*Huh?* I want to have another realtor's office, and I want you in my life forever and a big family. What about you, Sem?"

Skunk said, "That's it? Let's go have some drinks, and you can follow me downtown."

Skunk was holding Adana's hand, looking at her face turn red. She was trying not to look at all the half-naked women, but they were pretty and thick as hell.

Adana said, "OMG, Sem! I've never been to a gentlemen's club before. I need some shots."

Skunk said, "What's up, Ax?"

Ax said, "What's up, fam! I see you brought your mom's favorite."

Adana said, "I'm everybody's favorite, fool. How have you've been, Ax?"

Ax said, "I'm good. Y'all here to party?"

Skunk said, "Let us get a VIP room with the best bottle in this piece."

Skunk hit the flame, while he watched Adana's head go up and down to the music. He kept blowing the smoke at her so that she could get a contact. Soon, as he laid his head back, he felt her stand up. *What the fuck is she doing*, Skunk thought. She was moving her body to the music with no rhythm at all.

Skunk said, "Shid! Take them clothes off and do that."

Adana said, "If that's what you want, baby?"

Skunk said, "You know what you're doing a li'l bit. Damn! That booty moving, though."

Adana said, "For you, it does."

Skunk said, "Leave the panties on."

Adana took off her dress and left her panties on like instructed, then started dancing in front of him all slowly, rubbing her body.

Skunk motioned for her to come closer. He placed his hands on her hips, pulling her down toward him for her to sit on his manhood.

Adana said, "This what you want, Sem?"

She pulled her panties to the side then sat down on him and started moaning loud as fuck as if this was her first time.

He squeezed one of her nipples and sucked the other while she bounced on his dick, and he loved the sounds she made.

Skunk said, "Damn! This what you do for me?"

Adana said, "Yes, Sem! I'm all yours...I love you."

*****

Tara followed their asses right to Cupid, ready to bust the fucking building down, but they had security at the front door checking everything.

She looked at the shining lights flashing AMATEUR NIGHT, WINNER FIVE HUNDRED DOLLARS FIRST PRIZE, so she took off the button up and tied up the white tank.

She pulled her hair in a messy seductive bun, put on some lip gloss, snatched her bra off, then headed straight to the door, holding in her tears.

Henry said, "What's up, mama, twenty for entry? You're too pretty to pay."

Tara said, "Thanks, hun! Here to win that five hundred."

Henry said, "You are too pretty for that, and it's free if you are competing. Have fun. Hope you win."

Tara said, "Thank you!"

Tara went straight to the bar and got a double shot of vodka, not having a feeling in the world right now. She slammed it then asked for another round and a beer.

Her mind was stuck, but her body took off walking fast as hell, looking for him in the main areas. When she didn't see him, she got even more pissed and went to the bathroom to roll up some flame.

She saw Ax walk from the VIP area, and she turned her head real quick and noticed they had a security guard at the entrance to that bitch. *Fuck*, Tara thought.

She was mad as fuck, and her mind was racing so fast, she grabbed one of the strippers. She asked for a dance in the VIP because she knew that was the only way to get by this buff-ass bouncer in his tight ass T-shirt.

Stripper 1 said, "That'll be two hundred to get to the back, beautiful."

Tara handed her the money quickly, then the stripper took Tara by the hand and led her to a whole new section that she'd never seen before.

Tara said, "It's nice back here."

Stripper 1 said, "They just added on and redecorated, so all this is new."

Tara snatched her hand back and went straight to the room with the smoke and knocked on the door. They couldn't hear shit over the music anyway.

Stripper 1 said, "We can go right here, miss! That sign says occupied."

Tara said, "I'll give you five hundred dollars. Please!"

Stripper 1 said, "Hell yeah. For what?"

Tara said, "To shut the fuck up! Give me ten minutes before you call security. Okay?"

Stripper 1 said, "I will, but the door isn't locked, for our safety. Go right in, and take your time."

Tara handed her the money and opened the door and saw this bitch riding her fiancé's dick, with her tits all in his mouth.

It was so smoky in the room that they didn't even notice Tara had opened the door. She politely walked over and swung her fist so fast that Skunk and Adana didn't know what the fuck was happening.

She kept throwing punches until Adana jumped up off the floor, trying to fight back. Tara hit her in the head with the beer bottle, so Adana got fazed a little.

Skunk just sat there like he had seen a ghost until he caught hold of what was going on. "Damn! Tara, stop it," Skunk shouted.

The stripper stepped to the side so one couldn't notice her in the cut. She didn't call for help because Tara paid her well for the night.

Skunk was trying to separate them, noticing Tara had them hands punching like she was a professional hood boxer. As they swung, Tara was letting her know who the fuck she was.

Tara said, *"Bitch, I know, you know about me! Bitch. Bitch."*

"Get this bitch," Adana screamed. *Got dammit*, Skunk thought because he didn't know what the fuck to do. Busted or not, he wanted to finish fucking Adana.

Skunk looked at the stripper and yelled for her to get security. Ax and security finally made it to the back, trying to help Skunk get Tara off Adana.

Tara said, *"Why you propose to me, Skunk? Or, are you Sem right now?"*

Adana said, *"Bitch, wait until I catch your ass."*

Skunk said, "Take your ass home, Tara! We're not talking about this right now."

Adana said, "Yeah, go home! Dumb ass…"

Tara said, *"Oh! You're gonna send me home. But you're staying with Ms. Doggy Face?"*

Tara ran straight for Skunk swinging, but he grabbed her arms, knowing damn well she was too short to even get to his face.

Adana said, *"Fuck you, bitch!"*

Tara said, *"No, Doggy! I'm his bitch, and you're fucking him."*

Ax said, "Damn! Adana, go put your clothes on and sit down somewhere."

Tara said, *"Sit, Boo Boo, sit! Matter of fact. Go fetch another dick somewhere else."*

Skunk said, "Ax! Fam, take her home, please? Fuck it! Call a cab."

Ax said, "Which one?"

Henry said, "Is everything okay back here?"

"You're late," Adana said. Skunk smirked at Ax as he escorted Tara to the front door, making sure she got in her car and pulled off.

He went back into VIP to talk with Adana, and she was putting her clothes on and crying when he walked in the room.

Skunk said, "I'm so sorry this happened to you."

Adana said, "She's your fiancée, Sem? I don't know what made me think…I could get you back. This bitch bust my head open. *Fuck!"*

Skunk said, "Let me take you to the doctor? Your shit is leaking. Damn!"

Adana said, "Going around the question. Is this bitch your fiancée?"

Skunk said, "Chill with all that bitch shit. Let's go wait in the front for the cab."

Adana said, "*Oh wow!* Now you're protecting her? Yeah…let me go to the front. This is too much."

Skunk said, "Quit crying! Hold the ice on your face. Look, neither one of y'all is bitches. I didn't know she was following us unless I would have left you out of this."

Adana said, "*Not answering the question! Are you her fiancé, Sem?*"

Skunk said, "Whoa…bring your voice down, Adana. I don't know who the fuck you yelling at, but we're friends, and she's wrong for busting your shit open. I don't have to answer to neither one of y'all."

Adana said, "Excuse me! I'm mad as hell! My nut got interrupted, then my head open. The man I love is someone else's fiancé, and my parents are going to ask questions. Damn!"

Skunk said, "Quit saying that fiancé shit, emphasizing the shit. I'm fucking her and you. You just got back in town. I was excited to see you. My life was not put on hold for no one just like yours wasn't. Quit trying me, and I'm going to deal with her."

Adana said, "Do you love me, Sem?"

Skunk said, "Come on now! I love both of y'all, and you're going to stay with me too."

Adana stormed to the front to wait for her cab to arrive, and Skunk was right behind her. "Wait, Adana," Skunk shouted.

Bang. Bang. Bang. Bang. Bang.

Skunk said, "*What the fuck! Get down! Get down, Adana!*"

All you could hear was Adana screaming, security ducking and looking around to see which way the shots were coming. *Bang, bang, bang, bang, bang.*

Skunk started shooting in the air because he didn't know which way it was coming from to let whoever know he stayed strapped. *I hope this is not Tara*, Skunk thought. He heard the tires burning rubber, so he knew they pulled off. He stood up in time to see that it wasn't Tara's car.

Skunk said, "You okay? What the fuck!"

Adana said, "*She did this! Sem…she's crazy.*"

Skunk said, "Stop it! We don't know who did this. Go to the hospital. I'll see you later."

Skunk was so furious by the fact his brother just got shot coming out this bitch and now this shit. He didn't want to think Tara did the shit, so he made sure nobody at the club called one time.

CHAPTER 25

Isaiah
Trying to Deal

Isaiah said, "I've been staying here with my brother until this shit dies down. What I don't understand is why you left like you had something to do with this shit?"

Samaya said, "I was scared, Sai. I need to find out who killed my baby."

Isaiah said, "What baby?"

Samaya said, "I was carrying our baby, Sai. This shit is getting to me."

Isaiah said, "Why didn't you tell me? I'm not some bum-ass nigga."

Samaya said, "Really! I didn't even know until the doctor told me."

When Terrence knocked on the door, they both just looked at him.

Terrence said, I need to speak with you both so come to the office, please?"

Isaiah said, "Let's go get this shit over with."

Terrence said, "Samaya and Queen, I need the truth. Look at these pictures and tell me how you know these people. They're trying to kill you, and I need to know why."

Samaya said, "*Is that Jai sitting with Chad? What the fuck!*"

Terrence said, "How do you know him? His real name is Charles, and his younger brother Chad died in the first robbery."

Samaya said, "Chad tried talking to me a few times at the club, but that's it. They look identical! What the fuck is she doing with them?"

Isaiah said, "When was this?"

Samaya said, "Way before you bought the club, Sai! Which one tried to rob us? I told you that I saw one of them at the club before."

Isaiah said, "Something like that! It looks like we need Jai in this meeting of the minds."

Queen studied all the pictures and waited for names to be said. "Quit shaking your leg," Samaya whispered. "I'm anxious, cousin," Queen replied softly. She knew they were the ones that fucked up her cousins, and she was coming full force.

The door opened, and Ishmael brought Jill in and sat her away from Queen and Samaya across the room.

Queen got up and looked at the pictures again then nudged Samaya to look at the picture with Jill and Rocky standing in front of her building.

Samaya saw Jill's face in a pile, and she jumped up so fast and leaped over Isaiah's lap and landed punches all in Jill's face, and Queen politely moved to the side so she could whoop her ass with more space. Samaya went to grab the vase off the table to bust her face open. Terrence grabbed her arm. "Isaiah, get her," Terrence exclaimed. "*We don't need a mess on the floor. Damn!*"

Jill folded up screaming for help, but the guys let Samaya wear that ass out a little bit.

Jill said, "*Get her off me! Ishmael.*"

Ishmael said, "Ishmael, my ass! That was my niece or nephew."

Samaya said, "*Bitch! You killed my fucking baby. Whore bitch!*"

Queen wanted to jump in so bad, but Merch was holding her back, and the way he cuffed her made her forget all about the shit she saw him doing.

Samaya was hurting her to the point Terrence motioned for the guys to break them up with his perfect ass. Terrence looked like he didn't want to fuck up his manicure, but he didn't like seeing women fight.

Merch said, "Get your girl, Isaiah! Chill out, Q! I'm not letting you go."

Isaiah grabbed Samaya and held her in the corner until they picked Jill's punk ass up and sat her in the chair.

Jill said, "*I didn't do anything! Ask Kala!*"

Samaya said, "Bitch! Fuck you and Kala! Da fuck I want to see her for?"

The pain medication had Ishmael so high, he wanted to throw dollars on their ass for performing because he didn't believe any of the females. He just looked and shook his head in disgust because he knew Jill was wrong for setting his family up, and the girls, he hadn't figured out yet.

Isaiah said, "Bae, I can't let you kill the girl! Plus, she's going to tell us what we need to know."

Swen said, "Better her than me because I'd stomp the truth out her punk ass."

Terrence said, "Wake up, Jillian. We need to talk, sweetie!"

Swen said, "Throw some water on her ass. Wake the fuck up! Come back to the light."

They all laughed so hard, they had to wait a few minutes, then Jill opened her eyes and started singing like a hummingbird.

Jill said, "He made me do it! He made me do it!"

Terrence said, "Who? Why mess with this family? And for what?"

Jill said, "Rocky...Y'all stole his money and briefcase!"

Isaiah said, "*For...what?* Is this a script they told you to tell us?"

Swen said, "My nephews don't have to steal a motherfucking thang. She's talking about that fat peeping fucker, right?"

Jill said, "Rocky said you'll have his money and a box. He told them boys he'd pay them well if they got his stuff back."

Swen said, "This bitch stalling!"

Ishmael said, "She can stall all she wants. She's not leaving!"

Terrence said, "Jillian? Come on. We need more information."

Samaya said, "*Come on, Jillian. He made you do what?*"

Isaiah looked at Queen then glanced at Merch like, *You hear Samaya's voice changing*, and they all knew she was dead-ass serious. She scared Terrence, too, because he looked around the room, making sure no guns were visible or in reach of her.

Jill said, "He made me start following Samaya that day you threw all that money on her."

Isaiah said, "*Me?* Damn!"

Jill said, "Yes, you! He wanted all her money and yours once he found out who you were."

Samaya said, "*Come on, Jillian... There's more! We're giving you a chance to come clean.*"

Ishmael said, "So, when I met you that day leaving the restaurant, that shit was a setup?"

Jill said, "Yes! My family did some bad things, and he's holding it over our heads."

Isaiah said, "Terrence? Didn't you say they were married?"

Terrence said, "Yes, I did! Look at this picture. Do you know this woman sitting with your brother? We know your brother was one of the robbers who died. Is this some revenge type shit?"

Jill said, "No! That's my brother Charles. His identical twin died in the robbery. I don't know that lady. Never seen her before."

Samaya said, "So you sent him to talk to me? *Let me go, Isaiah! Please...let me get this bitch!*"

Jill said, "I'm so sorry that happened to you, Saria. I didn't want to go to jail."

Queen said, "*Why...they fuck with Tara, bitch?*"

Jill said, "His sons been after you and Saria for years. After Chad met Saria, he couldn't bring himself to harm her and go along with their plan."

Ishmael said, "And, you couldn't even tell me, huh?"

Before Queen could get to her, Merch swooped her up off her feet and carried her to the other side of the room, knocking shit over.

Skunk came storming in the room, trying to figure out why Merch was carrying Queen, and Isaiah was holding Samaya. *I should have handled it my way*, Skunk thought. He looked at Jill, then looked straight at Ishmael. "*Damn!* Who beat her ass?" Skunk shouted. "This crazy-ass woman right here. Samaya, calm down," Isaiah replied.

Samaya said, "Bitch saying my name like we're friends."

Jill said, "They started following her again because of him."

Skunk said, "*Who, me?* What did I do?"

Jill said, "He was told you pulled the trigger that killed his boys. He wanted everyone you loved."

Queen said, "*How does he know what went on in that house? Quit lying!*"

Merch said, "Q, let the girl lie. I mean, talk. Damn!"

Terrence said, "We need to know everything about Rocky, and you're going to help us."

Swen said, "How many is it of these monkey muthafuckers?"

Jill said, "I don't know!"

Samaya said, "*Listen to this bitch lie. How the fuck you don't know or never seen this lady if you followed me? Get the fuck out of here! Please let me at this bitch, bae.*"

Skunk said, "Right. How would they know what went on in that house unless someone is talking?"

Isaiah said, "I know for a fact none of us said shit."

Queen said, "If they're following us, they knew that wasn't my cousin's house then."

Samaya said, "Now it sounds like the bitch trying to insinuate it was me. Bae, let me go, please?"

Jill said, "Rocky's son's been wanting you, Saria and Queen. Rocky wouldn't let anyone mess with his girls."

Queen said, "Bitch, quit saying 'his girls' as we belong to his ass. You're his girl, the fuck!"

Before Jill could respond, Isaiah whispered in Samaya's ear, "Get that bitch, bae," and he moved out of the way.

Samaya dashed across the room so fast and punched her in the jaw. Before she could stomp her, Terrence grabbed her. "Get her, Isaiah," Terrence said.

Jill looked at Ishmael like he was supposed to help her ass, but he turned his head in disgust. Jill tried to swing back this time, but

Swen stepped in and pushed Samaya back. "What the fuck is you doing," Swen shouted.

Ishmael said, "You killed a baby, Jill. Damn! Was any of my other friends working with you?"

Isaiah said, "Who else works for Rocky beside his sons? Who else do we need to know about, Jill?"

Jill said, "Kala, his other sons, some girl at the club, and my brothers. But we were forced into this."

Queen said, "She singing now! Trying to save her family's ass."

Merch said, "Jill? Why did he come after my family?"

Jill said, "Y'all took his shit! He mentioned a box and a briefcase full of money. He told his goons to follow you and find his shit. I'm not lying to you, Ishmael."

Ishmael said, "Don't be saying my name like I'm cool with this shit, shawty."

Isaiah said, "*Where are they going next?*"

Jill said, "*Here.* They probably outside or followed somebody here."

Swen said, "That's what I've been waiting to hear. How does he know where my fam live?"

Merch said, "Rocky came looking for you at the club, Jillian. Said you told him that's where you were going. Why are you lying to him, or you lying to us?"

Isaiah said, "What does he have on you?"

Jill said, "Kala helped me get away from him. She told him that to keep him off my tracks. I've been staying with her these last few days."

Swen said, "Sounds like we need to bring Octopus Jaws back in here."

Isaiah said, "Unc! Please let this girl talk. Quit handing him the flame!"

Swen said, "Well, maybe she can suck the truth out her ass. Do y'all agree?"

Queen said, "Who, Swen? Who's Octopus?"

Swen said, "The girl with the big jaws and deep throat."

Merch said, "Terrence, finish, please! Take the bottle! Unc, done for tonight."

Terrence said, "Y'all need to stop beating on the girl. She's not going to be able to talk with no teeth. *Damn!* Now, tell us what he has on you so that we can help your ass?"

Queen said, "*We're not helping shit.*"

Merch said, "Be quiet, Q! Let's get to the bottom of this shit!"

Jill said, "A cop pulled me over in an undercover car and raped me. I got hold of his gun and shot him dead. Rocky's fat ass was standing right there like he didn't give a fuck. He made me marry him and work in that damn club for his silence."

Terrence said, "*Damn!* Why didn't you tell somebody? I've seen the tapes in the box and pictures of everything but a wedding."

Jill said, "I don't know! I called my brothers to come help us get rid of the evidence. Rocky took the gun, and my brothers drove him into the ocean. Since then, he's made us do some fucked-up shit."

Isaiah said, "So, you are just used to killing people, huh?"

Samaya said, "*Right!* Punk ass…"

Terrence said, "Were you there when they got rid of the car and body?"

Jill said, "Yes…I sat in the car, and I didn't tell him where you lived, Ishmael. They followed all of you after leaving the club. I told Rocky that I saw the box at the club. I'm the only one that you guys would allow in the building, so they sent me. He's looking for me now, and I didn't tell him shit."

Isaiah said, "The ocean, huh?"

Terrence said, "We can help you. Show us where the car got dumped. I need the gun and your help to get it, Jillian. That's if you need this shit from over your head."

Ishmael said, "You can stop it with that Ishmael shit! Who else has he done this to?"

Jill said, "Rachel's family helped him rob a local gang member named Seth for his money and drugs. They found out his dad works for the governor. That's why he's trying to run. Rocky's been black-mailing Rachel, making her do crazy shit now."

Isaiah said, "How did Rachel get caught up in this shit? She's just a waitress!"

Jill said, "I just met her with Kala. One of the men sent her to meet Rachel at her job."

Samaya said, "Who's Rachel, Sai?"

Isaiah said, "I'll tell you later!"

Ishmael said, "I'm getting tired of hearing this shit. Their coming here, right? When?"

Jill said, "I don't know! He was supposed to get the box from me. He probably thinks I left the state."

Swen said, "All this 'I.I.I.I don't know' shit getting on my last nerve."

Terrence said, "Hmm. Should we know where you're going just in case?"

Jill said, "I came to Cupid looking for you one day when you didn't answer, Ishmael. I was about to tell you everything, and he knew it. I tried to, seriously!"

Swen said, "And my nephew said quit saying his name, Jilly!"

Terrence said, "You tried what? Quit crying. We're going to help you."

Jill said, "Everybody started shooting, so I ran off. After we hooked up this time, I was going to tell you. I've been here, so I don't know what the plan is now."

Samaya said, "*Ishmael. Ishmael. Ishmael. Girl, please, please! How did you meet Rocky?*"

Everybody wanted to laugh, but Samaya's voice was sounding more and scarier as hell each time she spoke. "That's a good question," Swen murmured out.

The crazy part was every time Samaya talked or said anything, Jill looked panicky. When anyone else spoke, Jill looked right in their face, worried.

Swen said, "Shit! You all done let the beast out. Ask her some more shit, Saria."

Merch went to laugh, but Queen covered his mouth because she knew Samaya and Isaiah were hurt, and she was ready to end it for her cousin.

Terrence knew there was some truth to what Jill was saying, and he also knew she was covering her ass.

Terrence knew Samaya dealt with Chad, but she didn't think he had a twin. And he saw the anger in her face when he showed Jill the picture.

Merch said, "They're trying to rob strippers, drug dealers, and tried to get us. These some crazy, loose-brain, do-whatever-type niggas."

Jill said, "I tried to tell you after you bought the club. When he saw me, he grabbed me by my hair and pulled me out the back door. I overheard him talking to one of his sons that night before."

"Why didn't you call him? Dummy!" Samaya said. "Good question," Swen said.

Queen said, "*Yeah, yeah, yeah!* They want to help you, but I'm gon' hurt your ass just like you did my family, Jillian."

Jill said, "Kala came to warn you, but you shot at her, Queen."

The men knew she wasn't lying about the club incidence, but they still didn't trust her. "We're getting somewhere now?" Skunk said.

Terrence said, "I'm going to have one of my workers go with you, so you can show us where this car got dumped. Did this cop have a uniform or badge? When did this happen? Was it on the news or in the paper?"

Jill said, "No. Rocky said he was a cop, so I believed him. Two years ago, they drove the car off the south side drop that everybody hangs out. I've never seen it on the news or in the paper."

Samaya said, "Still gonna sit yo flap back ass there and not tell us how you met him?"

Jill said, "*Oh my gosh! If y'all seen the tapes, you should know!*"

Samaya said, "What tapes?"

Isaiah said, "We'll show you later."

Terrence said, "Do you know the gang members they robbed? Where is Rachel? I can help her too."

Terrence picked the picture up then put it in her face. When Terrence answered his phone, he told the caller, "Bring her in," then hung up.

Merch said, "Damn! Don't make her eat the pictures, Terrence. Damn!"

Ishmael said, "Let her eat 'em. She's good at it."

Terrence said, "Ishmael, please stop! Do you know this lady with your brother? Jill, drink this water. Come on, we need information. Just how y'all followed them and gathered info, we need to hear this shit right now."

Isaiah said, *"Don't get quiet! Tell the got damn truth."*

When the door opened, Jill thought she saw a ghost because Kala told her she didn't know them like that.

Everybody's mouth dropped open. Terrence wanted to see how everyone reacted when she came in.

Swen said, "Everybody, this is Octopus Jaws!"

Kala said, "Whatever, Uncle Willie!"

Jill said, "I saw her with Samaya and Tara when I was following her for Rocky. She had so much business that he wanted to rob her too."

Kala said, "You didn't see me with shit!"

Jill said, "No…the girl in the picture. She said something to us one night when she showed up to the club. He had me following her and putting notes on her car to scare her. I found out she had a twin later on. I followed her a few times after she brought clothes to the club."

Terrence said, "Well, you are not going anywhere until we identify this dead cop. My friend just dropped off some pictures for us to see. She'll go along with us to find this car."

Swen said, "Hey, friend!"

Kala said, "Friend, my ass! I dropped that package off already, Terrence."

Terrence said, "Really? That was fast."

Kala said, "You need to go as if nothing happened, Jill. If Rocky finds out you talked to us, he'll kill you. Don't try to run when my guy takes you to the spot where the car is. I've recorded everything you said."

Swen said, "Look at her face, friend! She can't say nothing happened, but she got her ass whooped."

Kala said, "Friend, my ass! Now, stop capping."

Terrence said, "Thanks, K! Where do you think the gun is at, Jillian?"

Jill said, "He has a safe in the wall at his house he thinks I don't know about."

Swen said, "There you go, keep it up! What else does he have at the house?"

Ishmael said, "I want his ass to come in this bitch so that we can light his ass up. I'm tired of this shit."

Swen said, "That's what the fuck I'm talking about, nephew. Let's get this shit over with."

Merch said, "We need that safe. You still haven't told us who this drug dealer is?"

Swen said, "Jaws? Can you handle that?"

Skunk said, "Come on, Unc! Leave that girl alone."

Terrence said, "Look through this pile of the people that died around that time. This pile is the people he's related to, and this pile is his friends since high school. These are the people we've seen him talking to the last few weeks, and this pile is Rachel's family."

Swen said, "Fuck she get all these pictures? Is she the people?"

Jill was confused because she knew Kala was working for Rocky and his family. Hell, she even fucked Charles a few times. How she got on their side was wowing the fuck out of her.

Kala was handing Terrence all of Rocky's information from his favorite color, to his hangouts, and his teenage shit.

Jill even thought this bitch was the people the way she planned this shit out. She wanted to say something, but she was outnumbered and tired of getting beat on knowing damn well she wanted to fight back.

Skunk said, "I've sat and listened to all this irritating shit. Why did they fuck with Tara? My baby didn't have shit to do with that club, a briefcase, or a damn box."

"What the fuck," Kala shouted as she saw Queen put that thang to her head. Everybody stopped talking and looked at Queen, hoping she didn't pull the trigger.

Merch said, "Whoa! Bae, chill! Come on, bae! Let us get all of them at once. I promise you. I'll get them, Q! Put the gun down!"

Samaya said, "Look around the room, Queen. Think about this!"

Queen said, "I should let loose on yo ass, you punk-ass bitch. She is lying about all this shit!"

Jill fell to the floor hard as hell, and everybody just let her ass lie there while Queen was holding the pipe to Jill's dome.

Queen turned around and pointed that bitch at Kala. Then everybody in the room looked like they didn't know what was going on. "You a punk bitch too. I know about you, bitch! Now, why did you really come to my shit?" Queen said in fury.

Kala's eyes started tearing up, because she was stuck and couldn't do shit. "Why are you fucking with my family? You chipmunk-face bitch," Queen shouted.

Merch said, "Stop it, Q!"

Terrence said, "*Okay! Calm down! Kala, get the fuck from out of here! Come on, Queen! Hand me the weapon. Please let me get all their ass for you...*"

Swen said, "Let Quebie shoot they ass."

Merch said, "Unc, stop!"

Isaiah stepped in and took the gun from Queen and took the ladies to a different room while Terrence, Skunk, Swen, and Ishmael stayed with Jill.

The girls got mad as hell, but the other brothers knew what he was doing. He helped Jill clean up her face and made sure she ate. Then they looked through the pictures together and gathered information.

He knew she couldn't concentrate with all the fighting, yelling, and Kala was a distraction, so he wanted to make her feel comfortable. She started pointing people out in the pictures, giving dates, and singing again like a true friend.

Ishmael said, "You're going to text Rocky like you were scared. Tell him you think we found out about you."

Swen said, "Why is she crying? Look, we're not scared of Rocky and his sons. Just tell him you hid from everybody. Okay, jukie!"

Jill said, "This the cop right here…Why is Kala here?"

Terrence said, "Are you sure, Jill? Kala is here for everybody."

Ishmael said, "You're not in no position to ask questions."

Jill said, "I know how you feel. Do you know, Kala?"

Terrence had his guy get pictures of all the employees at Cupid, screenshots from the videos, Rocky's family members, some mug-shots, and mixed them in with the other photos, then lied to her about who they were.

When she pointed them out, they were the men from the videos they found at Cupid, and he wasn't surprised. Terrence had Ishmael get his brothers quickly so that they could see this shit.

Terrence said, "Look at this here! Now tell me what you know about Kala?"

Merch said, "Ms. Amateur Night, huh?"

Ishmael said, "I don't want to hear shit else from her."

Terrence said, "Bro…we need to hear this!"

Isaiah said, "Come on! My baby died behind this shit!"

Jill said, "Kala was asked to follow the girls from the beginning, so his sons could rob Saria and Queen. Everybody knows that they got money hid in a warehouse somewhere or something. After this shit kicked off with Rocky's stuff coming up missing, everything got turned around."

Isaiah said, "Kala's on her way to the club. Let me call Ax."

Terrence said, "Jill? You're trying to tell me that his sons know about this nasty shit?"

Terrence played the video, then threw the photos on the table, and she covered her face in disgust. She didn't want everyone see-ing what she went through and the other innocent people getting tortured.

Ishmael said, "*Damn!* This man sick."

Swen said, "Turn that shit off! I'm not about to watch this sick shit."

Jill said, "No. They don't know about him. This man connected with important people. That's why everyone is scared of him."

Merch said, "Well, I know of Seth! Once he finds out Rocky had something to do with his shit getting took, he's not gonna give a fuck about who he knows."

Swen said, "I need to know what's up with this Kala broad, Terrence?"

Jill said, "Are sure she's going to the club or maybe going to tell them we're all here? The little time I've known her, she'll do anything for the highest bid."

Skunk said, "Why Tara?"

Jill said, "When Kala saw she owned a shop, she got jealous and told them about her spot. Ask Tara about her fight with Kala."

Skunk said, "What fight?"

Jill said, "I told you we followed them to school and everywhere else. Kala was furious because Tara had more than her. We went to meet up with Rachel and ran into Tara."

Terrence said, "You can go with him, Jill. He'll bring you to another room without the other ladies."

Isaiah said, "I called Ax and put him up on game. Fuck this!"

Terrence said, "Look. I had my boys do a background check on Kala ass too. She knows them, but I don't know how yet? She's following dick and money only. Setting people up is not in her blood."

Swen said, "What would make her snitch on her friend's family? I don't fuck with people like that, seriously."

Isaiah said, "This whole time they were after the ladies. Then we stumble onto a hidden treasure of freaky shit and guns."

Skunk said, "Bitch-ass nigga should have come in the club and asked for his shit."

Ishmael said, "I'm with Unc on this one. Why would she tell?"

Terrence said, "Okay. I took her to my office after the club that first night, and my wife caught us fucking in my office. She's the second woman I got caught up with, so the divorce is final."

Merch said, "Damn, bro! She got some good-ass neck though."

Skunk said, "Damn, she does! Hope you don't love her, bro?"

Terrence said, "Come on, bro! I love the way that fat ass sits up like that."

Skunk said, "Long as your boy Mint keeps an eye on her, we're good."

Swen said, "Damn! Merch told me about her octopus grip. She done had all y'all? She's playing both sides. She's probably fucking them also."

Ishmael said, "She didn't suck or fuck me! She looks sneaky as fuck. Looking like she's always thinking about a plan."

Merch said, "She can plan to get fucked up! Good head or not, I'm not playing about my family."

Swen said, "When your pops said, 'Don't mix business with pleasure,' this is what the fuck he meant. You can't be fucking these females and they work for you. They know all your damn business. *Naw, nephews, naw!*"

Terrence said, "They're leading all the bullshit to your houses and businesses."

Swen said, "If this private investigating shit doesn't go right, I'm handling this shit my way. *That's a promise, Terrence.*"

Terrence said, "Hmm. My investigations stopped my brothers from getting questioned about the first robbery. Self-defense! My plan will work."

Swen said, "*You pretty motherfucker! Did yo investigation stop my got damn nephew from getting popped? Get the fuck out here, with that diploma shit!*"

Isaiah said, "Whoa, Unc. We didn't know none of this was going to happen. Let's chill and get this shit over. I'm not about to have my best friend arguing with my fam."

Terrence said, "It's all good, Isaiah. I understand where he's coming from. I'm pissed as well."

Swen said, "Look. Don't think I don't know about that slick sarcasm shit you trying to slide past my ears, young boy. Dumping these niggas in the river is self-defense in my book."

Merch said, "Unc! Come on! Terrence not like that. Skunk… quit passing Unc the flame. He's tripping already."

Swen said, "*I'm not tripping shit! I'm observing this* 'I'm pissed as well' *type bullshit!*"

They all started laughing, but when Swen saw Terrence smirk, Swen stood up and staggered a little. Isaiah caught him and helped him sit back down. Isaiah took the liquor bottle from his uncle. "No fighting," Isaiah said.

Skunk said, "Well, I need to switch this shit up before y'all start fighting. Somebody shot at me, leaving the club. *Hold on!* I didn't want any of them females knowing shit. I waited to say something."

Swen said, "See...I don't need a degree to shoot this mutha-fucka. *Let's go!*"

Isaiah said, "I thought we had everybody already!"

Terrence said, "Somebody is lying!"

Swen said, "*Seems like it! Go get that octopus-mouth bitch and the jilly-hickle-bee-looking muthafucker.*"

They all wanted to laugh so bad, but the way Swen's eyes looked, they knew he was furious. He was ready to hurt somebody over them on the strength of their father.

Skunk said, "Unc? You're coming with me! Let's go talk with Tara."

Ishmael
Really, Though

Merch went to Cupid and kicked it with Kala until Terrence called him. He made sure she was drinking and flaming so she wouldn't know what hit her when the truth came out.

Queen didn't like the fact that he had to be with the bitch all night hearing Swen call her "octopus," putting that shit together, but her cousin's revenge was more important.

*****

Terrence, Skunk, Zach, Mint, and Jill went to the area where she said the car is. Terrence knew the bitch wasn't lying about being raped because he saw the video in Rocky's collection, but he knew her dumb ass meant lake.

*****

The dead mystery cop she pointed out from the stack of pictures wasn't dead. Terrence didn't tell her, because he needed leverage over her head. He had Zach arrange a meeting with the dead cop to make a business proposition that involved getting rid of Jill.

*****

Terrence found out about Rachel's little sister Riley. He never expected Rocky to go after her innocence, but she was in one of the recent photos. Zach took pictures of her coming out his trap house and men coming and going.

Jill took them to Rachel, and Riley and Rachel was so pissed at Jill when she saw she'd brought them. They had to keep Rachel from fucking her face up more. "*They're here to help us,*" Jill shouted. Rachel was frightened until Terrence explained everything to her "She showed him where I lived," Rachel cried out. "Please help us!"

Riley said, "I don't want to go back to that hellhole."

*****

Swen had Jill call Charles, Reggie, and Roger while he sat there listening to every word coming out of her mouth, making sure she said what Terrence told her to a tee, playing with his pipe.

If Jill didn't follow the instructions, they made sure she knew they had the gun and the recovered car to hand over to the people if she didn't follow the plan.

*****

Jill was nervous when she approached Reggie because he was a hothead like Queen. Charles, Reggie, Roger, Rosso, and Roswell all listened to Jill as they drove to the spot.

Jill said, "Look! When we go in, be quick, because his graduation ceremony is for two hours. Did y'all leave the phones at the house?"

Roger said, "We're not stupid, bitch! Look like somebody dog walked yo ass."

Charles said, "Chill, nigga! Now, let's dog walk in and out this bitch rich."

Reggie said, "I don't need that long. We can catch their ass leaving the ceremony."

Rosso said, "Can't believe this nigga trusted you with the key. Dumb ass!"

Jill said, "*Fuck you*, Roger!"

Roger said, "No! You got fucked up…"

*****

Merch already knew Jai was game for whatever he wanted, and Kala was going, too, after he flashed all that money in her face. Kala was ready to suck some shit when he told them they were going to his house. "Let us go where we can have some privacy," Merch demanded.

*****

Zach said, "What's up, man? You're Rocky's guy, right? He told me some good things about you."

The dead mystery cop said, "Yeah! That's my man. So, you heard Jill was running her mouth, huh? I'm glad you caught this bitch before she started telling some shit."

Zach said, "Hell yeah! I'll make her disappear for this much money. *No problem!*"

The dead mystery cop said, "We're using finger motions now? Money is no problem."

Zach said, "Yeah! She's trying to snitch on us too. We'll be there in a few minutes."

The dead mystery cop said, "I told Rocky to let her go a long time ago. She knows and seen too much already."

Zach said, "Some people don't understand dead weight."

*****

Before they got to the driveway, her brother pulled her to the side. "Did you tell them who I am?" Charles asked. "No, I didn't," Jill whispered in disgust.

Jill said, "Be quiet and follow me this way. The safe is in the dining room behind this picture."

They followed behind her, and Charles stayed at the front door looking out as they crept around the corner. When Jill turned the light on, they all froze. "What the fuck," Reggie said.

Charles felt something cold on the back of his head, and he already knew what time it was. "Go, bitch," Ishmael said.

Charles said, "What the fuck is going on?"

Isaiah said, "We're going to do this a little different from what the fuck you bitch niggas did. *Samaya and Queen, take the pistols from these fools.*"

415

Ishmael said, "*Nigga, take a seat with they ass! Here's Mr. Charles.* Ladies, help me tie them up."

Samaya said, "Sit yo pussy ass down and quit acting tough. Bitch!"

Reggie said, "Yeah! I got you, Saria…"

*****

Zach and the dead mystery cop pulled up and went straight into the house. His signal was to come in when the light was on.

Zach said, "This snitch bitch right here around the corner tied up. You got gloves?"

The dead mystery cop said, "Yes, I do. Always come prepared, my nigga."

When they turned the corner, the dead mystery cop saw Seth standing over in the corner with a smirk on his face of satisfaction. When he looked at Jill, he put his face down in disbelief. Before she could attack him, Zach picked her up and carried back to the corner. "You'll have your time with him," Zach said in her ear.

Jill said, "*I…I thought you were dead? Bitch…*"

Seth said, "Sit yo punk ass down with the rest of these fools."

Ishmael said, "Check his ass, Zach! Tape and tie his hands."

Seth said, "So, you are a cop now, Ethan?"

Jill said, "Rocky told me he was a cop. I thought you were dead? I can't believe this shit!"

Everyone started looking at the man tied up in the chair with his face covered with a potato bag. When he started moaning, he realized he couldn't move and tried to rock himself out of the chair. "Calm down, buddy," Seth whispered.

Queen said, "Buddy has a lot of explaining to do."

*****

Merch walked in Ishmael's house with the ladies all giggly. He slapped Kala on her ass. "That's going to cost you," Kala said. "I bet it is," Merch whispered. After he found out about her scheming ass, he wanted Queen to get the bitch in the worse way. Jai was so drunk, she couldn't wait to fuck Merch with another female, besides Queen.

Merch said, "Turn right there. My room down to the right."

When Kala turned the corner, she almost ran when her enemies of her enemies were on the floor with their hands tied up and their mouths taped. She was shocked at what to say, and the way Swen looked at her, she was scared for her life. She didn't think Terrence would betray her; after all, they did together and not tell her about this meeting.

Rachel was staring at Kala, hoping she didn't tell them she gave up Queen's information.

Rachel said, "Riley, they'll never be able to rape us or make us turn tricks anymore."

Jai said, "Chuck? What the fuck is going on here?"

Everybody looked straight at them, and the only word you heard from everyone was "*Damn! Rape?*" "They're out of pocket, nephew," Swen said, knowing he knew already.

Terrence said, "His name is *sick*-ass Charles. You should find out more about a man before you start fucking and sucking him within days."

Jai said, "I can do as I please."

*****

Ishmael walked off to his room. When he came back with Jez, everybody looked surprised. "Damn! It's two of they fine asses," Swen shouted out. Jez ran straight to her twin "Why are we here," Jez whispered in Jai's ear.

Jai said, "What the fuck is going on? Sis, are you okay?"

Terrence said, "Ishmael? What's going on, bro?"

Ishmael said, "They got the wrong man locked up for this shit. She can change that by hearing this sick shit."

Didn't anybody know that Ishmael was bringing Jez to confront her stalker face-to-face and to give her comfort as he promised?

Queen said, "What is she doing here? This some other shit!"

Tara said, "Hold on! We both were victims to these assholes, and she deserves to be here, period."

Jez said, "What the fuck! That's Chuck!"

Terrence said, "Listen! We need to get this shit over."

Ishmael walked around them, pulling off their tape to hear what the men had to say, not noticing the nervousness in the room getting heavy.

Terrence made sure he put the tape in his pocket because of DNA. The men thought they were going to rob someone, so they already had on gloves, and do-rags were covering half their faces, which made the plan go easier.

Mint walked over and poured water on the man with the mask on. When he started choking, all you could hear was mumbling.

Ishmael said, *"Shut the fuck up! Fat ass!"*

Seth pulled the mask off. "So…where is my shit, Rocky?" Seth said. When he pulled the tape off his mouth, Rocky was stuttering and pretending as if he couldn't speak.

Mint said, *"Wake the fuck up!"*

Seth said, *"Look at me, pussy! Ethan, you're playing the role of a cop now? Motherfuckers on tape doing nasty shit. Then, you set me up, bitch?"*

Ethan said, "It's not like that! I didn't have shit to do with none of this."

Seth said, "Shut the fuck up! Where my shit at?"

Seth slapped the shit out of Ethan and walked over to Rocky, then put his pistol in his mouth. "Y'all like playing cops and robbers, huh," Seth muttered out in anger.

Rocky couldn't believe that they were playing the tapes in front of his family. They couldn't believe what they were seeing, so they just put their head down in disgust.

Rocky started crying and moping like a baby. "What the fuck are you crying for?" Seth said. "Dad, this is some crazy sick shit," Rosso said.

Isaiah said, "How does it feel being on the other side?"

Samaya said, *"You're behind the death of my baby, Rocky!"*

Rocky said, "*Please…Seth? Ethan set that robbery up. He told me where the money and product was.*"

Seth said, "*Shut the fuck up, Mr. Ricardo.*"

Ethan said, "*Nigga! You and Chad set up everything. Quit lying, motherfucker. You wanted Jill, so you and Charles paid me to set her up.*"

Ishmael said, "Truth is coming out now the shoe on the other foot. No point in asking who shot me. All of you are pointing more fingers than you have. Keep singing."

Jill said, "*No. No. You're my brother, bitch? Why?*"

Charles said, "*Fuck you, bitch!*"

Rosso said, "Ethan, you paid us. So, how in the fuck we even know about his shit? You never said it was his. *It don't matter anymore. Tell the truth.*"

Queen said, "*Well, we know all y'all had something to do with something. It really don't matter.*"

Rocky said, "I didn't have anything to do with none of this shit. I wanted my belongings back. Ask Kala."

Samaya said, "I heard you wanted my money."

Kala said, "Don't ask me shit!"

Ishmael said, "These are the people that hurt you and my family. Now you've seen and heard the truth, let me get you and Jai out of here."

Jai said, "*Hold on! Charles said he was a detective. Lying ass! And to think I was fucking a thief and rapist.*"

Charles said, "*Fuck you! I don't know this bitch!*"

Jai said, "Son of a bitch!"

Jai ran across the room and tried to kick him, but Zach grabbed her up off her feet. "What the fuck are you trying to do," Zach said.

Jez said, "Is this why you came looking for Queen, Kala?"

Queen said, "Excuse me?"

Kala said, "Fuck you! Cat-face ass."

Jez said, "That man and Kala came and messed up my sister's shop looking for Queen and Samaya. Tara already beat that ass. You don't want none again…"

Terrence said, "*Get the girls out of here, now!* Samaya and Queen, stay."

*****

Zach took Tara to the hotel, then dropped Rachel, Riley, Kala, and the twins back to Seth's warehouse, and Teisha met up with them. Teisha was instructed to keep an eye on them until the men came.

Jai still didn't get a chance to holler at Merch as she wanted. She saw Queen mean mugging her from across the room. "I'm getting you, bitch," Jai thought she saw Queen mumble, so she stopped looking at him and her.

Terrence said, "Let's get down to business. I'm ready to go!"

Jez couldn't help but think about having an innocent man in jail, and how he pleaded his innocence that day.

*****

Rachel and Riley were happy to be free from torture, but mad they had to ride in the car with Jill and Kala.

Tara was mad as hell she had to leave but also pissed she had to sit in Skunk's face thinking about him sucking a bitch's titties, to the point she couldn't even say anything.

*****

Isaiah said, "Mr. Ricardo? You're responsible for my baby's death, and that shit's not sitting right with me. Hell, your own kids died behind some bullshit. You are taking people's innocence, you nasty fucker."

Rocky said, "No...I just wanted my shit back."

Ishmael said, "We found guns and tapes! Quit making it seem like we took some money."

Seth said, "But you took my shit! My shit didn't belong to you, Negro. Quit it with that fast-talking shit!"

Rosso said, "You said they took a briefcase and money, then you're raping people?"

Charles said, "Look! I'll tell you everything. I'm not about to go ouuuu—"

Before Charles could finish his sentence, *boom, boom, boom boom.* "Asshole" was whispered softly by the shooter. *Boom, boom, boom…boom. Boom.*

Terrence said, "*No…no…no. What the fuck!*"

Swen said, "It's about time! I was getting sick of looking at they rat asses."

Seth said, "*Got damn, my nigga!*"

Terrence said, "*Aww, shit!*"

Charles started squirming on the floor, trying to lift his weak arms to point before he could move any limb. *Boom. boom. boom.*

Merch said, "*Damn! This wasn't part of the plan.*"

Swen said, "Somebody had to do it sooner or later."

The room got silent, then Terrence walked over and grabbed the pistol because he trusted no one, and he didn't want to get caught in the cross fire or the court system. Terrence turned and looked at everybody in the room like, *Another mess I need to clean up.* "This stays in this room," Terrence said. "It's okay…Give me the gun!"

Ishmael said, "Go take them clothes off, then put on one of my shirts. Hurry up! Bring all the dirty clothes back to me. *Hurry up!*"

Samaya and Queen stood there in a daze watching Ishmael put everything in a bag. Mint, Seth, and Swen started gathering everything up.

Terrence said, "*Damn!* We wanted to find this man's shit."

Seth said, "You clean up here, then I'll deal with the rest. I'll find my shit! Jill punk ass know where it is."

Terrence said, "It wasn't supposed to go like this. The man was about to speak!"

Swen said, "What? Speak another lie! Don't nobody have time for all that? Especially for someone who does this type shit to people."

Ishmael said, "It is what it is! Fuck it! Let's get this shit over with."

Queen said, "Why didn't his sons say shit? Charles didn't either."

Terrence said, "Charles tried."

Ishmael said, "They were embarrassed. I wouldn't have said shit either."

Samaya said, "All their ass nasty. Da fuck! Like father, like sons."

PART 6

Who We've Created

CHAPTER 26

Samaya
Numb

Before Teisha started questioning the ladies, she had separated them into different rooms. She noticed a lot of bullshit with Jill and Kala's story when they were together, but Rachel was either dumb or playing dumb.

Jill blamed everything on Kala and Rocky, but the only problem was Jill knew way too much about everything.

Kala told some truth until she started dodging around, getting dicked down. Teisha saw her leave Cupid a few times trying to get paid for her services from everybody.

Kala said, "Why they bring me here?"

Teisha said, "What made you go to Queen's house? You said, 'She shot at me.' I mean, y'all ain't friends."

Kala said, "I went to talk to her. Rocky wanted to know if she saw his belongings. *The bitch just started shooting. She didn't even see me. And no, we're not friends. I don't like the bitch.*"

Teisha said, "Well, damn! Didn't mean to anger you, Kaka. How did you know where she lived?"

Kala said, "It's Kala. Ask Rocky, shit! I need something to drink. You're questioning me like you're a detective or something."

Teisha said, "I'm not questioning shit! I'm talking to you. You're just answering with free will. Besides, you don't see me writing shit down, do you?"

Kala said, "I thought you worked for them? I'm ready to go!"

Teisha said, "Naw, girl. They got me waiting for them in this damn warehouse. I overheard that other girl in the purple telling them some shit about you. I'm tired of answering questions as well."

Kala said, "Bitch, can't tell them too much. She gave me Queen's address, and Rocky went to the bitch house after they got shot up at Cupid."

Teisha said, "That's why I don't have female friends now. They talk too much for me. I fought Queen and her punk ass cousin at Cupid, girl. They tried to jump me."

Kala said, "No, bitch! You're lying. They act so tough. That's why I fucked her man."

Teisha said, "I don't know who fucking who when it comes to the men."

Kala said, "Girl, Merch sexy as hell. Anyways, they said once they finished we'll be good to go home."

Teisha said, "I don't know about all that leaving shit. You might have to talk with Terrence first."

Teisha got up and walked off. Before entering the other room, she called Terrence. "That Kala bitch, a setup, setup. I'll call you back," Teisha said and hung up before he could say anything.

*****

As soon as she swung the door open, she grabbed a chair and pretended to cry. "I can't take this anymore," Teisha sobbed. "These motherfuckers believe anything a bitch tell them. I told them I didn't have shit to do with none of this shit. That bitch Kala in there telling all the business. Have you met Tunisia?"

Jill said, "No. But why are they messing with you? Don't cry! You didn't have anything to do with this shit. I'll tell them."

Teisha said, "I'm sorry, I'm Tay. What's your name?"

Jill said, "It's okay. I'm Jill! I've been here waiting for them to get finished so that I could go home."

Teisha said, "*Oh no! I can't talk to you. That girl Kala said you're behind all this shit. Why did they put me in here with you? Oh my gosh! They're going to think that we know each other or something.*"

Jill said, "*Hold on! She's lying.* She's the one breaking up marriages, fucking all them brothers and their enemies. Rachel's dizzy ass handing out addresses. They bet' not be saying my name."

Teisha knew none of them or what the fuck they were talking about, but she knew a sneaky lying-ass snitch. She knew Jill would snitch like a bitch if the finger pointed at her.

Teisha said, "She said you and Samaya had this planned, then she started crying hysterically. I told them Rocky planned all this shit."

Jill said, "Who the fuck is Samaya? Kala only wants to know their dick sizes and how much money she can get. Rachel's dumb ass sucked dick for a few dollars in a restaurant with her punk ass."

Teisha said, "That other girl said she saw you with Queen, and don't nobody like that smart-mouth bitch."

Jill said, "I'm about to go smack them for real, for real. Where are they? Them bitches know the truth behind what Rocky wanted. His nasty-ass videos."

Teisha said, "Hold on! I'll show you. Did you hear about his sons? That's fucked up!"

Jill said, "All their asses is crazy and thirsty. I told Terrence they've been plotting on Saria and Queen. They were following them for a long time. Hmm, how did you get involved in this?"

Teisha said, "Hold up! I'm about to go get them."

*****

As soon as the door closed, Teisha called Terrence back. "Jill a dumb bitch! She was doing as told, but hiding something," Teisha said and hung up. Terrence looked at his phone. "I don't see how they deal with this bitch," he whispered.

*****

427

Samaya was crying like a baby, feeling happy and disappointed at the same time, thinking if she weren't a dancer, her baby would be alive.

She's come face-to-face with the devil himself, not knowing she was working with him at the club for years. She'd never thought Rocky was this stupid and nasty, with his horny, humping-around ass.

*****

Merch said, "Y'all can stay in this hotel room until everything dies down. We'll make sure you have everything you need. Queen... Queen?"

Queen said, "What? Damn!"

Merch said, "Don't what me! What the fuck are you daydreaming about?"

Tara said, "Why do we need to stay in the hotel owned by y'all?"

Skunk said, "Because we're trying to keep y'all safe."

Merch said, "Like I said, you're staying here for a while, and I'll have someone drive you around until this shit calms down."

Tara said, "I'm not staying here, period. What the fuck are we hiding for?"

Skunk said, "You will if I tell you to, Tara. Let something happen to my baby. That's yo ass. *Now, period that!*"

Merch said, "We don't know who the fuck these niggas are and who they were working with. It's just for safety. Damn!"

Queen said, "I'll stay for a few days, but I'm not about to stay cooped up in a hotel."

Merch said, "What the fuck you mean? You were running, and now you're a superhero? Get the fuck out of here."

Queen said, "*I was running from yo ass!*"

Merch said, "Let's get something straight. You weren't running from me. Scary ass!"

Queen said, "*Fuck youuuuuu!*"

"*What mothafuccc—*" Merch said. Before he could finish his sentence, Samaya and Isaiah were running in the front. Merch choking the shit out of Queen's ass, and Samaya started punching him in the back of his head. "Get the fuck off her, dude," Isaiah shouted. Skunk grabbed Merch's arm before he hit Queen, and Isaiah held Samaya.

Merch said, "Watch your mouth, Queen! Samaya...back yo ass up! Much as shit I've done for you and your family."

Samaya said, "Don't be pushing me, Merch! I'm not that bitch!"

Merch said, "And, I'm no punk either, *Samaya!*"

Tara said, "*Dude, you're tripping!*"

Skunk said, "Shut yo ass up! Didn't you bust somebody's head open with a beer bottle?"

Tara said, "*You mad? You mad, huh?*"

Tara dashed at Skunk, but Isaiah grabbed her ass real quick, knowing Skunk would never hit a woman "*Sit your pregnant ass down,*" Skunk shouted. "Whoa. Whoa. Chill, baby girl," Isaiah whispered.

Samaya was surprised at what she heard and looked at Queen. "You bust somebody's shit, sis?" Samaya said, giggling. "That's a felony," Queen mumbled softly.

Skunk said, "Yeah, it is a felony! Luckily, I told her not to press charges."

Tara said, "*You're gonna keep playing with me, huh? You should have let her.*"

Tara tried hard to get at Skunk, but Merch stood in front of her and let her tag his chest. "You like that bitch, huh?" Tara kept yelling over and over.

Skunk said, "Have a seat, Tara! You don't want to see the other side of me..."

Tara said, "*I already saw you sucking! So, what's the other side?*"

Skunk stood up and started walking toward the door and acted like he was leaving.

Samaya said, "*Tara, oh my gosh!*"

Tara said, "*What the fuck!*"

Merch said, "Got damn! Bro, do that shit again for me!"

Tara said, "Fuck you, Merch!"

Isaiah said, "Y'all need to calm down. I know everybody still shocked, but arguing and fighting ain't going to change shit."

When they turned around, Samaya was swinging at Skunk, and before anybody could make it to them, he backed up and shoved her to the ground. Queen went to throw the lamp at him, but Merch snatched it before she could release it.

Tara just stood there still in shock that Skunk slapped her. *That shit hurt my heart more than my flesh*, Tara thought.

Isaiah said, "Merch, you and Skunk need to leave right now."

Skunk said, "Naw! They got me messed up."

Samaya said, "What's the matter, Queen? Quit crying!"

Queen said, "We don't have to stay here in their shit?"

Merch said, "*Because I said so! Now, shut the fuck up!*"

Skunk said, "I'm pretty sure you didn't have a problem fucking in this *shit, huh*? I'm gone before they call their crazy-ass aunt."

Merch said, "Bro, you a fool!"

Skunk said, "The bitch is crazy! Tell them, Tara! You better be lucky she's your aunt. Don't get quiet now, Ms. Heavyweight Boxer."

Samaya said, "Really, Skunk? You just went all the way there. *Damn!*"

Queen said, "Sure did! Dick was good, but I'm not running anymore, Master Merch. And, Skunk, you can slow that tongue down about my family. *Bro!*"

Tara said, "Queen has a point, and I don't need babysitting or spankings."

Samaya said, "We don't have to, but it's a good idea, ladies. Let's lay low for a few days."

Merch said, "You're damn right, I'm master. We shared our first piece of pussy here, remember, Q?"

Queen said, "This bitch said 'spankings,' and Master just broadcasting the daily pussy news."

Samaya said, "*Can y'all please stop?*"

Isaiah said, "Yeah, this is going too far. I don't want to hear about no dicks and pussies right now."

Merch said, "I'm gone, bro. Call me when you're ready before I am on the news."

Queen said, "Make sure your fiancé is right on your side when you're escorted out with the flashing lights and cameras."

Merch said, "And you're gonna be on the other side with yo—"

Isaiah said, "Enough…Bro, I'll call you later…"

*****

Isaiah reserved a room for them to have some privacy. He had some questions for Samaya, and he wasn't into everyone being in his business.

Isaiah turned on the music and flamed as he watched her fall asleep on the couch. *We would have had a beautiful baby*, Isaiah thought.

He ran some hot bathwater with bubbles, added some oil, and lit some candles. When he went back into the room, he picked Samaya up, carried her into the bathroom, undressed her, and helped her into the tub.

Samaya was so sleepy that her body went limp as he washed her hair a few times and rubbed her back and body. She kept opening her eyes as the water hit her body that he splashed on her softly, and he politely brushed his hands through her long thick hair.

Samaya lay across the bed with her head over his warm chest, looking at this handsome man of hers. *What would the baby have looked like*, she thought.

When Isaiah felt the warm water hit his chest, he knew she was crying, so he rubbed her hair softly and hugged her tightly as he flamed the pain away temporarily.

Isaiah said, "They're fighting with all this shit going on. You okay, baby? Seriously."

Samaya said, "They killed our baby, Sai. I didn't even know I was pregnant until they told me in the hospital. That did something to my heart. I've never felt this type of void."

Isaiah said, "Baby, don't cry! It's going to be all right, come on."

Isaiah wiped her tears off her face, then he kissed her juicy bottom lip slowly as he continued to wipe the tears from her cheeks. He held her chin. *Oh my gosh, don't look at me*, Samaya thought as she lifted her face to indulge into the kiss even more. When their eyes connected, she felt his motherfucking soul snatch her heart with a link.

He guided her to lie on her stomach while he massaged the lotion over her entire body slowly. That shit was feeling so good. She couldn't hold back her emotions and started crying even more. *What the fuck is he doing to me*, she thought.

"Turn over. It's going to be okay," Isaiah whispered in her ear. He leaned over, bit her nipple, and started playing with her nipple ring with the tip of his tongue.

When he noticed that she was crying hard, he backed up a little and hugged her. She thought, *This is what a hug feels like from a man who loves you*. That's when she knew he was her backbone, and she had to be his without a doubt.

Isaiah said, "Quit crying, it's going to be okay, Samaya. I'm not going nowhere."

Samaya said, "I don't know what to do? Where am I going? I don't even have a place to live anymore. Then my poor baby. *Why?*"

Isaiah said, "We'll find you a place to live that's simple shit. I got you! Hell, I don't have a house no more."

Samaya said, "You own this big hotel. You bought the strip club without telling me. What else are you hiding from me?"

Isaiah said, "Where is this shit coming from? I'm not about to start arguing and fighting like them. That's not my style."

Samaya said, "These big houses, nice cars, hotels, and buying clubs?"

Isaiah said, "Excuse me? I'm not hiding shit! I'm a grown-ass man with affairs happening all the time. Buying a business means I'm hiding something seriously?"

Samaya said, "I don't know what to expect after being beaten up and robbed. I'm sorry, my mind all over the place."

Isaiah said, "Let me explain something to you. I didn't know you had a problem with my wealth or asking me questions. We've been fucking around. You could've asked questions."

Samaya said, "My hustle is all I ever knew, and for the man I'm falling for to buy the club I'm working at is sneaky."

Isaiah said, "Sneaky, huh? My family owns a lot of properties, companies, stocks, and some more shit. When did it become your business what we owned? Maybe you're hiding something from me. You did run."

Samaya said, "I'm not hiding anything from you. I ran because I was scared of what the outcome was going to be after all this. Then you're talking to me like I'm not shit. I didn't ask for this to happen. You asked me to stop dancing, and I did."

Isaiah said, "Quit assuming shit! Talk to me and ask questions. I have nothing to hide from you. My brother wanted to buy the club. It's not even my forte. Investing money to get money, yes, indeed."

Samaya said, "Who are you? Where all this money come from? What's the relation between us? Did you ask me to stop dancing because you bought the club?"

Isaiah said, "No! I didn't want everybody seeing mines. Look, we're past all that. We were about to have a baby.

Samaya said, "Past what? You said ask, and us having a baby wouldn't have changed the fact I don't know enough about you."

Isaiah said, "Whoa, whoa, let me answer one question at a time. I'm Isaiah. I'm showing you how to get the money as I do. You're mines, Samaya. Like us."

Samaya said, "Us, huh?"

Isaiah said, "Let us not argue, and we just lost our baby. Then this other shit just happened. From now on, do your normal routine. We can define us as time goes by."

Samaya said, "I danced for a living, remember? That was my source of income and routine."

Isaiah said, "Let's start from where you left off. First, we need to find a place. Second, when you start college, everything will fall into place. Be patient."

Samaya said, "Being patient isn't putting money in my pocket."

Isaiah said, "Bae, shut up! Bring that ass here so that we can release all this stress. We're going to need to see a therapist after all this shit."

Samaya said, "I do not need to see shit! Ain't nothing wrong with me."

Isaiah said, "You've been through a lot lately. Might help. Come here!"

Samaya said, "You can go with me. Put another baby in me, Sai!"

Isaiah said, "You're not listening. I said we're going, damn! Bring that ass right here. If the equation is right, it'll be a girl."

Isaiah grabbed her ass, pushing her down harder onto his manhood, watching her boobs bounce. "I want a boy, so hopefully, my calculation is on point," Samaya moaned. He missed how she rode his dick, and she missed him. "You can have whatever you want. You keep bouncing like that," Isaiah replied.

*****

That morning before Isaiah left, Samaya made sure he left some bands for them to get around. He also talked with Mint so he could watch the ladies while they were out handling business.

*****

Mint knew the ladies still were nervous about what happened, so he tried to make sure they were comfortable as possible. He was paid nicely to stay around them for a while, and a few weeks had passed in no time.

Mint said, "What's the plan for today?"

Tara said, "Oh my gosh! I can't do this shit! I'm going to my shop to pick up some things, then I'm going to stay with Mom's irritating self."

Mint said, "You know I can't take you to your family's houses."

Queen said, "Girl, I'm coming with you."

Samaya said, "So, you heifers think y'all leaving me here with Mint?"

Mint said, "What's wrong with me? I'm getting paid nicely to keep you safe."

Queen said, "You left us the first night. Was it good?"

Samaya said, "Hush! I don't kiss and tell."

Tara said, "My pregnant ass be needing some homemade food. Plus, I'm still pissed I caught Skunk fucking that bitch. They better be glad they check you at the door. But I'm going to the shop he bought for me with his abusive ass."

Samaya said, "Why didn't you hit him instead of her?"

Queen said, "I would've shot both they ass."

Tara said, "She knew about me, and she was the closet."

Samaya said, "Bitch! quit playing. That quiet nigga would have shot yo ass."

Tara said, "I thought about that too! Queen, you didn't laugh when Merch was choking yo ass. Haha, that!"

Queen said, "That shit didn't hurt. He chokes me harder when we're fucking."

Mint said, "Okay, ladies…Let's change the subject."

Queen said, "Call my aunt and tell her we're on our way. My ass is starving. Plus, Merch hasn't said much to me anyway. Probably with one of his bitches."

Samaya said, "I don't have time for Isaiah coming over there looking for me. Now he wants to get a place together like we're married."

Mint said, "Don't do it unless you're ready."

Queen said, "Anyways! If he doesn't contact me soon, we're finished."

Samaya said, "*See, bitch!* Quit saying that shit around me, and Merch will fuck you up! I'll fuck you up! That baby is innocent. Give the baby to me, hell!"

Queen said, "I'm scared, Samaya! I don't want to be a single mother with my baby having a stepmom and shit. I'm not pregnant, for the last time."

Mint said, "They got power over y'all!"

Tara said, "*Well, I'm keeping my baby! I don't give a fuck if Skunk is not in this baby's life! Period.*"

Samaya said, "Queen, call him and quit arguing with that man. Give that baby a chance."

Queen said, "Here we go with all this sad and simple shit. You call him! *I'm not pregnant. Damn!*"

Tara said, "Call Merch, Samaya! Call Skunk, too, while your at it."

Samaya said, "Y'all mad! Don't get mad at me. Da fuck!"

Mint said, "Now, they got y'all arguing at each other."

Samaya said, "*Oh my gosh, Mint! Shut up.*"

Queen said, "Mint, take me to my aunt's house, please?"

Tara said, "*Please, Mint! They're stressing me out.*"

Mint said, "My instructions were to take you back to the hotel after running errands."

Samaya said, "*What instructions?*"

Queen said, "*Instructions?*"

Tara said, "*Instructions, my ass!*"

Samaya put her pistol to his head. Queen turned and looked at Tara like this bitch done lost her mind. Tara shook her head and held her stomach. "This is accessory," Tara said.

Queen laughed so hard. "456908 push, please," Queen said in a burst of laughter.

Samaya said, "*Motherfucker, please! The instructions changed! Now take me to my mufucking mama's house right now!*"

He turned the car around fast as hell, not even playing with his life. *I should hit this tree and make this bitch fly through the window,* Mint thought.

Mint said, "*Samaya!* Put that thing down before it goes off! This fucking car gonna flip over and kill all our asses and babies too."

Queen said, "This shit done made my fam snap!"

Tara said, "Sis, you are experiencing a little bit of a perinatal after distributive shock or something. You need to breathe!"

Queen said, "Bang! He's dead, and we'll all be crippled or dead. Samaya, chill!"

Tara said, "Queen, stop it! This shit is not funny at all. Sis, give me that thang before you black out and do some dumb shit."

Samaya said, "When we get there, you can call whoever gave you the instructions. Tell them we said we're not leaving, and you're welcome to stay if you want some homemade food. *Your choice!*"

Mint said, "*Shit!* Let's eat some homemade food by Auntie Tamyra. Should we go grocery shopping first?"

Queen looked at Samaya like, *Bitch, you lost your mind*, and Tara just giggled because she knew her sister wasn't playing.

How does he know my mama's name. Ain't sitting right with me, Tara thought.

Mint wanted to pull over and dump Samaya in the river, but he knew she was going through some new shit. Plus, all their asses were packing, and he knew he'd have to lay them all down, mentally fucked up and all.

Queen said, "*Damn! Damn!* We're pulling pipes to go eat some homemade food."

Tara said, "*This bitch got juice now!* Samaya, sit your ass back. I want my life and my babies."

Samaya said, "Nobody is running my fucking life. If I want to visit my damn mama, I will, the fuck. Take us to the grocery store, please? Can't come empty-handed. On her side of town."

*****

The ladies cooked while Sammie and Mint played the game in the living room smoking flame.

After a few shots, Mint felt at home and didn't bother to call none of them, including Terrence.

Tamyra had set up the couch for Mint to sleep on because he refused to leave from by the front door. He hadn't had a decent night's sleep since all the traveling and following them began.

He was aware of his surroundings because he had watched the house already, and he noticed Tara peeking around the corner at him constantly. Queen said, "What do you keep looking at him for." "Just because he's watching the door doesn't make it any better for us," Tara replied. "No reason to be nervous," Samaya said.

Sammie said, "Get some rest, son…I'm gonna need you to rest so I can get my rematch tomorrow."

Mint said, "I got you! Thanks for the hospitality, much appreciated."

Tamyra said, "You're always welcome, baby."

When Samaya went to check on him, he was sleeping like a baby, so she took his car keys and slept on the couch across from him. She slept with her thang under her pillow in case he called his friends on her.

*****

That morning Samaya saw Tara rushing toward the front door. Before she could get out the main entrance, Samaya grabbed her by the arm "Where are you going?" Samaya whispered so no one could hear them.

Tara said, "Why? You need to ask that nigga in there how he knows our mama name. We didn't say it yesterday. Now let me go before we both wake the whole house up, cra-cra."

*****

Samaya just stood there standing over this man as he slept, and the whole house was quiet. She was thinking about a plan to get away with dumping his ass at the club in a gift box.

"*What the fuck,*" Mint yelled out, but she put her hand over his mouth. "Damn, nigga, yo breath stank," Samaya whispered. "Shhh! Now tell me how the fuck you know my mama, bitch? Now speak! if you yell, muthafucker, I will shoot you dead."

Mint said, "I know your whole family, Samaya. I've followed you and found you. I made sure the men that hurt you and your family was brought together and handled. I watched your parents so that Rocky couldn't bring harm to them. He was here on several occasions looking for you, and I chased them off with your parents not knowing shit."

Samaya said, "You were hired by whom? Do you work for yourself? Did you find all of them? Did I say something funny?"

Mint said, "You can start a question with a W if you'd like. I'm not with that crazy shit."

Samaya said, "Who the fuck are you then? I'm not playing with yo ass!"

Mint said, "I have partners, and we own an investigation company, and that's how I found you and know of your people. If need be, we can look for the rest of them and kill everybody that was ever associated with him. Can you make some coffee, cra-cra?"

Samaya said, "Fuck you! And I know you like my cousin. You better not hurt her."

Mint said, "Samaya, go make some coffee or something. You're already scrambled, so no need for scrambled eggs."

Samaya said, "Whatever, nigga! You'll be cracked and scrambled in no time you keep fucking with us."

*****

Toonie came in and saw Samaya standing over this man covering his mouth, looking at him with her pipe at his temple. She stood there and watched the whole thing ensue, and neither one of them heard her creep into the house. When she had heard enough, she went upstairs because she never heard Samaya sound or act like that, and it scared the shit out of her.

Jai
Games

Jai stayed at her parents' house with Jez until she got the call from Merch that everything was cool.

She still didn't understand being questioned by his friends, but she answered everything so that she could leave in peace.

She felt that Jez was disturbed by everything, and feeling guilty about having the wrong man convicted made her stay and keep an eye on her.

Jai didn't give a fuck about the shit going on, as long as her twin got justice. She still wanted to see Kala about that shit so that she could have clarity.

Their parents were so happy to have Jai home, they didn't ask any questions or have a clue to what just went down in their daughter's life.

When she saw Chuck sitting on the floor, she almost kicked him in the face to think he lied about his name and he had something to do with her twin getting hurt. Jai felt as if he deserved everything coming to him and more if he did that to his sister.

*****

Jai went to get coffee then called Kimberly to meet her at the shop so they could get caught up on back orders.

Kimberly said, "I'll call her and let her know you're here."

The man said, "Don't do that, I'll surprise her!"

Kimberly said, "She's going to love the flowers."

*****

Jai looked at her chocolate friend sitting in her office chair, wanting him more than ever before.

Forgetting about all the bullshit that just happened, she smiled so hard, all her teeth were showing.

He grabbed her neck and pulled her head toward him. "How can I help you, sir?" Jai whispered with pleasure. "You already know what I want. Take that shit off," the man demanded.

Jai locked the door, and he was behind her pulling and pushing her head toward the door.

The more she moaned, the more forceful he got, and she loved it. She started taking her clothes off slowly, doing as he said. While she was taking it all off slowly, he pulled her panties to the side and went full ham.

Jai said, "Oh my gosh! I've been missing you!"

When he grabbed her chin and pulled her toward him, she started unbuckling his pants and moaning to the enjoyment of his grip around her neck.

The man let her soft, manicured hands take his dick out. He watched her place it right on the tip of her tongue and slowly grip the tip with her lips. When she stopped doing that, she sucked his tip then opened her throat to let it all in, choking vaguely. "Got damn," the man moaned, just enough for her to hear. "You need to teach classes on this shit," he said as he clenched her hair and let her do her.

Before he could bust a nut, he pulled back, motioning for her to turn around onto the desk. When she bent over, he put her right leg onto her desk. She felt the tip of his dick on her clitoris and moaned loudly, not giving a fuck about customers or employees.

The man let his dick sit there to see how long she could take it, and he chuckled because he watched her ass squirm wanting him, moving around, trying to make it go in. She grabbed his dick within seven seconds trying to push it in herself. "Don't play with me! Put it in, Daddy. I miss this dick," Jai said.

He knew she couldn't wait that long, so he pushed his manhood in and watched her enjoy him more than any other female, but the feeling isn't mutual. Watching her throw it back made him stroke harder, and her juices began flowing like a river.

The man said, "You like that, don't you?"

Jai said, "*Yes, Daddy, yes!*"

The man said, "This shit getting better each time."

The man chopped it up with Jai before he left, and she went on with her day as usual, feeling no remorse for fucking the shit out of him.

*****

Jai said, "Nice for you to come in and help, sis."

Jez said, "Girl, you know I wouldn't leave you hanging. Hello, Kimberly, how are you?"

Kimberly said, "I'm good, but horny after hearing your sister get hers on in the office."

Jez tried not to spit her coffee out laughing so hard, and Jai had a shameful look on her face. "Plus, he was fine," Kimberly said. "Really! I'm sorry, girl," Jai replied.

Kimberly said, "It's okay! It sounded like you were about to make a dick challenge video."

Jez choked on her coffee again it spilled all over her shirt. "Yo ass funny." Jez giggled.

Jai said, "Sis, getting coffee all on the fabrics."

Jez said, "I'm sorry, I'm sorry, but that shit was funny."

Jai said, "Your ass needs some dick to loosen that ass up."

Kimberly said, "*Who? Me?* Girl, I get the dick on a regular, plus, my man doesn't play that shit."

Jez said, "I'll stay a virgin until I meet the right one. Besides, I think sex is overrated."

Jai said, "*Girl!* You mean this man buying phones and you haven't even let him smell the pussy? Hell, she got to meet the family and everything."

Jez said, "He hasn't smelled it. *Ugh, sis!* He bought the phone so that we could stay in contact. Mom always picking up the other phone when I'm on it. If he didn't buy it, I was."

Jai went to grab the phone out of Jez's bag and show it to Kimberly, but Jez smacked her hand hard as hell. "Don't play with me, wet cooch," Jez uttered.

Jai said, "*OMG, sis! What the fuck! Where the fuck you get that from?*"

Jez said, "It's pretty, huh? When the notes were getting put on my car, Tara bought it for me to have protection."

Jai said, "*Damn!* I see y'all pretty close. Don't let Mom see that shit, or she'll freak out. Dad might think he has a son finally."

Jez said, "We're besties! I'm going to work at her shop again. Daddy always treated me like a boy anyway."

Kimberly said, "I'll be over to see you with all this hair. I hate combing it."

Jez said, "Looks like both of you need to get your ends chopped off..."

Jai said, "I'm happy for you! I'll be over there. For the record, I hired Kimberly to replace you when you graduated, and I have another lady coming in later for an interview. Sis, let me talk with you in my office please."

Kimberly said, "I hope I like the new chick, and she better get the coffee right."

Jez said, "Somebody is jealous, I see. I'll train her in before I start school."

*****

"What's up," Jez said, as she closed the door. "What do you think they did to Chuck," Jai whispered. *That nigga gave some good head*, Jai thought. "I'm just glad it's over with," Jez said, pulling out a lighter to flame. "What the hell," Jai shouted. "Let me hit that shit," Jai said.

Jai said, "I can't believe Chuck or Charles was a fraud. What you think they did with him?"

Jez said, "The less we know, the better. I'm not about to ask their asses either, so quit asking me about that shit. It's over with!"

*****

Jai went home, cleaned up, went over her designs for the four models, drew some extra ones just in case, sipped her wine, and called

443

Kimberly. She hadn't got Kimberly's sizes due to all the conflict that was going on, so she called for her to come over.

Jai called all the models and made sure they knew to come by the shop tomorrow for their fittings. She had Kimberly go pick up some cheese, crackers, water, and wine for the ladies for when they came.

This event was one of the most significant events they had every year, and everybody was going to be there.

That's how Jai met some famous designers a few years ago that made her push her style. They gave her some valuable tips on designs, materials to use, information on how to make a look that everyone will know that it's your work.

*****

The doorbell rang, and she ran to the door in a hurry. "Hey, girl," Jai said in a soft tipsy voice.

Kimberly walked in with a one-piece green spandex short outfit on and some wheat Timbos. She smelled like a fresh garden being hit by the sunrise light shine. "What's up, girl." Kimberly giggled, knowing Jai was tipsy.

Jai said, "Would you like a drink? Come over here and let me see what these new designs do for your figure."

Kimberly said, "Thank you! I need a drink after what went on tonight... You just did these tonight? That's quick, girl. Red will look good on my skin tone. Let me finish this drink, then I'll try them on. Do you mind?"

Jai said, "Take your time. I'll finish up these last alterations on these few designs for you to try on. If you don't mind me asking, what happened?"

Kimberly said, "My supposed-to-be man side chick called me on an app. She sent me some pictures and screenshot messages. He just got a power dick because we fuck all the time."

Jai said, "Kimberly? Men and women do as one pleases, so I can't take sides. Besides, everybody wants sex if it's been a six-year or one-minute relationship. One thing I do know is that feelings come and go by each individual."

Kimberly said, "He should have told me then. Bitch was so pretty, I would have fucked and sucked her myself. He didn't allow me to ride with him or let alone show him how deep my loyalty was."

Jai said, "I'm running into a lot of 'ride or die' chicks...giving too much energy into some bullshit that ain't even worth it. Reverse that shit! Ride and die for yourself. Fuck that! That's why my feelings are in check. Don't get attached, so I can do me and leave."

Kimberly said, "What the fuck? No...I loved this man, Jai! I would have done anything for this man."

Jai said, "Tell me this. The love you feel for a child, your child. Can he get that same feeling? Seriously!"

Kimberly said, "I love our child more when you put it that way. We've been through so much together. Why would he cheat?"

Jai said, "Ask yourself! Why am I asking questions about how he treated me when I know who I am. Girl, come out this trance and love yourself first. The kids come first, period."

Kimberly said, "We only have one child together. Thanks for the input, but...I like how this fits. I might have to buy this one. Tell me, why are you here alone?"

Jai said, "I like it this way. I'm in control of me. We'll go with these two you like and put it with the others. We can call it a night. Thanks for coming by on such short notice."

Kimberly said, "Do you ever think you'll fall in love? I know you are attracted to nice-looking men. I'm sorry, I shouldn't have said that. No dissing."

Jai said, "It's fine. I don't know about love. I want someone that wants and feels the same way about me, as I do them. And, I'm attracted to men and women."

Kimberly said, "I know, right! When I got home from work today, all his stuff was gone. I had the locks changed because he took his keys. I need another drink!"

Jai said, "Don't cry, Kimberly. You're a beautiful woman as well. Have you ever cheated?"

Kimberly said, "Of course not! From the messages she sent, they've been messing around for years. Way before our baby."

Kimberly finished her third drink and hit the flame, so she was ripped. When she sat on the bench to take the outfit off, Jai leaned over to help her so she wouldn't tear it. "Oh, thank you," Kimberly slurred.

Jai was mesmerized by her soft, beautiful buttered-down skin. Before Kimberly could stand up all the way and pull her bodysuit past her hips, Jai's hand brushed against her nipple. "*Oh, damn!*" Kimberly said. When Jai saw that she liked it, she gently pushed her back down on the bench and pulled her suit back off.

Jai put her face in between her thighs, and the wetness began the more Kimberly opened her legs. Kimberly lifted her legs over Jai's shoulders, letting her indulge into her pearl, and all the pain and stress went away for that moment.

Kimberly said, "Jai…yassssss, hmm, please don't tell anyone."

Jai said, "Shhh!"

Kimberly pushed Jai's head into her woman valley, not giving a fuck if she was breathing or not. Jai reached up and grabbed her nipples, squeezing them as the man did to her, knowing the feeling was pleasing.

Listening to Kimberly force a moan of satisfaction made her stop because something wasn't right. When she looked at her, it looked as if she was troubled. "What's the matter," Jai asked.

Kimberly said, "Oh my gosh, Jai! We shouldn't have happened. Your skills are most definitely better than his, but you're a woman."

Jai said, "Come and let me show you what to do, Kimberly. Let your tongue follow the motion of my hand. I'll move your head slowly, okay?"

Kimberly said, "Girl, don't laugh at me."

Kimberly moved her tongue the same way that Jai's hand moved. Jai could tell from the way her head moved she was an amateur with her tongue skills. Jai didn't give a fuck as long as she was pleased, and Kimberly returned the favor.

Jai said, "Slow down, Kim! Imagine you're eating a popsicle or sucker…Oh, yes…"

Kimberly said, "Wait a minute! I'm doing this with you with ease. I always told him no."

When Jai heard her phone beep a few times, she pushed Kimberly's head back. "Get up," Jai said as she felt her walls relax in disappointment. Kimberly rolled off her knees to sit on her butt, watching Jai look at her phone, smiling. She pretended to look at her phone as this woman turned her feeling off wanting pleasure like a pro. *Do not watch her,* Kimberly thought.

Kimberly said, "That must be a man texting the way you're smiling?"

Jai said, "You don't get it! A feeling is a feeling of a man or woman. It's all on how we decide to take it. You mean to tell me you denied him head?"

Kimberly said, "Yes, I did! I took this man for face value and what he had to offer. I thought I pleased him in every way. He begged me to have this baby."

Jai said, "Did he eat your pussy? What did you have to offer him? The baby is a blessing, so don't ever second-guess that."

Kimberly said, "Yes, he did. I gave him a baby and I. So, if I had sucked his dick, he would have stayed?"

Jai said, "Look, working in the shop, I've seen men come with no money and ready to spend their last dime on women. The sad part is when I meet the women, they're mad, rude, ungrateful, and then wonder why all the cheating is happening, thinking somebody owes them something, but it's an eagle trip. I bet the other girl sucked it."

Kimberly said, "Don't nobody owe me shit! The question or point is to be aware of what a person's intentions are upfront. Now, I understand what my father meant by being aware and don't be blinded by what someone else thinks love is."

Jai said, "Your daddy must know the truth? Feelings come and go. That's why I want someone that feels the same way as me."

Jai walked Kimberly to the door, and when she opened it, the man was standing right there. "What's up?" the man said.

Jai said, "Kimberly? I'll see you tomorrow. Thanks for all your work."

The man said, "She can stay!"

Jai looked at the man sideways, knowing damn well she was going for anything he said. "I need to get home," Kimberly said softly. "Call his ass! I bet he doesn't answer," Jai replied. "Relationship problems," the man said.

Kimberly turned around and walked back in with them, not knowing what the hell she was about to get into. "He didn't answer," Kimberly mumbled. She was so mad that she called him, knowing he was with her.

Kimberly sat in the chair watching Jai dance to the music while the man hit his flame with his fine ass. The man motioned for Jai to walk over to Kimberly, and she leaned over and pecked Kimberly's lips. "Don't worry about him," Jai whispered. He watched them kiss as Jai started to undress Kimberly again.

The man walked over and stood behind Jai, caressing her ass as he watched them kiss. Kimberly lay back onto the couch and looked at him as Jai indulged into her valley. Kimberly felt a different type of pleasure as the man stroked Jai from the back, giving her valley more gratifying pressure.

The man told them to switch positions, and he couldn't wait to smash Kimberly's fine ass. Jai looked at him as he went to push himself into Kimberly, and they both moaned out of pleasure, but before they climaxed all the way, *bang. Bang. Bang. Bang. Bang. Bang. Bang.* Glass was shattering everywhere as the drunken women realized what was happening.

The man said, "*Get the fuck down!*"

Jai said, "*Oh my gosh! What the fuck is going on?*"

The man rushed over to the window looking, but whoever did it pulled off by the time he got over there to shoot back.

*****

Mint said, "*What the fuck! Who lives there?*"

Samaya said, "*Girl…what did you see?*"

Mint said, "Why the fuck are you shooting at them? Damn!"

Queen said, "Don't worry about it. You work for him, so if you tell him you were with me when this happened, what do you think will happen? The choice is yours."

Samaya said, "*This shit crazy!*"

Queen said, "And he's nasty as fuck!"

Samaya said, "*Queen? Say something!*"

Mint said, "Let me clarify something! I get paid well for doing a favor. And I'm not scared of shit or a snitch. I'm just wondering, why give someone that much energy?"

Queen said, "Energy, my ass! Take me to my TT's house."

Samaya said, "More like *feelings*! Here, Mint, take the flame."

Mint said, "Pulling, pointing, and shooting is an action. Feelings are what the fuck we saw him go in there to get. If you had taken that same energy to walk up there and knock, you could have a feeling with their ass."

Samaya said, "Well said, but I would have done the same thing."

Mint said, "Not if you find the right man. Here, Queen, take the flame and relax."

Queen said, "Yeah…let me hit the flame! Always coughing with yo no-lung-having ass."

*****

Jai rushed to the shop that next morning, finishing her last touch-ups, not giving a fuck about nothing but being on time.

Kimberly was so nervous from all the shooting that she watched Jai prance around as if nothing happened. "Where'd you go last night," Kimberly whispered to Jai so Jez couldn't hear. "Let's not do this here, or mention it to Jez," Jai said effortlessly.

After everyone left, Kimberly went to Jai's office to talk with her after she locked up. "Hey, how can I help you," Jai said as she continued to fumble through her purse.

Kimberly said, "When I went home last night…he pushed his house key under the door."

Jai said, "Don't cry! It's going to be okay. Where is the baby?"

Kimberly said, "He took him! He texted me saying some shit about attention, so I left. I work for our family."

Jai said, "I've never been a relationship, so I don't know what to say. I'm sorry!"

Kimberly said, "Girl, this the last time I get played. Fuck this! Then my lease ends at the end of the month. Damn!"

Jai said, "Do you have money saved up? If so, you shouldn't let this shit stress you out. I'll have my friend help you move if you're planning on leaving."

Kimberly said, "I should disappear and make his ass chase me. Hmm, what are you doing, Jai?"

Jai said, "Finishing where we left off last night. Do you want me to stop?"

Kimberly said, "No! Oh, my...Damn!"

CHAPTER 27

Queen
Confused

Queen kept running to the bathroom, running the water because she didn't want anybody hearing her. "She doesn't know who's house she's in," Tamyra said.

Queen said, "Auntie, that coffee smell is making me sick. OMG!"

Tamyra said, "I would offer you some, but it's not good for the baby."

Tamyra sipped on the coffee and walked off, not noticing that Queen followed right behind her.

Queen said, "How do you know, Auntie? Samaya told you, huh?"

Tamyra said, "Baby, you have that glow all up in here. Then you can't keep anything down running to my bathroom every time you smell or taste food since you've been here. That's called being pregnant!"

Samaya said, "Oh. She told you, Ma? That must mean she's keeping it. By the way, Mom, Tara is upstairs throwing up all over your bathroom.

Tamyra said, "Girl...you're not killing no baby over here. Besides, Merch loves you."

Queen said, "Everybody is judging me! I hate, Merch."

Tamyra said, "Queen? Don't say that! The baby is innocent."

Queen ran off crying like a baby right past Mint. "He doesn't love shit," Queen shouted. "What's wrong with her," Mint said.

Tamyra said, "Yeah. She's pregnant, and that baby got her emotional."

Mint said, "Damn! She's pregnant, again?"

Samaya said, "I'll go talk to her. Mint? Let's go talk for a minute."

Tamyra said, "Let her be, baby! How are you feeling this morning?"

Sammie said, "Baby…give me a cup of coffee and leave the girls alone."

Tamyra said, "Hey, baby, Tara is upstairs sick."

Samaya said, "*Hi, Dad! I'll be back, Mom.*"

Why did he say again with his good investigation ass, Samaya thought. Samaya ran off behind Queen and jumped in the car with her and Mint.

Queen had been calling Mint a lot to come pick her up, but this time she had him take her to the car lot. She tried paying Mint every time, but he wouldn't take the money. "Y'all like my sisters now," Mint said. "You mean homeys," Queen replied. "Shit, I'll be your sister." Samaya giggled.

*****

There wasn't anybody about to stop her money from coming in, so she went driving around in her new Dodge Charger looking for a strip club.

She looked at some condos that had security until she found the one she wanted, being picky as fuck. She went through the same people that sold her town home. By the end of the day, they had all her information, and she had her keys.

Mint said, "What's up, Q?"

Queen said, "Can you come over?"

Mint said, "To your aunt's?"

Queen said, "Can I finish, please? Mint…"

Mint said, "My bad, Q! Just surprised you are asking your homey for help."

Queen said, "I need a man here when they drop off my furniture. I feel safe with you around."

Mint said, "Send me your location, homey?"

*****

Queen said, "You can send him up. Thanks."

When Mint saw her standing in the doorway he was impressed. Mint said, "How are you, homey?"

Queen said, "Hi…Thanks for helping me. I really appreciate you taking the time out of your schedule to help me. I know your family probably needs you."

Mint said, "I'm an only child with a lot of aunts, uncles, and cousins. My parents live in Minnesota during the summer, then travel during the winter months. When I finished college, I moved out here with my cousin Terrence, and we started our own business."

Queen said, "What kind of business? If you don't mind me asking."

Mint said, "We own our law firm with a line of private investigators. I see you're doing good! You got all this from dancing?"

Queen said, "I see you've been investigating me, so there's no point in telling you about me because you already know my family? You said 'again.' How do you know that?"

Mint said, "Investigating is what I do well. Either you didn't go through with it when you last went to your appointment, or you got pregnant again."

Queen said, "I slipped up again! I don't know what to do after seeing that shit the other day."

Mint walked to the kitchen and poured his loud on the counter, breaking it up, as he watched Queen swish around in her tight-ass jeans. "I'm sorry, may I flame up in here?" Mint asked.

Queen said, "You can flame, homey! Tell me about this investigation gig. Would you like something to drink?"

Mint said, "Yes, please! I'm the one who found you, Queen. I was never investigating, just finding."

Queen said, "I guess! How did you find me? Let me hit that?"

Mint said, "If I tell you, I'd have to put you on my payroll. Seriously, the same way you find dude's ass."

Queen said, "Are you serious? I know his routine, so I follow him."

Mint said, "He must have known yours also because we go off what the clients give us. What you got to eat?"

Queen said, "It's an Italian dish in there from earlier. Mint? Do you have a girlfriend?"

Mint said, "Where did you get this cheese pizza from? This shit looks good, Q!"

Queen said, "Don't ignore me, fool….What's so funny? Do you?"

Mint said, "Come sit and eat with me. Why call me out my name? I'm no one's fool. You got some juicy-ass lips. And this shit is good."

Queen said, "Yo ass high! Now, everything is going to taste and look better. It's this nice pizza joint a few miles away."

Mint said, "I don't have time for a relationship right now. Damn! Slow down and save me a piece. So, what are you going to do now, Q?"

Queen said, "You keep calling me Q. That's cute. I found a place like an hour away to work. I'm going to try out tomorrow evening. Hopefully, my skills are good enough for their club. How'd you find me, Mint?"

Mint said, "Can't tell you my secrets. Besides, all that shit you're doing is unbalanced."

Queen said, "Mint, please! You going with me or not?"

Mint said, "Do Merch know you are going to dance? You're too pretty for that, Q."

Queen said, "Fuck him! I'm grown, and what does me being pretty has to do with me hustling?"

Mint said, "You are pregnant, again. Don't do that to the baby if you're planning on keeping it. You're a beautiful young woman with your whole life ahead of you. Switch up and do something different for a change."

Queen said, "Anyways. Did you tell anyone that you were coming to help me?"

Mint said, "Yes, Merch! No, I didn't!"

Queen said, "I see you got jokes. Come watch me dance tomorrow?"

Mint said, "No! I want to see you do something productive with yourself. If I wanted to see you dance, I would have you dance for me right now."

Queen said, "Okay, Okay! Dancing is an art, Mint. I'm making money, and what's not productive about that?"

Mint said, "Did you finish high school?"

Queen said, "Yes, I did! Samaya made sure of it."

Mint said, "Other than dancing, what other things are you good at?"

Queen said, "I like cooking, writing, helping people, fashion, and fucking. *OMG, look at your face! You're not laughing now?*"

Mint said, "That's a start! If you cook like your aunt, you could start a business. If you like fashion, you could sell clothes. Helping people has a wide range of jobs. If I help you, can you promise me you won't dance until you have the baby? If you're not making money, we'll figure something out. What you think, Q?"

Queen said, "*OMG, Mint! I'll see what it do!*"

Mint said, "I'm about to get out of here, and thanks for the pizza, Q."

Queen said, "It's late. You can sleep on the couch. Let me get you some blankets."

Mint said, "Thanks. And dancing is a skill, and fucking is an art."

They both cracked up, knowing Mint would argue to make his point, so Queen just let his philosophy win.

Queen said, "Thanks for setting up my furniture."

Mint said, "Damn! If I get more hugs like this, I'm moving in."

Queen said, "You need to quit playing with yo fine ass."

Mint said, "I'm not playing about it. I wouldn't lie to my homey. Go get some sleep, so I can see what you look like in the morning."

*****

Mint saw her walk to the bathroom with a towel wrapped around her a few times before he went to sleep, knowing the baby kept her running. His dick got hard every time he saw her prance through the hallway, hoping her towel would fall.

He felt the covers getting pulled off him, so he opened his eyes and saw Queen's beautiful naked body standing in front of him. He leaned over and pulled her at the waist toward him so that she could sit down on his face. He let her ride his tongue until she squirted, but as he went to stand up, he got light-headed.

Queen said, "Mint? Mint? *Wake up, Mint! Your alarm is going off. Mint!* Would you like some coffee?"

Mint said, "Damn! I was dreaming, my ass off. I don't drink coffee, but thanks."

Queen said, "I see somebody's excited. When you calm down, I made us some breakfast."

Mint said, "All that ass, why wouldn't I be? Good morning, beautiful."

He grabbed her onto him, wrestling around on the couch. "Stop, Mint! You play too much," Queen said, giggling. "Oh, you're fighting back? Let me up, so I can see what you made," Mint said.

Queen said, "Stop it! You grabbed me! Ouch, quit tickling me, Mint."

Mint said, "My tickling hurts now? Come here!"

He went to pick her up, but she fell back onto the couch, looking straight into his eyes. She kissed her finger and placed them on his lips, and as soon as he went to back off, Toonie said, "Ahem. Ahem. Excuse me! Why would you give me a key if you are going to be in here doing all this Hollywood love shit? *So…cut, cut, cut! Take two when I'm not here. Thank you!*"

Mint said, "Hello, miss!"

Queen said, "Oh, shit! Don't get her started."

Toonie said, "*Don't 'miss' me!* Why are you here?"

Mint said, "Excuse us? We were playing around."

Toonie said, "Whatever! I'll be in the back waiting for y'all to get done acting or role-playing."

*****

When Queen arrived at Extreme Gentle's Club, she noticed that a few of the girls were ashy; had cellulite, worn-down shoes, dusty clothes; and looked tired.

Toonie said, "Okay! What are we doing here?"

Queen said, "Bitch! You'll be okay! Just use this if needed. Hold on! Do you know how to use it?"

Toonie said, "Since we're using that word so lightly. *Bitch!* Do you know who my mama is?"

After the manager escorted her to the dressing room, she immediately got dizzy from the heat, but she waited patiently for her turn to show out.

Toonie said, "You don't look so good! I don't understand why you are here!"

Queen said, "Seriously, Toonie! Get a grip and hit this shit! It's moola to be made."

Toonie said, "I'm not a crackhead! Thanks anyway."

Queen said, "I'm not a fucking crackhead! Herbs come from the earth."

Toonie said, "It's to each's own! Let me quit playing. Let me hit that shit?"

At the time, she wasn't thinking about her baby, so she flamed as usual. "Don't tell anyone about this," Queen said. "What the fuck is there to tell?" Toonie replied with an attitude.

After she gave DJ K two hundred dollars, he liked her hustle already, knowing he had to provide an introduction that would get the men's attention. "You keep doing that, and I'll bring out the red carpet for yo pretty ass," DJ K said.

DJ K said, "*Extreme*…Let's welcome the *beautiful, sexy* Q to the stage. Representing for the amateurs on the north side. Let's see if she has what it takes to make the cut, fellas."

Soon as the music started playing, everyone looked because her choice of music was faster than usual, so they knew her ass was about to move or crack under pressure. "What the fuck," Toonie whispered under her voice, trying to ignore the man trying to talk with her and pay attention to Queen twerking on the stage.

Queen walked out slowly and stopped every few feet to twerk to the music and to rub her boobs. She started smiling as the men approached the stage, so she grabbed the pole with both hands. Her ass cheeks were bouncing and shaking one at a time to the beat, going up and down simultaneously. Then she swung her body onto the pole and flipped her body upside down, twerking in the air, holding herself up.

Most of the men in the club walked over to the stage, throwing money and screaming for more, and Toonie went to pick up her money as instructed.

DJ K said, "*Q…is doing her thang, fellas!*"

When she saw more of the men walking up, she turned her body back upright then dropped into the splits, making her ass cheeks drop to every dollar she saw fall. She swung her legs up, went on all fours, and started throwing her ass in a circle.

Dude 1 said, "*Got damn! Baby girl doing that!*"

Dude 2 said, "*Man…she the baddest bitch in this camp.*"

Dude 3 said, "Roll over, and let us see the front?"

Dude 1 said, "Chill out! She's a keeper, for a real nigga."

Dude 2 said, "*This nigga about to fall in love again.*"

Queen watched Toonie pick up her money because she knew Toonie wasn't used to doing this type of shit, but she looked amazed and disgusted at the same time.

Queen was trying to hear what the guys were saying, yet the music was too loud, and her body kept moving as she saw the money fall.

When she exited the stage and headed toward the back, she noticed one of the guys approaching her. "Excuse me, miss! Excuse me!" Dude 3 shouted, trying to make his way through the crowd swiftly so he could follow up behind her.

Queen was ignoring Dude 3 because money was her main focus. When he grabbed her arm, she turned around fast as hell. "*Excuse me! Why are you grabbing on me?*" Queen demanded. "No harm meant. Let me spit at you for a minute," Dude 3 replied.

Queen said, "I'll be back out. Let me go freshen up."

Dude 3 said, "Freshen up?"

Queen said, "Like…wipe my pussy, spray perfume on, and change."

Toonie said, "Q, come here? *Now!*"

She flamed, took a few shots, and put on her one-piece turquoise leopard suit with fishnet stockings and slipped on her black three-inch heel boots. "Queen? Quit trying to dodge me. We need to talk right now. Fuck!" Toonie said.

Queen went walking around looking for the gentlemen that wanted private and lap dances. Toonie was watching Queen on the sideline. *What the fuck is going on? Did my mama tell her? I need to call my mama right now*, Toonie thought as her mind was racing.

*****

Dude 1 came and asked for her to go to the VIP room, and she stood looking up at him in a trance, like she didn't hear shit he said. "Who are you," Queen asked. "I'm Tracy," Tracy said in a friendly manner.

Queen said, "Nice to meet you, Tracy."

Tracy said, "You as well. Follow me!"

Tracy was mesmerized by her beauty. "Why do you dance," Tracy asked, as she danced in front of him. "Don't do that," Queen replied. She leaned over and started whispering in his ear and he put a stack of money in her bra. "What are you doing here?" she asked. "My boys brought me here," Tracy said.

Queen stopped dancing and looked at him, "I'm sorry, Q," Tracy said as he pulled more money out of his pocket. "Thanks,"

Queen said as she continued to dance for him. Noticing he was looking at her face instead of her body made her stop dancing again.

Tracy said, "Q, sit here! I want to talk to you."

Queen said, "Look, I'm working! My time is money, Tracy. You're fine as hell, but my money comes first, and that's not an issue with me."

Tracy said, "Thanks for the compliment, and I could buy this whole damn club, but I want you. Take this and talk with me for the rest of the night."

Queen said, "This is a lot of money for just talking, Tracy. Now what?"

Tracy said, "Put my number in your phone and tell me why you're here?"

Queen said, "For the money! You are blowing my high with all these questions. I asked you who are you, then you tell me your name. Again, who are you?"

Tracy said, "I'm me! When I want something, I always get it. You're the most beautiful woman I've ever seen besides my mother, with this deep-colored skin tone."

Queen said, "Thank you! I never heard that before. You're very confident. Oops! I meant vain."

Tracy said, "You got jokes! Here, I got flame. Let me roll for you. You like them skinny or fat?"

Queen said, "Oh, okay! You got jokes, too, I see."

Tracy said, "Not like that, mama. Get your mind out of the gutter. Some folks have baby lungs, and some are professional at this shit."

Queen said, "I'm in between. So, you know I'm a dancer. Who or what are you? What's funny?"

Tracy said, "A man with a plan. Just because you dance doesn't mean that defines who you are. This shit is a hustle, not a career, mama."

Queen said, "Well, I guess I've been hustling my whole life."

Tracy said, "It might be good to alleviate that shit off your chest. You're not that old."

Queen said, "Well, I've been hustling long enough. I'm still waiting for your answer."

Listening to this slow, smooth-talking man had her in a daze, but that shit was sexy as fuck. The more he flamed, his use of proper English became more slurred.

Nor did he dress like Merch. However, he was just as handsome, a little taller, better physique, and paid apparently.

Queen said, "Don't be calling and texting me all the time, either."

Tracy said, "No, mama. That's why I said put my number in your phone, because you're doing all the calling."

Queen said, "Am I going to have females chasing me, fighting, and calling me? I don't have time for that."

Tracy said, "You don't have to worry about all that. I would never put anyone in a situation that I wouldn't want to go through. I'm not for all the drama."

Queen said, "So...you can buy the club, huh? That's real forward."

Tracy said, "Why lie? It's the truth. Damn! You got some nice-ass lips. Do you have any kids?"

Queen said, "Shit! I can buy this bitch too. No kids. Thank you, and your lips are a nice size also."

Tracy said, "That's what I'm talking about, mama. Don't be afraid or hide what you can do. I'm proud of you."

Queen said, "It does feel good speaking up about myself knowing where I came from."

Tracy said, "Expressing yourself motivates you to want more. That shit makes me grind even harder every day for mines."

Queen said, "You have kids?"

Tracy said, "Thought I did. The test came back after two years of lies, and he's not mine."

Queen said, "Why'd it take so long? Poor baby."

Tracy said, "He started looking like the other man. The sad part is my mother knew it, but I was in denial."

Queen said, "I'm sorry for laughing. That's not cool."

Tracy said, "Naw, you good. I was still helping until his real daddy stepped in his life."

Queen said, "See…That's why we got attachment issues now. Loving someone for whom they are then they're taken from you. Poor baby going through this shit at a young age. How do you feel? Are you okay?"

Tracy said, "I'm good! Thank you. Nobody has asked me that yet, thanks. Everybody thinks that shit is funny until their lights about to get cut off or they need some gas."

Queen said, "Oh my gosh! Silly self, is there anything else you want to talk about before I go?"

Tracy said, "Will you marry me?"

"Don't answer that," Toonie shouted as she stepped in the VIP room with them. "Q, or whoever you are, let's go, now" Toonie demanded.

Queen said, "Girl, calm yo ass down! I'm coming…"

Tracy said, "Call me, Q!"

*****

They just sat there at the table looking over all the paperwork as tears ran down Queen's face, and Toonie waved for the waitress to bring more tissue. Queen wasn't letting up, and Teresa just sat there, looking and hoping they were tears of happiness.

Teresa said, "*What? Why are you looking at me like that?* Okay, let me lower my voice."

Toonie said, "Mama? I told you this was not a good idea."

Teresa said, "They don't know you. Plus, I don't like their sneaky asses. They think because they got money my nieces are gonna jump when they say."

Toonie said, "Let's leave and talk about this in private. Kya, quit crying, please."

Teresa said, "I was overthinking and didn't know what to do. I followed my first or fifth thought. Shit! I don't know!"

Queen, Samaya, Teresa, and Toonie sat on the balcony flaming and taking shot after shot. Samaya kept reading the papers over and

462

over in disbelief that Teresa handled her business while they were running from something she bought.

Teresa said, "Please don't be mad at me, Kya."

Queen said, "Can y'all stop calling me by my government name. Damn! I'm not mad at you, just never thought of this."

Samaya said, "How did you know they were selling the place?"

Toonie said, "Well, I went to audition. I went back to see why I didn't receive a callback. Some dude named Ax was there. Before I performed for him, he got a phone call, and I overheard him talking. Did I say something funny?"

Queen said, "We all know you did *not* audition. At least he bought it."

Teresa said, "When she told me, I found out who was selling it, and I bought it."

Samaya said, "How'd you come up with this much money without going to the storage unit?"

Queen said, "I'm ecstatic right now. We hit their ass for that much money, and I didn't even know."

Teresa said, "You told me that wasn't your case, and all the licks added up. I mean, everybody was coming to me for his flame."

Toonie said, "Mama said, 'Feelings flooded you and your thoughts were clouded,' so she figured she get the club back."

Samaya said, "Damn! Smart move, TT!"

Queen said, "Toonie? Why didn't you tell me before I went onstage?"

Toonie said, "I tried! When you started twerking, and all that money fell, I figured we needed to make money back we spent on this investment."

Samaya said, "Hell naw! Now that's some smart pimp shit. Did she bank?"

Toonie said, "Hell yeah! I started to audition…Mama, tell Kya the other information."

Teresa said, "Did you know that he kept some of his money with that school, bitch?"

Queen said, "How did you find out?"

Toonie said, "Ummmm! I befriended the bitch! She's cool, and she talks a lot."

Queen said, "Why didn't you tell me? Is this the fiancée, bitch?"

Teresa said, "That's her lying ass. She told Toonie that Merch wouldn't meet her parents, or go to the next level."

Queen said, "So, she's on the street telling lies about mines marrying her ass."

Samaya said, "I see why y'all didn't tell us. What else did you find out, Toonie?"

Toonie said, "First, I came up with the idea of hitting them where it hurts, but these niggas are rich. I found out enough to know that this little club is like chump change to them. Oh, by the way, Ax don't remember shit!"

Queen said, "Yo ass silly! When can we take over?"

Teresa said, "They have a month to get out! Like the contract says, everything stays in the club and we can change that stupid-ass name from Cupid to Lovely Vines right."

Toonie said, "Oh, yeah! Ishmael and Ax think y'all had something to do with the robbery. Some girl name Teisha was running her mouth to me when I waited for Ax."

Queen said, "I can't stand that bitch."

Toonie said, "Well, she isn't fond of you either, and she talks too much as well. Come to find out Ax is hating on his family, and we could use this shit for an advantage if the shit comes to it."

Teresa said, "That's right, daughter! Family first...Be careful because I saw the other side of them."

Queen said, "Damn! I thought you were just some quiet-ass little girl!"

Toonie said, "Family first! I only went there to see what had y'all stuck doing dumb shit."

Samaya said, "Slow your tongue down! Your thoughts are coming out your mouth saying too much!"

Toonie said, "Aren't you in love with Isaiah? He got you stuck with his sneaky ass."

Teresa said, "Toonie, stop! I'm not about to let nothing come in between my family."

Queen said, "How did you have time for all this?"

Samaya said, "Naw, fuck that! Sneaky how?"

Toonie said, "I rode around with y'all and hung around them. They don't know who I am or Queen's real name, so I figured we put the club in her name. Did you ever meet Rachel? Looking at your face, you didn't know she was topping Isaiah off at the restaurant. Wasn't she at the house meeting that went down?"

Samaya said, "Are you serious? I was pregnant by this nigga. He swore it wasn't…"

Toonie said, "See! What are you crying for again? His innocent ass swore it wasn't another woman, huh?"

Teresa said, "*Give me the flame! This shit got you running yo mouth!*"

Toonie said, "I'm sick of these muthafuckers hurting my cousins. Now, I know how you can get more money if you stop crying and listen to me. Please!"

Queen said, What the fuck! I know what I'm doing. I've been doing this for a minute."

Samaya said, "Right! Teresa, you put her up to this?"

Teresa said, "Hell naw! She saw the money, so she mentioned buying the club and getting the schoolgirl. That's it. Hit this shit and quit accusing me. I didn't even know she had game."

Toonie said, "Look at this! I got all this from talking…Oh, yeah! Queen, do you even know who you were dancing on?"

Queen said, "What bitch! You a snitch?"

Toonie said, "Nope! Telling people what they want to hear is a fantasy in their head, and they pay me. Where you show them what you are working with and tease them."

Samaya said, "Smart, but I can't stand yo ass."

Queen said, "So, the money goes right into your account?"

Toonie said, "Yup! No picking money up off the floor."

Teresa said, "The floor money fed yo ass too."

Queen said, "I want to know who this dude is?"

Merch
Doing as I Please

After that night, Merch went to his mother's house until his house sold and waited to hear from his lawyers that everything was cool.

He didn't bother with any of his female friends or the selling of Cupid, not trusting a soul to the point he wanted to replace them all.

*****

Toonie said, "Now, let the games begin with his sweet ass."

Samaya said, "Where yo mama at?"

Queen said, "You're gonna quit talking about my baby like that."

Toonie said, "Girl, please! They own this building, and I'm about to show y'all what you didn't know about Mr. Sweetie."

Queen said, "Samaya, get your cousin crazy ass before she gets slapped."

Toonie said, "How the fuck am I crazy and you're the one having weird-ass dreams?"

Samaya said, "Glad she found somebody else to tell that shit. He just pulled up. Let's wait to see if one of his girls show up."

Toonie said, "Nope! We're about to have the same shit as them in a minute. We're out!"

Queen said, "We can be out, but my dreams be feeling real as fuck. So, therefore, they're real and worth telling you both."

Toonie said, "Who dreams they're in a tub getting head from your black man, and his head comes up once, and he's white specifically. Not only that, he's drowning while eating your pussy and lives after you make his favorite breakfast. Hope you climaxed."

Queen said, "Don't forget he had pretty brown hair, bitch."

Samaya said, "Oh, she climaxed! The best she ever had and the shit confused her so badly she woke up, fucked the shit out of Merch, and cooked his fave breakfast."

Queen said, "Fuck y'all! That shit is real. Ha, ha, ha...Try this flame!"

Samaya said, "If that shit got you dreaming like that, I'm good."

Toonie said, "I'll pass also! Fuck around and dream we're all some dolphins getting chased by some damn brother sharks. Wake up eating tuna cakes and shit..."

*****

Merch went to the hotel looking for Queen to find out the room was empty, so he called Isaiah to see if he knew where the girls were. Isaiah told him Mint was keeping an eye on them until everything calmed down, then he called Terrence for his number.

Merch's text to Mint: "Mint, this Merch."

Mint's text to Merch: "What's up?"

Merch's text to Mint: "Where is Queen?"

Mint's text to Merch: "at her aunt's crib."

Merch went to knock on the door, but Sammie swung open the door and hugged him so hard, hoping that the checks started coming back in. "*Hey, nephew! How are you feeling? You're looking hungry. Come, eat!*" Tamyra shouted.

Sammie said, "Come in, young man. How's it going? We're sorry to hear about your brother."

Merch said, "Hello, family, I'm good! Thanks. How are you doing? Lovely? I would love something to eat."

Merch already knew what he was getting into when he came over. He knew he was going to be sitting for a while, so he brought some flame to chop it up with Sammie and play the game.

Queen barely went around her family when Merch stepped into her life because he had her running the streets with him. Her family thought he was the best man ever because he supplied her with money and flame for their habits. Plus, she kept her auntie with payment other than what her daughters provided.

Samaya said, "What's up, black ass? Coming to choke some shit?"

Merch said, "Nothing much! Let me talk with you for a minute?"

467

Samaya said, "What's up? You know damn well you get on my nerves."

Merch said, "Shut up! Haven't seen your cousin in a while. Her phone is going straight to voice mail. Do you know if she went to the doctor yet?"

Samaya said, "She went shopping. My mom sent her with a long list. Let me try calling her for you, black ass."

Merch said, "Thanks, Saria…"

*****

Samaya's text to Queen: "Bitch! Merch here looking for you… We told him you went shopping."

Queen's text to Samaya: "Tell him I'm on my way."

Samaya's text to Queen: "Bitch! Bring some bags…he looks mad."

*****

Samaya said, "Merch…she on her way back, and she left her phone in the car. That pregnant shit got her ass slow."

Merch said, "Aight!"

Queen arrived. Merch quickly grabbed her hand and led her to the porch so they could have some privacy. She could see the emptiness in his eyes and anger from her not answering the phone, but she wanted him to feel what she felt.

Merch said, "What's up, Q? I know you have seen me calling your phone? Have you been to the doctor yet?"

Queen said, "Take your hand off my throat. Merch, stop!"

Merch said, "You better be lucky we are here."

Queen said, "After that shit happened, I have just been thinking a lot. I've been staying with my family until this shit dies down between us. No, I haven't been to the doctor."

Merch said, "You're playing with me, right? You need to make that happen immediately."

Queen said, "*Stop choking me!* I will! So, where do we go from here? I don't want to be a single parent, Merch."

Merch said, "What's that supposed to mean? We pick up from where we left off!"

Queen said, "What? Fucking, threesomes, and riding around? Stop pulling my fucking hair."

Merch said, "Shut up! Look, slow your roll. First, I didn't force you to do shit. We did it together. Riding around bought that last house you sold and the vehicles. You don't have to worry about me not being there. I'm going to always take care of you and her."

Queen said, "*Wow!* How many hers is it?"

Merch said, "That's all you got to say, Queen?"

Queen said, "I don't have time right now."

Merch said, "If all that was a problem, you didn't say that in Vegas when you were sucking my dick? Now, you don't have time. What don't you have time for?"

Queen said, "*Why the fuck you keep coming at me disrespectful-ass shit?*"

Merch said, "Lower your voice! We loved each other until this shit happened. You ran with my baby, or is it mines?"

Queen tried to jump up and hit Merch in his face. Before she could land a hit, he grabbed her hands and held her down on the chair. "Let me go," Queen shouted. "Everything is all about you and your females. If it's not empowering Merch, he disrespects you. *And, yes, I sucked the skin off that muthafucka! You know this your baby! Let me go!*"

Merch said, "Bring your voice down. Tell me what you don't have time for, because all this wow shit about to stop!"

Queen said, "My baby doesn't have time for sharing her daddy with all these other chicken heads."

Merch said, "That's it? Calm down before you scare the baby. Let's go to my car!"

Queen said, "I guess! I've been thinking about my future a lot lately. I'm thinking about taking classes at the community college so my baby and I will be straight."

Merch said, "Get in and shut the door! Let me know how much you need."

Queen said, "I'm not about to be doing all this fighting shit with you, Merch."

Merch said, "Look at these crooked fuckers."

Queen said, "*Who?*"

Merch said, "Detective Thomas and Phillips is walking up to your auntie's house."

Queen said, "The last time they were here they asked Samaya who was she running from, and this bitch said herself, and they left."

The last time, Merch thought. "Tell your aunt to quit calling them about Tara, and they'll stop coming," Merch said. "How do you know all that?" Queen replied.

Merch said, "My lawyer told me. We need to know what's going on with my baby."

Queen said, "I thought you were more worried about your females."

Merch said, "You keep saying 'females'! I don't have females. When it comes to my family or baby, don't nobody comes before the people that mean the most to me."

Queen said, "I can't tell! Merch? Why haven't I met your family besides your brothers? Are you married or something?"

Merch said, "No!"

Queen said, "Do they even know about the baby or me?"

Merch said, "What's with all the questions? You never asked me anything about me but quick to ask for money. Queen? What's my favorite color? What's my real name? Hell, you never asked about my parents, but I don't know yours either like that."

Queen started crying like a baby, and Merch just held her in his arms as he watched Samaya shut the porch door in their faces.

Merch said, "Sometimes, we let money take over our hearts."

Queen said, "Your favorite color is gray, Milan. I know your parents or moms don't like me. I know more than you think. I've watched and listened to you for years. I loved you."

Merch said, "Damn! I love you too."

Queen said, "Really? Okay! Who else are you fucking?"

Merch said, "What the fuck, Queen! I love you, damn! Nothing else matters."

Queen said, "When did this start? You are not supposed to be ashamed of the people you love."

Merch said, "I watched you blossom into this beautiful young woman that always had my back doing any and everything to please me. I'm sorry…for not listening lately."

Keep my mind focused! Toonie told my ass not to get mushy, Queen thought.

Queen said, "I'll see you later. This shit is not going anywhere… Let me go! Merch, stop choking me. What the fuck!"

Merch said, "You'll go when I tell you to. Shut the fuck up! You didn't say that shit when we were fucking. What's wrong with you? *I love you, Queen…*"

Queen said, "Okay! I'll see you later if you have time. When's the last time you saw Jai? Can I get the truth, please!"

Merch said, "You keep playing with me, I see. I'm looking for us a house now, and answer your phone, so we can go look at it together."

Queen said, "Okay! I hope it's big enough for our family. Ugh! Stop trying to kiss me."

Merch said, "Go on in the house! I'll call you later!"

*****

As soon as Merch pulled off, Queen jumped back in her ride and hit the highway, heading to the mall to get some new household items, and her phone kept ringing. *I hate turning my music down while driving,* Queen thought. When she saw it was Mint's fine investigating ass, she answered, yet she wanted it to be Tracy.

She texted Tracy earlier before Samaya had texted her about Merch, so she patiently waited. *If Toonie were right, I hit the jackpot with both their caring asses,* Queen thought.

Mint said, "What's up, Queen? You at home?"

Queen said, "Nothing. On my way to the mall. I'll be home later to change before I go to work. What's up?"

Mint said, "What mall? I'm meeting you."

*****

"Glad you came because I need help carrying all this stuff," Queen said as she sent Merch to voice mail. "Make his ass chase you" was all Queen heard Toonie repeating in her thoughts as she sent him to voice mail again and again.

Mint didn't give any emotions in his face when the cashier said the total paying each time and watching her ignore her downfall. "You're doing things like a boss," Queen whispered so that Mint could hear her. "When I'm with a woman, she'll never have to pay," Mint said with passion.

*****

Merch just looked at his phone in cynicism, wanting to go back to her people's house and pick up the cashier check he dropped off for Queen's tuition. He had too much pride to go back and face her family, so he called again. When it went to voice mail the second time, he hoped she was laying low and getting some rest for her and their baby.

*****

Queen said, "*Stop! Stop! Stop!*"

Queen was running fast, hitting the corners of the kitchen. "Oh my gosh, Mint" Queen shouted. "Bring yo ass here," Mint said, giggling. He was chasing her around the house, trying to get her to loosen up, live, and smile more.

As soon as he caught her, he swept her up and carried her back to the room. Placing her on the bed gently as she gazed into his eyes, "Now let's finish here," Mint said.

Queen said, "You play too much. Pull the sheet down! Smooth out the wrinkles! No. Put that pillow over there."

Mint said, "Do you want me to get yo ass again?"

Queen said, "*No! No!* No…"

Mint jumped over the bed and grabbed her and pinned her down on the bed and bit her neck. Queen giggled like a little girl at the pleasure she never felt from a grown-ass man. She looked up at him. "You play too much," Queen muttered softly. "Thanks for buying everything. Let me up so I can cook for you."

Mint pushed her back down softly and kissed her top lip. "Welcome, you deserve everything you want," Mint said. "Get up so I can fix some food," Queen replied softly. "Wait…wait…Oh my gosh! Mint? I'm gonna be late for work."

Mint said, "Do you need me to go? If you're going to do it, let me protect you."

Queen said, "Protect! I thought you investigated only."

Mint said, "I can do both if you want me! Do you want me to stop?"

Queen said, "I'm good! I already have someone going with me. Why are you looking like that? It's not a man, Mint. That feels good!"

*****

Queen was driving to work when her phone beeped. *Tracy*, Queen thought. The text said, "don't go in, wait for me in the parking lot."

When she saw him approaching, she unlocked the door, and they exchanged greetings as he got comfortable. "I hope you don't send me to voice mail," Tracy said. "Oh, it's not like that," Queen replied. "He dropped the check off," Queen smiled as she read the text from Toonie. *This girl is slick smart*, Queen thought.

"I see a busy woman," Tracy said. "It's my cousin! I'm telling her not to come right now," Queen said with a smirk on her face, knowing she was sending Merch to voice mail and texting Toonie at the same time.

Queen said, "What's up, T?"

Tracy said, "I see they hired you. I like your ride, and it fits you well. How much money do you think you'll make tonight, lil mama?"

Queen heard Toonie's voice again in her head, "*You put yourself up there and get that bread! Price tag they ass!*"

Queen said, "Looking at the parking lot, five hundred a car, a thousand or more on the stage, and then VIP. Why?"

Tracy said, "Take this! Is this enough for you to follow me?"

Queen said, "Follow you for what? I'm not fucking or sucking now. Besides, I don't know you like that."

Tracy said, "You're right! I'm not on none of that, lil mama. I'm trying to get to know you. If it's too soon, I'll understand."

Queen said, "Okay! Give it to me! First, where are we going?"

Tracy said, "We can go in your car if it would make you feel better since you have your strap and all."

Queen said, "I see yours too. Let me see your ID so I can see who you are."

Tracy said, "I'm not gonna hurt you, but here, take a picture of it! Like I said before, we were interrupted the last time. Will you marry me? I want to treat you right."

Queen said, "Where to?"

*****

Zach just sat there looking at people come and go out of their aunt's house, but no Queen. When he got out of the car, he started walking toward the house, slowly looking around. The house door swung open, and he saw everyone coming out of the house cheerful, so he turned around quickly and jumped back in his car.

Zach said, "She's not here, my man."

Merch said, "You sure? She might be sleeping."

Zach said, "I've been out here all day and night. Then everyone is coming out of the house and leaving."

Merch said, "Can you follow them for me?"

Zach said, "I have an idea, but it's going to cost you."

He banged on the door for a few minutes, and nobody answered, so he decided to pick the lock. *Going back into my teenage years when I was dumb*, Zach thought as he heard the click.

He walked through all the bedrooms, then checked the whole house. It was empty, so he headed back to the front door, and as soon as he shut the door and turned around, he saw a beautiful woman walking toward him. She was too close for him to go back in without her hearing the door, so he picked up a paper off the floor. *Knock. Knock. Knock. Knock.*

Zach said, "Oh! What the heck! You just scared the mess out of me, miss."

Toonie said, "If you knock any harder, you're going to break the door down. May I help you, sir?"

Zach said, "Oh! I'm here to share the good news."

Toonie said, "Not now, sir! Come back when my family gets back. They need to hear it. See you later!"

*****

"What's the code to the gate?" Queen asked. When the gate opened, she was surprised at the driveway and this big beautiful house they pulled up to. "Is this a mansion?" Queen said. "Yes, lil mama," Tracy said. "You can bring your piece if you want. That shit sexy as hell to me."

Queen said, "Shit! I was…You can bring yours also."

When he pushed the door open, the aroma of soul food hit her face. "Hope you are hungry," Tracy said. "Let me see if the kitchen is clean first," Queen said as she sent Merch to voice mail. As soon as Queen blocked his number, she was giving all smiles to another man's family. She wanted to share that feeling with the man she loved and his family, but the voice mail should be full in the morning.

Tracy said, "Pops, this is the young lady I was telling you about, and this beautiful woman right here is my mother, Ada. Queen, meet my parents, and my sisters are coming later."

Queen said, "Hi, Ada and Pops. Nice to meet you. Your food smells so good."

Tracy said, "My mom is one of the best cooks in America. I'll show you her garden later."

Ada said, "You are beautiful like my baby said. Nice to meet you as well. Take a piece of chicken, try my macaroni, and the rest will be done shortly."

Queen said, "Thanks so much, Ada. I'll stay right here with you until it's done."

Pops said, "Baby always trying to feed people. Nice to meet you, young lady. Help yourself to a drink or something."

Tracy said, "Come! Let me show you around the house and my space. These all my little cousins, and they don't even see us when they're playing the game. I'll introduce you later."

Queen said, "This is a nice house. Do you even know how to swim in that big pool? That's the biggest Jacuzzi I've ever seen."

Tracy said, "Come in! Let me show you who I am."

Queen said, "Wow! I've never been in a studio before. It's nice, Tracy."

Tracy watched Queen roll the flame, but he noticed she didn't take her piece from under her jean jacket yet. He saw that she kept looking at her phone, so he decided to keep her busy.

Tracy said, "When I go in the booth, I need you to push this button. When I wave my hand up, push this button."

Queen said, "Record...and pause! I gotcha! I feel important."

Queen sat watching this man spit facts like he was talking about her life. When he came out of the booth, he played around with it. "Can you sing?" Tracy asked.

Queen said, "Oh my gosh! No...You sound good!"

Tracy said, "Get in there, and say what comes to your mind first. Ain't nobody here, so quit being shy."

"I'm not shy," Queen said and went straight to the mic. "I want you to repeat what I say, softly," Tracy said. When she put on the headphones, she could hear him more clearly. "Okay! Let me hear it a few times," Queen yelled, not knowing she was loud as hell.

The music went silent. Queen looked as if she touched something. "Say that shit a little slower, ma," Tracy said. "Next time, give me a wave or something. Thought I broke something," Queen shouted. When she came out of the booth, Tracy handed her the flame. "Listen to this," Tracy mumbled with smoke coming out of his mouth.

I roll with a real one
We flame to keep the pain away
I roll with a real one
We flame to keep the pain away

Queen said, "*Wow!* That's me. I must admit we do sound good together."

Tracy said, "After my man put his magic touch on it, it'll be on the radio. You are going to be a little star. Now write a verse and spit that shit. Make sure it's something relating to the hook."

Queen said, "You play too much! I can say a lot right now."

Come, come flame with the real, because I'm the realest
You could be around, check on Queen, check about Queen
Flame to think of a plan, stay, hustling to stay above water

Tracy said, "Damn, lil Q! Slow it down just a lil bit. Go!"

Come on now, come on now
He's telling me to slow down
But I'm the best at what I do!
I flame with the real because I'm the realest
You could be round, check on lil Q, lil Q, the best
Never slowing it down, keep it going, Mr. T

Tracy said, "*Damn! Lil Q spazzed out.*"

*****

Merch said, "Man, you playing with the word?"

Zach said, "I didn't know what the fuck to say. Glad she didn't want to hear my version."

Merch said, "If she didn't come out and wasn't in the house, she's moving around."

*****

Queen said, "I turned my phone off and went to sleep as you told me. I was spotting, so I went to the doctor earlier. They told me to stay off my feet for a while."

Merch said, "I already know Teresa ain't gonna tell me shit, so I didn't even try to call her mean ass. What else do you need?"

Queen said, "I found a condo for a reasonable price. We need somewhere to live because I can't stay with my aunt forever."

Merch said, "Just for you and the baby? I'm sorry for everything I've done to hurt you, Queen. I'm here for whatever you need."

Queen said, "What about our baby? I'm not sharing you with any other females."

CHAPTER 28

The Club
The Wrong One

Skunk didn't sit well with how security let Tara get in VIP, so he had a meeting to let everyone know that Cupid was sold and closed until new management took over.

*****

Ax said, "Detective Thomas and Phillips came looking for Rocky, said they needed to talk to him, and I asked them for what, but they insisted if he came around to give them a call."

Skunk said, "Mr. Thomas and his partner some noisy fuckers, and everybody knows them from around the way. They came questioning my girl sister about leaving the hospital. They asked her was she running from Rocky's fat stomach ass."

Ax said, "They acted all surprised when they heard it was under new management. Thomas was doing all the talking then I heard Phillips says, 'He must be on the move.' When they walked off, I made sure they left the building."

Skunk said, "They know he had something to do with these robberies. Nasty bastard."

Ax said, "I let Teisha loudmouth ass go assist at the car wash until she learns how to deal with people. All that fighting isn't good for the business."

Merch, Ishmael, Isaiah, Swen, and Terrence were on their way to meet up with Skunk and Ax at Cupid.

Skunk said, "I'm not buying this type of business no more. It's drama all the time."

Swen said, "A little drama with females is cool, but all that extra shit gots to go!"

Ax said, "Not our problem anymore. It's sold, and Seth said he handled everything else."

Merch said, "We could have had a ladies boxing night all the fighting they were doing in this bitch."

Ishmael said, "That shit does sound about right. Put that shit right in the middle of the floor."

Isaiah said, "I might have looked into that, but it sold quickly."

Swen said, "If y'all got my nephew Isaiah agreeing, that shit a moneymaker."

*****

Sunshine didn't sit well with getting fired, so she pulled up to Cupid trying to sweet-talk the security guard.

Henry said, "How may I help you, beautiful?"

Sunshine said, "I'm here to speak with management?"

Henry said, "Baby girl, you know they fired all the staff. You need an appointment to meet with them in a month or so."

Sunshine said, "Them? Where's Ax? This shit is not cool!"

Henry said, "Orders are to only let the important people in."

Sunshine said, *"Much as I sucked that nigga's dick, he gon' fire me?"*

Sunshine walked off cursing mad as hell that they let her go. When she saw Merch come out the back door, she jumped back out of the car and approached him.

Before he could get to his car, she touched his shoulder, and Merch turned around so fast with his metal. "Get that thing out my face, nigga," Sunshine shouted.

Merch said, "Why in the fuck are you walking up all fast and shit? And watch that nigga shit!"

Sunshine said, "Calm down! I need to ask you something."

Merch said, "Bitch! You calm the fuck down! What the fuck you want, little butt?"

Sunshine said, "Quit calling me that! You know my little ass can still make this bitch move."

Merch said, "What's up, Sunshine? I need to get back in here."

Sunshine said, "You know the new owners?"

Merch said, "Why? That's none of your business!"

Sunshine said, "What the fuck going on with this new club? They fired my ass for no reason out of the blue. If you know them, you can get my job back?"

Merch said, "Go somewhere else! Give me your number with a valid driver's license."

Sunshine said, "What you need all that for, the fuck?"

Merch said, "I can give a good word to the new owner. The fuck!"

Sunshine said, "Maybe...I should go across town somewhere else, like Queen did. This shit for the birds."

Sunshine started walking off and talking shit at the same time because she mad pissed at whoever fired her.

Merch said, "What the fuck you say? Bring yo ass back over here, lil butt."

Sunshine said, "*Fuck you, Merch! Thought we were better than that?*"

Before Sunshine could get into her car, Merch grabbed her around the neck and turned her face toward his. "Now get the fuck out the car," Merch said.

Merch said, "Bitch! You know better than talking to me like that? You done lost your fucking mind. Now what the fuck you say?"

Sunshine said, "Merch! Let me go, crazy ass. You're doing bedroom shit. You horny, nigga?"

Merch said, "Oh! Do you like being choked? What the fuck you say about Queen?"

Sunshine said, "I'm going to dance with Queen across town."

Merch said, "What's the name of the club? Give me your information so I can run a background on your ass, and don't tell her you told me anything."

Sunshine said, "So, I can have my job back?"

Merch said, "You work for me from now on. Follow me in so I can get your information. I'll let you know what to do next and when you can start."

Sunshine said, "What's the point of giving you all my information?"

Merch said, "Shut the fuck up! I need to know who I'm dealing with."

Sunshine said, "All you had to do was ask. My name is Susanna, I'm twenty-two years old, and I'm from Florida."

Henry said, "*You good over there, boss?*"

Sunshine said, "Look at this late security-ass puppy. *Yeah, he good!*"

Merch said, "Don't tell anybody about our arrangements, and I'll make sure you're taken care of."

Sunshine said, "I get flame from her. That's all."

Merch said, "Well, from now on, I'll make sure you're good."

Sunshine said, "We exchanged numbers that day, then I left because that club was nasty and the men were rude."

Merch said, "Queen's a big girl. She can handle it. Call me later after you finish up here."

Sunshine said, "How much I'm getting paid for my deeds?"

Merch said, "Hey, Chaste, this is Susanna. Can you get her information and make sure it comes to me when it's back. Thank you! Susanna, call me later."

Chaste said, "Yes, boss! Hello, Susanna, come with me."

Sunshine said, "Hi, Chaste, you can call me Sunshine."

Merch said, "Go on 'head, Susanna! Chaste, give her my number. Thank you."

Sunshine said, "*Ugh!* Yo ass is so irritating. You'd be fine if you weren't so mean and rude."

Merch said, "And you'd be bad if you had some ass. Go on 'head, lil butt!"

*****

Toonie had arranged for a walk-through with her people only to make sure the Cupid owners had left everything per contract. She checked file cabinets, cabinets, closets, behind the bar, storage units, and the dressing room, trying to find anything they had left.

Toonie said, "Can I help you? We're closed right now?"

Sunshine said, "I came to see if Merch was here. He said I started today. What's so funny?"

Toonie said, "This club is under new management, and I don't know a Merch."

Jez
Truth

Jennifer said, "What's gotten into you just leaving like this?"

Jez said, "Mother, I'm sorry for leaving without telling you. I need a life besides school and work."

Jennifer said, "Who is he?"

Jez said, "Mom...what are you talking about?"

Jennifer said, "I've had that same look in my eyes when I met your father, so I know. What's his name, baby?"

Jez said, "Ishmael! He's a nice man. He bought me this phone, and we went on trips."

Jennifer said, "Trips? Did he finish school? Does he work? I hope he's not a drug dealer like my sister's son."

Jez said, "Stop it, Mom! He just graduated college, owns his own business, and he's not a drug dealer mom."

Jennifer said, "Okay. What does he look like?"

Jez said, "*Mom*...you and Dad turned him away when he came to see me at the hospital."

Jennifer said, "Okay! That's a tall fine man put together well. Where'd you meet him?"

Jez said, "Making a drop for Jai downtown."

Jennifer said, "That figures. Well, I would like to meet him since he's turning my baby out."

Jez said, "Maybe we should give Jai some credit, Mom. You are always jumping down her back. Mom, Ishmael is not turning me out. He's giving me feelings that I've never had."

Jennifer said, "Well, they let that janitor go after they found out some new information. I feel bad for the man. We put in a letter of recommendation for him to get his job back."

Jez said, "I feel bad we didn't know at the time, but all the evidence pointed to him. See how you care about the feelings of a stranger accused wrongful, but Jai is your daughter, Mom."

John said, "Now! Now! Jez? Your mother cares, but you are going to watch your tone when talking to my wife."

Jennifer blanked out, not hearing shit John said, and smacked the shit out of Jez. He was able to grab Jennifer before she could swing again. "*Watch your mouth,*" Jennifer shouted.

Jez ran off, crying at the fact her mother always got defensive whenever someone told her the truth or defended themselves.

Then her father forever took her side for any and everything, except for when he beat her. That's why Jai left at seventeen and never turned back, and she was beginning to start her running.

Jennifer said, "Thanks, baby! They said someone sent them the information. I'm just glad it's over with."

John said, "We need to talk about my girls and you getting along."

Jennifer said, "What are you saying? They're spoiled and disrespectful! I'm not going. Stop, John! Please let me go, John!"

John said, "You're gonna act like this shit didn't happen? *Now let them be, Jennie!*"

*****

Jez jumped in her hooptie, turning the key to hear the engine rattling, jerking, and some more shit. She called Tara to let her know she was running late.

Tara said, "I'm doing someone's hair right now, hun, unless I'd come. Told you to get a different car, girl. Call your guy."

Jez said, "I don't want to bother that man. I'll just catch a cab."

Tara said, "If he wanted to get wet, he'd have no problem calling you. Bitch, please."

*****

Jez's text to Ishmael: "Hi Ishmael."

It took him fifteen minutes to text her back. As soon as she went to dial the cab number, his text came through.

Ishmael's text to Jez: "baby girl, what's up?"

Jez's text to Ishmael: "My car won't start Ishmael, and I need a ride to work."

Ishmael's text to Jez: "Give me a few minutes, then I'm on my way."

Jez's text to Ishmael: "Okay, I'll be sitting outside my parents' house in this white beetle."

*****

Ishmael pulled up, and saw Jez sitting in this beat-up-ass car, wondering why this beautiful woman didn't have a nice ride. He noticed her parents sitting on the porch, looking at their daughter get in his car.

John said, "This is your fault they're running, always fucking up!"

Jennifer said, "*Stop, John! Please stop…*"

*****

Ishmael said, "Baby girl, lift your head. What's wrong?"

Jez said, "Me and my mom had a heated discussion which led to her slapping the fuck out of me."

Ishmael said, "Damn! Sorry to hear that! Do we have time to stop for coffee?"

Jez said, "Yes, I have time! I'm my boss, and my first client is scheduled for ten this morning."

Jez watched him drive the whole time. She loved his smell and the way he dressed.

Ishmael said, "I'm normally at school. Since graduation, my mornings are free until I find something that I like doing. I'll drive you around until then."

Jez said, "You're playing, right? I'll find somebody to fix my car. Why are we pulling in here? What kind of a coffee shop is this?"

Ishmael said, "Relax, baby girl. I got you! I'm joking, any-ways…I work every day."

Jez said, "Are you working now?"

Ishmael said, "I see you are not always so serious. That's good. My time accounted for, and I'm working on what I want."

Ishmael couldn't even get out of the car, and James came dashing up. "*Hey! My favorite customer! What's up, Ishmael?*" James shouted.

Ishmael looked in the car and told Jez to get out of her car. "What's up, James?" Ishmael said with the biggest grin on his face.

James said, "*Wow…You're a beautiful woman.*"

Jez said, "Hello, thank you, sir!"

Ishmael said, "How's the family doing?"

James said, "Great! Thanks for asking! How can I assist you today, Ishmael?"

Ishmael said, "My girl needs a new ride. Can you help me out?"

Jez said, "Ishmael? Let me talk with you for a minute, please."

Ishmael said, "I already know! You don't want me to buy you a car. Long as you're my friend, I would expect for you to look out for me when I need help. My father taught me to treat people how you want to be treated, and your lady should never want for anything. Jez? Let me treat you right. I'm a man first, before anything. Put this wall down, so I can treat you how a woman should be."

Jez said, "Ishmael…Thanks for making me your girl. That's nice, and this is a big gift. My parents would trip about me taking such a big gift."

Ishmael said, "Who said this was a gift? I'm investing in what I want, which is Jez, and you're a grown-ass woman. Maybe it's time for you to make your own decisions. Let's look around, bae."

Jez picked out an all-white 2018 Audi A4 sedan. *Why is this man spending more money on me than I ever spent on myself,* Jez thought.

Ishmael said, "I see you have exquisite taste."

Jez said, "I don't know what kind of car this is. I like it though."

Ishmael said, "It fits you fine! Look…you don't have to worry about any of this."

Jez said, "I've never had anyone do such nice things for me. I don't know how to feel or what to say, Ishmael. The trips and hanging out is fine. Here he comes!"

James said, "So, whose name should I put this in?"

Ishmael said, "Put the car in her name and use my insurance until she's ready to switch it."

James said, "How would you like to pay for this car, my man?"

Ishmael went to his trunk and came back with the money he was supposed to have deposited. James smiled so hard, you could see all his teeth. "I'll be back to get the paperwork," Ishmael said. "No problem," James shouted.

Ishmael said, "Meet me at the coffee shop around the corner, baby girl."

Jez pulled up behind Ishmael, still in disbelief this man just bought her a new car just like that with no hesitation. "Why are you crying?" Ishmael asked. "Come on! Get out the car," Ishmael demanded in a soft tone with his hand out.

Ishmael said, "You don't owe me anything. You don't have to tell anyone I bought this car if it would make you feel uncomfortable. Hell, tell them it's a rental."

Jez said, "How am I going to repay you?"

Ishmael said, "I'm not looking for repayment. Quit crying and let's go get some dark roasted coffee."

Jez said, "I'm not uncomfortable with it, the total opposite. I feel different when I'm with you."

Ishmael said, "Different, how?"

Jez said, "I feel complete when I'm around you, and I've never been...Never mind!"

Ishmael said, "You've never been with a man before? I know that already, J."

Jez said, "How? Is it really that obvious?"

Ishmael said, "Know that I know. And I didn't buy you a car to get in your panties. I want all of you. Go to work and call me later."

Jez said, "How can you afford to buy me a car just like that? With cash!"

Ishmael said, "Is that all you want to know? I told you, I'm a legit businessman that doesn't sell drugs."

Jez said, "I'm sorry. Never had anyone do anything nice for me besides my parents. Then the first guy I ever give any play happens to be rich, buying phones and cars."

Ishmael said, "Nothing to be sorry for, and quit all that rambling on and learn how to accept and give."

Jez said, "What happened to those people at your house?"

Ishmael turned to face her, and he looked at her, then grabbed her face softly. "What you don't know, the better," he said softly.

*****

Swen said, "It's the other sister that knows too much."
Seth said, "Doesn't matter to me. They both were there."
Swen said, "Well, whatever you decide to do about the situation, make sure my nephew is not with her."
Seth said, "Looking at this shit! Maybe we should let your nephew deal with her, seeing he's all tender for the bitch."
Swen said, "Yeah! He's more involved with her than I expected. Buying cars and shit."
Seth said, "I'll just have my guy keep an eye on the other one because the bitch saw everybody."
Swen said, "Fuck her! It's not like these skully punks gonna get some breaking news type shit."

*****

As soon as Jez parted ways with Ishmael, she went straight to the boutique to see her sister before going to work.
Jai said, "Damn! She slapped you? I've always walked away. You're turning into a little disrespectful idiot. Surprised Daddy didn't punch yo ass."
Jez said, "I'm not worried about them beating me. The way he beat her ass all our life, I'm surprised she's still with him. Now she's taking it out on us."
Jai said, "Shouldn't you be at work? I have a full schedule today."
Jez said, "Come outside with me for a minute. I need to show you something."

*****

Swen and Seth just sat there watching everything they were doing from the jumping around, hugging, and looking in her new ride. "You're right! They're in love with these girls," Seth said as he pulled off.

*****

Jez said, "I just called him for a ride, and he took me to get a car."

Jai said, "So…what are you nervous about again? Seriously. I think he likes you."

Jez said, "Do you think they're trying to shut us up about what we saw?"

Jai said, "Naw, bitch! I wish one of their asses would bring me to a lot. I'd pick out my dream car. Sis, I think he likes you. Besides, we didn't see shit!"

Jez said, "Excuse me? But, you are dumber than I thought."

Jai said, "Never dumb! But, I didn't see shit! Let's leave it at that, and I hope they come with me a hush bag or gift."

Jez said, "I guess, but this is not funny. I gotta go, see you later, love."

CHAPTER 29

Tara
It's Whatever

The doctor told Tara to avoid stress because it was causing the bleeding, so she moved some of her things to the shop. She stayed there for a while and didn't let anyone know she was sleeping there, or her plans.

She wasn't scared after they caught everybody. They didn't tell her what happened after she left, but she knew they weren't coming back. *This stressful bitch needs to quit calling me*, Tara thought. "Here comes the other 25 percent of my stress," Tara whispered to herself.

Tara said, "Mom…sit! You're always cutting your hair. Let it grow…Good morning, Jez. You are looking cute today."

Jez said, "Hi, Tamyra. Hey, Tara. Thanks…"

Tamyra said, "Hey, Jez, how are you doing? Tell your friend to listen to her client and cut my hair."

Tara said, "Well, Daddy told me to stop cutting it."

Tamyra said, "Well, your daddy can run his other baby mama. Damn! I mean business."

Tara looked at her phone screen then sent Skunk to voice mail again. "He needs to call that other bitch," Tara said. Every time he called, it made her relive through that night all over again.

Tamyra said, "You're speaking out loud. Stop it!"

Jez said, "Tara always speak out loud! Cut your mother's hair, girl!"

When she heard the baby's heartbeat at her appointment that morning before going to work, it made her so happy. It almost made her not give a fuck about what Skunk did, but she still made the necessary calls.

She couldn't wait to see that bitch Adana again. Knowing she knew about her and the fact she runs to his mama's house, telling everything she hears, made her furious. It made her want to run and tell his mama what she saw at Cupid, but she'd probably cheer on Adana.

Tara said, "Hold on, Mom. I'll be right back!"

Jez said, "You okay, sis? I've seen that look before."

Tamyra said, "That baby got her running to the bathroom every fifteen minutes."

Tara said, "I'm fine. I'll be right back!"

Tara rushed off to the bathroom because she started feeling wet again, so she was trying not to hold her stomach in front of everyone. Noticing blood on her tissue again, she felt the cramps getting worse. She didn't pay it no mind because it wasn't a lot like the last time, and the doctor told her it would happen after her checkup.

Tara said, "Sorry, Mom, I'll be done soon. So we have other siblings from Dad, huh?"

Tamyra said, "*No*, I'm just talking fast! Aww, shit, look who's walking in."

Tara said, "Fuck him!"

Tamyra said, "Watch your mouth! Don't let him hear you talking like that. At least let me get to my nine first...*Hey, Skunk!*"

Skunk said, "Hello, Ma. I see my baby got you looking lovelier than ever. What's up, Matthew?"

Matthew said, "What's up, Skunk? Let me holla at you before you leave."

Tamyra said, "Thank you, son!"

Tara said, "I saw you and your baby in the VIP, so please don't mistake me for her."

"Oh, shit," Jez whispered and looked at Tamyra. Tamyra started tapping Tara's leg under the sundry for her to quit getting jazzy, but Skunk couldn't see her doing it.

Skunk said, "Let me talk with you in private, Tara. Please."

Tara said, "Where are we going? To the VIP? I don't have time right now."

Skunk said, "When you have time, we can go if you want to. Quit playing with me, Tara."

Tara said, "*Fuuuu! Ouch!*"

Before she could get the words out, Tamyra had pinched her leg hard as hell. The few people that were in the shop looked over at them, wondering what was going on.

Skunk said, "You okay? Is it the baby? *Say something!*"

Tara said, "Naw, nigga! *It's you! Please leave!*"

Skunk said, "If I leave, you are coming with me to talk. *Got dammit!*"

Tara said, "This is not the right time, Skunk. I have customers, dude. Please leave and make an appointment with my receptionist."

Skunk said, "Don't call me 'dude'! I will pick you up and carry yo ass out of here. Keep playing!"

Tara said, "Make an appointment, please! Should have carried your ass home or carried my ass in the VIP instead of your side chick."

Skunk said, "Excuse me, Tamyra! I need everybody to go outside for a moment while I talk to my fiancée. Right now!"

Matthew said, "*Okay! Everybody, out! You heard the man!*"

Tamyra said, "You should lower your voice security. We heard my son-in-law. I'm not going anywhere. Now, try me if you want to!"

Tara said, "Okay! Okay! We can talk in my office. Damn! Jez, can you take over for a minute. Thanks."

They turned the corner, and Skunk pushed her into the office, slamming the door behind them. "Yo mom ain't tough," Skunk muttered as he was pushing the door behind him. "Go tell her mister," Tara said softly with a laugh.

Tara said, "Don't push me! Cheating-ass liar."

Skunk said, "Shut yo ass up! Don't ever call me 'dude' either. Let me see that damn phone. Didn't you see me calling? Why didn't you tell me about your doctor's appointment this morning? It's my baby too! You are mad at me! Doesn't mean I can't be involved in *our baby's life.*"

Tara said, "Your tone is scaring the baby. Stop yelling…"

Tara shrugged her shoulders as if she didn't care or didn't know how to answer the bullshit she thought was coming out of his mouth.

Skunk said, "*Quit shrugging your shoulders and talk! What did the doctor say?*"

Before she could roll her eyes, Skunk grabbed her around the neck and pushed her head back onto the chair.

Tara said, "Stop it! They gave me these pills. I guess they got vitamin D in them since mine is being given out in the VIP."

Skunk said, "Yo ass amusing! From now on, I need to know everything, Tara. Appointments also! Do I make myself clear?"

Tara said, "Let me go! I hear your monkey ass. Will your new chick come too? I mean the baby's stepmom?"

Skunk said, "Do you want her too? I can arrange it! Quit asking dumb shit!"

Tara jumped up fast as hell, swinging at Skunk, shouting, "Asshole," but he grabbed her hands again. She got him a few times in his face because he was sitting on the desk with his head bent down, looking at her.

He didn't see it coming, but he knew she was acting too calm to let that shit slide. "Stop, Tara! Stop," he yelled as he held her down until she stopped trying to swing. As soon as he let her hands go, she started swinging again. "*What the fuck,*" Tara said as she cried out.

Skunk said, "Baby, I'm so sorry for hurting you and breaking our bond over some pussy. I didn't know what was going on with all these robberies and who was behind it. Shit had my mind all fucked up. She caught me slippin' in a moment when my mind was everywhere."

Skunk said, "You need to control yourself…"

Tara said, "That's no excuse! *You should have come to me. That's control.*"

Skunk said, "Baby, quit yelling and fighting before you hurt the baby and yourself."

Tara said, "*Oh! Only Sem can hurt and choke me, right? You let your mom and family talk about me! You don't give a fuck about me or the baby! Let me go, Sem!*"

Skunk said, "I was torn thinking your family had something to do with my brothers being robbed and shot. I didn't want to lose you behind this shit! Baby…I'm sorry! Baby, please forgive me?"

Tara said, "*That's no excuse for giving my dick away! I thought they had something to do with it too. The fuck! But…you rather ignore me! Then go fuck a bitch! Then have the audacity to say bond. I would have done anything for you. Then, I see this punk bitch riding you in a club you bought.*"

Skunk said, "Fuck that club! I want you back, Tara. Even if it takes for us to start all over again."

Tara said, "*Why? Why? Why, Sem? You hurt me bad! It's going to be hard trusting you, so I can't.*"

Skunk said, "What can I do, Tara?"

Tara said, "I want the truth. I know it's going to hurt. But fuck it!"

After Tamyra heard all the scuffling and yelling, she grabbed her purse and stood by the door. "What are you doing," Jez asked. "Making sure I don't have to blaze a muthafucka," Tamyra whispered. Jez stood right behind her like she was about that life, knowing she couldn't shoot shit. When they heard them move, they both ran off quietly and sat down like they weren't listening.

Skunk said, "I know! Please give me one more chance? I'll make it up to you. I'm so sorry, baby."

Skunk went to the bathroom in the office and came back with a wet cloth and cleaned her face.

Tara said, "Do she know your family? Did you give her any money or gifts? How many times did y'all fuck?"

Skunk said, "She knows my whole family. I've never given her shit. We had sex a few times. Honestly!"

Tara said, "Now the bitch family family. Do you love her? Please, don't go around the questions."

Skunk said, "I'm not in love with her. I love you, Tara…"

Tara said, "That's not what I asked you, Sem. If you loved me, you would have come to me and not let some random pussy distract you."

Skunk said, "I've known this girl since we were kids. I'd be lying if I said I didn't care about her, but I'm deeply in love with you."

Tara said, "If you care about her, that means you can fall in love with her if you already haven't. I can't do this anymore with you."

Skunk said, "*Fuck that bitch! I'll tell her that in your face.*"

Tara said, "*And!* That don't stop feelings. Was she a bitch when you were fucking and sucking her?"

Skunk said, "Tara…Damn! I love you! Forgive me as I would you."

Tara said, "I wouldn't cheat. You'd kill me if you found out I fucked someone. How would you feel if you walked in and I was riding a dick? *How'd you feel? Huh?*"

Skunk said, "Don't play with me. I'd fuck him up and you… Who's Donald?"

Tara said, "Where she at then? So I can finish beating that ass."

Skunk put his hands over his face in disbelief, because he saw Adana throwing hands back after she got up. *I should set that shit up*, he thought. He knew Tara would shoot her, and he'd have to live with her secret. *She didn't say who Donald was*, Skunk thought.

He wanted Tara back. His father would never leave his family even though he had joined two women in the hood holy matrimony.

Skunk said, "You need to stop all that fighting while you're pregnant. I'll be here to talk with you after you close up shop. Jez came back. That's good."

Tara said, "I'm going to my mom's when I leave. I'll text you with the next appointment. It's just too soon for me to forget this bitch riding your dick. I can forgive you, but if you had come to me about how you felt, you would have seen that we both thought the same shit."

Skunk said, "Baby, I'm sorry! I'll never cheat again!"

Tara said, "Our relationship was built on a solid foundation, and you allowed it to get cracked. I would have talked to my family about any assumptions we had."

Skunk said, "I'm going to rebuild that foundation. Trust me…"

Tara said, "Really, Sem? I trusted you before and got hurt. I'll call you later."

Skunk said, "Let me know what it cost."

Tara said, "That's the problem. My heart is free."

Tara tried walking out the office, then Skunk grabbed her hand, trying to make her turn around. "Come here, baby." Then she pushed him away. She wanted to tell him about the information that she took out of his phone, but she still wanted to see how the other chick looked. She wanted to know what her relations were with him.

Tara said, "Stop trying to kiss on me. I don't know where your mouth been."

Skunk said, "I'll take that! That ass looking right in them leggings, though. Damn!"

Tara said, "Always! I need some money for this plastic surgery. This scar on my face got to go!"

Jez was flat ironing her hair when they heard the door open, and the other stylists and clients were acting like they didn't hear anything. They all waited for Skunk to leave before they quit acting like mannequins. "Y'all is silly," Tara shouted.

Tara said, "*Y'all can quit fronting now!*"

Jez said, "You okay?"

Tamyra said, "Wish y'all stop stressing my grandbaby out with all that fighting and arguing. It's not good."

Everybody started laughing hard as hell because she just told on herself. "I didn't do shit! I just sat here," Tamyra whispered.

Tara said, "I already knew you were listening. I'm good, Mom."

Tamyra said, "All the banging and yelling. Hell yeah! I was ready to kick the door down, but I sat here."

Tara said, "That was me attacking his cheating ass."

Tara was watching him talk to security outside, wondering why his quiet ass didn't say anything when he heard the scuffling in the back.

Jack said, "Girl, boo. Everybody cheats!"

Jez said, "So…how's security around here?"

Everybody laughed hard. "That's one of his friends, so you know he's not gon' do shit. Jack? Everybody don't cheat. That's a lie," Tara said in one breath without pausing.

Jack said, "Honey, please! We don't catch them all the time."

Tamyra said, "Whatever he did can wait until you have the baby, I'm sure."

Tara said, "If you walk in and see a bitch riding your fiancé's dick. How would you feel?"

Jack said, "*Oh, Lawd! Cut his ass.*"

Tamyra said, "Watch yo mouth, Tara! That baby got you without a filter."

Tara said, "Sorry, Mama! But this nigga got me messed up!"

Jez said, "I'll finish your mother, and you can go rest in the back."

Tara said, "Thanks! I need to make a phone call. I'll be right back."

"You see this shit, man," Seth muttered out of anger when he saw Skunk coming and leaving the shop. Swen didn't know what to say, because he didn't even know she had opened the shop back up.

*****

Matthew said, "Thanks for that package. My boy Jesse wants to work security part-time when I'm not here."

Skunk said, "Welcome, bro. I'm still looking for a few more people for this new spot. Let me get his information so that I can arrange a meeting. I'll be back here when she closes, so I'll holla with you then."

*****

Swen went to get out the car, and Seth grabbed his arm in confusion. *I'm about to tell their ass something*, Swen thought. "Look at this shit, man," Swen said.

498

Seth said, "We were following her. I didn't know your family dealt with these females like that. What was the point of them bringing them?"

Swen said, "The females were beaten up and robbed as well. But they're all out here comfortable like some crazy shit didn't just go down."

Seth said, "That sounds like a setup! Could they walk after the robberies?"

Swen said, "Hell yeah! Their pretty faces beat up! That's it."

Skunk
At It Again

"Come over here and put that fat muthafucker right there, baby girl. Quit playing with it and let me see what it do, homey."

Adana said, "You play too much, homey, lover, friend…"

Skunk said, "I'm not playing! Come shake it!"

Adana said, "Let me make sure the door is locked!"

Skunk said, "Ain't nobody coming to my mother's house with no BS."

Skunk watched Adana ride his dick until she started giggling, then he knew she was about to nut. "Oh my gosh," Adana whispered softly.

He motioned for her to stand up and turn around. He assisted her in bending over the chair with her ass in the air. He pushed the back of her head softly forward, gripping her hair while stroking her softly as she started moving her ass in a circle to his rhythm.

Skunk said, "Quit crying! Damn, this pussy warm…"

Adana said, "*Shhh*…Come on, Zaddy, get this pussy!"

She moaned that shit out, and it made him feel some way, and he started stroking from side to side, slapping ass cheeks, squeezing nipples, and pulling hair.

Skunk said, "Throw that ass, homey!"

Adana said, "Homey, quit talking and give me that dick."

Skunk said, "You got some good pussy, Adana…*damn*! You've been holding out on me all these years."

Adana said, "Whatever, homey! That was good! Let me roll up some flame."

Skunk said, "You've been flaming a lot lately?"

Adana said, "I guess! Shit's relaxing! It's taking my mind off these stitches."

*****

Tara got tired of waiting for him to come, so she called her family to pick her up. "I'm sick of this shit," Tara mumbled.

Tara said, "Queen? How in the hell do you know where she lives?"

Queen said, "I have my resources and skills. They live next door to his mama. I followed Merch over here one day, then he led me to these realtor sisters."

Samaya laughed hard, noticing that Tara didn't crack a giggle or smirk. *So, it's two of these big booty bitches*, Tara thought.

Tara said, "Then, all this 'Baby, please' shit! He didn't come back to the shop the other night. What the fuck!"

Samaya said, "*Oh my gosh! Look at this, bitch!*"

Tara went to pull her pipe out the glove department, and Queen grabbed her hand. "TT said, 'Turn the anger into money, baby.' Now, put it back," Queen said.

Tara said, "*Let my hand go!*"

Queen said, "Get the money. I know how you're feeling, cousin, but this bitch or Skunk isn't worth it. Let's get this bitch another day."

Toonie said, "Yup! Let's go!"

Samaya said, "What's the point of sitting out here? Let's walk up there."

Tara said, "That's his car she's getting in? The bitch sold him the shop for me. The bitch came by the shop to drop some papers off, acting all surprised when she saw me. I knew I saw this bitch before."

Samaya said, "*Let me out this fucking car!*"

Toonie said, "*Stop this dumb shit! Calm down...and let's think. Shit!*"

Queen said, "*No. Let's follow these skanks to see where they take us. Now, both y'all trigger-finger asses sit back.*"

Tara said, "Whoever told you about her spot, can they tell you where he lives now? He barely goes to Cupid anymore after I caught him fucking her in VIP."

Toonie said, "Y'all wrong! They don't own Cupid anymore, Tara."

Samaya said, "Aw, hell no! Why didn't you tell me, sis? Girl, slow down before they see us. Oh, they sold the club to Queen."

Queen said, "How did you know he was at Cupid with her?"

501

Tara said, "I've sat and followed his ass a few times. I need to find out what chaste's relations is to him."

Samaya said, "*fuck Chaste?*"

Queen said, "*Right!* This nigga got a power dick."

Tara laughed a little bit, and Samaya shook her head, thinking about Isaiah's power dick. Toonie was so pissed that they even fucked them, period, so she didn't laugh.

Tara said, "I went through his phone right after we fucked."

Toonie said, "Samaya said, 'Let's go out to eat.' Now we're giving these men our time again. Shit never fails."

Skunk waited for Adana to come back from the store so he could bounce. He noticed a missed call from Chaste wanting to meet up with him to discuss her plans; he asked her to get together.

He ignored Tara's calls because he had already dropped the money off to her mom for the surgery, and she was fighting too much.

Skunk's text to Chaste: "Let's meet tomorrow around nine at the coffee shop."

Chaste's text to Skunk: "Okay."

She watched her chop it up with another dude before getting out of the car. "I guess she has game," Toonie said, and everybody laughed.

*****

Tara said, "Let's go in the store with this bitch."

Toonie said, "What are you crying for, Tara? Don't fight this girl! It's his doing…"

Tara said, "*This bitch knew about me!*"

Queen said, "You got me crying now. Fuck it! Let's go!"

They jumped out the car rushing to get her before she got to the car. Before Adana could see what was happening, Tara rushed her, swinging so fast, she bust her stitches back open. "What the fuck you want," Adana shouted as she swung back. Tara knocked her in the mouth, then Anema jumped out of the car to help her sister.

Anema tried to run up. Queen punched her in the nose, and her shit started leaking. Anema was fazed but managed to keep up with Queen. "Back up, bitch," Toonie shouted. She pushed Anema into the car and made the door shut.

Samaya saw Queen dragging Anema, and she went to help Tara. "I got this bitch," Tara shouted.

A few people came out to break it up, and some were recording because they didn't give a fuck. Tara was on a mission to beat ass any means necessary for being burned. "Take the car," Tara shouted to Samaya. *What the fuck*, Samaya thought as she started the car.

Adana tried to run up and stop Samaya from taking the car, but Toonie shoved her right back into Tara's punches. "Get that bitch," Toonie said.

Tara snatched her by the hair, pulling her down to give Samaya time to pull off. Before she could stomp her, "Let's go," Queen shouted. Samaya had started pulling off in Skunk's car then pulled next to Tara's ride. "Come on," Samaya shouted.

Tara said, "*You mines now! Now, walk to VIP, bitch!*"

Adana said, "*Fuck you!*"

Tara jumped in the car with Queen. "Pull off! I'm done with this bitch," Tara said as she cried from anger.

Queen said, "What? My cousin stepped to the other side. Gang gang in this bitch! Were we taking his car?"

Samaya said, "Where to, sis?"

Tara said, "*Y'all follow us, sis! That's my fucking car! That bitch can walk home.*"

Queen said, "Okay, cousin! You're cra-cra, for real, for real… Didn't the doctor tell you to take it easy?"

Tara said, "Did you see Toonie trying to sneak and be 'bout it? My baby is just fine. I know what you did yesterday. Did you tell anyone you should be taking it easy?"

Queen said, "What's so funny? I'm not ready for all this…And how do you know?"

Tara said, "I saw you leaving…Yes, I thought about it, but I love her. I'm not doing this anymore, either. He used to be worth my time, but not like this."

Samaya and Toonie jumped out of the car and got back in the car with them, and Toonie was acting nervous as hell.

Samaya said, "My sister gang gang! Are you okay, Toonie? Never mind, let me leave you alone."

Toonie said, "Did y'all ever hear about their father? Okay! Ignore me…"

Let me give my fiancé a heads-up, Tara thought.

Tara said, "I took my car to where you were supposed to come back the other night."

Skunk said, "What are you talking about, Tara? Baby? Hello? Hello? Damn!"

Adana called Skunk.

Adana said, "*This bitch just ran up on me again!*"

Skunk said, "Quit yelling and tell me what's going on? Tell your sister to be quiet."

Adana said, "Your ex-girl just jumped out of the car with some females…fought my sister and I. Then took your damn car. *Now, we're—I'm stuck!*"

Skunk said, "Can you get home?"

Adana said, "I left my car key in my top drawer next to my bed."

As soon as they got in the car, they were yelling and screaming. "Sem, do you know these girls?" Anema asked.

Skunk said, "Yes, I'm so sorry this happened. I will deal with them. Okay, Adana?"

Adana said, "What makes this bitch think she can keep sneaking me though. And, she's pregnant. Why the fuck is she fighting? Dumb bitch!"

Skunk said, "Hold on! We're going to keep the name-calling between y'all. Don't talk about her like that in front of me."

Anema said, "*Hold on! This bitch just took your car. Had her dumb-ass friends fight us over you!*"

Skunk said, "Slow down, Anema! You, too, Adana. I just told yo ass I was handling it."

Skunk had already called Merch to come to get him from his mom's house. When he saw him pull outside Adana's house, he was hoping Tara didn't follow them there with this shit.

Skunk said, "When I handle this shit, Adana, I'll hit you up."

Adana said, "Whatever! On my way back to the hospital. *Ugh!*"

Merch couldn't stop laughing at the fact his brother was banging Adana in his mom's empty house. "Never took her for the empty-house hookup," Merch said." I know Tara followed her, because Queen and Samaya put her up to this," Skunk shouted. "I believe they had something to do with it," Merch replied. "Let me hit that shit," Skunk said.

Merch said, "How the fuck did she get your car?"

Skunk said, "They had to follow her. I don't even feel like fighting with this girl tonight. Fuck that car!"

Merch said, "They out here acting like the black angels."

Skunk said, "Bro, you silly. They're out here wildin' out."

Merch said, "I can't believe Ms. Innocent repoed your shit. All their ass stay strapped! So, we're going to let her keep that bitch for the baby. I don't know why the fuck I bought that gun for Queen's crazy ass. Seems like she started acting tougher."

Skunk said, "Right! Shit! I didn't think Tara had this side to her. This baby got her acting crazy. I fucked up and bought her a gun, too, bro."

They both started laughing. "Probably watching us now," Merch said, as he exhaled his flame.

Merch said, "Damn! They beat up my Anema fine as too?"

Skunk said, "Ay, bro, take me to go grab one of Ishmael's cars? I need to be out of sight. I can't believe she just took the car from my side bitch."

Merch said, "How the fuck she in the same area as this girl, bro? Her shop and mom's crib on the other side of town."

Skunk said, "I'm not about to question her crazy ass right now. She tried fighting me the other day, like, fuck the baby. My boy Matthew told me her business is doing good. She has some nice-looking staff working there."

Merch said, "Heard Queen shaking her ass across town."

Skunk said, "While pregnant? Damn! They don't give a fuck about nobody but themselves. Does she know that you know about the other abortions?"

Merch said, "Trying to be sneaky about the shit, not telling me. On another note, I'm supposed to be meeting up with Seth."

Skunk said, "His fees are extremely high as hell."

Merch said, "Fuck it! We don't have to worry about that club anymore or them people. I'll pay him with ease."

Skunk said, "Right! Fucking with these crazy-ass females, we might need him again. It looked like they tried to kill the girls."

After Skunk got the keys from his brother, he left and went straight to his hotel to get some sleep. He made sure to tell the staff that he wanted no visitors or calls unless from his family.

*****

Skunk looked her up and down for a few minutes. He never saw her in anything but jogging pants and T-shirts. *Got damn*, Skunk thought.

Chaste said, "Hi, Sem. How are you?"

Skunk said, "I'm good, Chaste. What's with the big hug this morning? I like your hair and suit."

Chaste said, "I'm good, thank you! Well, I have a layout of the business proposal and location. If you look right here on the map a lot of the businesses which brings people, and people bring us revenue."

Skunk said, "Okay! I like that you are getting straight to business. Would you like a coffee first?"

Chaste said, "Yes. Sorry, I need to run this by you. They're showing this place today at ten thirty."

Skunk said, "Well, let's get the coffee to go."

Chaste jumped in her new Cadillac Escalade EXT with an all-white two-piece skirt suit on, looking like a straight businesswoman.

They arrived downtown. Skunk watched her switch until they reached their destination *Damn, that ass juicy*, he thought. They waited with a few more people until the realtor arrived discussing the layout. "This is a nice building," Chaste said. "I see you have good taste," Skunk replied. "I did a lot of research on this building compared to the others," Chaste whispered.

Skunk saw Adana walk through the door with sunglasses on, and he already knew he didn't have to compete with other potential buyers, then he thought about last night.

Adana said, "Hi, everyone, thanks for coming. You can take a brochure and look around. I have some refreshments set up. If you have any questions, please feel free to come to find me."

Chaste walked through the office area, discussing who would have what office and how many other associates could work there in the future. Skunk followed right behind her, listening and watching her point out little fine details.

Skunk said, "Let's go talk numbers."

Chaste said, "Hi, Adana, my name is Chaste, and this is my business partner, Sem. We have a few questions."

Adana said, "Hi, Chaste, and how are you, Sem? Buying more property, I see."

Skunk said, "I'm good, Adana. You didn't tell me you were showing this place?"

Adana said, "Yes. I'm covering for one of my coworkers because her car got stolen yesterday."

Chaste said, "Okay! Glad to see y'all know each other. Do you both need a minute, or can we get to business?"

Adana said, "I'm here to meet, greet, and sell. How can I help you, Chase?"

Chaste said, "Really? It's Chaste, for the record."

Skunk said, "Are they willing to come down on the monthly rent?"

Adana said, "The owner is trying to sell the place, but he hasn't received any offers. He's trying to rent out each space with a jacked-up price for rent to make extra money."

Chaste said, "Now we're talking business. Thanks."

Skunk said, "What the numbers look like to buy, Adana?"

Chaste said, "We would have to hire management for the whole building if we buy it."

Adana said, "Or you could sell each business their portion of the property, which the last owner wouldn't do. Now he's up in his ass with bills."

"She knows her shit! I like that," Chaste whispered. "I like it too," Skunk said.

*****

"Look, it's just you and me here, and I'm not letting you do some dumb shit," Toonie said. "Is he buying this bitch a building too," Tara whispered.

Toonie said, "You're gonna stop fighting over him. If he bought that shop for you, he'd buy you more than that. You're pregnant, right? Girl, please!"

Tara said, "Maybe he will. I can't stand looking at him right now."

Toonie said, "Make up some shit! Say you want to open another shop. Hell, say you need a yoga shop! Get creative on his ass and make these females wish they were you. Da fuck!"

Tara said, "Well, I sent a text saying I need another building. Let's see how smart you really are..."

CHAPTER 30

Isaiah
Business Only

Skunk called Isaiah to meet up with him and Chaste at the office building to look over the numbers, and Adana waited as usual. Chaste wanted to explain how much they could profit off the building, but Skunk let her know she had to convince Isaiah first.

Chaste said, "I hope she doesn't sell it! I like this location."

Skunk said, "Don't worry about that. It's ours. My brother will get us a better deal if he finds any discrepancies."

Isaiah and Skunk went to the side and discussed what they'd think would be best and invited Chaste to a meeting after Isaiah read it over.

When they finished, Isaiah went to their mom's new house where they all had been staying since they sold their homes, and she loved every moment of it.

Isaiah hadn't seen Samaya in a while, thinking about how everything went down, right before Rocky started talking. That made him suspicious, so he kept investigating her ass on his own, and didn't mention that he suspected her to his brothers.

Isaiah didn't have proof that she was trying to shut the men up, yet they got smoked before they could tell. Knowing his brothers, they'd make her disappear, and her losing the baby had her acting different, so he stayed quiet.

Isaiah called for a meeting at the hotel to meet up with the family before making decisions on his own because they were starting to be careless about what they bought.

Isaiah said, "Man, I heard the whip got repossessed?"

Skunk said, "That's some other shit! Then text me about another building."

Merch started choking off the flame from laughing. *She can have it too*, Skunk thought.

Swen said, "Well, nephew, if she's running around beating on your other girls, that's a bad look for you."

Skunk said, "She's my fiancée, and the other girl is my friends. We have sex."

Swen said, "No matter what title you put on it, they're still women that we sexed. Either you get an understanding with what you want from them unless they're going to keep at it."

Isaiah said, "That's real. I'm not going for no female following and fighting me, and all my friends. That girl could have been a business partner or something."

Ishmael said, "She caught them fucking at the club."

Swen said, "Well, damn! Nephew, ask yourself. Can I live with one woman for the rest of my life?"

Skunk said, "I've never thought about it like that. I don't know. I love Tara, though. Fuck!"

Merch said, "Them females wild ass fuck. Tara got them hands because Adana's face looked beaten like she got jumped."

Isaiah said, "I used to think Dad was something. After hearing all this shit makes me want to be just like him. His women never fought, had kids the same age, and all he did was take care of everything."

Swen said, "That's called communication and direction."

Skunk said, "And some good ass understanding. Tara is not going…"

Isaiah said, "I get it, Unc. With the right direction, they need no understanding. If you communicate the laws before anything, then directions will be followed."

Swen said, "You must have paid attention. Real shit! Skunk? Have you ever talked to her about it?"

Ishmael said, "Get rid of them and get all new chicks. I—"

Skunk said, "Nope, Unc.! Tara's not going anywhere. Back to business."

Isaiah said, "Talking about business! That buy downtown is a good one."

Merch said, "I'm glad we sold Cupid. That was a nice profit. I don't have time for no offsprings coming back making a part two sequel and shit."

Ishmael said, "We need Ax to manage this new building Skunk buying for Chaste fine ass."

Skunk said, "It's not like that! She's about her paper, but she does clean up well."

Isaiah said, "We'll only make quick money if we buy it. I went to Adana's office, and the owner finally came down on his offer. It's not the right spot for a firm, but that spot down the street from our hotel is finally selling their building. It's not connected to anything, and their asking price is reasonable."

Skunk said, "When can we see it? She'll like that."

Isaiah said, "We can see it tomorrow morning. If we buy it with cash, they won't even put it up on the market. Another thing I need to mention. Somebody just bought a car, money for school, and another building."

Skunk said, "I still want the other building as well. I have an idea for it."

Ishmael said, "Yes. I did, bro!"

Isaiah said, "Shit! Did you buy your brother a car? Let's hope this one doesn't get repossessed!"

Skunk said, "Bro, stop it! He bought his new girl a car."

Ishmael said, "Bro, you're crazy, and I can't believe Tara just took your shit! Then bro gave her money for another building."

Merch said, "And beat his side piece ass…I thought she was the normal one."

Swen said, "I heard about trigger finger, Queen."

Skunk said, "Come on, y'all. Let's finish up. Oh, Merch paid for school! Isaiah can't say too much, because he's paying Samaya every day not to strip."

Isaiah said, "They all have trigger fingers, Unc. Didn't you talk with Seth?"

Swen said, "I told him to stop by after the meeting."

Merch said, "Oh, now we're done talking about spending our money because Isaiah got mentioned. Okay!"

Isaiah said, "Okay! Okay! We have enough money to do as we please. I get it!"

Skunk said, "Ax, Chaste, and Teisha will join us in a minute. I decided to let Teisha work at our office to get some training. A lot of customers are missing her vibrant personality."

Merch said, "I talked with Sunshine. She thinks we still own Cupid, so I told her to keep an eye on Queen for me and I'll get her job back. I hear Queen's across town shaking ass again.

Ishmael said, "Hold on! They're just moving around with ease."

Swen said, "So, what are you thinking? She is pregnant, right?"

The door swung open, and all you could hear was Teisha's loud-mouth ass. "Here she comes," Isaiah said.

Merch said, "What's up, Ax and Tee?"

Teisha said, "*That's all you see, boss? Okay, nigga!*"

Merch said, "Hello, Ms. Teisha!"

Everybody arrived, and they laid down the rules as they flamed and waited for Seth to show up.

Isaiah said, "Well, Teisha, I looked at the wage we offered you. Are you fine with that?"

Teisha said, "*Hell yeah! This job is for how long? Y'all keep switching my shit!*"

Ishmael said, "Excuse me. Let me step out and take this call. And...do you have to speak so loud?"

Ishmael came back in the room, and everybody was looking at Seth smile at Teisha like they were some damn emoji characters.

Teisha said, "Hi, Seth! How are you doing?"

Seth said, "What's up, T? I'm good."

Ax said, "Hold on! Seth? What did you do to make her talk in a normal tone?"

Seth said, "Aw, man, it's not like that!"

Teisha said, "I'm gone! Call you later, Seth."

Isaiah said, "We have another business building opening soon, and we're going to need a manager to oversee everything going on with all the units. Here are the layout and my plans for the building. I'll give you a few days to look it over and get back to me with any ideas."

Skunk said, "Bro, I'm gonna need that building. Let Ax be the manager of the firm."

Ax said, "Does this mean I'll only oversee that business as well?"

Isaiah said, "Yes! Do you have time? With your business about to start."

Ax said, "Yes. I'm fine with this. Thanks, fam."

Ishmael said, "What's up, Seth?"

Seth said, "Hate to ruin the promotions. Do you think these ladies can be trusted?"

Isaiah said, "We haven't signed off anything yet."

Merch said, "I don't trust none of them."

Skunk said, "Tara said she thought they had something to do with it. After everything unfolded, I thought it was all Rocky's doing."

Seth said, "Most females would be sitting still after some shit like that. They're running around all worry free."

Ishmael said, "I just got off the phone with Terrence."

Swen said, "I hope his weird ass don't come here. Let me leave first!"

Ishmael said, "Unc. You don't like him, but he's the one that told me Lia was the people."

Merch said, "That's why she looked like she was taking notes. Punk bitch!"

Seth said, "Damn! I see y'all know how to pick 'em."

Ishmael said, "I'm not doing shit illegal. I don't have shit to worry about, plus, they wanted Rocky off the streets."

Isaiah said, "Fuck that! This shit over with apparently, we're still dealing with them."

Swen said, "I still don't like him! Have you ever noticed how he held the flame, nephew?"

Merch said, "How he hold that shit, Unc? This shit funny…"

Isaiah said, "Please don't get Unc started…"

Skunk said, "He investigated the ladies also and didn't find out shit."

Ishmael said, "Well, I've never pillow talked about anything. All she ever did was suck me off."

Seth said, "Fuck it! Was she doing it like that? I would have recorded her ass."

Isaiah said, "I think we should give her ass a job and watch they ass."

Merch said, "I don't want people knowing my damn business."

Ishmael said, "And I don't want Jill around me like that. Shit was strictly a pussy call."

Isaiah said, "Yeah, you're right! I'm just saying they wouldn't want anybody following and watching them."

Skunk said, "This shit got me thinking now. Look at how long they worked with him. Long enough to get trained."

Swen said, "That's what I wanted to talk about because I need all of you to leave these girls alone."

Ishmael said, "Did y'all see when the dude went to talk at the meeting, she let loose on his ass."

Isaiah said, "Come on now! They raped this girl."

Skunk said, "Thought I was the only one that saw that shit."

Merch said, "Damn! They raped my homey? That's why she sounded like a monster."

Seth said, "Either they're hiding something, or she got tired of hearing they ass speak."

Merch said, "Can't shit happen to the girls right now. Now, if some shit hit the fan, their punk ass going down."

Swen said, "Shit! That shit is not funny! Merch, you're right."

Ishmael said, "She smoked his ass!"

Isaiah said, "They killed her baby! But I saw that shit too!"

Seth said, "Makes sense to keep your enemy close. Just be careful…"

Isaiah said, "She's not an enemy. On some real shit. I thought we were going to have to do an exorcism. She sounded fucked up!"

Seth got his package and left with his head held up high, not giving a fuck about what they said. He knew he had to get in good with Teisha to stay up on shit.

Swen said, "Now that nigga gon' let me finish. I was tipsy, but I heard that pretty boy say Samaya was friends or something with a Chad. Now, do you think it's a good idea to trust them?"

Merch said, "Okay, listen to my theory if they set this shit up. Why in the hell are they still following and beating on people? What did they gain out of this shit happening?"

Isaiah said, "Not a damn thang!"

Skunk said, "They keep fucking with me. Somebody gonna catch a case."

*****

They just sat there, wondering if they should go in or sit outside. "Fuck it! I see a few people we know that came and left," Tara said. Samaya just shook her head knowing damn well Isaiah would snap if she barged in on him.

Samaya said, "I have too much to lose right now. What the fuck are we going in there for, and you know his mom moved to a new house?"

Tara said, "No, I didn't know! I wish Queen were here! Come on! I want to see the look on his face when he sees me."

Samaya said, "Tara, pull off! Didn't the doctor tell you to stay away from stress? I heard he just gave you a check for another building, and you're still tripping? Maybe we should have brought Toonie's smart ass. Let's go!"

*****

Isaiah went to pick up Samaya at her aunt's house, but when he pulled up, Detective Thomas and Phillips were exiting the house, and Samaya had to be the one shutting the door.

515

He waited for them to pull off, debating if he should go in or not, but he called Ishmael first. *I know one of them took my briefcase,* Isaiah thought as he called Ishmael.

Isaiah said, "Bro, I just pulled up to Tamyra's house, and Samaya was letting Detective Thomas and his partner out. Should I go ask what they wanted, or should I not say anything?"

Ishmael said, "I would wait to see if she mentions it first."

Isaiah said, "Fuck this shit!"

Isaiah pulled off and went to his mom's old crib. As soon as they saw him come through the door, they all laughed and passed him the flame.

Isaiah said, "Y'all flaming? Must mean Moms is out of town?"

Skunk said, "They went to see Pops, so you know they're not coming back soon."

Merch said, "We're sitting here waiting for you to call us, and you walk in."

Isaiah said, "The lawyer told her ass she didn't have to speak with them. Then I see this shit!"

Ishmael said, "They want to know why she left the hospital, nothing serious."

Isaiah said, "I was about to go steal bro keys out that bitch."

They laughed so hard, but Skunk just sat there looking high and confused.

Merch said, "That's some real gangsta shit!"

Skunk said, "Bro, if she was that bad to take a car from another bitch, she can have it. Give it to my baby!"

Ishmael said, "Straight up! I'm not fighting over no materialistic shit. And, if my side bitch let you beat her up, she's not making the team."

Isaiah said, "Let's fly to Vegas tonight? Right now!"

Merch said, "I'm game. I need some new friends."

Skunk said, "Let me call Mom!"

Ishmael said, "Any females coming?"

Isaiah said, "Just us! We haven't traveled since all this bullshit started."

Merch said, "Bro ass going down there to see Ruth country ass."

Ishmael said, "I forgot she moved to Vegas."

Isaiah said, "Nope! I'm good on her. She was too much for me."

Skunk said, "I'm ready! I'll just let Ax handle the business until we return."

Isaiah locked up the house and asked his mom's neighbor to keep an eye on the house and get her mail until she returned. When Anema saw him standing in the doorway, she just put her head down in dismay.

Samaya's text to Isaiah: "Hey Isaiah, what happened to you picking me up?"

Isaiah's text to Samaya: "This meeting is taking longer than expected, so I'll call you when it's over."

*****

"Do you see this shit?" the girl muttered, and the other woman was in agreement with her. "Let's do this shit," they both said at the same time.

Ishmael
Moving On

Ishmael sat at the poker table for hours winning and losing. He turned his ringer off so he could concentrate, not noticing it was Jez calling him. He was trying not to think about her knowing that he liked her character and how she carried herself, but she was too close to her twin's friends.

When he found out about Lia, he thought about calling Seth to get her ass, yet she gave him a lot of information, and that saved her ass. He thought about changing his number so Lia couldn't call, but he knew she could get it anyway, and that made him leave it be.

*****

The poker dealer said, "Sir. Sir. How many cards?"

Ishmael said, "One, please!"

Ishmael pushed all his chips in. *I need to make my money back,* Ishmael thought. "All bets in?" the poker dealer said. Three people backed out, and one opponent remained, and Ishmael knew he was bluffing. He laid his cards down. "Here you go! Royal flush," Ishmael said with a big smile.

Poker dealer said, "Ace high, straight flush. Wow!"

Ishmael saw the other player's face when he slammed his cards down, and they were pissed. *"We have a winner! Congratulations, sir!"* the poker dealer said. The poker dealer was happy with his generous tip.

Merch said, "How much you start with, bro?"

Ishmael said, "Fifty K! I've been sitting here the whole time."

Merch said, "Bro just won 150,000 dollars. Teach me how to play this shit?"

Isaiah said, "I lost a thousand! I'm quitting for the night."

Merch said, "Bro been playing since he was in diapers with Pops. Now you can buy Skunk a ride."

Ishmael said, "Where is Skunk? He must be playing the slots! Granny ass!"

Isaiah said, "Bro being cheap because he has money to buy a car in his other accounts."

Merch said, "You know he never plays anything else. Over there fighting the older people for machines. Look at his drunk ass!"

Skunk saw his brothers approaching. *Here they shit-talking ass come*, Skunk thought. "Get off my machine, young man," the old lady said in an angry tone. "I've won fifteen hundred so far! *Haha*," Skunk replied to the old lady.

Merch said, "You be arguing with them? You know their machines marked."

Skunk said, "She can have it now that I'm leaving. Let me go try to win this car."

Isaiah said, "Ishmael came up 150,000. He can buy your cheap butt a car. Your ass drunk!"

Skunk said, "Bro our lucky charm. Move so my new friends can watch me win."

Ishmael said, "They watching his ass. Soon as you get up, they running for this machine."

Skunk said, "Damn, bro, always winning big, then quit! Fuck it, and go for the million on their ass."

Ishmael said, "I'm not giving them the money back. Never! I'll come back when it a new dealer and players."

Merch said, "I'm going back to the table to play twenty-one. These old ladies are going to whoop yo ass over this machine any minute. Let's go, Skunk!"

Isaiah said, "I'm coming with you, so I'm not in the way when they bum rush his ass."

Skunk said, "I'll go! If I don't win off the first few hands, I'm walking away."

*****

Ishmael called Jez back after he settled down in his luxury room they gave him for winning.

Jez said, "Hi, Ishmael. *Oh my gosh! I miss you.*"

Ishmael said, "Well, hello, beautiful. How's it going?"

Jez said, "I love this new car. It rides so good. My parents were upset, so I told them you let me use the car until mines got out of the shop. I've been calling you to show you some good news. I got my own apartment, and I bought my first couch and bed today."

Ishmael said, "Baby, quit lying to your parents. You're grown, and they need to understand that. What I do for you shouldn't ever be hidden because I want to do it and more. Let your mom be her and move on. But congratulations."

Jez said, "They don't treat us like we're grown. I see why my sister left."

Ishmael said, "Long as you stay under their roof, they're going to be in your business and treat you like a child. You took a big step, and I'm happy for you."

Jez said, "I had to move when my clientele got up at the shop. I still need to finish school, so I didn't get anything pricey. Didn't want to go over my budget with bills. Anyways, when will I see you again?"

Ishmael said, "When do you want to coincide?"

Jez said, "Now! I miss your company."

Ishmael said, "I'll see you when I return home unless you jump on a flight to see me."

Jez said, "A flight! Quit playing! Where are you?"

Ishmael said, "Catch a cab to the airport then call me when you arrive. I'll have the confirmation number, and don't bring anything but your ID. When you land, I'll have a cab bring you to me."

Jez said, "Oh my gosh, you are impulsive! What about work?"

Ishmael said, "You're on spring break! You're a cosmetologist. That means you are your boss, baby girl, remember! Don't tell anyone, and this is between you and me."

Jez said, "How can I tell something if I don't know where I'm going?"

Ishmael said, "Smart-ass be looking for the cab."

Jez sat on the airplane, amazed at the feeling he gave her, knowing she didn't have a care in the world. *I really can't wait to hug and smell his cologne,* Jez thought. She thought about how he picked her up off the ground like her daddy did when she was a little girl, and that made her heart warm.

Ishmael called downstairs to the desk clerk, making sure the porter brought Jez up to his room when she arrived by herself.

He also put in an order for the kitchen to bring up steak, chicken, shrimp, veggie trays, fresh fruits, different salads, juices, water, candy, flowers, vodka, and champagne.

The maid brought extra towels, soap, sheets, a housecoat, and pillows.

*****

Jez walked in the casino looking at all the people screaming for joy, lights flashing, and machines making noises.

She approached the desk, and the lady reviewed her ID as instructed by Ishmael. *It's me...Damn!* Jez thought. She wasn't surprised that the lady was waiting on her like she knew her or something.

The clerk motioned for the porter to assist Jez upstairs, then she called his room to inform him that Jez was on her way upstairs. *Good customer service, I guess,* Jez thought as she strutted off.

Ishmael said, "Come in, baby girl! My baby, beautiful."

Ishmael handed the porter a tip. "Thanks, sir," the porter said, smiling from ear to ear from Ishmael's generosity. *Bitch better get out of here with that cheesy shit,* Jez thought. "Welcome," Ishmael replied with gratitude.

Jez ran up and jumped in his arms. She was hugging him like a little girl wanting to see her zaddy. As soon as the door closed, she saw the porter's face of dissatisfaction with her performance.

Ishmael loved how she indulged in him as no other female has ever done. He carried her through the room as she squeezed her legs around his waist, and he cuffed her ass, as her body wanted.

Jez said, "Hi, Ishmael! I like a clever man."

Ishmael said, "Look, I have some food and drinks for you. I didn't know what to get, so I ordered a little bit of everything for us."

Jez said, "I saw so many lights and people having fun. I've never been here before or out of that state. I'm happy you sent for me. I've never felt so important or special."

Ishmael said, "Baby girl, it's okay! Do you want to go down-stairs and gamble? I know exactly what to do! Come follow me!"

*****

The spa attendant said, "Come in, come in, beautiful people. How may I help you?"

Ishmael said, "Hello, miss. We want the whole treatment!"

Jez said, "Hello, miss."

The spa attendant said, "Same room for massages?"

Jez said, "Yes. Thanks."

The spa attendant said, "Follow me, and I'll show you where to change. You'll come out this way, and I'll introduce you to your massage therapist."

Jez said, "Thank you."

Ishmael said, "Thank you, miss."

After their massages, they sat in the chairs and sipped cham-pagne while the manicurists did Jez's hands and feet. *He just handed the manicurist the nail polish*, Jez thought. Being forward made her feel some way, but she liked it.

Jez said, "Why don't you get your toes done?"

Ishmael said, "I'm good on that, baby girl. The massage was enough for me, but this is about you…"

Jez said, "Why is this place open so late?"

Ishmael said, "This the city that never sleeps!"

They sat on the bed, and she watched him flame. *Why? Why? Why must everybody smoke?* Jez thought. When he blew the smoke in her face, she giggled and choked a little bit.

Jez said, "Stop, Ishmael! I don't smoke anymore."

They talked for a while then watched movies until she fell asleep on his chest. She rolled over, noticing he had covered her up and went to the oversize chair to sleep.

She went to the shower. Not wanting to put on the same clothes, she threw on the robe and stood in front of the mirror, coaching her-self. *Bitch! You can do this. Do it like the girls on the videos*, Jez thought.

She started walking over to him, and her stomach quenched as she got closer, not knowing what to do or expect.

After a few shots of tequila, a warm feeling and boldness overtook her. She bent over and kissed his forehead, then tapped his shoulder.

"*Wow*," Ishmael mumbled as she stood there in front of him looking like a wet edible snack. "Wake up and come to the bed, Ishmael," Jez said softly. *I want you next to me*, Jez thought. "Look, baby girl. I know you're a virrr—" Ishmael tried to say, but her robe dropped, and he followed her right to the bed.

Jez said, "I want you, Ishmael."

Ishmael said, "I want you too!"

He watched her beautiful body lie down. *I can't take her innocence*, Ishmael thought. Something about her made him think about feelings, and for once, he liked it. He grabbed her hand, so she could stand up in front of him as he sat down on the bed.

Ishmael said, "Let me show you something. Relax, Jez!"

He pulled her closer, and he started sucking her nipple. He squeezed the other one softly, then rotated and did the same with the other nipple. She moaned and grabbed his head, then he pulled back and looked at her in the eyes.

Ishmael said, "Do you like that feeling?"

Jez said, "Yes, I do! OMG…"

Ishmael said, "Do you want me to stop?"

Jez said, "No! My insides are doing something. What's so funny, Ish?"

He started at it again with her nipples, loving how she grabbed his head. He went to touch her clitoris. "Oh my," Jez whispered slowly.

That gave him the okay to move his finger in a circular motion. *It's almost ready*, he thought as he pushed his fingers inside her. She moaned out loud, and he had to look at her again.

Ishmael said, "What does your body feel like?"

Jez said, "Can't explain it! It feels so good and relaxing."

Ishmael said, "Have you ever touched yourself?"

Jez said, "No…Ick!"

Ishmael said, "Lay down! It's okay to know the body. That's why you're here sounding like a baby wolf and shit. Quit laughing and open your legs for me."

"I'm not a damn wolf, crazy." Jez laughed. He opened her legs and looked at this beautiful woman knowing if he refused her, she'd think he didn't want her.

"You want me to stop?" Ishmael asked. Jez moaned, "No" real softly as his lips touched her in ways she'd never imagined, and his hands did magic tricks to her inside. "*Hmm. Hmmm. Oh my gosh, Ishmael,*" Jez moaned.

He loved watching her body squirm knowing the best was about to happen. "*Oh my gosh, Ishmael! Oou—wait...oou—wait... Something is happening,*" Jez shouted in a confused, but pleasurable tone.

Ishmael said, "You are okay? It's called foreplay. What you're feeling is an orgasm. If I stop, you'll never know what it feels like."

Jez said, "I'm okay, teacher! What are you doing?"

Ishmael said, "Hold my head! That'll help you take your mind off it a little bit."

He put his arms around her legs so she couldn't run. When her legs started shaking, she moaned out loud. *I hope she doesn't start following me like Queen's crazy ass,* Ishmael thought. He saw a tear roll down her face and turned his head as if he didn't see it.

Jez said, "Oh my gosh! It feels like my body is numb. What should I do now? Teach me how to please you, Ishmael."

Ishmael said, "Come here! Find you a rhythm that you're comfortable with."

Jez said, "It's too big to put it all in my mouth like the girls do on the videos. Why do I need rhythm? Why are you laughing at me?"

Ishmael said, "You are not going to put it all in your mouth, baby girl. You do some shit like that, I'm getting up. Look, take your time with it. Never mind, do as you feel with no teeth."

When the penis got all the way hard, she looked scared and amazed at the same time, but her mind was telling her to run.

Jez said, "Is it going to hurt when you put it in?"

Ishmael said, "At first! If you can't take it, say stop!"

Jez said, "I don't want you to stop! I want you to be my first for everything, Ishmael."

That shit turned him on, He said, "Open your legs some," then got on top of Jez, trying not to go so fast, putting his manhood in, and he still heard a popping sound. "Ouch! Keep going Ish," she whispered.

When he listened to her demand, that shit hit his ear and made him go in without hesitation. She made him want her more passionately and to keep her around forever with that ear-whispering shit.

She gave out a loud moan as if she was crying, and he backed up and looked at her before pushing himself all the way inside. She scratched his back while pulling him into her body so that he couldn't see her tears. "I'm a grown woman. Remember, Ish," she said with pride. *Scoot over some, so I can throw this ass as they did in the video,* Jez thought.

Stroking her slowly, not wanting to hurt her, he gave her enough to let her know what she's been missing.

He felt her walls tightening up, so he made sure they both climaxed at the same time. She watched him turn over onto his back, sitting up slightly, "Oh my gosh! All that was in me?" Jez said. "Not yet! Come sit down on it," Ishmael demanded as he guided her as he sat up a little in the bed and pulled her to him.

He started sucking on her nipples to take her mind off the pain. "Damn, baby girl. Don't hurt yourself," Ishmael thought as he watched her try to go down on it.

He slightly grabbed her hips to guide her a little bit as she went halfway down then up with his help. "Are you okay," Ishmael said.

They finished having sex. He flamed, and they ate, watched TV, and fell asleep asking each other questions and comparing on who was brought up more strict.

*****

"*Oh my gosh! Ishmael, look!*" Jez shouted. "*What the fuck is wrong,*" Ishmael asked. *I'm bleeding! My period already came this month*, Jez thought. "Baby girl, you got your cherry popped," Ishmael said.

*****

"*No. No. No. No, this can't be happening,*" Ishmael shouted out in anger, looking at his brothers' confused faces. Once their mothers got the news, they were going to be upset, so they had everything moved to their new house before they got back.

They talked with the people and let them know they didn't want it to go into an investigation. Skunk and Merch had to deal with the neighbors. Skunk made sure Adana and her family wouldn't tell their mothers what had happened.

Ishmael said, "What the fuck is going on here? I'm not okay with this shit!"

Isaiah said, "I thought Seth handled all this bullshit?"

Merch said, "Hell naw! We hired Terrence to find all these motherfuckers. Now, if these bitches got something to do with this? I'll kill them my got damn self..."

Skunk said, "Bro, you ain't doing shit! The question is who the fuck knows where Mom Dukes live?"

Ishmael said, "Y'all gonna keep underestimating these females?"

Merch said, "Queen pulled up to her aunt's crib in a nice-ass whip. I heard she has a condo and a new job. I'm watching some shit! Then she's buying motorcycles and shit."

Skunk said, "Tara hasn't bought shit! She still lives with her mama, and she stays at the shop some nights."

Ishmael said, "You just got fucked up in that bitch! Now, you're comfortable enough to stay there? Come on now!"

Isaiah said, "Samaya still with her mama, and stays with me most nights. Honestly, I won't be checking up on her like that."

Ishmael said, "Only good thing is our mother's shit is insured. The fucked-up thing about this, whoever did this watched us leave."

Skunk said, "Who knew? I didn't tell anyone...What is y'all looking at me for?"

They all looked at Skunk and said, "The neighbors," simultaneously then shook their heads in shame.

Skunk said, "They're not that crazy, fam!"

PART 7

What's the Truth

CHAPTER 31

Samaya
Making Moves

"Excuse me, miss," the man said as he picked up a baby bottle and showed it to Samaya, "What? Damn!" Samaya said. "What the fuck do you want? You need to leave!"

Seth said, "If you don't cut me in, I'll let your sweet little family over there know what you did and your boyfriend."

Samaya said, "What set are you from? I've never heard of a real nigga trying to blackmail a bitch. Are you serious?"

Seth said, "Just so you know! Them females all pointed the finger at you and Ms. Queen. Only thing you can cut me into is that little pretty pussy."

Samaya said, "You and Swen old asses need to stop following us. Now, pussy that!"

Samaya walked back toward Tara, Queen, Teresa, Toonie, and Tamyra and acted like she was shopping for decorations for Tara's baby's room.

Samaya said, "It's some cute stuff over there, Tara."

Toonie said, "I saw you getting your play on. He's handsome, but you could do better…"

Samaya couldn't stop thinking about her baby every time she picked up clothes. When she started crying, Tamyra rushed over and hugged her. "It's okay, baby," Tamyra whispered in her ear.

Tara said, "Told y'all it was too soon. Let me find some contractors to come do the baby's room."

Queen said, "Sorry, girl, I shouldn't have told you to come. She's not due for a while. We can always come back. Right, Tara?"

Toonie said, "*'Right, Tara,' my ass! Coral already told me what you did! So quit fronting!*"

Teresa said, "Always running your mouth! He told you that as a friend."

Queen said, "I can't stand his ass! No wonder he's been dodging me."

Toonie said, "Who pretends to be pregnant? He's worried about her! Shit is sickening!"

Tamyra said, "It's okay, baby. God has a plan for you. Let's go until you feel better."

Samaya said, "I'm good! Let's get what we came for. Seriously, I'm okay, Mom. Quit looking at me like that, Mom."

Tamyra said, "Child, you go from crying to smiling within minutes. You're not okay."

Tara said, "Samaya, come on! Let's go before you have an emotional breakdown. We can share my baby girl."

Toonie said, "Have you talked to Merch lately? Doesn't he think you're still prego?"

Samaya said, "Toonie, shut up! Damn!"

Queen said, "Toonie? Why are you coming for me little girl? Fuck Merch, Coral, and you! Now, talk that!"

Tamyra said, "Y'all sound ridiculous! Queen, you don't have to lie to family. Toonie, be quiet!"

Queen said, "I didn't want to disappoint anyone. For one, I didn't tell anybody to begin with."

Samaya said, "I want my own baby, Tara. Your baby is going to be spoiled by us all, and I can't wait to be an aunt. Imagine if I had his baby and he's not answering now? I'd be stuck doing this single-parent shit!"

Tara said, "You're starting to sound like Queen. I'm ready to go!"

Tamyra said, "Samaya, stop beating yourself up. You're not pregnant, so all that 'what if' needs to stop now. Give the man a chance."

Samaya said, "I was going to call him but he stood me up the other night."

Queen said, "They're in Vegas kicking it. Tell her Toonie."

Samaya said, "Girl, how do you know?"

Queen said, "My friend! And little bit right here."

Toonie said, "You just said, 'Fuck him,' but your friend is telling you everything."

Samaya said, "Who Mint? Why is he telling that man's business? To get in the panties?"

Teresa said, "Dry snitching! Toonie, my sister told you to shut up already. Now, be quiet!"

Queen said, "Mint doesn't tell me shit! Sorry about my language, aunties."

Tara said, "He'll do whatever Queen wants. Mint loves you, Queen. Besides, I see the way he looks at you."

Tamyra said, "Well, Mint called me last week and told me he bought a new building. He would love for me and your father to open up a soul food restaurant. Guess my food was good to his belly."

Samaya said, "Why didn't you tell me? That's cool. I told you, your food is delicious."

Toonie said, "He's sharing his knowledge and wealth, which some people don't do. That's all I'm saying."

Tara said, "Mom? Why are you just now telling me this? I've been with you all afternoon. Let's go to the food court. I'm hungry."

Teresa said, "I'm gonna leave. I need to make a run. Toonie, you're coming with me!"

Teresa started walking off, and Toonie followed her. *Like you're not gonna tell them, Mom*, Toonie thought.

Tamyra said, "I thought he was bullshitting at first. Me and your father still was thinking about the offer. We can't afford another rent payment right now."

Samaya said, "Mother, when someone makes an offer like that, you don't pay rent! Me and Tara pay your taxes on your house anyways. You play too much!"

Tamyra said, "Your daddy just got laid off last week, so this is a blessing."

*****

Queen said, "Well, Merch called me a few times, but I sent him straight to voice mail. I'm not sharing him with anybody. Until he leaves the side pieces alone, I'm done talking to him."

Tamyra said, "These men love y'all, and you treat them wrong. Did you know he had other females from the beginning?"

Queen said, "I've always thought he did. I never seen any. We were together all the time."

Tamyra said, "You expect for him to change just like that? If he's with you all the time means they're part-time."

Queen said, "Auntie, oh my gosh! Tara, help me out!"

Samaya said, "I've never saw Isaiah talk to another woman nor have one approached us. I'm not sharing either! It's some good men out here that don't do all that running around."

Tara said, "I felt the same way in the beginning. Good luck, sis! Mom…please don't look at me like that."

Queen said, "The few times I followed Merch got me hurt. Shit, made me hate him."

Tamyra said, "*Really?* Too much energy used on a man. You're only going to see something that will hurt you, baby. That explains why you don't keep the babies."

Samaya said, "Let's finish up here so we can go look at this condo."

Queen said, "Samaya? You're a snitch! I'm not telling you shit else."

Tamyra said, "Baby, she didn't tell me anything. Never do! I watch and observe very well."

Queen said, "Okay, Auntie! Did you tell her what you did, Samaya?"

Samaya said, "Yo ass silly! You mean, we, we?"

Tara said, "If they're in Vegas! Why the fuck he keep texting me?"

Tamyra walked through the condo looking around, checking for anything. *I know dancing alone isn't getting them a life like this,* Tamyra thought.

Samaya said, "I like it! What do you think, Tara?"

Tara said, "It's nice! *Oh my gosh! I gotta go!*"

The realtor said, "This condo cost more than the other two I showed you downstairs. The top floor has a slight price change. It'll go fast, so take my card and contact me if you want it."

Samaya said, "I'll take it! Here's a cashier's check. Who do I make it out to?"

The realtor said, "Oh! I see you've done your homework! Make it out to Tillman's Enterprise Incorporated. May I ask your profession?"

Queen said, "A very well-paid ex-dancer. Her man plays pro basketball for Moseq."

Samaya said, "I'm a professional dancer, Lisa. Any more questions? Here's your check."

Lisa said, "No more questions, and thank you. Here's your keys! I'll see my way out!"

Samaya said, "Thank you! Thanks, Mom…"

Tamyra said, "Your father is downstairs. Call you later! Love y'all."

Tara said, "Congratulations, sis, but I have a client meeting me in an hour. Love you!"

Samaya said, "You're lying! Mama gone now! I saw how your face just dropped. What's going on?"

Queen said, "*Tara? Say something, Tara?*"

Tara said, "Their mother's house got robbed when they were out of town. Mint said he tried texting and calling us but we didn't answer. Oh my gosh!"

Samaya said, "Damn! I thought this shit was over with?"

Tara said, "Wow! To think I thought y'all had something to do with the first robberies, but y'all was with me that night."

Samaya said, "*Tara? Why rob their ass if they're giving us the money?*"

Queen said, "I hope you didn't say that shit to Skunk. Merch doesn't know about me dancing yet or my condo, and let's keep it that way. Let them deal with they mothers' issues."

Tara said, "First of all! I didn't know you were back dancing. Secondly, I don't talk to Merch or Skunk about you. I'm not with him anymore."

Samaya said, "Well, I'm going with you tonight. I need to make some of that bread back. You sure it's some ballers in there?"

Queen said, "Bitch! I make money every time, seriously. I bumped into Sunshine!"

Samaya said, "Ugh! I don't like her. It's going on four hours, and this man hasn't called or texted me back. I see why females…Never mind."

Queen said, "Have abortions? Follow they man? It's okay to talk about it! We all have our reasons for the shit we do. Don't look at me like that, Tara. Yo monkey ass started following Skunk too!"

Tara said, "I don't know! Why is he telling us though? Fuck them!"

Samaya said, "*No!* I didn't mean it like that, Queen. I'm so angry right now that I wanted this man's baby. My feelings are every fucking where, and we just talked about this shit. I cried in this man's arms and everything. Maybe he just wanted his dick wet that night."

Queen said, "You know, I don't give a fuck! They were some pretty decent licks."

Samaya said, "Fuck what, Queen? My feelings are hurt. I'm not a crazy bitch, either! Let me hit that shit?"

Queen said, "*That's my bitch! Fuck feelings! It's just a feeling!* Come back to the light!"

Samaya said, "Girl, you're so silly! I need some dick! This nigga needs to get out of his feelings for real before I call Tyrrrr—"

Queen said, "Me, too, girl! Let's go get this money, Saria."

Tara said, "Yeah! Go get the money. I like y'all better when you're chasing the paper, paper."

*****

That morning Samaya went to her mother's house because Queen and Mint were getting on her nerves chasing each other through her condo. She heard Mint say they're trusting the wrong people around them.

*****

Tamyra said, "You're here early! Come have some coffee with me, baby. Tell me what's going on?"

Samaya said, "Good morning, Mom. I don't want you to accept anything from Mint. We can't have any ties at all with them. We barely know him."

Tamyra said, "You're pregnant by him again? Aren't you? That's more than ties, Samaya. Come with me to the shop."

Samaya said, "Yes, I am. I'm not going to ask how you even know. I take it that you and Daddy signed a contract with Mint already?"

*****

Samaya just sat there looking at Tara do all this extra shit to their mother's head, and Tamyra was so excited. "It's coming together," Samaya said. "Sis, why you dye her hair red? Oh my gosh!"

Tara said, "Jez colored it! It looks good on Mama."

Tamyra said, "I like it! Where did she run off to that quick? My roots need touching up."

Tara said, "She texted me and said she'll be here this weekend. Hopefully everything is okay. Her mom beat her up, and her daddy just stood there."

Samaya said, "Damn! Girl, please...She probably needed her ass beat."

Tamyra said, "Well, okay! Where is my son-in-law? I see his car outside."

Samaya said, "Remember, Queen said something about Vegas, Mom? She heard that Merch went to Vegas. The monkey went with."

537

Tara said, "Yeah! He did. He left the car here with me until he got back. But they arrived home a few nights ago."

Samaya smiled at Tara, knowing damn well they were about to put the car in storage after their mama left.

Tara sold it to the highest bidder, and kept the money for the other building he gave her. "He can go suck some more titties if he wants," Tara said as she handed the teller the cash.

*****

Samaya said, "I went to see Jai the other day, and she was acting all weird. Damn! Here comes Toonie."

Tamyra said, "Toonie came to pick me up! Thanks, baby! Love you both…"

Tara said, "Jack? Can you style my sister please?"

Ms. Jack said, "*Yasss, honey, come on!* You're so fine, I might go back to dating women."

Tara said, "Be nice, Ms. Jack! Besides, you don't have enough money for her."

Ms. Jack said, "That's funny to you? I own oil companies, and gold mines in Africa."

Samaya said, "Sis told me you're cold at what you do. I need something new. Give me bounce and layers, Mr. Jack. Thanks."

Ms. Jack said, "*It's Ms. Jack*, sweetie!"

Samaya said, "Okay! Okay! My mistake…I need some blonde streaks also, please."

Tara said, "Don't cut all her hair off. She's tripping."

Samaya followed behind Jack as he switched over to the sink.

Ms. Jack said, "I'm just going to layer it. I'm not cutting all this girl hair off, Ms. Tara. The blonde will match your skin tone."

Samaya said, "I'm going to find me a new man tonight."

Ms. Jack said, "Honey, you can go with me tonight. Me and my best friends are going downtown to this new spot."

Tara said, "Don't invite my sister to one of your wild nights, Ms. Jack."

*****

Samaya went to pick up some outfits from Jai and noticed Queen's car outside, so she pulled off when she saw the sign flipped over. *Will be back in thirty minutes, my ass,* Samaya thought.

*****

"How may I help you," Samaya said, watching the receptionist hold some mail in her hand. "Here's Isaiah's mail," the receptionist said as she stood looking at Samaya in a daze.

"You can sit it on his desk. Thank you," Samaya said. "Does Mr. Isaiah know you're in here?," the receptionist replied in disbelief that a woman was in his office for the first time.

Samaya said, "Girl, if you don't get yo—"

Isaiah said, "Hello, Agnes! There my baby goes…"

Agnes smiled hard as hell when Isaiah walked out of the bathroom. When she saw him walk over and kiss Samaya, she turned her lips up. *Punk bitch*, Agnes thought.

Samaya was on her ass, and she could tell she was furious, so she grabbed his face and made it a wet kiss.

He hugged Samaya, and Agnes turned and rushed out of the room. "Good day, sir," Agnes said. After the door shut, Agnes realized he didn't say anything and got furious.

Samaya giggled as Isaiah picked her up and carried her around the desk. He sat her on the desk in front of his chair and pushed himself between her legs.

Samaya said, "Your friend is mad! Can I get an office down the hall and teach dancing classes?"

Isaiah said, "This is a different type of building, but the men might like it on their lunch break. Damn! You have some soft hands. I like the new hairdo."

Samaya said, "Glad you like them, Daddy. I think we should lock the door."

Isaiah closed his eyes, getting all into the kiss, and Samaya glanced at the mail that said, 'Urgent,' and pulled back. She waited for him to open his eyes. *This is a weird bitch*, Samaya thought.

Samaya said, "That girl just stuck her head in here peeping. Ugh…I saw her through the mirror."

Isaiah said, "Ms. Agnes is something else. Let me lock this door…She's never seen anyone here besides clients and my family, so this is new to her."

"I think you should open this," Samaya said. As soon as he rushed back to her, she was holding the envelope in her hand. "Well, damn! Detective Samaya," Isaiah said with a slight disappointment.

Samaya said, "I don't have to be a detective to know that you're surprised. What's the matter?"

Isaiah said, "*Wow!* How in the fuck? This can't be true!"

Jai
Between Us

Jai watched her beautiful brown body lie back slowly as she pushed her legs open just like the man do her. Jai started licking her clit in a circular motion, watching Queen moan and squeeze her own nipples. "You're getting good at this girl," Queen said.

She watched Jai's head go up and down, thinking about Merch the whole time. Jai stood up and looked at Queen, "I can't do this anymore," Jai said. Queen grabbed her hand and tried to push them between her legs, but Jai backed up. "Stop it, Queen," Jai muttered, knowing she wanted Merch instead.

Queen said, "Bitch! You are getting good at this."

Jai did just as Queen told her. *This woman really got a hold on me*, Jai thought. Jai finished and went straight to the bathroom to clean up, and Queen followed right up behind her.

Queen said, "Open your mouth, bitch?"

Jai said, "Queen? What are you doing? I'm sorry for whatever I did."

Queen said, "Open your mouth, bitch! Suck it like you do my nigga's dick, bitch."

Queen shoved the pistol into Jai's lips until she opened her mouth. Jai cried out in embarrassment and fear.

Queen said, "Bitch, if I ever see him pull up here again, I will kill yo punk ass. Look, bitch! Look! Yeah! I saw him coming and leaving all times of the day and mornings. What the fuck I tell you the last time? Thought I was playing? Now, suck this bullet, bitch."

Jai said, "Queen! Queen! *Queen...Queen! Snap out of it!*"

Queen said, "Damn! I spazzed out for a moment. Give me a towel please?"

Jai grabbed Queen and started at it again before giving her the towel. "That head got you dizzy! You want some more," Jai said.

Queen said, "Bitch, shut up!" I gotta go..."

*****

541

Jai cleaned up the shop and went home to prepare for the second round of the designers' show.

Being one of the top three finalists, and she wanted first prize so bad to open another store, she had to be on her A game.

Jai jumped in the shower, then took a few shots, went over her finished designs, made out all her checks for her models, and just looked at the phone.

He was one of her weaknesses, so she tried avoiding his text and his other half.

Merch's text to Jai: "you up?"

Jai's text to Merch: "getting some rest, I have another show tomorrow."

She sat in front of the fireplace, watching and listening to the wood crack, thinking about the last several months of her threesomes. *The wood just got burned out from the flames just how they're doing me since I've hooked up with them,* Jai thought.

Merch's text to Jai: "come open the door."

*****

Jai said, "Where have you been, stranger?"

Merch said, "Don't start with all these questions. Where is your linen closet?"

Jai said, "Well, hi, Baby Daddy! How are you doing?"

Merch walked to the bathroom to shower, and she followed him. "I thought you got rid of it," Merch said. "I'm just playing," Jai said in a low tone.

Merch said, "Quit playing with me, Jai. Take this and go learn how to roll."

*****

Samaya said, "Quit crying, Queen! You're gonna keep hurting yourself by following this fool. How did you know he'd be here?"

Queen said, "Merch has a routine, and I took this file from Mint."

Samaya said, "Let me see this shit. Oh my gosh! How and when?"

Queen said, "I took it from his trunk when he was driving us around like some damn kids."

Samaya said, "It's got everybody's address. Glad I moved. How'd you really know he was back?"

Queen said, "I called him back to see what was up. It went straight to voice mail. Something told me to watch this bitch Jai. I've seen him at her shop a few times, and he spent the night with the bitch."

Samaya said, "I'm about to go knock. She is my friend!"

Queen said, "If they think we had something to do with the last robberies, that means they think we hit his mama's house. We invited her to the room, so I take blame for this shit."

Teresa said, "You're staying in this car. This man just dropped her money off for a tuition to yo mama's house. She needs to keep asking for shit. He's doing him right now, and he doesn't owe her shit but to take care of their fake baby."

Queen said, "I can't do this shit!"

Teresa said, "Once y'all go knock on the door, then what? Run in shooting at motherfuckers fucking? Then the money going to stop coming. If you know he's lying, then lie to his ass. He's not committing a crime here, ladies. Get that money and quit allowing your pussy to control your feelings. Just how you got his ass, you can get the next nigga to pay you."

Samaya said, "Auntie, damn! She's in love!"

Teresa said, "Love makes you cry and follow people? If she wants him, she needs to trust him and talk to the man. She's chasing, fighting, and shooting at bitches over some dick and some more shit."

Queen said, "Fuck it! I'm about to go knock! I'll say Samaya sent me."

Teresa said, "After I said all that! For what? To see him hugged up with another bitch? If he opens the door naked, what are you gonna do?"

Queen said, "*Fuck it! I'm gone! I need a new car!*"

Teresa said, "Bitch might be making him some clothes or curtains for his mama's new house."

They laughed so hard, Queen had to pull over. "How do you know his mama got a new house," Queen said.

*****

Jai was nervous and running around until Jez and Kimberly showed up. They assisted her with styling hair, doing makeup, and dressing up her models.

Jez said, "What the fuck is he doing here?"

Kimberly said, "Your friend came to support you. That's real nice."

Jai said, "Lower your voice…Who are you talking about?"

Jai saw him hugging one of the temp models and got nervous and mad at the same time. She didn't have time to call Samaya so she wouldn't bring Queen as her plus one because she was trying to be the number one for the night.

Jez said, "That's clearly not Ms. Queen."

Jai said, "Sure isn't! I really don't want no drama here."

Kimberly said, "What does Queen have to do with anything?"

Jez said, "Damn! She's all excited to see him. Look how she's hugging and kissing that man. We should go over and say hi. Girl, how is drama coming from saying hello?"

Jai said, "No! I don't have time for this. Let's finish!"

Kimberly said, "He's fine as hell though. I'd fuck him!"

Jai said, "Kim, get the fuck out of here with that. Secrets can be told or exposed."

Jez said, "Why are you so pressed, sis? What am I missing? Are you okay, Kim? Both y'all faces are red!"

Jai said, "I'm not pressed! He's clearly taken by many, so why bother. I'm here for business only. And Kim is fine."

*****

Samaya walked in with an all-white dress on, complementing her legs, feeling herself and flamed up. Gloss was popping and couldn't nobody tell her shit, because she was ready to walk the runway her damn self.

Samaya said, "Hello, sir! Could you please escort me to my seat?"

The attendant said, "Hello, miss! May I see your ticket. Thank you, right this way, miss. You're a VIP guest. Your waitress will be right with you. Enjoy the show."

Samaya waited until the show was almost over before calling Queen to tell her she saw Merch's car being valet parked when she arrived. She needed Jai to win for the sake of her pockets also, so she waited to call Queen.

*****

After Jai did her last walk with the models, she went to the back to greet as usual. When Jai saw Samaya approaching, her face turned pale with a fake smile.

Jai said, "Hey, Samaya! Hope you enjoyed the show?"

Samaya said, "Hi, ladies. I loved it. You're looking beautiful as always."

The temp model that Merch was hugging was on the stage with all judges at the time, so Jai knew Merch was in the crowd watching her. Little did Jai know, Samaya was looking for his ass too.

Samaya said, "What's going on after this, Jai? Call me if you have some free time. Give me a hug, girl. Congratulations!"

Jai said, "Thank you so much! I'm glad you made it. Did you bring anyone with you?"

Samaya said, "Queen came, but she's waiting in the front for me. Call me later. Bye, ladies!"

Jez said, "Jai? What's wrong with you? You're looking all pale and shit. You're supposed to be happy right now."

Kimberly said, "Girl, you look sick!"

Jai said, "I just don't want any drama here."

Jez said, "You keep saying that! Let's finish up in here and leave."

Samaya met Queen at the door showing the attendant her plus one and went to the side and waited to see some shit.

Samaya said, "Girl, when I walked up and said hi, Jai turned pale. Then I said you came with me, and that bitch almost fainted. If they're fucking around like this to the point where he's coming to her events and shit, he must like her."

Queen was listening, but not paying any attention to Samaya because she was scoping the room, looking for his ass.

Samaya said, "I saw his car being parked. I'm not tripping, fam."

Queen said, "Hold on! Hold on!"

Queen pulled Samaya to the side and stepped out of the way to be seen. "What the fuck are you doing," Samaya said.

Queen said, "Girl, this the slinky bitch from the hotel."

Samaya said, "Is this bitch kissing him?"

Samaya tried to grab Queen, but she took off too fast and grabbed Samaya around the arm, making her come with, "Oh, shit," Samaya muttered.

Queen said, "Hi, I'm Holly, and this is my assistant, Ray. You did a wonderful job. How long have you've been modeling?"

India said, "Ooh, I'm India! Thank you. Who are you again?"

Queen said, "I buy for my boutique downtown. I work with a designer, and she loved your walk. Nice meeting you, India. You're a lucky man, sir."

Merch's and Samaya's mouths dropped open. They just knew Queen was about to let them have it, and Jai watched at a distance, and she was surprised any swinging didn't start.

Samaya said, "Bitch! Oh my gosh! You played that shit well. I thought you were about to snap."

Queen said, "I heard Auntie Teresa in my head saying, 'Get the money,' so fuck him. Jai was looking, too, punk-ass bitch. Let's go, fam!"

India rushed over to speak with Jai, and to her surprise Merch was right with her with a blank look on his face. "Jai, may I intervene, please," India said.

Jai said, "Yes! How may I help you? And good job, thanks for everything."

India said, "Welcome. My friend would like to know how much for the dress?"

"Excuse your friend and I for a moment. India, right?" Jai muttered as she and Merch stepped to the side.

Jai said, "Look. I don't know what's going on, but she was referred to me by an agency last-minute type shit, because her designer lost in this competition. Another thing is I'm not Queen. If you think my dress cost the same amount as that cheap-ass room we fuck in, that's an insult. Tell that puppy-face bitch to take my shit off right now! What the fuck is so funny?"

Merch said, "Didn't Terrence tell you to start checking up on who you give that pussy to?"

Jai said, "Fuck you, Merch!"

Merch said, "You're gonna be fucking me tonight in that cheap-ass hotel that I own, Ms. Jai. Now, how much is the dress, so she can wear it when she meets us tonight? Your sister is calling you."

Jez said, "*Jai, answer your phone! Snap out of it. Jai…*"

Merch said, "Yeah, snap back to reality! Ms. Jai…"

Jai said, "Yes, this is she. Excuse me, sir? What do you mean on fire? My whole shop? I'm on my way!"

*****

Jai cried as she watched the firefighters put the fire out. *It couldn't have been Queen. No way she'd make it across town that fast*, Jai thought.

Jez said, "Sis, let's go. This shit is depressing. They'll call you when they're finished."

Kimberly said, "Come on, girl!"

Jai said, "*How? How? Why me?*"

Kimberly said, "Somebody blowing you up."

Jai handed the phone to Jez because she was crying too much.

Jez said, "Hello, how may I help you? Yes! *When?*"

Jai said, "Why are you looking like that, twin? Why are you crying?"

Jez said, "Twin, it's the police! The neighbors saw your door wide open and called them."

Jai said, "I locked my got damn door. What the fuck is going on?"

Jai arrived home. Everything in her house was ruined, and they left the water running, poured bleach over most of her clothes, and knocked holes in the walls. Luckily, the firefighters were able to put the fire out before the whole house burned down.

Jez said, "Twin, what's going on? You got blood running down your legs. Kimberly, help me get her to the car!"

Jai said, "Girl, my stomach hurt! I can't take this right now."

CHAPTER 32

Queen
No Direction! No Feelings!

Queen, Samaya, and Mint went looking at small buildings for them to buy for Tamyra's second location and Queen's dance hall.

Mint took Queen to open a bank account earlier that morning so she could put some of her money up. It took some convincing from Samaya to do it because she wasn't trying to listen to Mint.

Mint said, "This building isn't connected to anything, so it'll cost more. You want something where the music won't bother the neighbors."

Queen said, "Samaya? What do you think? I like it."

Mint said, "It'll work. I'll make some calls to hold it until we look at the other buildings for your mom."

Samaya said, "I like the last one better! We wouldn't have to redo the whole building. Plus, this one needs everything."

Mint said, "It'll be your design, though. Let's go see the other showings and get something to eat."

*****

Queen and Samaya went to her house, waiting for Mint to call with the good news.

Samaya said, "That's fucked up! That girl shop and the house burned down on the same night."

Queen said, "Fuck her! Why do one if you're not gang gang to do the other. Well, I've seen too much today."

Samaya said, "Ay, Queen, stop it! Her shop burned down, house robbed, and on top of all that, she lost her baby."

Queen said, "What the fuck you just say? 'Baby'? Aw, hell naw."

Samaya said, "Yes, baby!"

Queen said, "This bitch was pregnant? Aww, hell naw!"

Samaya said, "I thought you knew already! What are you crying for Queen?"

Queen said, "We both were pregnant by his ass at the same time. I can't do this, Samaya. I can't…"

Samaya said, "It's okay, Queen. It might not have been his. What about the other men she was fucking. Charles, Donald, and Seth!"

Queen said, "Damn! So, she fucked Seth? When?"

*****

Mint brought over Chinese food for them, the papers for them to sign on their new investments, and the latest properties for sale.

Mint said, "I'm proud of you two ladies. Whoa, Queen, you can't drink that."

Queen said, "I'm not pregnant anymore, Mint. You didn't hear the news?"

Mint said, "Queen? Come on, baby. It'll be all right. Don't hurt the baby because things aren't going according to your plan."

Queen said, "Samaya? Can you tell him! *Hold on! That's me! Turn it up…Oh my gosh!*"

Samaya said, "I'm going home to get some rest. Love you guys!"

Queen said, "You don't believe me? Listen, Samaya!"

Mint said, "I'll walk you home, Samaya. Queen, I'll be right back."

Samaya said, "I'm a big girl! You stay here, and I'm gone."

Mint said, "Why do you beautiful women carry pistols around like that? That shit is not sexy!"

Queen said, "When you are a dancer, it comes with the territory. Mint, you can leave also? I need some time to myself. Thanks for the food."

*****

Queen and Toonie walked up to Queen's door to find Mint and Samaya at her door, waiting for her. "What they want," Toonie said.

Samaya said, "I thought you were in there ignoring us. Where are you coming from?"

Mint said, "Let's go look at this property, Queen?"

Queen said, "I need to rest for a moment. I was up all night, and I'm sleepy. Y'all go without me. I trust you both."

Samaya said, "Well, we own the building already, so you get some rest. We'll be back to check on you. Let me get that new number before I go?"

Queen said, "Don't give it out, please! Oh, by the way, I'm about to be rich."

Mint said, "Your man is looking for you, and he seemed kinda excited."

Queen said, "I don't have a man!"

Samaya said, "He called my mom's house too. What's going on, Queen?"

Queen said, "*I don't care anymore! I need some rest before I go to work.*"

Toonie said, "Let my cousin through, please! She famous."

Samaya said, "Toonie, shut up! Kya, who wrote you this check?"

Mint said, "Let me see is real! Damn...who wrote you this check?"

Queen said, "All that time I was chasing dead weight. My hook on this song is number one on the charts. Told y'all that was me!"

Queen flamed then went straight to sleep. She was so out of it, she didn't hear the alarm go off for work. When the sound finally woke her up, she rushed to shower, then lay across her bed flaming and watching television.

Queen said, "*Stop banging like that! What the fuck!*"

Samaya said, "*Open the door, fam?*"

Queen said, "Girl, quit banging on my door like that?"

Samaya said, "I think they know?"

Queen said, "How, bitch? Are you high or something? We covered all of our tracks, and besides, we would be dead or in jail."

Samaya said, "Why Isaiah acting funny?"

Queen said, "This nigga got you paranoid, girl. They all act funny. Look at Merch and Skunk funny swinging-vine-dick asses. Quit mentioning that shit to me before I start tripping with you."

Samaya said, "You missed work last night! Had me calling you all night and morning. I was worried and shit!"

Queen said, "I'm not worried about them niggas. They can't do anything more to us than we can do to them. Period."

Samaya said, "Forgot your ass gang gang in this bitch. Fuck it! Gang gang in this bitch."

Queen said, "Maybe he's dealing with losing his baby different from you. Personally, these niggas can take as many trips as they please, but I will shoot to kill they start questioning me like a pussy. I'm not Rocky!"

Samaya said, "I got your half of the insurance check from the fires."

Queen said, "Glad you invested in that nasty bitch shop. Auntie flipped all the flame from Nyala's crib, and we let them dudes keep everything else from Jai's crib and his mama's house."

Toonie said, "Glad to see you woke her up, and I still can't believe you're a singer. And, she didn't know about her soon to be mother-in-law's house. Thanks, Saria!"

Samaya said, "Seriously? Damn! Let's deposit the check first...I can't believe it either."

Queen said, "How long were you standing there listening and shit?"

Toonie said, "Long enough! This whole time I thought y'all was dumb as fuck. I need to tell y'all something."

*****

The ladies met up with Mint at the café over north to discuss a business plan he came up with after they all left the bank with Queen.

Mint said, "I need to run you ladies over to this building."

Queen said, "I'm not feeling this dancing anymore especially if this check go through. We need to hurry and meet up with TT before she does some more dumb shit."

Mint said, "I already stopped her from running in Chaste's crib. She's on her way."

Toonie said, "Cousin, look! That check cleared. Oh my gosh! I need to call Tracy and get you on another track. Sing some shit to me, bitch..."

Queen said, "She really put an app on her phone for my account. Thanks, Toonie!"

Samaya said, "Yo ass silly as fuck! Mint? Take us to get her some paper and pencils? I'm with you on that one. *Sing, Queen. Rap it or whatever.*"

Mint said, "Let me write her up a contract first, so she's not getting the short end of the stick. We need royalties in this camp."

Toonie said, "Nigga! 'Camp'? I thought my ass was corny?"

Mint said, "I will be corny as hell if my baby keeps getting some hundred-thousand-dollar checks regularly."

Toonie said, "Baby? Boy, stop it!"

Samaya said, "We need to start investing in our future. I'm not planning on shaking my ass my whole life, or ever again. I did what I needed at the time to get ahead for us."

Queen said, "I'm not that old, and long as it pays, we're good. I'm gone, y'all. Call me later, Samaya."

*****

Queen went home to get prepared for dealing with the new coworkers and clients, and that shit took a lot of her energy. When she started, it seemed like all the men were into her, but they wanted a bitch to break their backs in fourths like a measuring cup for a dollar or two.

Queen stopped to pick up some cigarillos and gum from the corner store before heading to work. *I need some dick*, Queen thought.

Female 1 said, "*Bitch! You thought you did something at the club?*"

She turned around, holding her waist, ready to blow any bitch about that life. When she saw the girl, she already knew the deal, because she had five females with her to amp her punk ass.

Queen said, "Bitch, please! Don't get pumped up full of slugs."

Before Queen could make it to the car, Teisha ran up, and Queen smacked her ass down with her thang.

Queen said, "*Anyone else want this bitch? Run up!*"

Teisha said, "*Fuck you, bitch!*"

Queen said, "*Get up and talk shit, bitch! I'll fuck you better than yah nigga, bitch. Now fuck that!*"

Teisha said, "*What, bitch? Throw them hands!*"

As soon as Queen starting throwing her hands, Teisha couldn't keep up, and one of her friends started running up to help Teisha, and Queen pulled that thang out again.

Queen said, "*Try me! I don't do jumping, skinny bitch! And y'all can catch this lead too! Try me!*"

Queen got in her car and pulled off. Teisha was still talking shit with her punk-ass cheerleaders, and Queen rolled her window down. She let her thang off a few times in the air like cheap fireworks, and them scary friends of hers scattered like roaches.

Seth said, "This bitch just let loose on their ass. I need a bitch like that."

Swen said, "My nephew said she was crazy."

Seth said, "You're right! If she wanted to kill somebody, she'd done it a long time ago."

*****

She arrived at work, and the parking lot was full, which meant more money for her. While she waited for Samaya, she flamed and took a few shots to loosen up.

Walking around the club talking to some tippers to butter them up, she did a few lap dances until it was her time to hit the stage.

DJ K said, "*We got Ms. Sexy Queen coming to the stage. We are in for a good show! So, get ready, fellas and women.*"

She saw him walking up when she looked back at herself twerking, so she knew he was about to lecture her, "*K? Turn the music off! You see me, motherfucker! Turn it off,*" Tracy demanded. Everybody in the club looked at him in confusion.

Queen said, "What do y'all want?"

Tracy said, "I know that check went through. What are you doing here?"

Mint said, "Look at this contract, Queen. You're set, baby girl. You don't have to dance anymore."

Teresa said, "Shit! If you like strip clubs, we can buy this one also. Matter of fact! Who owns this shit?"

Tracy said, "I do! But she can have it…Fuck it! We can shoot videos here."

Samaya said, "Okay, then! Cousin, we own shit now. We don't have to do this anymore."

Toonie said, "Can't y'all see she's sick! She's stuck! Tracy? Let's get her in some twerking videos as soon as possible? Thanks."

"*Shut up,*" they all said to Toonie simultaneously. "Is this contract real? Damn," Queen said. "Yes," Tracy replied. "We're gonna look it over tomorrow," Mint said.

*****

Lil Q
Hook. No feelings. Hook
I could have sworn Samaya wiped a tear from the
    truth told on my first featured track
I cry every day in my heart to keep the hustle alive

JPay call from my little brother, hustling easy before
*   he fell victim to the trap!*
What you know 'bout that
Chasing behind some empty balls that led me to
*   have*
Lost memories, in the brand-new tubes of no life
*   at all*
I cry every day in my heart to keep the hustle alive
Empty-ass life dancing without a cause
Now, try me! Try me!
I don't give a fuck about you or your feelings at all
Now pay me! And, hook the next trick, pole tricks
*   and all*
I cry every day in my heart to keep the hustle alive

Tracy said, "Damn, K! We're gonna have to break that down. You can pause too."

Queen said, "I'm just saying shit! Let me know what we should keep."

Toonie said, "*I like* 'I cry every day in my heart to keep the hustle alive.' *What?*"

Tracy said, "Nothing! You got a good ear."

Tracy
Hook. No feelings. Hook.
No feelings coming as raw as it gets
I cry every day in my heart to keep the hustle alive
DNA after four years, what the fuck you thought
Quiet as kept, the brand-new tube been paid for by
*   a few of my dead presidents at fault*
Never dizzy, I already took that walk. No visits! My
*   own money on my books*
I cry every day in my heart to keep the hustle alive
Quick to hook, have 'em dangling. No feelings,
*   quick to hook*

Toonie said, "What was that shit? I heard too many hooks. Let's do this over...Tracy, we're gonna let a female sing the hook, thanks!"

Merch
The Light

Merch said, "That's her! I thought she was doing all this crazy shit. And, she's in the studio making music and number one videos."

Skunk said, "Tara won't answer her phone. I went to her parents' crib, and they sold it."

Isaiah said, "Look at this shit! This why they're not answering phones and moved."

Ishmael said, "Did you know she could sing, bro?"

Merch said, "I never asked! Shouldn't she be showing by now?"

Swen said, "The question is when and where did she meet him?"

*****

Merch watched her head go up and down behind his phone as he watched Queen in this video. "Damn," Merch mumbled. "You like that," Sunshine whispered as she tried to continue. "Get up," Merch said.

Sunshine said, "I told you! She doesn't sell shit anymore, and that rapper done took her out of the game. I told you he be here on Saturdays doing videos."

Merch said, "I told you to get her number? That's him! Hold on!"

Sunshine said, "*Wait! Wait! Wait...Merch, stop! Wait...*"

Merch jumped out of the car and walked up to the dude like he was a fan. "Can I holla at you," Merch said. "Who you looking for, nigga?"

*****

He watched as Queen walked down the aisle with their daughters throwing the flowers and her father holding her arm, bringing her to him.

As he pulled the veil over her face, he started crying, knowing he was finally going to get his wifey back. "I do...I do...I do...," Merch said.

They stood under the waterfall, and he loved how the water was flowing off her skin and making him love everything about her. "Queen, why are you so bright," Merch cried out. *Beeeeep…beeeeeeep.*

Dr. Coe said, "*Clear…Wait…wait…Shit!* Come on, son! *Clear.*" *Beeeeeep.*

Dr. Coe said, "*I got you…Hold on…Shit! Clear…Shit!* Okay! Thought I lost you, son. Come on, team, and let's get these bullets out of him."

*****

Janice was cleaning Merch up and noticed that Dr. Coe was looking over his colleague's work to see if he was pleased as usual.

Nurse Janice said, "I'll call ICU to get him a room together."

Dr. Coe said, "I'll handle that! Just keep an eye on him. Thank you."

All the nurses were scrambling around in the room, but Janice knew who he was. Dr. Coe must have known also the way he directed his staff to help out unusually, and Janice knew something was odd.

*****

Sunshine said, "*Look. Who own this muthafucker? I need to see them right away!*"

Sunshine looked puzzled as fuck. *Why is this bitch here*, Sunshine thought.

Samaya said, "Can I help you? It's Sunny, right?"

Samaya laughed and turned to walk away. "*Merch, just got shot up looking for Queen,*" Sunshine yelled out as she broke down crying.

Samaya said, "Don't come here lying to get at my cousin. Tell him to leave her alone!"

Sunshine said, "*Are you crazy? Where is Queen?*"

Samaya said, "What hospital he at, damn? Here she comes. Fuck!"

Queen said, "What did you do to her, Samaya? Why is she crying?"

Sunshine said, "Merrr—"

Samaya said, "Shut the fuck up! Merch got shot! She said he was looking for you, and I don't believe her."

Queen said, "*Talk, bitch! I will snatch your brain through your scalp!*"

Samaya said, "Whoa, you can't do this in front of everybody."

Sunshine said, "He went looking for you at Extreme. He got shot a lot of times. He's in the hospital. Come on, Queen. Let's go!"

Samaya said, "She's not lying, and I'm sorry. Nurse Janice just texted me. Let's dip!"

Samaya was speeding and watching Queen at the same time. The look on her face was pale, and Sunshine was in the back crying more than Queen.

Queen said, "How did he find out about Extreme? Sunshine, you need to talk, before I blow yo got damn head off, bitch!"

Samaya said, "Before you shoot the bitch, let me pull over by the lake. I don't need any evidence in my shit."

Sunshine said, "He paid me to keep an eye on you. I didn't tell him shit! I just mentioned you worked there."

Queen said, "Who shot him? *Bitch! Who shot him?*"

Sunshine said, "It was too dark to see. He jumped out of the car and walked up on a crowd of men. All I heard was gunfire, so I called the ambulance."

*****

Teresa just sat there looking at their ass tell her what they just did and how she was going to cover for them, which just wowed the fuck out of her.

Teresa said, "Them people are private, and the way the moms looked at us made me want to slap them bitches and what made her come to the club."

Samaya said, "Are you okay, Queen? I'm glad he's living. Why did he hire Sunshine punk ass?"

Queen said, "I don't know what to think. Why did he come looking for me after five months."

Toonie said, "Seriously! He thought you were prego. He watched the video and saw you weren't growing. *Duh.*"

Samaya said, "Toonie, not right now! Not now!"

Teresa said, "Don't look at me! Y'all know she's been like this her whole life."

Toonie said, He said they're moms go to church on Sundays. Samaya can text Nurse Janice, and you can sneak in to see yah boy. *Bam!"*

Queen said, "I can't stand you, but that's a good idea."

Samaya said, "Have y'all talked to Tara? She disappeared on all our asses."

Teresa said, "Oh my! Toonie, don't start with your storytelling."

Queen said, "She sold everything and moved on. She'll be back! Skunk fucked her mind up."

*****

Nurse Janice met them by the hospital locker room. "If you're a snitch, please leave now," Nurse Janice said. "Stop shaking and put in the code," Samaya replied. "Girl, I've never done any crazy shit like this before," Nurse Janice whispered.

They changed into some scrubs. Queen put on a hospital gown and got in the wheelchair, and they pushed her to the therapy room like a patient.

Queen said, "I hope this works!"

Samaya said, "Why you put all that lip gloss on? Try to look sad!"

Queen said, "I can't be looking all dry when I see my baby."

Nurse Janice said, "Oh, fuck! Oh, fuck!"

Dr. Coe said, "Good day, ladies!"

Nurse Janice said, "*Hello, Mr. Coe.*"

Samaya said, "How far is it? Damn, girl, it's some fine ass docs in here. I'm signing up for school after this."

Queen said, "Oh my gosh! Look at my baby! He looks fucked up!"

Nurse Janice said, "Oh, shit! Please don't cry. That's going to draw attention to us. I'm gonna go tell them I need to give him his meds so that they can leave the room for a minute."

Samaya said, "Okay, here we go!"

They looked at each other for a moment; then Queen fell out crying onto his chest as he lay on the bed helpless.

When he wrapped his weak arms around her ahead, he bent his head over and placed his face onto her head. Samaya and Janice started crying like babies. "Awe, bitch! Where the tissue," Samaya said.

Merch said, "I'm sorry, Kya. For not getting to know you! I should have known your favorite food, color, and what you wanted out of life. I love you."

Queen said, "I love you, too, Milan! We have to go before we get her fired. She'll give you our numbers. Come on, y'all!"

Samaya said, "Bye, nigga!"

Nurse Janice said, "Bye, nig—I mean Merch! Come on, Queen."

*****

"Mom, I know she's the one for me. I love her," Merch said as he watched his mother cry for him and the fact that he loved a stripper.

Marsha said, "You don't know what you're saying. The drugs have you irrational right now."

Skunk said, "Come on now, Mom. Let's leave so that he can get some rest."

Marsha said, *"He's shot up because of her. And I'll kill that bitch myself!"*

Skunk said, "Whoa, Mom, let's go because your angry right now."

As soon as she swung the door open, she pushed past Swen, knocking him into the door. "Y'all done brought the old Marsha back," Swen said. *"Fuck you,"* Marsha replied and didn't give a fuck about who heard her.

Skunk said, "What the fuck! I've never heard Mom curse. You better tell Queen to hide out!"

Merch said, "Mom ain't gonna do nothing!"

Swen said, "What, nigga? Aww, shit, my bad, nephew! Shid! Yo mama is no punk! Yo mama done cut, stabbed, and…"

Skunk said, "Unc, *stop*! I don't want to hear about my mother's war stories. That shit will mess up the thoughts I have of her being innocent."

Merch said, "How is she innocent and she let daddy move her in with his wife? Come on now, bro! They're all pimps."

Swen said, "See, now y'all bringing some other shit into the mix. I told y'all that's an understanding. Now leave it alone. She is cold with that thang, doe! Queen fine ass better be careful."

Skunk said, "You need not speak on that again. It sounds like you've used up all your breath for the day. Get some rest, bro!"

Merch said, "I'm trying to get out of here to fuck on something…that I'll lose breath over!"

*****

"Jean, there's no talking to me right now. Move out of my way," Marsha shouted. Jean was trying her best to hold her back until Ax walked in.

Ax said, "Auntie, I got this! I promise."

Marsha said, "*I need to know why my son went looking for her? If he loves her! Why did he have to find her? Then she should know who shot him! Now they can't find the other bitch!*"

Jean said, "What her? And what bitch is she talking about, nephew?"

Ax said, "*Jean? What are you doing? Marsha!* Let me find them first."

Jean said, "She doesn't have time for this pillow-talking shit. She's coming with fire about our boys. Damn!"

*****

The nurse aide said, "Milan, how are you today? My name is Lily, and I'm your aide for today."

563

Merch said, "Could be better! How are you?"

Lily said, "I'm good. Thanks for asking! Do you want a shower or bed bath today? Are you hungry? We need you to try and eat something."

Merch said, "You're welcome. But I'd like to use the whirlpool with some flame, please."

Lily said, "You are silly! I'll get you something up here to eat after your shower. Your wounds aren't healed enough for soaking. Sorry, Milan."

He sat in the shower chair, feeling helpless as this woman lathered soap on him. She washed him thoroughly and rinsed him with pride and not holding her hands out. That made him look at women different for some reason, and only a few would understand.

Merch said, "Lily, thank you so much. I needed this."

Lily said, "It's okay, Mr. Milan. I like helping people, and it's my job. Let me take you back to your room so you can eat for me."

Merch said, "This blanket is warm, thanks."

Lily said, "Here we are! I ordered you some soup and crackers, salad, strawberry Jell-O, and some green tea. Are you in any pain? If so, I can go tell the nurse."

Merch said, "I'll eat the soup. Yes, I'm in pain! Can you give me my meds, though?"

Lily said, "I'm not a nurse yet. When I'm a nurse, you'll be long gone from here."

Merch said, "Where are you from, Lily? Are you married?"

Lily said, "I'm from Alaska with no husband. Why do you ask?"

Merch said, "Beautiful woman, no ring, caring, and smart. Who wouldn't want to know!"

Lily said, "Well, your call light is here. Push this if you need anything. I'll let the nurse know you ate and need pain medication, Milan."

*****

Nurse Janice said, "Hi, Milan, how are you today?"

Merch said, "What's up? I'm feeling a little better today. How're your friends doing?"

Nurse Janice said, "They're good! Do you remember when Samaya came here?"

Merch said, "Yes, I do? Shit! Her, my brother, her sister, and her friend. What about it, Janice?"

Nurse Janice said, "This cop asked me to find out what happened to her, and that's how I knew who you were. Your family has been prevalent around here and theirs."

Merch said, "What's your point in telling me this? Does Queen know who shot me? That's all I want to know! Ask her that, Nurse!"

Lily said, "Hi, Milan, your light was on. How can I help you? Hi, Janice."

Nurse Janice said, "Hello. I'll step out. I'll get that information for you, sir."

Merch said, "Must have been a mistake. I'm good, Lily, thanks."

CHAPTER 33

The Club
What

Samaya said, "Did he say who did it? How many times did he get shot?"

Nurse Janice said, "Four times! They're looking for the girl now. He doesn't remember anything up to being shot."

Queen said, "Hit the flame and loosen up, Janice. It's some nice-looking men downstairs because y'all look lonely as fuck."

Samaya said, "Queen? Don't you want to hear this?"

Queen said, "I love him! That doesn't mean I forgot about all the shit I saw. I saw that girl at the hospital before we left."

Samaya said, "Fuck it! I don't even want to know which one."

Nurse Janice said, "Even if you did see a girl, they can't see him! His mother's rule. He thinks you know who did it, Queen."

Queen said, "If I knew, he'd be dead. I don't fuck with half-ass killas...I'm going to find out, though."

Nurse Janice said, "I know all women are different, but you'll leave him if he cheated? I guess my understanding of love is dissimilar. I thought forgiveness played a role in everyday life?"

Queen said, "Well, Ms. Cupid! As a woman, oops, I meant human, we can only deal with so much before we snap. I'm grateful that you helped me sneak in to see Samaya and Merch in the hospital, but a liar I will not do. Remember me when I was eighteen?

You're the one that told me I was burning, Ms. Janice. I should have listened to you back then."

Samaya said, "Whoa, whoa, I didn't know niggas was out here leaking. Damn! Can we discuss love on another day, and the rules, please?"

Queen said, "When he saw me, he could have asked himself drugged up or not. Don't send some random chick to ask me shit."

*****

They watched the girls killing it on the stage, and Nurse Janice was starting to come out of her shell after a few drinks. Janice slammed her empty shot glass onto the bar then took off to the stage.

Samaya said, "Look, Queen!"

Queen said, "What the fuck is he doing here? Go tell her to leave!"

Samaya said, "I don't know! But they don't need to see her here."

Samaya snatched her by the arm and started pulling her for the back door. He was tripping over chairs and people, "*They're here*," Samaya shouted in her ear as they rushed out the back door, jumping into her ride.

Nurse Janice said, "Who are you talking about?"

Samaya said, "Merch's family! Why in the fuck did she bring him here? I'm gonna go drop you off, and don't say shit to anybody!"

Nurse Janice said, "What the fuck can I say? I didn't see shit!"

Samaya said, "Did you bring my package? And this stays between us!"

*****

Teresa said, "*Don't be pushing me, mufucker! Told yo ass she wasn't here.*"

Ax said, "*Shut the fuck up! Where the other bitch?*"

Teresa said, "Nigga, you better watch yo mouth! Pussy ass pulling guns on a *female!*"

567

Ax said, "Where the fuck is Sammy, Sarire? Whatever her fucking name is? Or, that Queenie bitch?"

Teresa said, "I told yo monkey ass!"

Bam, boom, bam.

Teresa said, "What the fuck? Y'all crazy…"

Queen said, "*Damn!* I don't know why they sent his punk ass. I thought it was all of them the way she said it."

Teresa said, "He walked in here like he was hitting a lick. I hope this nigga isn't dead! What did he want?"

Queen said, "This gun got his little ass thinking he's tough. Doesn't he look like a baby monkey?"

Teresa said, "You sound all jolly and shit! What the fuck is going on?"

Queen said, "Honestly, I'm high as hell. If I hadn't hit him, you'd probably be dead, Auntie!"

Teresa said, "Whatever the fuck you tried, don't do that shit again…We're gonna leave his ass up here until the club close."

Queen said, "Something, because I'm not going to jail over his little ass."

*****

Teresa said, "This nigga heavy as hell! That has to be his car! Do the alarm thingy or something!"

Queen said, "Yup! There it goes! *What the fuck, TT!*"

Teresa said, "He started moving! He is gonna wake up in this bitch with a headache. We're gonna leave him in the car?"

Queen said, "Yes! He pulled a gun on you. And I'm not trying to have back problems carrying his bulk ass."

Teresa said, "What? You want to drive his ass in the river or something? We got too much shit under our belt already."

Queen said, "We're selling the club! I don't have time for midgets pulling guns on people, and this shit right here."

Teresa said, "Who is that?"

Queen said, "That's Toonie! She done lost her mind! Auntie, go get her!"

*****

Marsha said, "Told you we should have gone ourselves. I'm getting to the bottom of this."

Jean said, "Po' child, slow, just like his mama. Them girls probably beat his ass."

Ishmael said, "Why didn't you tell me before you sent him? Moms, y'all can't start missions not knowing what the business is to begin with."

Marsha said, "Do you know who I am? Please tell him the truth, Jean."

Jean said, "Damn! You done made her mad…She waving hands and shit…Marsha?"

Ishmael said, "Mom? Come back and talk to me? Please?"

Marsha said, "*Who broke in our house?*"

Jean said, "Son? We've done all this before you were even thought of, so don't talk to Mom like that. Talking about why, I can't believe you are questioning our judgment."

Ishmael said, "I'm sorry! I Didn't mean it like that, Mom. Mom, come here, I didn't mean it like that. I'm sorry, we don't know who broke in."

Marsha said, "You didn't contact the people, because you thought it was them girls? Didn't you? Look at me?"

Ishmael said, "We don't know! If I thought it was them, I'd say something, Mom. Mom, I don't even like them women."

Jean said, "Who would know we moved and left some of our stuff there? Did anyone know we left town?"

Marsha said, "Tell us the business from the beginning. Everything!"

Jez
Puzzled

Jez went to work back with Jai part-time until she found something of her liking. Every beauty salon was either ghetto or messy when she walked in.

Ishmael said, "Maybe I should go in and look because this is the third one you've walked right out of. What's up?"

Jez said, "Okay, they're too loud in this one. Then the last one, the barber, was smoking with the customers. The one before that, the females were sitting on the man's lap."

Ishmael said, "Well, you can't keep going to random people houses that you barely know."

Jez said, "Can you take me here, please? Let me go talk with her and see what she recommends."

When they pulled up, she asked him to come in with her for the first time. "I don't understand why you don't just rent a building or buy one. And get workers," Ishmael said.

Jez said, "Hi, Sarah! How are you doing? Sarah, meet Ishmael. Ishmael, this is my old teacher Sarah."

Sarah said, "Hi, Jez. Nice to meet you, Ishmael. I'm okay, nice seeing you again. You've graduated already! Are you coming to take my job?"

Jez said, "No. No. I'm trying to see if you have any friends that are hiring?"

Sarah said, "Well, you usually have to wait a year after you graduate to be a teacher, but I need help here. If you work under my license, it'll work. The pay isn't much, but you could always have your customers come here and pay rent monthly."

Jez said, "Whoa! Okay, thanks! I'll call you later..."

Ishmael said, "Nice meeting you, Sarah. Excuse us! Let me talk with you for a minute, Jez."

"What's that look about, Ishmael," Jez said as he lifted her face with his hand to look at him. "Tara is gone! You're either gonna spoil yourself like she did you or start working somewhere," Ishmael said.

Jez said, "I'm gonna quit working for my sister, then start here and go to school part-time."

Ishmael said, "What's your future career? Hairstylist, clothing designer assistant, teacher's pet assistant, or part-time student? All this running around is not good for you?"

Jez said, "Well, damn! You are harsh. Yes, I miss Tara, but I was not spoiled. Honestly, what the fuck did I sign up for because I like doing hair."

Ishmael said, "Well, stick with hair and pick up classes when you have time. Find a place that you can rent out without being stressed."

Jez said, "I wouldn't even know where to begin. I just got my first apartment."

Ishmael said, "It's still early. Let's go to my office, so I can see what you are working with."

He just sat there looking over the papers, looking at her every other second. "What," Jez asked. "It's not that bad. Let me see what I can do," Ishmael said.

Agnes said, "How can I help you, sir? Oh, your mother is on her way."

Ishmael said, "Agnes, I told you that you don't have to call me 'sir.' May I have the latest printout of our properties, please? Thanks!"

Jez said, "I saw her sitting there, but I didn't know you had a personal receptionist. She's young and pretty."

Ishmael said, "We just hired her a few months ago. She's a pretty decent worker…"

Agnes said, "Here you go! Would either of you like some coffee or water?"

Jez said, "I would love some coffee. Thanks, Agnes."

Ishmael said, "Come over here and sit with me, Jez. We can look them over and go see some later."

When Jean came off the elevator, Agnes waited to see her mistress come off behind her. *Wow! She's alone*, Agnes thought. "Hello,

Jean. Ishmael is waiting for you," Agnes said. "Hi, Agnes…I hope he is," Jean replied. "Oh, it's a woman in there," Agnes whispered.

*****

Ishmael said, "Come in! Mom, are you knocking?"

Jean said, "I was told to knock because you have company. Hello!"

Ishmael said, "Hi, Mom…Meet Jez. Jez, this is my mom, Jean. Say something!"

Jez said, "Nice to meet you, Jean…"

Jean said, "Nice to meet you as well! If what he said on the phone is true, we need to leave and get drinks on me…Shit!"

It was her third drink, and Ishmael knew when his other mother arrived they were going to try to tag team him. *Here she comes*, Ishmael thought. *Damn, they fucked up her pretty face*, Marsha thought as she had a seat.

Jean said, "We just looked at a few of our properties. Ishmael wants to turn one into a saloon for his baby Jez."

Ishmael said, "Hi, Mom! Jez this is my other mom, Marsha."

Marsha said, "Nice to meet you! Nice choice, son. I know everything, Jez. I want to meet with your sister if possible?"

Jez said, "Thanks! About what?"

Ishmael said, "Thanks, Mom…Jez, I told them about the notes, the females, the club, and incident at the shop. They both know about Vegas. And—"

*****

The only thing that was holding her back from ultimately moving out was the few items at her parents' house.

Moving closer to campus was one of the most significant moves she made since leaving with Ishmael on a secret vacation, and she was ready for a change without being under her parents' roof.

Jez had her earbuds in listening to her music as she shoved her books in her backpack. As soon as she swung her bag over to the bed, she felt a hard blow to her head, and she fell onto the bed, and another blow followed it.

When she grabbed her head, she went to turn and look, but the blow had her dizzy. All she saw was her mother's face behind all the madness, crying in the hallway tied up next to her father that lay on the floor helpless with his mouth taped up.

Jennifer said, "*What do you want? Leave my daughter alone!*"

The janitor said, "*Fuck your daughter! What I look like putting notes on her fucking car? For what?*"

Jennifer said, "Oh my gosh! We're so sorry. Please don't kill us!"

Janitor said, "*You fucked my life up, you little whore!*"

Jennifer said, "*Please don't hurt her! Please stop hitting her!*"

Janitor said, "*Shut the fuck up! She ruined my life!*"

Jennifer said, "She didn't know who did it! Please don't hurt us! We have the money."

Janitor said, "Well, she won't be able to fuck up anybody else's life!"

Jez lay there as the warm wetness ran down her already fucked-up face, watching the janitor run over and kick her mother in the stomach. John swarmed on the floor helplessly as the tears ran down his face like a waterfall.

Janitor said, "*I don't want your got damn money, bitch!*"

Jez said, "I'm sorry! I'm sorry! Please stop! *Leave my mom alone. Daddy…OMG…Please stop!*"

Janitor said, "*This is your fault! I hate lying muthafuckers like you!*"

Tears started mixing in with the warm wetness and blurred her eyes, but the coldness of the metal made her see enough as the janitor went to stomp her mother's head. *Bang. Bang.* "Aaaah!" *Bang.* "Aaaah!" *Bang. Bang.* "Aaaah!" *Bang. Bang.* "Aaaah!" "*Stop…Stop… Stop,*" Jez screamed. *Bang.* "Aaaah!" *Bang.* "Aaaah!"

*****

Ishmael sat waiting for Jez to wake up as he sipped his tea and read the paper gladly it was the janitor on the front page as dead and not her. As he read on, he knew she would need comforting in so many ways.

He made sure her room had orange marigolds everywhere, and he had the water sounds playing as it bounced off the quietness of the room walls.

Ishmael had his lawyer talk with the people, so she and her family could have some peace of mind.

Nurse Fern said, "Hello, sir! I'm Fern. I'll be her nurse until this evening."

Ishmael said, "Hello, Mr. Fern. Thanks."

Nurse Fern said, "You have it real relaxing here. Let me know if I can get you anything?"

Ishmael said, "What is that you're giving her?"

Nurse Fern said, "Just some saline to keep her nourished since she hasn't had an appetite since she's been here. Are you her husband?"

*****

Jai walked in and saw her flowers in the back surrounded by *all these ugly orange things*, she thought.

She looked at Fern play with the tubes as if he was doing something, and Ishmael sat and looked as if he was her damn husband already.

Jai said, "Hello, everyone. How's my sister doing?"

Nurse Fern said, "Hello, miss. Your sister is fine. She's getting caught up on some sleep."

Ishmael said, "Hi! How are you doing?"

Jai said, "I'm mad that my sister keeps coming to the hospital behind dumb shit. Thanks for asking though! Nice flowers, what a surprise. Her favorite!"

Ishmael said, "You are right! Weren't you just in the hospital? Sorry about that! Are you feeling better?"

Jai said, "I'm good! How's your brother, if you don't mind me asking?"

Ishmael said, "He's stable...He has a long stay in the hospital and recovery ahead."

Jai said, "Thanks for getting my sister a private room. I really appreciate this."

Ishmael said, "No problem! Anything for my baby."

Jai said, "You bought my sister a shop, a car, and a few phones. What's up, Ishmael?"

Ishmael said, "That's none of your business. What your sister shares with you is enough, because I don't owe you or anybody else an explanation on how I treat my baby. And, I most definitely don't owe anyone an explanation on how a man treats a woman, Jai."

Nurse Fern said, "Ahem. I'll return shortly…"

Ishmael said, "Thanks for all you do, Fern, and I'll be here when you return."

Jai said, "Is there something funny, Fern? Good day."

Nurse Fern said, "I'm gonna take my degrees on out of here. Good check! Oops, I meant good day…"

Jez woke up and lay there, listening to everyone talk. *Damn! Ishmael checked her ass*, Jez thought. She didn't open her eyes, because she didn't want to be bothered by anyone. Nurse Fern saw her open her eyes and shut them real quick, so he didn't say anything as he left the room.

Jez noticed all the orange flowers, but she was still bothered by the whole situation, and flowers couldn't stop the thought that she shot at somebody.

*****

Jez didn't want to hear anything the doctor was saying. Ishmael stepped in and talked to the doctor for her. He set it up to where Jez would go to his home, and he would have everything set up for therapy.

Jai said, "Sis? Are you okay with this?"

Jez said, "I don't want to talk right now, Jai."

Ishmael said, "I know you're upset about everything, but—"

Jai said, "*No. No. No. I can't take it anymore!*"

Jez said, "Where is my mother? I'm glad you set everything up, but I need to see my mother first. Jai, where is my daddy?"

Jai folded up in the chair and started crying out, knowing her sister was unaware of what had happened. The rest of the staff ran in the room to see what was going on, and Jai immediately stormed out of the room crying.

Jez said, "Ishmael, what happened? Please tell me what's going on."

Nurse Fern said, "Is everything okay? We don't need you all worked up, Jez. Let me get your vitals, too, please?"

Jez said, "I thought I was leaving? What's going on?"

The doctor said, "You are! We need to talk to you for a moment. Jez? Do you mind if we talk while he's in here?"

Jez said, "It's Ishmael! Yes, he can stay. He's my husband! Am I dying or something? Damn!"

The doctor said, "No. But I have some bad news!"

CHAPTER 34

Tara
Me, Myself, and I

Tara just sat there reading her book and occasionally looking up to see the waves on the ocean brushing past the rocks.

She found out about everything going on and started selling everything, including her shop and didn't look back.

She didn't even tell her parents where she went, because they would have told everybody, including Skunk.

She wasn't accepting no form of stress in her life, and if it meant cutting her whole family off, so be it.

Coral said, "I'm so glad I came. I met a nice man this morning. Are you hungry? Tara?"

Tara said, "I'll eat some fruit when we get back home."

Coral said, "Tara, you know this isn't home. We can't stay here forever. You know that man will come looking for you."

Tara said, "If he were going to come, he would have been came. Please don't bring him up again. Besides, I'm making good money off these single-parenting groups I'm holding."

Coral said, "Well, I do like working with you, but I need a raise if we're staying here. I need my spot soon as you have the baby."

Tara said, "I found another house, and you'll love it. I'm going to need you to keep an eye on the nanny when I'm busy...Quit laughing! I'm serious, Coral!"

Coral said, "Nanny, my ass! Skunk mothers is not going for all that, missy."

Tara said, "What makes you think they're going to be a part of my baby's life?"

Coral said, "He stressed you doesn't mean he'll be a bad father. IJS!"

Tara said, "No, you didn't just spell the alphabet mixed up?"

Coral said, "Did you just call me stupid? I know, I said that shit right? Are you really gonna walk away and not fix the alphabet?"

Tara said, "*You're talking in third person...I'm gone, sweetie!*"

*****

Tara went over her applications before the meeting started because she wanted to know a little bit about everyone. She planned an open group meeting. That way, no one had to wait in a long line. Each person could speak with her and socialize with others while waiting.

He knew Tara had money when she bought a building and put it in his mother's name. Grants were coming in for the people attending, so she didn't have a problem with paying him more.

Coral was in charge of buying all the office supplies, decorating the office, ordering items for the attending parents, and finding workers for the kids that attended. He called a babysitting agency and had everything arranged before the meeting. The babysitters helped with setting up the rooms per ages and shopping for supplies.

Coral said, "Hey, Tara. I need to see the applications, so I can see if they got some skills. I need help doing all this?"

Tara said, "I've met the other young ladies you hired, and they're nice. I'm going to be doing all the paperwork from now on, so I need all the receipts. What do you need help with?"

Coral said, "Tara? How do you know how to do all this grant shit?"

Tara said, "Look, before you came down here, I took a few classes on how to write grants, and I already knew who I wanted to help, which made it easy for me. Thanks for letting me use your mother's name. That will keep Skunk from knowing and messing with me about my baby."

Coral said, "Bitch. I knew you had money, but damn, you're buying buildings and shit. Where this class at?"

Tara said, "I didn't buy the building with that grant money. Coral, quit playing with me! You know I had money already. And, I'm paying you out of my pocket."

Coral said, "You sold everything? I can't believe you sold that shop. How?"

Tara said, "I'm not a dumb bitch! I had everything put in my name. Nigga, you are acting like Queen didn't give yo ass some money."

Coral said, "Yes, she did! I'm serious, though. He put the house in your name too?"

Tara said, "Coral…Just because a motherfucker gives you money to shop doesn't mean you have to spend the shit. Best believe if he wanted to marry me, I had access to everything."

Coral said, "All this time you were the smart bitch! Damn… Okay! One more mixed alphabet question, please? Don't look at me like that?"

Tara said, "I'm not about to tell you how much money I have. Here, this is for you, and we're going to look at the house tomorrow. So, why are you looking at me like that now?"

Coral said, "Damn! Am I reading this right? Damn! Then you put a check in this bitch? Okay. Okay. Well, never mind my question! How can I be of your assistance today?"

Tara said, "You play way too much! I found a cleaning company, so you don't have to worry about that. Let's go open the doors."

Coral said, "Tara? Did you take that man basketball money? I need to know what we're up against. Okay. Okay. Sorry, don't look at me like that!"

Tara watched the parents walk in, looking over the sheets for them to know what to do and what they had to offer them.

After a few people talked with Coral, Tara came from around the corner to greet and answer questions. She looked at the name tags, so she could put a face with the application as the people walked by her. She was so amazed at the turnout, and more people came than expected, so she had to go print off more applications. "Miss, I can help you. Miss," the man said.

Tara said, "I'm sorry! What did you say?"

Andy said, "I'm Andy Mower! I see you are tired. I can help you. I came for—"

Tara said, "Sorry! I'm Tara. Maybe I should put on a name tag like everyone else. I need more copies of the application. A few more people showed up."

Andy said, "I sure will have a seat, Tara! Word of mouth carries around here. We don't get much help around this area. Thanks for showing up. It looks like the baby is due any day? You should be resting."

Tara said, "I'll rest later, thanks! Mr. Mower, you have a one-year-old daughter named Ty'Anna. Is she here in the day care?"

Andy said, "You did your homework. No! She's with my mother."

Tara said, "I wanted to know about the people I'm meeting. How much longer do you have of schooling?"

Coral said, "Umm. Mr. Andy? Let me get the applications that are printed already and leave Tara be. Matter of fact, since you're helpful, Come help me with the second part of the application so that these people can talk with Ms. Tara after."

Tara sat and talked with each individual, and after the tenth one, she informed Coral that they were going to need more help.

Coral and Andy helped interview the rest of the people and gave out gift cards. Tara made sure she wrote Andy a check before he left, and asked him to come back.

*****

Tara walked out of the house, going down the path to the motherhouse, and Coral was right behind Tara questioning the realtor.

Tara said, "What do you think, Coral?"

Coral said, "I like it! Where the nanny gonna stay?"

Tara said, "Yo ass silly! She is going home!"

*****

Tara was shredding papers when Coral walked in. "Mr. Andy Mowers is here to see you," Coral said and walked off. "Come in, Mr.—" Tara tried to say before he cut her off.

Andy said, "It's just Andy! Thanks for seeing me in such short notice."

Tara said, "That's fine. Thanks for the other day. We were unprepared. So you said part-time, right?"

Andy said, "Two days is all I need, and this can go for a college credit also. About the other day. Word of mouth carries, and maybe you should set up a schedule, and see people individually."

Coral said, "I'm sorry, y'all! I'll be right back. I'm going to get more gift cards. I'll be back in a few."

Tara said, "See you later! I wanted to get it all over with, but that was a hot mess. Come, let me show you where you'll be working, and we can discuss your pay. *Ouch!*"

*****

Bang. Bang. Bang. Bang. "*Get down,*" Coral yelled. Everyone was yelling, falling, and running away from the men that stormed in the building shooting.

When Tara saw the people rushing toward her with blood rushing down, their helpless bodies crying for help, she rushed for the back door. "Where the fuck you going," Skunk said. "How did you find me," Tara screamed out.

*****

Nurse Emma said, "Tara. Tara. Wake up, Tara. Tara, dear. It's okay! Wait, Tara! You're okay…Look at me! You're okay, dear."

Tara said, "Where am I? The people were…"

Nurse Emma said, "You and your baby daughter is fine. You are at the hospital."

Coral said, "Tara? You fainted, and Andy had to rush you to the doctor. Bitch, you scared the shit out of us!"

Nurse Emma said, "*Ahem*….Language, please! You have a beautiful baby girl. We had to rush and deliver her because you fell pretty hard on your stomach."

Tara said, "Can you go get her please! Thanks."

Coral said, "*Ahem that!* Let me shut this door! Tara…what the fuck happened? You were okay up until I left the office. She was trying to wake you up just now, and you were fighting her ass."

Tara said, "I was thinking about Skunk, and some weird shit happened at the Hope Community Center, then I woke up here."

Coral said, "*Uh-uh!* If he got you shaking like that. I hope his ass don't pop up! You're still strapped, right? Da fuck…"

*****

Tara just sat and looked into her beautiful face, rubbing her hands softly as she still didn't know what to call her.

Tara said, "How long does she have to be in this incubator?"

Nurse Emma said, "What's her name? She's adorable! She'll be done in three hours yet."

Tara said, "Her name is Zoe Eve. And thanks. She's so little… Why are you crying, fool? You're so irra!"

Coral said, "Bitch, this shit is touching my soul. My stinka butt is perfect! And you almost died!"

Nurse Emma said, "Ahem Language around the baby! I'll be back to check on you, Ms. Tara."

"I know you decided not to have a nanny, but she's good," Coral whispered. "Listening to you and Andy tell those horror stories about abductions and beatings, I've changed my mind," Tara said.

*****

Coral stood and looked at Tara around the hospital curtain. "Oh, shit! Nigga, you scared me," Coral shouted. "Well, quit standing here crying and go say something," Andy said.

Tara said, "His crybaby ass always crying. They're taking her out the incubator in a few. She had jaundice, Coral! I told you she's okay!"

Andy said, "She can have a playdate with my little angel. How are you feeling, Tara?"

Tara said, "I'm good, Andy, Thanks for asking! I hear you have everything going swell at the center. Thanks so much!"

Andy said, "No, thank you! You're a blessing sent right on time for my little angel and I."

*****

Tara was so happy to be home with baby Zoe Eve that Coral brought the office home for her to work, and Andy helped him run the center.

They hired new staff, and Tara was there via video to have a part in it. She made sure she did a background check on everyone, including the ones from the temp agencies.

*****

Coral said, "I'm so glad we hired you. I don't know if I could have done this all by my lonesome. Thanks, Andy."

Andy said, "What's up with Tara? Does she have a man? Never mind, I'll ask her. My bad."

Coral said, "You're right! You're bad. Look, you seem like a decent guy, but only them people ask questions behind folk's back. And, a real man would ask her himself. Besides, Tara is rich, rich, and I don't know if she's into men like you. My bad...I shouldn't have said that."

Andy said, "I'm gonna go to my office and finish up. Good day!"

*****

Andy made a house visit to meet up with Tara to discuss the new guidelines he came up with, but he needed her approval first.

Tara loved having Andy and Coral around for company, but this day was different from the other days. Andy didn't realize what he had handed her "That's a nice donation, Tara," Andy said as he watched her face go blank.

Coral walked in with some tea ready to gossip, noticing Tara was looking weird. "What you say to Ms. Tara?" Coral said.

Andy said, "Tara. Tara. Tara. What's the matter? I gave her that check! It's a blessing, right?"

Coral said, "Let me see! *Oh, shit! When did this come?*"

Skunk
On a Mission

"Why do you need all this space for one person," Adana asked. "Tara, my baby, and you," Skunk said.

Skunk said, "Anything else?"

Adana said, "Oh, that's how we're doing it? Then I need my room. Where baby mama at?"

Skunk said, "You get the numbers right, and I'll worry about the rest."

Adana said, "I'm moving in, and just a minute ago, your brother accused us of robbing your mother. Did they ever find out who did that?"

Skunk said, "You know I'm not discussing that with you. Don't mention it again! Matter of fact, leave!"

*****

Skunk left the hospital from seeing his brother, and he called one of his close friends.

Skunk said, "I like what you did with the office. Decorated nice, and I see you picked the most prominent office. Thanks for reaching out to me on this proposition.

Chaste said, "We have some clients already, and everything is going accordingly. Sorry to hear about your brother. I know that hit hard."

Skunk said, "Thanks. He's doing better. That business I asked you to handle for me, I need another favor. However, you or whoever found out, I need you to find this girl that went on the run. She was there when my brother got shot, and he can't remember dude's face."

Chaste said, "Anything for a friend. Come here, Sem?"

He just knew she was about to give in to him. He wouldn't stop her either the way she wore them suits, because he's been wanting to tap her out. "Give me a hug, Sem" Chaste said.

Skunk said, "Damn! You smell nice, and thanks, Chaste."

Chaste said, "You are squeezing me hard, Sem."

Omar said, "*Ahem!* Am I interrupting something?"

Chaste said, "Oh, no! It's not like that! Sem, meet Omar. Omar, meet Sem. Sem is my friend I was telling you about."

Omar said, "I see! Friends being friendly!"

Chaste said, "Sem, quit laughing…"

Skunk said, "What's up? Nice to meet you, Omar. We're just business partners."

Omar said, "Friend or business, I see what it is."

Chaste said, "*Omar? Wait!* Sem, quit laughing."

Skunk said, "Go on and chase his ass! If you knew he was coming, why jump in my arms?"

Chaste said, "I'm not chasing him! I hugged my friend because he's going through something…Oh my gosh! He just walked out! Anyways, what's her name, and give me as much information about her as possible."

Skunk said, "First, we need to get an alarm system, or lock the doors when we're closed. He just walked up in here with his sensitive ass."

Chaste said, "That was my sensitive booty call. Fuck!"

*****

Zach said, "I told you not to contact her! Here you go."

Skunk said, "Wow! She had a girl. She's so pretty and little. Zoe Eve…that's a beautiful name. Did she leave yet?"

Zach said, "She has too much going on to up and leave. If I'd known you were gonna send her money, I wouldn't have wasted my time having her followed."

Skunk said, "What the fuck! I want my baby to be taken care of, but I didn't send her shit!"

Zach said, "Somebody did! Now, she's ready to run. What the fuck did you do to her?"

Skunk said, "Only person that knows where she is beside us is Chaste. She caught me cheating in the act!"

Zach said, "When are you going to see your daughter?"

Skunk said, "If I go, she'll run…I need to make things right."

*****

Skunk just sat there looking at the picture for hours, imagining her lying across his chest, and Tara walking around in her white cotton dress.

*****

Adana splashed the water at him, hoping he'd put the picture down and pay her some attention. She went under the bubbles and water, and almost choked trying to put his dick in her mouth. "Get up," Skunk said. "Yo ass trying to bob for apples and shit! Get your pretty ass over here."

Adana said, "Well, you won't let me see what you're looking at?"

Adana sat right on top of him and rode him in the tub, making the water wave and splash. He grabbed her ass and massaged her with the oils that flowed through the water to make it at ease, and he loved hearing her moans of enjoyment. "You're ready! Turn around," Skunk demanded.

*****

Skunk said, "Come on in, sexy! Did you find Omar? He stopped by earlier looking for you."

Chaste said, "Good morning. I hope you're not serious? I don't do jealousy very well."

Skunk said, "You should have gone to your office first."

Chaste said, "I hope he didn't send some flowers! Tell me, Sem! Anyways, this is for you, and that girl is nowhere to be found."

Skunk said, "You better go back on the other side of this desk and quit touching me before Mr. Sensitive walk in on you again."

Chaste said, "Anyways, you're looking nice this morning as well. On a serious note, the last place they tracked Suzanna was at the club. Merch had a background check on her already, so I went to the hospital to visit him. Terrence gave me a little information."

Skunk said, "Let's check it out! Did you find out who Donald was, and how long they were talking? I mean, is he the baby daddy? You're laughing!"

Chaste said, "That girl was playing. The guy that works in the flower shop told me she paid to have the flowers delivered, and wrote the message out. Donald is Tara! The baby looks just like you. Have you told your moms yet?"

CHAPTER 35

Isaiah
Something Has to Give

Ax woke up and started panicking when he realized that the water was swallowing the car. "*What the fuck*," Ax shouted. When he went to look for something substantial, he started panicking more when he noticed his gun was nowhere in sight.

Before the water subdued the car, he started rolling the window down, hoping and scared of what river or lake he was sinking in. As soon as the water hit his face, he took a deep breath and went out the window, fighting the strength of the water.

His fear of drowning made him swim like he was getting his silver medal, and if he got the gold, he was getting them bitches for sure.

As his head came over the currents, he swung his arms, trying to stay afloat, and looked for land. The darkness made it hard to see with the water hitting his face, "*Help...*," Ax shouted out, but he started swallowing water.

He started swimming fast and hard, but his arms started feeling heavy and weak after each stroke. "What the fuck! This boy is having a stroke," Jean shouted.

Isaiah said, "Mom, seriously? This is not funny!"

Marsha said, "Wake him up! Quit dashing that water on him. That's making him move more."

Jean said, "This shit is not funny. Let me stop! Is he paddling? Aw, hell naw!"

Isaiah said, "I found him in his car. I'm sorry, but he's having a nightmare or something."

Skunk said, "What was he doing there anyway? We sold the place. Mom, are you laughing too?"

Isaiah said, "Oh, now we're getting quiet? Y'all funny!"

Marsha said, "I was gonna go myself, and he decided this was over our heads."

Jean said, "Okay, let me stop laughing, but I wouldn't have come back all knotted up."

Marsha said, "Right! We sent him to look for that Queen girl. I need to ask her something."

Skunk said, "Are you ladies serious? What do you want to know?"

Marsha said, "Wake his ass up! I need a shot! Jean? Where is your stash? I'll be right back."

Isaiah said, "*Mama!* When did you start talking like this?"

Jean said, "Y'all don't know yo mother dearest because Marsha is a beast, son!"

Isaiah said, "Awh, hell naw…Y'all tripping!"

Marsha said, "What she say? I know you said something when I walked out."

Skunk said, "I can't believe my ears! They done went from sweet sweet to gang gang."

Isaiah said, "Mom, y'all need to stop tripping! We'll go get her…"

Marsha said, "Gang gang, my ass! They're tripping whenever they think they can get away with harming my children. Like I don't know what's going on."

Jean said, "They think shit sweet! Get they ass, Marsha."

Isaiah said, "Mama, stop amping her! Skunk…"

Marsha said, "I told y'all to stop dealing with them. *But no!* He's buying rings and buildings."

Jean said, "Don't forget he's taking bitches on trips, handing out cash, and let her set him up to get robbed."

Isaiah looked at Skunk like, *How the fuck they know all this*; then Skunk dashed the rest of the water on Ax. "Wake yo ass up," Skunk said. "Shake his ass or something." Isaiah laughed. "Whatever the fuck he smoking or doing, don't bring that shit in my house," Jean said.

Skunk said, "The way he's swinging, he most definitely fighting in his sleep."

Marsha said, "Naw, they whooped his ass!"

Ax said, "*What the fuck! Help! Help!*"

Jean said, "Slap his ass! Wake yo ass up, nephew!"

Ax said, "*Wait... Wait... How in da fuck? Auntie? Sem? Isaiah?*"

Isaiah said, "It's us! How are you doing?"

Marsha said, "It's clear you got banged up, but what the fuck were you smoking? Yo ass tripping!"

Isaiah said, "Mom, please stop talking like that. We will go get them."

Jean said, "It's too late for all that! She called your father."

Ax said, "*Them bitches bought the club right from under us!*"

Marsha said, "What are you yelling for? We're right here."

Ax said, "Their aunt Teresa bought the club in her name, I think. I set up a meeting and carried her ass to the club, and that's all I remembered."

Isaiah said, "I found you in the car sleep! One of the dancers called me and told me you were too drunk to drive."

Ax said, "I'm going to get them, bitches! I'm not going out like that."

Isaiah said, "I went to knock on the door after I saw you were good in the car, and they put a 'Closed' sign on the door. I was only trying to thank them for calling us."

Marsha said, "Thank them? Nope, I can't deal. Jean, do you still have a stash of flame?"

Isaiah said, "Mom? You all are taking shots and flaming? Skunk?"

Skunk said, "What else did you find out, Ax? Wait...wait... Look at this! Zoe Eve, my daughter."

They all looked at the picture then looked at Skunk then back at the picture. When they saw the tears running down Jean's face,

591

Marsha hugged her and took a shot with her free arm. "Mom, chill," Skunk said.

Jean knew that Marsha was upset because Tara was an ex-stripper, but that's how Isaiah Sr. got them, and she understood why she despised it so much. *If our kids knew what we did on them poles*, Jean whispered. "I already know," Marsha whispered to Jean as she handed her the shot.

Marsha said, "Where is she? She looks just like you when you were a baby, but cuter."

Jean said, "She's our baby! I want to meet her."

Isaiah said, "Bro, congratulations. She's so precious!"

*****

Isaiah watched her as they jumped in the truck and pulled off with a briefcase and duffel bag. He never thought he'd be following a female, but if Ax was telling the truth, proof was needed before he proposed.

She walked through the gate and couldn't believe what she was seeing. "How the fuck this bitch get a storage unit here," Samaya said.

Queen said, "What bitch?"

Samaya said, "I thought they killed that bitch? Hold the fuck up!"

"What the fuck are you doing here?" Queen shouted as she rushed Jill.

Samaya said, "Talk, bitch!"

Queen said, "Cuz, chill! They have cameras everywhere."

Samaya said, "Not in the unit they don't. Now, talk!"

Jill said, "The people gave this shit to Charles after Chad died, and he gave it to me. I wanted to see what was in here. We can see it's empty, so what was the point?"

Samaya said, "Queen, them niggas were following us. We were the intended target. You're going to follow us when we leave here like shit didn't happen. You hear me, bitch?"

Jill said, "Yes. What for? I didn't tell anybody anything. I told them everything you said to say. Kala is the one that told them some extra shit."

Queen said, "She doesn't know shit about me. We told you to fuck the nigga, not fall in love and get pregnant. Does he know yet?"

Samaya said, "Hell naw, she wouldn't be standing here with her punk ass. I thought Merch ass was the crazy one. Shit! Ishmael is off the chain, and he's in love with Jez crazy ass."

Jill said, "How am I the punk? I'm the one that put the cameras in the club for our safety and put our sex tapes out there for them to find."

Queen said, "You made them think he forced y'all to do that shit. How?"

Jill said, "I cried...Da fuck! I still don't get how y'all knew they were following you?"

Queen said, "Come on, let's go! This bitch is questioning us and sounding like the people."

Samaya walked through the building looking for anything that tied her to the club and Queen, and Jill shredded papers while waiting for everyone else to show up.

*****

Isaiah said, "Come now! I'm watching all their ass walk in the building. I'm waiting for y'all!"

Ishmael
Family First

Ishmael said, "If you can't pick the lock, kick that bitch down! They might see us, and I'm not getting shot by some sneaky cheerleaders."

Zach said, "Fuck it! Come on, this bitch open now! Please don't sleep on these bitches or soon-to-be wives."

Tee said, "Let me go first!"

The men looked into the office, and they were sitting around the table, looking like they were mimicking them. Isaiah held his hand up for them to let him go in because he knew they would shoot at everybody else, because they didn't like or understand them.

Isaiah said, *"What's up, Saria? Whoa. Whoa. Hold up! Saria? Put them motherfucking thangs down!"*

Samaya said, "What the fuck are you doing here? How did you get in?"

Queen said, "How the fuck did he know we were here is the question?"

Isaiah said, "We need to talk! *I'm not playing…Put the fucking gun down now!"*

Queen said, "Bitch! What are you doing? Samaya? Don't listen to him."

Samaya said, "Y'all chill! Auntie, let's chill. What do you want to talk about?"

Toonie said, "I told y'all we should have met somewhere else. This janky-ass club."

As soon as they sat back down and put their guns away, the men walked in, and all they could feel was the ladies' disappointed energy toward Samaya.

Isaiah said, "Chill! It's not like that! We want to talk."

Ishmael said, "Who shot my fucking brother, Queen?"

Queen said, "I don't know! Ask him! When I went to find out, I heard he walked up on somebody, and they shot him."

Ax said, "Why are you investigating?"

Tee said, "Who told you that?"

594

Ishmael said, "Probably Sunshine! That's why she's missing now!"

Jill said, "Kala told them!"

Bitch, shut up, Queen and Samaya thought as they both saw Ishmael zooming in on Jill. *She looks about eight or nine months*, Ishmael thought while doing the math and hoping he didn't slip up.

Ishmael said, "You're about to bust, aren't you, Jillian?"

Isaiah said, "Oh, shit! Where is Sunshine? She was there when this shit happened?"

Skunk said, "How the fuck would Kala know?"

Ax said, "They're all lying! They own this fucking club, and they killed Sunshine to keep her quiet. She probably had Merch shot!"

Queen said, "Like you said, 'probably,' you monkey-face bitch!"

Isaiah said, "*Whoa...whoa...Put them damn guns down!*"

Tee said, "These bitches think they're tough?"

Isaiah said, "Fam, chill out! Put the guns down! I need to know who shot my brother, and where is Sunshine?"

Samaya said, "Nigga! You a bitch...Da fuck! I'm not putting shit down until they leave!"

Jill said, "*Kala told me, and I told them about Merch!*"

Queen said, "I asked Merch myself who did this shit. The fuck I'm gonna shoot or get him shot for, and I left him alone."

Isaiah said, "When did he tell you? He can't have any visitors that is not on the list."

Queen said, "Call and ask him right now! He told the nurse to ask me to find out for him. Call him!"

Ax said, "I sure will *call him!*"

Skunk said, "He already told me about the visit..."

Teresa said, "I can't believe this munch-face nigga is acting tough. We just knocked his punk ass out!"

Ax said, "*Bitch...*"

Ax swung and missed Teresa's face by an inch. "You punk bitch," Ax said as Isaiah stood in front of him. Tee grabbed Teresa's arm so she couldn't shoot and stood ground in front of her. "Let me go," Teresa demanded, but Tee was too solid for her to nudge.

Samaya had her gun pointing right at Ishmael's head, and Queen had her gun at Isaiah's side. "Tell him to let her go," Samaya said.

Toonie said, "Oh shit! Look, ladies, if you wanted to buy this club for your men and I knew you were coming with all this drama, I wouldn't have shown it to you. Jill, I will have your check for you if I find a buyer for the property next door that Ricardo left."

Isaiah said, "Skunk? Can y'all please chill? Everybody, put your guns down!"

Skunk said, "Where the fuck are you going? Sit yo ass down!"

Toonie said, "Look, y'all tripping! I came here to sell the place to these ladies. Mr. Ricardo Simms didn't know he owned the other property until we went over some paperwork, and everything is going to Jillian since he passed. I don't have shit to do with all this mess!"

Skunk said, "Sit yo ass down! Quit rambling through them got damn papers, and shut up."

Toonie said, "Mister, I'm trying to find something."

Teresa said, "Now, let me go big ass? This nigga over here, smelling like money, coming to a gunfight with a room full of women!"

Tee said, "Shut the fuck up! Where the fuck is Kala and Sunshine?"

Teresa said, "Ask Teisha and Seth stupid!"

Ishmael said, "Who the fuck is the men they're buying the club for?"

Toonie said, "Can I speak with the gun out of my face! Thanks."

Toonie looked through and over the papers, making it look like she was trying to find something, hoping Ax didn't recognize her.

Toonie said, "Who is Milan and Isaiah? The message says, 'Samaya wanted to buy the club that was taken away from them as a gift.' This is ridiculous."

Ax said, "This bitch said 'who' like this a game show. Get the fuck out of here!"

Toonie said, "I sure will. Goodbye!"

Tee said, "Sit yo goofy ass down! Toon, Toot Too, or whatever the fuck yo name is!"

Teresa looked at Samaya, and Samaya looked at Queen, hoping this crazy-ass girl's plan would go through. Jill was so nervous, she felt the wetness between her legs but was too worried to say anything.

Isaiah said, "We sold the club! Samaya, what's going on?"

Samaya said, "Shit! I thought you wanted the club back, so I talked to her about buying it. I didn't know Jill owned the other side."

Ishmael said, "We had somebody follow you from a storage unit?"

Queen said, "So! Should have had somebody following Sunshine and Kala!"

Isaiah said, "Can everybody leave! I need to speak with Samaya."

Skunk said, "Hold on! Who is this Samaya?"

Samaya said, "Fuck! I don't know! Who is it?"

Ishmael said, "It's your niece, dumb ass! Even Tara is not fooling with y'all!"

Teresa said, "That's not my niece! You got, played!"

*****

Teisha said, "They're all in there now. I should go shoot that bitch in front of everybody."

Seth said, "I don't think that's a good idea."

Teisha said, "Why did you let Jill go? She was just as guilty as the other females."

Seth said, "So, you're questioning me now? Shut the fuck up!"

Teisha said, "Please, let me go! Sorry."

ABOUT THE AUTHOR

Tondria Leatrice was born in Minneapolis, Minnesota, in May 1972 to Ada and Richard. She is the oldest of her parents' four children. Her siblings are Richard, Calvin, and Dakar.

Tondria later had four children of her own: Marlon Jr. in 1991, Montrelle in 1992, Tashondra in 1996, and Demarco in 2001.

CPSIA information can be obtained
at www.ICGtesting.com
Printed in the USA
LVHW021214141021
700428LV00001B/8